Santa Maria

DEEP WATER

DEEP
WATER

Emma Bamford

Scout Press

New York   London   Toronto   Sydney   New Delhi

Scout Press
An Imprint of Simon & Schuster, Inc.
1230 Avenue of the Americas
New York, NY 10020

First Scout Press hardcover edition May 2022

SCOUT PRESS and colophon are registered trademarks of Simon & Schuster, Inc.

For information about special discounts for bulk purchases, please contact Simon & Schuster Special Sales at 1-866-506-1949 or business@simonandschuster.com.

The Simon & Schuster Speakers Bureau can bring authors to your live event. For more information or to book an event, contact the Simon & Schuster Speakers Bureau at 1-866-248-3049 or visit our website at www.simonspeakers.com.

Interior design by Jaime Putorti

Manufactured in the United States of America

10 9 8 7 6 5 4 3 2 1

Library of Congress Cataloging-in-Publication Data is available.

ISBN 978-1-9821-7036-3
ISBN 978-1-9821-7038-7 (ebook)

DEEP WATER

PATUSAN

1

When you spend as much time at the mercy of the sea as I have, your soul forgets how to rest. As a seafarer, your ability to react to the slightest change in the environment, be it internally, in the structure and seaworthiness of your vessel, or externally, in the conditions of the ocean and sky that surround you, means everything. Lives depend on how quickly you can act. And the one person who must always be most attuned to each creak of a bulkhead or slam of the hull, to a shift in the cadence of the engines or the howl of the wind, is the captain.

Even when I'm on my off-watch, lying asleep in my narrow bunk, my soul remains alert. So that December night I was already sitting up before my first officer had finished rapping his knuckles against my cabin door, was swinging my bare soles to the cool linoleum by the time he entered and saluted me.

"Sorry to disturb you, Captain." He had his feet planted wide, to counter the pitch of the ship in the waves. There was a near gale outside—the forerunner of a monsoon come early, climate change having sent nature's calendar askew.

"What is it, Yusuf?"

"Flares sighted, sir."

"Flares?" We were in the middle of the Indian Ocean, one thousand nautical miles from land in any direction—Africa, Sri Lanka, Sumatra—and even farther from our home port. There were no shipping lanes nearby; no fishermen would venture this far offshore. "Are you sure?"

"Yes, sir."

I reached into my locker for tomorrow's shirt. Pulled on my uniform trousers. "How many?"

"Two. Both red parachutes. Umar saw the first one as it arced down. We waited two minutes, then a second went up."

A gap of two minutes between the first and second. Red parachutes. Done by the book. I slipped on my shoes. "Any vessels showing on AIS?"

"No, sir. But we're picking something up on radar, seven nautical miles east-southeast. We thought it was just a rain shadow."

I returned with Yusuf to the ship's bridge. After the dimness of the corridor, the overhead lights were searing, and rap music blared from a phone. The air was spiked with spice and oil, and the spoor led to an illicit samosa wrapper by the bin.

Ensign Umar was hunched over the radar, examining the screen where the range rings glowed, green leaching into black. Rain clouds and the growing sea state created ghosts on the screen, coming, going, coming again, changing shape with every revolution of the radar antenna. On the windshield the wipers were set to maximum speed, and past the reach of their curves the glass was greasy with salt. Beyond, all was black.

I turned back to the radar screen. "Where's the object?"

"Here," said Umar, omitting the *sir*. I suspected the rap music was his fault; a lot of my men were just kampong boys, really. Village kids. Umar tapped the screen at five o'clock. I watched the blip, trying to discern a pattern in the jigging pixels, to find the constancy that would confirm the existence of a boat.

The rapper was still raging. "*No one learns, key turns, kick back pales, first time fails.*"

Music was banned on watch. Whenever I was on board, I switched off my personal phone and left it in my locker. Besides, even when we were within signal range, there was no one left to call me.

I blinked. "Ensign Mohammed Umar bin Rayyan. Turn that off!"

"Yes, Captain." He scrambled to the electronics panel, where his phone was on charge. He constantly had it with him, was always polishing the glass, checking it was still tucked safe in its protective case.

After he muted the music, there was a moment of blissful silence. And then I heard it. A call on the radio.

"—day, mayday, –ver—"

"Umar! The VHF."

He was already there, reaching for the fist mic with one hand and turning up the volume on the transceiver with the other. Static filled the bridge, rushing in my ears like the roar of water a drowning person must hear.

The call came through again. "May–, –day, may–ay." Everyone stilled. "—t *Santa Maria*, sailing ya– *aria*, sailing yacht *Sant– Ma–ia*."

"That's a woman," Umar said.

I glared at him, straining to hear. Had she really said *Maria*?

"—edical emergency. Require immediate assist—" the woman said, in English.

I took the mic from Umar and replied, also in English, "*Santa Maria*, this is Royal Malaysian Navy patrol vessel *Patusan*, over."

There was a crunch of interference, and I wondered if my transmission had failed to reach her. I waited, my finger hovering over the send button. Umar and Yusuf's eyes were on me. Mine were on the radar screen.

"Oh my God," she said, breathing distortion into her mic. She sounded British. "I thought you might be a mirage." She let out a noise, and I couldn't tell if she was laughing or crying. "I've been calling for days. Then I saw you on my screen. This is *Santa Maria*. I mean mayday, I mean over."

"Ma'am," I said, as clearly as I could, "I understand you require assistance. I need to know the location of your vessel and the nature of your distress."

The connection was stronger as she read out her lat and long. Umar wrote down the coordinates and nodded to indicate they corresponded with the blip on the radar. Yusuf changed our course.

"Please come," she said, and her voice broke. "My husband. He's badly injured. Very badly."

"Your vessel, ma'am. Is it disabled?"

"No, but he's hurt. He needs a doctor. Please hurry."

"We are on our way, ma'am," I said. "Our ETA is—"

"Two eight minutes," Yusuf said, in Bahasa Malaysia.

"Twenty-eight minutes," I relayed in English.

"Oh God."

The tremor in her words made me reach past Yusuf's shoulder to nudge the throttles forward. Seawater exploded against the portlights. I couldn't take us any faster in this sea state.

"Ma'am," I said, clicking down to transmit. "What happened? To your boat? To your husband?" There was just the soft *crrr* of white noise. I tried again, depressed the transmit button. "Ma'am? Can you tell me what has happened? With *Santa Maria*?" I released my finger, listened. Again, nothing. Was I sensing reluctance, or was I reading too much into an unsteady radio link? Perhaps she was tending to him, out of reach of the radio.

Depress. "Ma'am." My voice swelled with professionalism—my ability to switch off the personal had proved a blessing in recent years. "We are coming to you." Release. Although perhaps *benefit* was a better term, since I no longer believed in blessings. Depress. "My officers are trained in first aid." Release. I wanted—needed—to keep her on the line. Depress. "Ma'am, what is your name?"

A crackle. "Virginie."

"Virginie. I am Captain Danial Tengku."

"Help us." Now she was definitely crying.

Often, when I think of my wife, I wish someone had been there with her at that terrible time. She must have been so frightened. At least I could do something for this woman.

"Virginie. Listen to me. We will be with you as soon as we can. It is now"—I checked the bridge clock—"twenty-six minutes." She was quiet. "Can you hear me?"

"Yes."

"Good."

I let thirty seconds pass. "Virginie, are you there?"

She answered immediately. "Yes."

"Now our ETA is a little over twenty-five minutes."

While we steamed toward *Santa Maria*, I called her every thirty seconds, using her name each time, both to calm her, so she'd know she wasn't alone, and to build a connection, trust. Ten, twenty, fifty, fifty-two times I did this. Fifty-two—the number of weeks in a year or cards in a deck, the number of Penangites lost that fateful day.

"Virginie, are you there?"

"Yes."

Eventually, the drone of the engines lowered as Yusuf reduced speed. The *Patusan* lurched against the waves. I grabbed the flashlight and threw open the door to the deck. It was slippery, and I needed to hold on as I swept the churning black ocean with the beam. Nothing.

Then—*boom!*—the thick night was detonated, the sky lit white as day, and there, off our starboard bow, against a backdrop of star-censoring clouds, a sailing yacht was silhouetted, its sails and rigging flickering like a phantom in the guttering pyrotechnics of a dying flare.

Santa Maria. Maria—my wife's name.

I did then something I hadn't done for years. I crossed myself.

2

The support tender jogged and jolted in the open water. Umar was a good helmsman, turning the open-top boat to reduce the impact of the waves, but it was slow going, getting over to the sailboat, and we were all drenched right through.

I'd left Yusuf in charge on the *Patusan* and taken Umar with me, plus the ship's medic, Haziq. *Santa Maria*'s deck light guided us in. From this angle I could see it was a catamaran, and I was grateful for small mercies—its low freeboard would make boarding in this sea state easier. A rolling wave as tall as a building picked us up, lifting first the rear of the support tender, and then the middle and the bow, blocking my view for a moment, and we surfed forward, shunted by the force of the ocean.

Umar timed the approach to *Santa Maria* well, and Haziq boarded and made off the line.

"Stay in the tender," I ordered Umar. "I don't want to risk the line breaking in these conditions."

"Sir."

"And hold on tight."

I passed Haziq his medical kit and climbed out. I wasn't sure what condition the yacht would be in, but under my feet the engines rumbled steadily, and I knew it still had power, wasn't disabled and adrift. The sails had been furled and secured. We dashed up a short run of steps, crouching to keep our balance, and emerged at the back of the catamaran's cockpit, a wide, well-lit space decked in teak. On the floor between the helmsman's seat and a dining table were dark splashes and smears. Blood. I signaled to Haziq—we'd go inside.

Virginie was just through the glass doors in a crouched position, her back to us, each notch of her spine pronounced between the horizontal slashes of her bikini. She turned as we entered. Her eyes were shadowed, the sockets deep, and her limbs and middle were streaked a reddish-brown, the arms all the way up to the elbow. Beside her lay a Caucasian man, unconscious, and naked apart from a pair of shorts. Runnels of blood had blackened his face and neck, pooled above his collarbone. A bandage bound his head. Blood-stiffened cloths littered the floor.

Haziq checked his pulse. "Alive," he said.

Virginie looked up at me, confused, and I translated for her. "It's okay. This is my medic. He will help your husband. What happened?"

"Jake," she said. She started to shiver. "Jake is his name."

I didn't press her. Explanations could come later. "Is there anyone else on board, Virginie?" I looked around the saloon. Cushions had been thrown onto the floor, to create a kind of makeshift bed, and at the navigation station the VHF's fist mic was dangling, a black heart at the end of a cord. Everything else seemed to be in order.

She shook her head.

"Just you two?"

A nod.

I asked Haziq what he thought, and he said the man had lost a lot of blood and that we should move him to the *Patusan*, where we had better facilities. We could also get him to a hospital much quicker that way. I did a mental calculation—at top speed, it'd be about four days to Port Brown. Would he last that long? I asked Haziq, still in Bahasa.

He studied the unconscious man's face. "Possibly."

Virginie remained crouched by her husband. I explained we would take them onto our ship. "It will mean leaving your yacht," I said. "Do you understand?" She looked up at me with flat eyes. "Your boat, *Santa Maria*. We can't tow her that far. We'll have to leave her behind." What would abandoning ship mean to her? *Santa Maria* might be her only home. Some Westerners do this—sell their houses for the price of an entire village and live on a boat instead. This one was evidently worth a lot of money. "Virginie. You understand what I'm saying, about your boat?"

"It's not my boat."

His, then. Not the time to be getting into semantics. "Do you want to get some belongings to bring with you to the *Patusan*?" Her shivers had become full-body tremors. "Perhaps some clothes?"

She looked at her husband, shook her head.

"Your passports?"

"They're not here. We have nothing here."

Had she also suffered some kind of head trauma? "You must have some clothes on board," I insisted. Again, she shook her head.

I left her. In the starboard hull was a master cabin. In a locker, I found men's and women's clothing. I snatched up some dresses, a waterproof jacket, and went back into the saloon.

"Here," I said, draping the jacket around her shoulders. Goose bumps sprang up on her neck as I pulled my hands away. "You'll need this for the ride in the tender."

She pulled the edges of the jacket tight around her throat. I went to the chart table and lifted the lid. The ship's papers were tucked inside a plastic wallet, along with a few passports. I shoved all of the documentation into an empty grab bag, stuffed in the dresses, and rolled down the top. We would have to hold the *Patusan* in position until Haziq had stabilized her husband. Hopefully by then Virginie would be making more sense, and we could help her salvage more of her belongings before we left.

"Ready for the transfer?" I asked Haziq, who had put a neck collar on Jake and bandaged his head. He signaled to Virginie to put pressure on the bandage while he went to the tender for the stretcher.

A ship-to-ship transfer of a casualty is never easy, and oceanic swell and thick darkness only make it harder. As we loaded Jake into the tender and laid him on the floor, as we lurched back to the *Patusan*, as we offloaded him onto the ship, Virginie never took her eyes off him. Somehow she managed to ignore the ocean as it reared and roared and spumed around us and focused completely on her husband, gripping his fingers, whispering to him. Later, I'd doubt myself, but I remember thinking that was pure love, there; that was the way Maria had looked at me.

When we were all out of the tender, Yusuf, who had come down from the bridge to assist, took one end of the stretcher. Haziq took the other, and they started to march Jake off along the passageway. Only then did she turn to me. Her face was shiny with salt water, the jacket still clutched tight to her throat.

"Go to him," I said. "It's okay. He's safe now."

It lasted only a fraction of a moment, the look of gratitude she gave me before she scrambled off into the bowels of the ship, shedding the jacket as she went, but it was enough to engulf me in loneliness.

"You're safe now," I repeated, to the empty air.

3

I was conscious of Maria's shadow lingering beside me as I dealt with the extra work created by the unexpected turn of events. The ghosts of my lost children filled the bridge with the brackish scent of ozone. Normally I could command them all to leave me in peace, but that morning they were persistent, and even though I did my best to ignore them, they slowed me down. Therefore it was a while, after dawn had lifted the sky to gray, before I saw Virginie again.

The cook had laid out breakfast in the mess, so I filled two mugs with still-hot coffee and picked up a couple of rotis. In the sick bay, Haziq had set up the patient, who remained unconscious, on the hospital bunk. Virginie was clutching her husband's hand through the metal rail. She was still in her bikini.

Haziq understood my look. "She wouldn't wear any of those clothes you brought back," he said.

I put down the drinks and food. "Scrubs?"

He pointed to a locker. Inside were two shelves holding medication, and on a third, unisex medic's clothing packaged in cellophane. I opened a set and shook out a folded T-shirt.

"Here," I said to her. She took it wordlessly and slipped it over her head. It was green, and long on her, like a man's baju melayu top. My heart constricted. Sometimes, after we made love in the afternoons, Maria would pick up my shirt from the floor, wrap it around herself, and come back to sit on the side of the bed, her arms hidden by the fabric but her legs free.

I addressed Haziq. "How is the patient? And have you assessed her?"

He took the cellophane wrapper from me and crumpled it into a bin. "He's stable for now. Obviously we can't x-ray him here, but as long as he doesn't have a seizure or isn't bleeding internally, he should be able to hang on until we get back to Port Brown."

"And the wife?" She was ignoring us, watching her husband.

"She has no signs of injury. I assessed her for concussion, but she seems okay. Severely dehydrated, and in need of a few good meals. Looks like she hasn't been eating much."

I went back to the coffee and bread. "So, if there's no concussion, she's allowed to eat now?"

"Sure."

I lifted a cup, automatically countering for the movement of the *Patusan* beneath my feet so I didn't spill. After nearly four decades at sea, it was second nature. "Here," I said to Virginie, switching from Bahasa to English, "you must drink something."

When she didn't respond, I said her name and tapped the mug on the rail. The chime it made startled her out of her reverie. She stared at it, and I had the same feeling I'd had on *Santa Maria*, that we might be dealing with a traumatic response of some kind. I needed to find out what had happened to her and Jake; I'd have to make a full report first to my superiors and then to the appropriate authorities, especially if he died. Reports, inquiries, inquests—I've had more than my fill of those. But my first duty is always to human care. The rest can wait.

I offered her the mug again, and this time she took it, curling her fingers around the barrel. They were dark from the sun—darker than my own—her nails shell pink. After a moment she released her other hand from Jake's so she could wrap those fingers around the mug, too. Her shoulders were high, tensed, and she clung to the coffee. She took a sip, and then she tipped the mug right back and drained the lot. A little thing at the time, but later, once she'd told me her story and I understood better, I would remember how she'd done that, and it would make me think about how strong primal instincts are: for food, drink, shelter; to protect the ones we love.

I placed the rounds of bread, stacked in greaseproof paper, on the bed. "Here. Makan." It was what Maria would say when I was home on leave, putting in front of me a dish of nasi lemak or wantan mee; the captain of our home giving the same order to her husband that she'd give to our children: Makan. Eat.

Virginie pinched off a small moon and chewed tentatively. It was an effort for her to swallow, and her body bucked, but then she picked up the whole roti in both hands and bit deep, tearing into it again with her teeth before she'd even finished chewing the first mouthful. Both rotis vanished.

"Sorry," she said, bringing a hand to wipe oily crumbs from her mouth. Haziq passed her a paper towel.

"No need for apology," I replied. "It's good that you eat and drink. But now I think you should sleep."

I'd allotted her my cabin—as the only woman on board, she couldn't be expected to share. I'd hot bunk with Yusuf until we reached Port Brown. She fussed about leaving her husband, but I translated for her what Haziq had said about his condition.

"You must be strong for him, Virginie," I said, "and for that you need rest." I could see I wouldn't have to fight hard—she was stooping with fatigue.

I led her to my cabin. Her lids were already dropping as she saw me out. The lock turned with a click, and I hurried along the passageway and back to my work, my family at my heels.

4

I let her sleep for six hours. In the time she rested, the ocean calmed until it moved us as placidly as a mother swaying an infant. I never trust the sea when it's this even-tempered; I prefer when its full power is unfurled. At least then you know what you're dealing with, can't be taken by surprise.

The *Patusan* had been holding her position, waiting for the all-clear to leave for Port Brown. I wanted answers to at least some of my questions before we abandoned *Santa Maria* for good, so I carried some lunch to Virginie in my cabin. As before, she devoured it. The two bottles of water I'd left by the bed were empty, too.

She was in my bunk, the sheets puddled in her lap, the cup of tea I'd taken her cradled in her hands. I was upright on a chair I'd drawn nearer the bed, close enough to start a conversation, but not so close it was uncomfortable for either of us.

"A navy ship," she said. "They told us there was a navy ship, but that it wouldn't come. I was trying to get someone on the radio for two days. And then you came."

"They?" I asked. "Who are *they*?"

There was a knock at the door. Umar entered at my command.

"Sir." His deference surprised me, and also his salute—he never normally did that. He gave a curt nod to Virginie. He said in English, "You wanted this, Captain?" He passed me a handheld VHF.

"Ensign," I said, and this, too, felt performative. We were unused to having an audience. I switched to Bahasa. "When you have a moment, find a radar reflector, and fix it to the catamaran. Take Yamat with you." Yamat was my engineer. "Get him to wait with the tender while you do so." I could have ordered him to scuttle the boat, but it was worth a lot, there was nothing wrong with it, and I didn't want to get tied up in arguments with the insurers. "Also check the boat's AIS is transmitting. It wasn't showing up last night. Leave it on. Keep one engine on, but in neutral, so the battery bank stays charged for as long as possible. Who knows how far *Santa Maria* will drift when we abandon her? I want to reduce the chances of another ship running into her as much as we can."

"Now, sir?"

"Not necessarily. Before sunset, though. Radio me when you're there."

"Sir." He started to make his way out.

"And Umar," I added, "pick up some more clothes for them and also do a final pass through the boat before you leave, so that there is no need for us to linger once we get the order." He closed the door on his way out.

When we were alone, I started again. "Who told you about our patrol ship? And where were you?"

She dropped her gaze. When my wife and I talked—about anything: Aadam's schooling, happenings in the kampong, our plans for the future—I would have to wait while she considered her response. Her face would be cast down as she thought, and eventually I'd be rewarded with a glint from those tourmaline eyes.

"The others," Virginie said. "They told us about the navy ship. The others on Amarante."

So she had been to Amarante. Few make it there these days, but some of these foreigners are so persistent. I say foreigners, but what I mean is Westerners, because nearly all of them are Westerners, who think islands like Amarante are paradise, that a strip of golden sand is the utopia they've been searching for, and that it will heal all wounds. I suppose if a person's wounds are shallow enough, a touch of sunshine and a lungful of salty air might be all they need to heal. But for others, the cuts are too deep. And for others still, these beaches and the waters surrounding them lead to death, not rebirth.

I wanted to say all of this to her, but instead I told her we used to patrol Amarante several times a year, but that it was so remote, and resources were tight these days, and our remit had been changed by central command.

Virginie's gaze was still on her lap. Her shoulders were hunched again, her defenses clearly up, and I was unsure how to question her. I tried: "You and Jake went to Amarante on holiday?"

She blinked. "Kind of."

"And then he had an accident?"

Silence. She straightened the rumples in the sheets, smoothing the same piece of cloth over and again, as if she could flatten the waves on the sea. The best way to soothe troubled waters, Maria would say, was to pour oil on them—but there was no balm strong enough to help her that day.

I refocused. In the few brief conversations we'd had, this white woman and I, we hadn't yet discussed what had injured Jake or shaken her so badly. It was time to get to the bottom of things. "Virginie, what happened?"

She sucked down the tea, although it must have been cold by then. As she put the empty cup on the shelf next to my bunk, she nudged the photograph that sat there, and the rosary beads I kept on the frame fell off with a clatter. She picked them up, the cross nestled in her palm, the beads dangling beyond her wrist. Her head was bowed in examination; her sandy hair, which was cut short like a man's, dreadfully matted.

"Are you Catholic?" she asked.

"I was raised Catholic."

"Your English is very good."

"I went to an English-medium school. My father's mother was British. And you? Where did you grow up?"

"England, mainly. And France." Her attention went back to Maria's rosary. "My great-aunt used to have a set just like these." She pinched a bead between thumb and forefinger. "I thought you'd be Muslim."

"There are a few Catholics in Malaysia. We have you to thank for that."

"Me?" Then comprehension opened her face. "Ah. You mean colonialists." The beads draped across her fingers, she picked up the photograph. Even now, I can feel the way my mouth pressed into a firm line. "Sweet," she said. "Your wife and kids? How old are they?"

I hesitated. None of the crew ever asked me about my family. "Aadam, my son, was seven when that was taken. Farah, five." She hadn't asked Maria's age, but I added it. "My wife, thirty-one."

"Thirty-one," she said, and I detected a chink, a softening. "Same as me. And how long ago was this taken?"

"In 2004. On Merdeka Day at our home in Penang." The children had dressed up in red-and-white outfits Maria had cut and sewn from the Stripes of Glory. In their hands, plastic flags fluttered. "Four months before . . ."

She must have noticed that I stopped, but she didn't press me to continue. Instead she asked, "You live in Penang?"

"Yes."

"Does your son want to follow you into the navy? Or your daughter, even?"

A rip, dragging me off my course. I wanted to hold on to something, so I reached for the grab bag by my feet, the one I'd taken from *Santa Maria*. The plastic buckles clicked as I popped them open, the impermeable plastic creaked as I unrolled the opening. Inside, on top, were the clothes I'd packed; below, the passports and paperwork. I lifted it all out and piled it onto my knee. Virginie was still wearing the scrubs shirt I'd taken from sick bay. Perhaps now she was rested, thinking more logically, she'd feel more comfortable in her own things. It might even help her to open up more.

I unfolded a dress. Unconventional attire for a navy vessel, but at least it was longer, and would cover more of her legs than the scrubs did. I offered it to her. "Here. I brought it from your boat."

Her guard went up again. "I told you, Captain Tengku, *Santa Maria* is not my boat."

"Your husband's boat."

"Not his, either."

"Then you stole it?"

I intended this as a kind of joke, to try to loosen her, but she jerked away from me. The photo frame was still in her hands, and she rubbed at a mark on the silver surround with a finger. "Jake was in the water."

Behind me, Maria, Aadam, and Farah rose. "Where? At Amarante?"

She nodded, fingers on the photo frame again.

"And he hit his head?"

Another nod. At last we were getting somewhere. "How?"

"I'm not sure."

"On the hull? The rudder?"

Silence.

"Rocks?"

The muscles in her jaw worked. "I think maybe the prop."

If it had been a propeller, he was extremely lucky to be alive. And he should have known better than that. I'd had them down as pros; I'd seen her seamanship firsthand, in the operation of the flares, the solo handling of the sails, and I'd presumed that to be going somewhere as far offshore as Amarante, her husband must be equally knowledgeable. So what was he doing, swimming near a propeller? Something was off.

"Listen, you've got to understand something. Jake hates the water. More than that—he's frightened of it. But he got in it. For me."

Maria never learned how to swim. But we spoke about it and agreed that Aadam and Farah should learn. So that's why she took them to Pantai Pasir Panjang, to see the sea from the safety of the sand, to get them used to it.

I snapped back into work mode. Virginie's story was making little sense. "So you're telling me that your husband, who's frightened of water, jumps overboard, near a moving propeller, for you, for some reason?"

"He didn't jump."

"He fell?"

She shook her head, impenetrable again.

"He tripped?"

Another shake.

"Pushed?"

That time her head was still. I took it as a yes. "By who? Who pushed him, Virginie?" Had she? Was that why she was acting so oddly—not from trauma but guilt? "You?"

"No!"

"Who?"

"Vitor."

"Who's Vitor? Your crew?" The catamaran was easily big enough to warrant crew—one, possibly even two.

"They were fighting. Jake wanted the water, and Vitor wouldn't let him."

"I thought you said Jake was frightened of the water?"

"Not that water, the other water. Oh, I'm telling it wrong." She slammed the picture frame onto the bedding and brought her hands to her face, gasping against her palms. I picked up the photograph— luckily the glass hadn't cracked—and put it back in its place.

"I need . . ." She got out of the bed abruptly. "Where's the head?"

Averting my gaze from her bare legs, I pointed to the closed bathroom door. She slipped through and shut it behind her. I heard the tap running.

I put the dress and other clothing on the floor and turned my attention to the documents, the passports and the ship's papers. There were four passports. The first I opened was Brazilian, for a Vitor Santos, a white man. In the photograph his jaw was square, his skin tanned, hair dark. His date of birth made him forty-two—a little old to be working as a deckhand. Perhaps he was their skipper, and I'd overestimated her and Jake's skills. The second passport had a black cover, embossed in gold: República de Moçambique. The woman in the picture was not Virginie. She was black, her hair woven tight against her skull, extending into long braids. Teresa Mabote. Their stewardess-cook? The third passport was European, Portuguese, a white man's. João da Silva. The image wasn't so clear, but it looked like the man in the first passport. Corresponding date of birth. And the fourth was for the same man, but Mozambican again this time, Vicente de Sousa. Another birth date match. There were no passports for Virginie or Jake.

A squeak came as the bathroom tap was switched off. I slipped the ship's papers from their wallet and unfolded them. *Santa Maria* was registered in São Sebastião, Brazil, to Vitor Santos. I thumbed through the rest of the paperwork, looking to see if the yacht had been sold on. But nothing. It all tallied.

Not my boat, she'd said.

The bathroom door opened. Her hairline was damp, her features surprisingly composed for someone who just a moment or two before had been so distressed. The edges of the passport covers bit into my fingers. Who was this woman, and what had she done?

"I'll start from the beginning," she said, as she came out. "You'll understand better that way—"

I held out the ship's papers and first passport to her, photo page open. "Virginie, who is Vitor Santos? Why do you have his boat? Who is Teresa Mabote? And where are they now?"

She dropped to the bed. Her jaw was working, but no sound emerged; her focus was locked on the passport.

"Virginie, what's going on?"

She clamped her hands beneath her thighs.

"Virginie, answer me. Who is this man, and where is he? Have you done something to him?"

She started to rock back and forth, still working her jaw. It came first as a whisper, too soft to comprehend, but then it built to a murmur. Through the repetition of the phrase, which was timed to her movements, as if by the physical act of rocking she was forcing it out, I was able to discern her words, and the moment when I did so was like the drawback before a tsunami, that otherworldly pause when the water vanishes and all seems still and calm and silent before the destruction comes.

"It's all my fault. I killed them. Killed them! It's all my fault."

AMARANTE

5

The plane banked and Virginie put down her book to look out of the window. They were still over the sea. How she loved that cobalt shade of deep water—just looking at it filled her with energy, with life, with hope. In the seat beside her, Jake napped, and she almost woke him to point it out, but then she checked her watch. Let him rest. They'd be seeing it up close very soon.

She unbuckled her seat belt and leaned as far forward as she could, straining for a glimpse of land. The height and speed of the plane had a peculiar effect on the waves below, seeming to fasten them in time and space, solidifying the whitecaps. She spotted a yacht, impossibly small. Both sails were up, and it was heeled over, so it must have been moving, but like the waves, it seemed pinned in position on the earth. She wondered about the people on board—they were on a voyage, like her and Jake. Did they share the same dreams? Were they also seeking new beginnings? She pressed the tip of her finger against the window-pane. Ice crystals had formed on the outside.

Just before they started the descent, Jake woke, blinking groggily. "How long was I out for?"

"Couple of hours. We're nearly there." The huge smile he gave her mirrored her own feelings.

When they emerged from the controlled atmosphere of the cabin and started to descend the steps from the plane, the hot air brought enticing exotic smells: smoke, melting tarmac, and a vital, vegetal spice of tropical land, so different from the air in England. She paused and took a deeper breath. Would everything else be so different here, too? She hoped so.

Her foot left the last metal step and found the ground. Ahead, a line of bottle palms, their fronds rustling in the wind, flanked the entrance to a low-slung terminal. Despite the fifteen-hour journey, she was buoyant. Just one more hour, two at the most, and they'd be there. She turned and waited for Jake, who was halfway down the steps, carrying a wheelie case that wasn't theirs. On reaching the ground, he placed it in front of an elderly woman dressed in a long patterned tunic and head scarf. The woman thanked him in smiles and ducks of her chin. That was the thing with Jake: always thinking of others.

Virginie snaked an arm around his waist and leaned in. "Leaving me for another woman already?"

He puffed out his cheeks. "You've some stiff competition there." He kissed the top of her head, and together they followed the woman and the other passengers across the apron to the terminal.

It was late afternoon by the time the taxi stopped at the harbor. Waiters were preparing an outdoor restaurant for the evening's customers, setting out plastic chairs, laying tablecloths, weighing down piles of whisper-thin pink paper napkins with forks and spoons. They nodded to her as they worked.

Jake unloaded their luggage from the car. "I'll go find a water taxi to take us out to the boat," he said, adding the last holdall to the pile on the ground. "You okay to wait here with these?"

"Sure." She pulled some ringgit from her wallet. "Here." The notes she'd withdrawn at the airport were purple, red, and orange, colorful as money in a Monopoly set. "You might need to pay up front." He pocketed them, kissed her cheek, and set off.

Beyond the restaurant, the harbor brimmed with boats. Wooden longtails disturbed the tranquility with the loud tut-tut-tut of their outboard motors as they returned from a day's fishing. She pulled out her phone to take a picture. In the shot, the red and blue paint gleamed in the sunshine. With their almost vertical bowsprits, the longtails looked like tropical versions of Viking longships, back from plundering the seas, or the canoes of those other early seafarers, the fearless Polynesian explorers who set out on voyages thousands of miles long, trusting their fate to the winds and stars. She made a mental note to email her boss at the museum—former boss, really—and suggest he add something on Malay longtails to a display. She posted the photo, so her brother and sisters and their friends would see it and know they'd arrived safely.

At the far end of the sea wall the Malaysian flag fluttered on a pole, familiar and strange at the same time in the way it looked just like the Stars and Stripes until a hard snap revealed a yellow crescent moon and star in the canton. With the wind came the ozonic scent of the ocean, layered with diesel and the fishy stink of nets crisping under the sun, far more intense than the smells that blew in off the water near their flat back in England. Beyond the sea wall about twenty sailing yachts were at anchor, all turned with the tide to point toward the shore. She scanned the bay, but it was difficult to tell which yacht was theirs from this distance, which would be their home—the first they'd owned together—as they traveled for the next year, perhaps even two. Her stomach flipped. Imagine the places these boats might have been, what their owners had seen. Soon she and Jake would be the ones with stories to tell. What better way to get their marriage off to a good start?

The sun was relentless, and she eyed the shade cast by a broad banyan tree. Strangler fig, some people called them. She shifted their four bags underneath its spreading canopy and examined the aerial roots that had grown down to the earth in search of water. Remarkable, really, how nature could thrive as long as it was able to fulfill its basic needs: food, water, light.

The luggage had already picked up a coating of dust. Their whole lives—their new lives—were held in these four bags. Packing up the flat had been a lot of work, but as she'd watched the storage van round the corner, its indicator barely visible through the autumn fog, she'd felt lighter. It was an odd word, *belongings*, for things like pots and pans, armchairs, winter boots, photographs. It implied you needed all those items to feel you belonged somewhere, or with someone, and that without all that stuff you were untethered, an outcast almost. But things, even people, weighed you down. Apart from Jake. He never could.

A cat approached, a tortoiseshell, and nuzzled her calf. It was an adult, fully grown but tiny, little bigger than a kitten, its tail bobbed. It mewed, and she went to scratch behind its ears, hearing Tomas—*fleas, disease, unhygienic*. She stroked the top of its head, under its chin. It pushed its skull against her fingers a couple of times before losing interest, distracted by some spilled yellow rice on the grass by her feet.

She edged along a few grains with her sandal. "Here, little fellow, have it all."

At her name being called, she looked up. Jake was coming along the path, his hair streaked copper by the sun. "Good news. Found a fisherman to take us."

They picked up two bags each, and he led the way down to the dock, where a longtail was waiting, a fisherman squatting by the tiller. Jake swung the bags into the boat and Virginie climbed in. The longtail's narrow beam made it unstable, and it tilted alarmingly, causing her to land harder on the bench than she'd intended. Not very graceful. Embarrassed, she looked at the fisherman, but his hollow-cheeked face remained impassive. Once Jake was in, too, the fisherman yanked on the starter cord, firing the engine into a noisy rattle, and headed out into the bay.

The wind generated by the forward movement was a blessed relief, drying the sweat on her forehead and lifting her damp hair away from her neck. The fisherman, old, possibly as old as her father, but bony in his shorts and loose T-shirt while Papa was rounded by good living, pointed at one of the yachts anchored toward the back of the pack, and Jake nodded. As they drew closer, Virginie recognized the sail cover, but the boat looked more tired than the last time she'd seen it, the navy lettering of its name, *Lost Horizon*, faded to a stonewashed denim, furry algae clinging to the waterline. She shook herself mentally. None of that mattered, not really—it was just cosmetic. No need to focus on the little things; this was about the bigger picture. A bit of elbow grease, as Jake called it, and everything would be fine. And besides, the worn letters would soon be replaced when they renamed the yacht and put their own stamp on it.

The longtail drew alongside, and Jake stood and grabbed the rail, holding the two boats together.

"Pergi, pergi," the fisherman said, raising his voice over the clatter of the engine, flicking his hand, signaling her to climb onto the yacht. She hefted their bags onto the deck and scrambled up, the scorching metal of the toe rail burning her knee as she went. Jake had only one foot on the deck, the other still in midair, when the fisherman pushed off and revved his throttle, eager to return home before the evening prayer.

As soon as she got below deck, she was sweating again. The air down here was oppressively still, so layered with the stink of months-old mold and fuel and brine that it was almost solid, and she struggled to breathe. Jake opened the hatch and windows, but it made little difference.

"First job tomorrow, fit some fans?" she asked.

He pulled off his T-shirt. His skin was an English-winter white all over, ghostly looking. "Definitely."

Four months had passed since she'd spotted the online listing for the yacht. At thirty-six feet, it was the perfect size and setup for two, and such a bargain compared to what people were asking in the UK or Europe. She'd pointed it out to Jake, and a couple of weeks later, after an email exchange with the owners, an older Dutch couple, they'd found a good deal on plane tickets and flown out here to view it. They were confident that with Jake's boatbuilding experience and her countless summers on board her father's boat share they'd be capable of doing the survey themselves. They'd found the yacht in sound condition for its age, if, naturally, given their tight budget, a little worn. After a short negotiation with the Dutch couple, they'd transferred their savings.

She took a look around, squaring what she saw before her now with the mental pictures she'd held in her mind for the past few months. The blue bench-style settees, which ran along each side of the saloon, upright as church pews, were faded, but not yet in need of replacing. She opened the wooden cupboards above, welcoming the whisper of air against her cheek that the movement of the louvered doors created. It was a good job they hadn't brought much stuff with them from home because it was a meager amount of space, even compared to what they'd had in their small flat, and especially so compared to the wall of wardrobes she'd had in Paris. That bloody antique dresser of Tomas's—it was so huge it had dominated the bedroom of that apartment. Although it was worth more than this entire boat, she'd gladly have given it away; if she'd been allowed to, she'd have stripped all of the fusty inherited furniture out of that place, ripped away the heavy drapes, replaced everything with clean, modern pieces—a chest of drawers or a nightstand she could put her hairbrush onto, her glass of water, without fear. But that hadn't been her choice to make.

She closed the doors with a snap, shutting out the past. The walls were bare now the previous owners had taken down their things, leaving her free to decorate any way she chose. She pictured herself hanging mementos bought from beachside villages, collecting shells from every anchorage they visited, curating the tale of their travels. Tomorrow she'd pick up a local batik print to jazz things up.

The polished sole boards were smooth under her bare feet as she turned toward the back of the boat, into the narrow L-shaped galley that hooked around the starboard side. She opened the top-loading fridge, peered into the cupboards, tried the small gimballed stove. All were still in good working order. The sink was rusting where the salt-water tap had been allowed to drip, but a good scrub would get the marks out. Two paces beyond the galley was the cabin, with a high double berth. Not as wide as their bed at home, but big enough, cozy for two.

She retreated back through the galley on her way to the head on the port side. Jake was at the chart table, kneeling on the seat, flicking switches on the instrument panel. As she squeezed through, the boat rolled, riding the wake of a passing vessel, and she grabbed his calf to steady herself. She'd need a day or so to find her sea legs.

"I think the batteries are dead," he said, clicking away. "I swear they were working last time we were here."

The Dutch couple had left the head in a fairly clean state, she found when she ducked into the compact bathroom. She pulled the shower hose from its slot at the sink, where it doubled as a tap, and turned it on. Only a dribble. What she'd give for a cool shower—but no power meant that wasn't an option right now. It was cramped in there, and all at once she was too hot. She backed into the saloon and unzipped one of her bags, grabbing the first pair of shorts and loose T-shirt she could find. As soon as she lifted her hair from her neck to twist a band around it, she could breathe.

She rooted around the bag again, looking for the folder with their wedding photo. She'd only brought the one—her and Jake, a selfie taken by the river, their faces filling most of the frame in front of a tufted sky. She propped it on the shelf.

"Damn it," Jake said, giving up at the panel. The bottle of champagne she'd bought at duty-free was sticking out of her bag. He fished it out. She'd blown their daily budget on it but hadn't cared. "Just this once," she'd told him as they stood under the artificial 24/7 lights of the airport shop as people milled past, all on journeys to somewhere else. "It's a special occasion."

"We can't chill it," he said now. "The celebrations are going to have to wait a day or two."

She knew other ways to celebrate. She moved over to him. His chest was slick and the hair at his nape damp under her fingertips. He was salty when she kissed him, tasted of home.

"Think it might be too hot for this?" she said.

"Baby, it's never too hot for this." He put the bottle on the side and slid both hands up under her T-shirt.

That night they slept outside to escape the worst of the heat, curled opposite each other on the cockpit benches, the humidity heavy as a blanket. Woken by a fishing boat motoring across the harbor, she reached for Jake, but found only air before she remembered that they weren't in their bed in the flat. The realization jolted her fully awake, and she tossed and turned for a while before tiptoeing her way across the dew-damp teak to the foredeck. At the tip of the bow, she caught hold of the roped steel of the forestay and looked east, examining the sky for the first tint of sunrise. The high hills on the land were shadowed and woolly in the predawn grayness, and as the sky lightened, turning the hills a hundred shades of green, a single man's voice called the faithful to prayer.

6

Nearly a month passed without leaving the anchorage as they busied themselves fixing things on the boat. Jake's prediction of a day or two of work became a week, a fortnight, and then double that as job after job claimed their time.

As they replaced the batteries, fitted filters, and patched up sails worn paper-thin from years of wind and sun, it occurred to Virginie that no matter how experienced you were, there was always something new to learn about boats. She could sail—childhood holidays exploring the Côte d'Azur on the yacht her father shared with three others had ensured that. And her job at the maritime museum meant she'd learned to talk endlessly about pilot cutters, South Coast smugglers, and the salt-farming history of the oozy Hampshire lands surrounding Jake's hometown of Lymington. But she was realizing now how she'd been swept along by the romance and hadn't really considered this part, all the maintenance and engineering needed. Especially in a boat like theirs, an older one at the more affordable end of the scale.

Jake was in his element, stripping things down and putting them back together again, oily fingers hovering over manuals. By nightfall every evening his skin was sheened with sweat, his temples smudged with dirt. She always liked him best like this back home—just in from the yard in a T-shirt that showed the strength of his arms, in particular those definition lines along the edges of his triceps.

She never ceased to be amazed by his ability to understand how things worked. She'd witnessed it first a week or so into their relationship when her electric kettle had refused to heat up in the kitchen of the flat she shared with two other women. She'd sworn and thrown the thing into the sink. While she was rummaging under the counter for a saucepan, he rescued the kettle, pulled a penknife from his pocket, and started to take it apart. "It doesn't matter," she told him. "I'll pick up a new one tomorrow." He abandoned it with reluctance. Later that afternoon, waking from a nap after a couple of hours in bed, she found him back in the kitchen, screwdriver in hand, kettle parts scattered across the counter. Within half an hour, it was working. A couple of months later, when her car broke down, he spent an entire weekend getting it going. "You didn't have to," she'd said. "I could've taken it to the garage." He'd dangled the key off the tip of his finger. "I wanted to. And besides, now I don't have to worry it'll conk out again, leave you stuck somewhere. I know you'll be safe." Taking care—of things, of her—was a trait she found incredibly attractive in him.

Today was the last day of work, and her final task was to paint the boat's new name on the topsides. She'd be glad to see the back of *Lost Horizon*—it was far too negative. She tied their rubber dinghy alongside and stood in it, carefully timing her brush strokes with the waves and tracing out the name they'd chosen in honor of the ancient seafarers who'd first set out across the oceans, and also to mark their own imminent voyaging: *Wayfinder*.

She had finished the writing on one side of the boat and was filling in the downstroke of the *r* on the other when Terry came by in his dinghy. Terry was an older Australian they sometimes bumped into around town. A lot of the cruisers they'd met around here were like him, retirees with leathered skin and sun-faded shirts who'd traded their lives on land for dreams of adventure at sea as soon as their children had flown the nest. Many had been to amazing places, but now, two or even three decades on, they had neither the resources nor the inclination to move back to a more comfortable life ashore. They drifted to Malaysia because their pensions went further here.

Terry steered his dinghy close to hers and knocked his engine into idle. "Nice job."

"Thanks." She reloaded her brush to paint the curved top of the letter.

"That Jotun?"

It wasn't. She turned the paint can label out to show him.

"Always use Jotun myself," he said. "Expensive, but you get what you pay for."

She made a noncommittal noise. Terry was harmless, but full of unsolicited advice. Well into his seventies, he was no longer fit enough to take his boat out, and it languished permanently on a mooring in the bay. He was on his own; by the sound of it, his kids and grandkids never visited. And it seemed few around here were willing to spend much time with him, either. Often she saw people giving him a wide berth.

"You heading off soon?" he said.

A passing boat threw out its wake, making her dinghy bob. She lifted the brush away from the hull just in time. "Later this week, all being well."

"Still shooting for Thailand?"

Thailand was their first choice of where to take *Wayfinder*—great food, plenty of other yachts. She'd already dug out the pilot guide and put it on the chart table, ready for planning. "That's right, now we're all finished."

He cackled. "Finished, ay? You know things are never finished on boats." He laughed again, to himself more than to her.

She added the final daub of paint. "Done!"

A pop from overhead. Jake was coming along the side deck with the bottle of duty-free champagne in one hand, two cooler cups in the other. Perfect timing.

"Make sure you save a libation for the sea gods, keep them on your side," Terry said.

Jake tipped the tiniest amount into the water. "Precious stuff, this. That'll have to do."

Terry saluted him. "Well, I'll leave yous to it."

She waved him off before she climbed up. Jake handed over a cup and tapped his against hers.

"Hang on," she said, unlocking her phone. "Come here a sec." She angled the camera so the champagne and the sea behind them were in shot and leaned her head against his. It was a good picture, both of them looking happy and tanned—the sun was so strong here that by now even Jake's resolutely pale skin had picked up a touch of caramel. Before posting it, she added a label: *#inparadise*.

"I think we've earned a break," he said after she'd put down her phone and they'd taken their first deliciously cold sip. "No beans from a tin tonight. My beautiful wife deserves better."

"What, corned beef instead?"

"If you're lucky, you might get a tinned potato or two on the side." He leaned back against the cabin top. "What about the yacht club for dinner?"

Yacht clubs—never as glamorous as their name suggested. She knew that much from Lymington. The one here was no exception, and the food was pretty awful. But after a full day of working in the sun, she was too tired to cook, and she bet Jake was, too.

"Sure." She lifted her glass again. Tiny bubbles burst against her upper lip, their scent toasty, a little like apple sauce. "You'll have to get me drunk for their 'Western style' steak, though."

He wriggled his eyebrows "If that's a challenge, you're on!"

•   •   •

There was a handful of other customers at the yacht club: a trio of middle-aged Chinese men deep in conversation and four sailors crammed around the table nearest the plug socket, laptops on charge. She didn't recognize them—new arrivals, maybe.

She took a chair by the window while Jake fetched drinks from the bar. It had been dark for an hour, and the lights on the dock made orange stripes on the water. It was hard to imagine their old life now, the wet gray days when it was difficult to get out from under the duvet, the constant striving to keep on top of the working week's routines. Traffic jams, office politics, repetitive, pointless programs on the TV. And before then, before Jake . . . No—she didn't want to think of that; she didn't want those memories, those emotions, to travel here to this rainbow-bright, effervescent country. Better they stayed behind, in another place, another time.

On the table was a beer mat, its edges swollen with moisture, exposing the pulpy insides. She nudged it away. Life was so pleasant here, so free—they woke with the muezzin's call, did things at their own pace. She showered off the day's sweat as the sun sank below the horizon. Evenings were for eating, talking, and, once it was cool enough, sex. All as she'd wanted, just as she'd imagined. And now that the works were done, life would be even better. The fun could really start.

She checked her phone: a missed call from Mum, likes of her champagne post from her sisters, and replies from her brother, Philippe— *Not jealous AT ALL*—and her boss—*Tres bon (voyage)!*

Jake returned, a beer in each hand. "Sorry I took so long." He sat. "Terry collared me, on about some island. Heaven on earth, apparently. You know what he's like. Probably had a skinful." He glanced back at the bar. "Oh, heads-up. Incoming."

Terry was shuffling toward them across the tiled floor. He looked like he might have been in the yacht club ever since she'd waved him off earlier. "G'day again, Vee."

"Terry."

"Been telling your husband here about my island."

"Mmm, so I hear."

"I've been thinking this arvo, about yous two. And Thailand. And I don't reckon it's the right place."

"No?"

"It's all right, but nothing special, nothing you can't get right here. Bit run-of-the-mill these days, chocka with backpackers and hustlers looking to make a buck or two. Chocka with boats, too. Not like in the '80s—now *that* was a time to visit."

Unprompted, he pulled out a chair and settled at their table. She suppressed a sigh. There went her and Jake's celebration.

"Nah," Terry said, "it seems to me the pair of you know what you're doing. Like me and Eileen, back in the day. You got gumption."

Jake laughed. "Gumption!"

"Gumption." Terry's nod was slow, although it was hard to tell whether in confirmation or through drink. "Not like most young 'uns, all concerned with Apple this, Insta that."

Millennials were Terry's favorite topic, and he could easily harp on for half an hour. Better to steer him onto a different course. "So, this island," Virginie said. Under the table, Jake nudged her foot with his. *Don't encourage him*, the touch meant.

"I wouldn't normally mention it," Terry said, "but . . ." He knocked back the last inch of his beer. "It's not Thailand, this island, not by a long shot—it takes balls to go there. About as remote as you can get in this world."

"Hey," Jake said. "We've got balls. What happened to gumption?"

Terry paid no heed to his jesting. "It's a beaut, all right. Think of a travel agent's brochure or a postcard with a beautiful beach on it. Now multiply that by about a million. Except this one's not been—what do they call it—photoshopped."

"Really?" She met Jake's skeptical eye with a grin, yet kept her voice sincere. "That beautiful?"

"Soft white sand with only your footprints in it, palm trees, clearest water you've ever seen . . . the real deal. A few boats head there every dry season—only a few, mind. It's been going for years—a bit of a secret members' club." He tapped the side of his nose. "There's some club rules, but it's friendly. 'Course there's no shops, no yacht clubs, no air-conditioning—you won't even get anything on the radio. Though that's not what you'd go for, is it? It's pure nothing, you get me? You gotta be pretty happy with your own company. No stresses, no worries, all the time in the world. Yep—pure nothing, and yet everything."

When Terry wasn't looking, Jake winked at her. He had a glint in his eye. "Sounds fascinating, Terry," he said. "How do we get there?" She used her drink to mask her smile.

Terry reached for the soggy beer mat, tipped it on its side. "From here, it's three weeks or so, depending on your boat—yours is a thirty-six-footer, right?" They nodded. "So it's three days up to PB." He sailed the mat along his edge of the table, tracing an invisible route.

"PB?"

"Port Brown."

She laughed. "Doesn't sound very Malaysian."

"Named by the English. This island I'm talking about, that used to be British, too, but got handed over, you know?" He returned to his demonstration. "Now, in PB, you stock up with fuel, water, provisions—fill your lockers, your dunny, everywhere. It's gotta last months." The mat changed direction, set off toward Jake. "Then it's two thousand miles west-sou'west. For you, that'll be a good fortnight at sea. Now, beyond the island your closest land is Sri Lanka." He waggled his empty glass. "Five days off." The glass plonked down on the table in the corner farthest from his model boat. "But you won't be interested in anywhere else, for sure. And we're in the right monsoon season, so it's downwind all the way. Piece of piss." The mat picked up speed, coming to rest near Jake. "There's a natural harbor in the southwest corner. Drop your hook and"—he released the mat with a flourish, letting it slap down—"you can really start to enjoy yourselves."

It was only a silly game, but still the idea of setting sail made her stomach fizz. They'd be off in a few days anyway, the dreams they'd had at home coming to fruition at last. Jake's bare foot was resting on hers. She flexed back her toes so they touched sole to sole.

"You ever been?" he asked Terry. "To this Eden?"

Terry fished a pouch of tobacco from his shirt pocket and pulled a filter from it. " 'Course. Wouldn't be telling you this if I hadn't, would I? Every season for twelve years with the wife, till she got crook." He put the filter between his lips while he stretched out a cigarette paper on his knee.

So he wasn't all talk. "Twelve years?" she said. "Why so many?"

He looked up from the line of tobacco he was sowing across the paper. "Weren't you listening?" The filter, stuck to his upper lip, bobbed. "Why go anywhere else? Trust me—I've been to a lot of places, and none of them compares to this. I only wish we'd known about it at your age." He plucked the filter from his mouth, added it to his cigarette, and rolled. "I can't imagine a better honeymoon spot. Forget your all-inclusive Maldives deal. That's not real life. You want to test the mettle of your marriage, go somewhere like this. Forty-two years, we were married. Cast iron."

Forty-two years. She glanced at Jake. A lifetime. What would he be like in his seventies? "Whose idea was it to go there, Terry?" she asked. "Yours or Eileen's?"

He narrowed his eyes, deepening the creases at the corners. "Do you know, I can't remember now. But after we had a taste of it that first year, we bloody well went back soon as. There's something about the place. Not just the beauty. It's the rawness. The remoteness. Gets in your bones. Feels like you and her against the world."

"Survive that, and you can survive anything?"

He chuckled, a throaty smoker's caw. "Exactly. You can't beat memories like that."

Unlit cigarette slotted between his lips, he stood, chair scraping against the tiles. "I'd better be getting back." When he took her hand, callouses pressed into her skin. "Now, don't go feeling you have to listen to me, but it'd be worth your while. For sure." He released her and nodded to Jake. "G'night."

She watched him make his way across the floor. How easy it was to fall into the habit of judging someone by surface alone, even if you constantly reminded yourself not to. Her opinion of Terry had shifted as they'd talked, and now, looking at his departing back, she imagined him in his early thirties, full of brio and ambition, deeply in love with his new bride.

He was almost at the exit when it occurred to her that he hadn't told them what the island was called. She raised her voice so it would carry across to him. "Terry, what's its real name, your island?"

He stopped, one hand on the open door. "Amarante." He cleared his throat and, to her surprise, began to recite poetry: "'Immortal amarant, a flower which once in Paradise, fast by the Tree of Life, began to bloom.'"

And then he slipped through into the night.

7

Amarante. Virginie lay awake in their cabin, enjoying the air from the fan tickling her skin. *Amar-ante.* A beautiful word, sonorous. *Amour-ante.* A place of love, a place before love. A place to love.

Beside her, Jake slept. They hadn't stayed long at the yacht club after Terry left, had come back and fallen eagerly into bed. But she'd woken early, which was unusual for her. Normally she was the night owl, and at home Jake would come say good night as she carried on working at the kitchen table. The museum wasn't well funded, didn't have enough staff, so evenings were generally spent catching up. Her director joked that hers were the most thorough wall panels ever, but she didn't begrudge the extra time. The stories and artifacts the old mariners had brought back from their travels were fascinating.

Jake was the opposite, an early bird, and even at weekends, when the yard wasn't demanding his time, he'd be kissing her as dawn broke, off to crew for some boat owner in a race round the cans, or to help out with the kids' club Oppies and Toppers. Out here their patterns had synced, no doubt because of the even length of the days and nights at this latitude, and the laid-back lifestyle of the locals. Life in Malaysia operated at a much slower pace than anywhere else she'd lived. In

London, Paris, even Lymington, everything had always been frenetic, and she'd found it hard to switch off.

Immortal Amarant. She slipped out of bed and went to the chart table, where her phone was on charge. She typed in Terry's words. It was a line by Milton, his *amarant* missing the last syllable of Terry's island's name. She lifted the table's hinged lid and pulled out the stack of charts. They were secondhand, and the edges, as she thumbed through them, were soft, the paper musty. Europe, Australasia, the South Pacific. Then, the Indian Ocean. It was an out-of-date chart, a photocopy—how her father would have tutted—and it took a few seconds to understand how to read the faded black lines with the white spaces between them, the numbers, and the abbreviations *Sh* and *Co* showing where shell and coral lined the seabed.

She located where they were anchored now. Using her thumb and forefinger as dividers, she inched out a rough four hundred miles along the coast of the Malaysian peninsula. Port Brown. Okay. Then five times that distance west-southwest, skipping over the northern end of Sumatra. Should be . . . there. She jabbed a spot on the chart, peering closely. There was a black dot on the paper, but at this scale, where a thousand miles were reduced to a hand span, it was difficult to tell whether it was an island or a mark transferred from the photocopier. A magnifying glass didn't help. She riffled through the selection of charts until she found a slightly more recent version and checked again. Yes, there it was, a tiny island standing alone in the middle of the ocean. This chart had a label for it: *Amarante.*

In the aft cabin Jake stirred, and the fan was silenced with a click. He came through, and as he bent to kiss her, his hand was hot on her shoulder.

"Up already? Early for you."

"Couldn't sleep. Thought I'd look for Amarante."

"Terry's love island?"

"It's here. Look."

He leaned in. "Aha! Amarante." He picked up the chart and held it close to his face, then at arm's length, frowning. He pursed his lips. "Doesn't say whether it's paradise or not." It landed back on the table. "Coffee?"

The stove clicked, and he set the water on to bubble. She reached for the chart, where the fractured Thai coastline was caught along the right-hand edge. Maybe Terry was right, and Thailand wasn't the place to go. Those famous beaches turned into movie sets, all the tourists, the barefaced commerce. What adventure was there in that?

She thought of the world chart they'd pinned on their wall in the flat, how she'd brought home a pack of kids' stickers from the museum, little cartoon boats, and she and Jake had pressed them onto the paper in the places that appealed to them, dotting the bluest, most out-of-the-way, exotic places, building a fleet bent on escape and discovery.

Before she'd even fully formed the thought, she was saying it. "Jake, what if we went there? To Amarante?"

He was reaching into the cupboard. "What? Why?"

"Well, it sounded just like what we want. Beautiful. Quiet. Beautiful."

"You said that."

It was hard to put into words. It was more a feeling deep inside her, a radiating warmth, expanding light, excitement at what could be. She could admit she'd fallen for the promise it offered, but that would seem silly; better to appeal to his sense of curiosity, to the opportunity it presented. "And it could be interesting, right?"

He sifted through the fridge. The milk carton thunked as he placed it on the counter. "A secret island that's like heaven on earth and which you can only get to on your own boat? Come on, Vee. People have been spinning stuff like that for years."

His reaction surprised her—usually they were on the same page when it came to this trip. They hadn't been dating long when he'd told her about his plan to buy a boat. By then she'd already picked up on his obsession with explorer-sailors—his bookshelf was crammed with dog-eared copies of Slocum, Stevenson, Moitessier, Knox-Johnston. He'd even brought a few of his favorites, treasured since his teens, out here with him. She'd assumed he was looking for a challenge.

With their own yacht, they could go anywhere—so why not choose somewhere fresh? When she'd backpacked as a student, she'd always ridden the train to the end of the line, well past the usual hot spots, like Rome or Budapest. That's how she found herself in Lymington—and look what that led her to, *who* it led her to. How could you find excitement, or expect to change, to grow, if you did the same things all the time? Now she had the chance to try new experiences with Jake by her side, and the opportunity to go somewhere few people had been. She couldn't let this pass her by.

She said, "I know it's basically hearsay from an old yachtie we heard when we were a bit pissed."

Jake moved to the settee. He stretched out his legs. "Don't you think we should try something a bit more in our comfort zone first?"

"Come on. We're both more than capable. And you reckon taverna-hopping in the Med bores you. Wouldn't Thailand be just like that?"

He was pushing his hand backwards and forwards through his hair—it was his tell. He did it when he was unsure about something.

"We came away for adventure," she continued, twisting her wedding ring. This marriage was going to work. Jake was for keeps. "Isn't this the kind of place you always wanted to go to?" Jake's eyes flicked to his books. "How about striking a bargain? We go to Amarante now and Thailand afterwards. Or Bali, Sumatra—your choice."

He ran his finger around the rim of his cup, once, twice. "I don't know, Vee. I get what you're saying, but why can't we stick to the original plan? It's crazy, following directions given to us by a bloke we barely know, like some kind of children's treasure hunt."

Was that why he had a problem with it? Not Amarante as such, but the fact the idea had come from another man? She didn't think he was that kind of guy.

"And besides," he added, "it's so remote. Nothing there, Terry said. Do you always have to do things the hard way? Normal can be fun, too, you know."

"Hard, sure. But not impossible. It's not that different from sailing to Thailand—just a bit farther, a different direction."

"It's a little more than that."

"Of course it is. But we already did the difficult stuff, getting out here in the first place." At home: saving, planning, studying charts. Buying pilot guides, swotting up on the area, learning the unfamiliar monsoon weather patterns—spending every spare moment ensuring they were as prepared as could be. Among all that, making the actual decision to do it, to leave, was the greatest leap of faith. At any point, either of them could have backed out. But they hadn't. "I thought it was your dream? You made it mine, too. For better, for worse, we said, Jake. And this"—she tapped the chart—"*this* is the better, right here, right now. It's why we bought our own boat. It'll be fantastic. *Wayfinder*'s ready. We're ready. You never know—we might want to stay forever. A lifelong honeymoon."

She crossed the saloon to sit on his knee and encircled his shoulders with her arms. "We can go all *Blue Lagoon* and live in a straw hut we build on the beach." She kissed him lightly on the lips.

His hands came to her waist. "You'd look good in a grass skirt."

If he was making a joke of it, she'd already won.

He sighed. "You've really got your heart set on this?"

She nodded and kissed him properly. "So?" she asked while his eyes were still closed. "What do you think?"

He opened his eyes and held her gaze. "I think we do it."

8

Five days after first hearing of Amarante, Virginie stood by Jake at the helm as he maneuvered *Wayfinder* through Port Brown harbor. Local boats furrowed the water, laden with gas canisters, crates of soft drink, and enough passengers to sink their hulls precariously low. The people in the boats stared at the yacht as they passed.

She went below to try to hail the harbormaster's office for a third time. All she could get from the radio was static and conversations in Malay. During their time in Malaysia, she'd picked up a few words, but nothing more than standard greetings and the names of food items—kopi (coffee), air (water)—or basic places—tandas (bathroom), restoran (restaurant).

She stuck her head out of the companionway. "It's no good. I'm not getting anything."

"Okay, come up here and help me figure out where to go. I'll make another circle."

On their second rotation she understood that one of the smaller aluminum boats was trying to attract their attention. The driver was gesturing to *Wayfinder*, then pointing to a row of fishing vessels tied against the harbor edge. There—a gap between them.

"He says to go in there, near that wall," she relayed to Jake, and he turned the helm toward where she was pointing, where old car tires were chained to the concrete as fenders.

As they got closer, the acrid smell of dried fish caught in her nostrils. A horde of men appeared from under the shade cast by a crumbling breeze-block building to shout and scramble over the fishing boats and tell her, with beckoning hands, that she was to throw her lines to them. A few seconds of pushing and pulling, shouting and revving, and they were in, and the pack dispersed. Some men squatted under the tree again; others remained standing, rolling cigarettes, watching, but with no real interest.

After three days of constant motion at sea, the stillness on board was stultifying. She looked around. As this was a historic port town on a trade route, she'd expected colonial architecture, but this dockside area of Port Brown was ugly, dingier even than some of the places she'd seen that summer she'd gone inter-railing through Europe, after her father had shipped her off, wanting her out of his hair.

It had been raining all afternoon the day he gave her the ticket, and the swollen plaster walls of their old house had leached a dankness into the air. As it turned out, it wouldn't be the family home for much longer. It was just the two of them in the sitting room—although, of course, only she was sitting. He never sat, never remained in one place for long—it was a wonder he ever finished a painting, or that he managed to stay put for those first seventeen years of her life. "Here," Papa said, holding out an envelope, keeping his arm outstretched until she had no option but to accept it. Thick and creamy, and ridged beneath her fingertips, it was one from his office desk, used for sending invoices to clients. "Good girl."

He'd tried to make the ticket and small allowance seem like gifts, yet even as a teenager she'd recognized them as bribes, and the knowledge of his infidelity with the woman he'd been painting had discolored everything she saw on her travels. She'd sought out the ugliest cities, trying to match her surroundings to her mood. But not one of them had been as decrepit as this.

The few tin-roofed buildings around the harbor were molding in the tropical heat. Beyond the sheer-edged concrete that served as their mooring wall were the remains of a lawn, worn down to the odd tuft of yellowed grass and dotted with sun-bleached rubbish. A dun-colored pariah dog, its teats swollen, panted under the scant shade of a scrubby tree. A little way off, a toddler scratched his belly as he watched his mother wash dishes under a dripping standpipe. The air was thick with boats—the smell and noise and motion of them—and the sea was no better, thin slicks of diesel adding color to what was otherwise a filthy brown soup.

Tiredness washed over her as she fetched the boat's documents and their passports from below. "I hate it here," she told Jake as he passed. God, she hoped they hadn't made a mistake.

"Two days, tops," he promised, kissing the top of her head. "Then we'll be off." Thankfully he didn't seize the opportunity to say I told you so.

At the harbormaster's office, they waited in a corridor until a young Indian woman, glossy hair woven into a plait that almost reached her knees, called them forward and took the copies of their boat papers. The room they entered was bare, the only furniture a worn desk and chairs. No computer. An official, also seemingly of Indian heritage, was working at the desk. Without stopping he gestured for them to sit. Behind him, cracked window louvers let in flies, but no air. Virginie wafted her face with her hand. Jake's temple was streaked with sweat. Pinned to one wall of the room was a Malaysian ensign; next to it sagged a damp-stained map of the world, so old that the pink of the British Empire was the predominant color.

As the girl with the plait placed their papers on the desk, the official—N. Ahmad, according to the name plate before him—made a final flourish with his pen and sat up. He steepled his fingers so that the tips were level with his full mustache, then he rested his wrists against the edge of the desk and regarded each of them in turn. "You want to go to Amarante."

Jake spoke first. "Yes, sir."

"Your boat's name?"

"*Wayfinder*."

N. Ahmad shuffled the documents. "It says here a different name."

"We changed it," Virginie said.

"Change? Why?"

Was Ahmad his first name or last name? Would it be wrong to address him as Mr. Ahmad? Probably best to avoid names altogether, as Jake had done. "Well, sir, because we didn't like it. We wanted a new one."

"You changed on the boat? The writing?"

She pictured the letters she'd painted on the topsides and really hoped she wouldn't have to sand them off again.

"Yes," Jake said. "And on the register. On the internet. The paper copy hadn't arrived by the time we set off, but you see from the digital version here that it's the same boat." He leaned across the desk to stab a finger at the registration certificate.

"Changing name is very bad," N. Ahmad said.

Oh, Lord. Don't let them be stuck here in Port Brown for weeks, waiting on paperwork. Perhaps a woman's touch would help. She made her eyes wide. "Bad?"

"Yes, bad luck. Very bad luck to change name of the boat."

Jake snorted. "Oh, come on, I've—"

She laid a warning hand on his arm. He was about to protest that he knew of plenty of boats that had been renamed, that new owners back home did it all the time—how many postdivorce *My Half*s had they seen around the marinas? But this wasn't the time nor place to make a fuss.

"You have the fee for the permit?" the official asked.

She pulled her wallet from her bag. "Yes. I have ringgit or US dollars."

"Either is okay."

The man reread each document slowly. He opened a drawer in his desk, which scraped as he pulled. He took out a form. "You can stay two months on this island," he said as he wrote. "Permit is for two months only. After that, you must leave. Southwest monsoon is coming. Very dangerous. You understand?"

Two months would have to do. If Amarante proved as good as promised, they could always return next year. She looked at Jake, who touched her knee. "Yes," she answered. Across the room a fly zapper gave a sharp crackle as an insect flew into it. The dry body hit the floor.

With fingertips stained betel nut brown, N. Ahmad picked up a stamp. He changed the date on the dial and assessed them again, Jake, then her, the stamp hovering in the air above the permit. "In Amarante there is nothing," he said. "No hospital, no coast guard; only navy patrol boat once, maybe twice, in one year. No helicopter rescue. Radio not working, no phone, no internet. You understand?"

Sweat was gluing her shirt to the small of her back. He made it sound like a threat, but its seclusion was a major part of Amarante's appeal. If it was full of restaurants and tourists, they might as well be anywhere. She went to say yes, but the air in the room was dry, and her voice stuck in her throat, so she nodded instead. The stamp descended.

Before she could reach to take the slip of paper from his fingers, he was already bowed over his work again. As she and Jake left the room, two insects electrocuted themselves almost simultaneously on the zapper.

9

Insects were singing, sending their euphonic chorus out into the soft night. In the open-air restaurant, Virginie drank. First water to cool her throat, then wine, savoring the mineral taste. How glad she was to be clean and feel human again. Long hours packing several months' worth of food and other supplies into every spare inch of the boat had exhausted her, but it was a satisfying tiredness, the kind that made her limbs heavy, her movements languid. Across the table, Jake gave her a one-sided smile, equally worn out.

She eased down in her seat, thankful the sun was gone, and, with it, a little of the heat. Every restaurant in Port Brown was open air. This one was effectively a courtyard dotted with tables and chairs, with a bar and serving area at one end, and outbuildings near the road housing the kitchen, bathrooms, and, presumably, stores. No way at all to shut out the elements. What did people do here when the monsoon changed, when the fierce winds came and downpours flash-flooded the streets? Close for the season, perhaps.

Their food arrived—chicken curry, sharp with star anise—and they ate quickly, almost in silence. When a waiter came to take their plates, Jake lifted his empty beer bottle, and the man, Indian like the harbormaster, acknowledged the request with a slanted nod, head wobbling on his neck. He was dressed all in white, a clean high-collared tunic over narrow trousers. Once he'd walked away, Jake said, "He looks like a servant from colonial times in that uniform. You'd think they'd want to leave all that behind."

The waiter returned with a silver tray balanced on the tips of his fingers. He transferred Jake's beer and a fresh glass to their table. "More wine, madam?"

"No thanks. I'm fine." She lifted her glass an inch. A circle of condensation had soddened the paper cloth.

"Surely, madam." The waiter gave his slack nod again and left.

Behind Jake, on the far side of the restaurant, a string of colored bulbs swayed in a whisper of breeze. She looked from them to her husband. *Husband.* Six months on, the word still felt slightly out of place. She'd thought of Tomas as her husband for so long. Even though they'd been divorced three years, there was still a momentary dislocation whenever she looked at her left hand and saw the plain band there rather than the heavy sapphire from before. She needed to shake that feeling. She would, she determined, on this trip.

She sat up straight. Jake looked done in. "Do you want to get an early night?" she asked.

He yawned. "Sorry." He reached for her hand. "I didn't realize provisioning would hit me so hard."

She entwined her fingers with his. "Same here."

"Tomorrow will be more relaxed. We'll just buy the fuel and go."

Go—just like that, they'd be off. She felt that same kick of excitement. "Sounds great." A quick squeeze; then she stood. "Loo."

Her route across the restaurant and past the bar area took her close to the only other occupied table. The couple there were evidently tourists, but not English—a well-dressed tanned white man and a beautiful black woman in a red dress. The woman was about her own age, the man ten or fifteen years older. As Virginie passed, the man glanced up. Orang putih, as she knew the locals termed

Westerners, always noticed one another, perhaps because they were in the minority.

When she emerged from the bathroom, the beautiful woman was outside, talking in a low voice to two local men. They were on a motorbike idling in an alley between the street and the toilets, one scarecrow-skinny, ostentatious in lots of bling that clashed with his Manchester United shirt, the other very fat and all in black. They fell silent as Virginie emerged, and the woman hitched her evening bag higher on her shoulder. She looked fidgety, even a bit nervous, but perhaps she was just in a hurry for the loo. Virginie gave her a brief smile to say, It's all yours. The woman went in, and the bike drove off.

In the restaurant, the woman's companion had abandoned his own table. He and Jake were standing together, talking. "Making friends?" she asked when she got there.

"Good evening," the stranger said. He was tall—half a head taller than Jake—and the kind of attractive that suggests a well-heeled, cosmopolitan life: lean, tanned, clean-shaven. His snowy linen shirt was spotless. She couldn't quite place his accent. American, maybe, but with a hint of Spanish.

"This is Vitor," Jake said. "He's on a boat, too. Vitor, this is my wife, Vee."

"Or Virginie," she said as they shook hands. "Either's fine."

"Virginie," the man replied. She caught a flash of heavy watch. "Êtes-vous française?"

She replied in English. "Half. I grew up partly in France. But English is better, for Jake's sake."

"Apologies." The man dropped her hand and made a slight bow. "Jake says you are here on a big sailing adventure?"

She couldn't deny a thrill at the words. She indicated the harbor wall, where *Wayfinder* was tied up. "That's ours over there."

He grinned, then pointed to a different part of the harbor. "There is my baby. *Santa Maria*. Like the trusted ship of Columbus."

Of course. In the afternoon, after they'd returned from the bustling market, they'd seen a large catamaran glide in and anchor across from the fishing dock. She'd fleetingly acknowledged it was a beautiful boat and returned to concentrating on passing groceries to Jake without dropping them into the water. In the dark, now she knew what she was looking at, she could make out a masthead anchor light, its white gleam mingling with the few streetlights on the land behind.

"What brings you to Port Brown?" Vitor said, to Jake this time. "I do not think it is the beauty of this place."

"No, we just came to stock up. We're leaving tomorrow."

"For where?"

"Amarante."

"Ah." So he knew it—could even be en route now. What a stroke of luck that would be, meeting someone else heading their way. Before she could ask, his mobile rang. He silenced it and put it away. He gestured to their table—"Shall we?"

Wordlessly, she asked the same question of Jake. She'd like to stay, but if he wanted that early night, they ought to make their excuses now. He gave the tiniest shrug to say, Why not? They sat.

"I will buy more wine," Vitor said, and summoned the waiter. "Same again, and four glasses." Then he raised his voice, called, "Darling, come join us!" across the restaurant.

The woman—his wife? girlfriend?—was returning from the loo. She had the kind of figure Virginie always envied, finely built and long-limbed but soft. Ultrafeminine. Her hair was past her shoulder blades, woven into braids, half of which were pinned back, which suited her face, drew attention to the kind of cheekbones that caught the light. Up close Virginie could tell that her dress—red, yes, but a subtle shade—wasn't the kind you could buy in a high street shop. She was younger than Virginie first thought, not even her own age, maybe mid-twenties. Her choice of clothes and the way she held her body with a considered stillness made her appear older. Vitor introduced her as Teresa.

"Hello," she said, with a tight smile. Instead of offering a hand, she clutched her bag tightly, and Virginie, who had started to extend her own hand, had to quickly lift it away. Again, as she had outside the bathroom, she sensed an edginess in Teresa. Perhaps she and Jake were an unwelcome interruption to her evening, or she was ready to leave. But when Vitor pulled across a chair for Teresa and motioned for her to sit, she lowered herself into it.

The waiter brought the wine, and Vitor dropped a flush of notes on the table, easily more than enough to cover the bill. Drinks poured, he sat back. "So you are bound for Amarante. You know they call it the paradise isle?"

"You've heard that, too?"

He crossed one leg over the other. "An associate in Mumbai told me about it last year. He recommended I go there, but business . . ." He spread his hands. "You know how it is. I had some small problems in Rio. A delay. But now everything is fine."

So she'd been right, they were going to Amarante. And Rio explained the accent.

"You're from Brazil?" Jake asked.

The phone rang again—either Vitor was popular, or someone really wanted to get hold of him. He muted it. "I lived for many years in New York."

"And you, Teresa?" Virginie asked. "Are you from Brazil?"

Teresa was staring distractedly in the direction of the bar, her mind clearly elsewhere. Virginie tried again. "Teresa?"

She turned back. "No, I am from Maputo. In Mozambique." She drew out the *o*'s, rolled the *r* in *from*. "You know my country?"

Mozambique was one of the places she'd suggested to Tomas for their honeymoon, along with a road trip through the southern states of the US and a cottage in the Scottish Highlands. He'd booked a venerable hotel in Rome instead. "Far more civilized in Europe."

"That's a long way from Brazil," Virginie said. "Where did you two meet?" But she'd lost her again.

"Darling"—Vitor leaned toward Teresa—"it is not every day we meet fellow sailors." He put a hand on her thigh. "We should make friends, yes?"

He took his hand away, and as he did so, it was if she decided to relax and push whatever was bothering her from her mind because she dropped her shoulders and faced the table.

"Of course," she said, smiling, reaching for her wine. "You are right." She took a mouthful, but perhaps slightly too big a mouthful because it seemed an effort to swallow. She pressed her fingers to her throat, and when she could speak again, she added, "We are very lucky."

They talked like this for a while, in the way Virginie had done with other strangers on previous travels, sharing a pleasant evening and a feeling of being outsiders, asking shallow, safe questions and forming gossamer bonds designed to last an evening but no further. Vitor did more talking than Teresa, who mainly seemed to back him up, agreeing with points he'd made, without revealing much about her own opinions. But she seemed happy to be there, smiling and nodding, hiding her laughter in his shoulder when he translated a joke for her that she hadn't been able to follow in their fast, wine-lubricated English.

The first bottle stood empty, and they'd made good inroads into a second when their conversation was drowned out by a revving engine. Virginie looked up. A motorbike was driving into the restaurant, almost to the bar. The one from outside the bathroom? Both riders were helmetless, the belly of the driver pudging out the coat he wore backwards, as riders in Malaysia often seemed to do. He kept astride the bike, the engine thunderous, headlamp directed toward their table. The pillion passenger swung off. He was in a Man U shirt, jewelry. They must be the same men. What was going on? She looked to Teresa, who snatched up her purse, blinking fast in the sudden light.

The waiter ran over to the bike, shouting in Bahasa. The passenger grabbed his lapels. Although slender, he was the taller man, and the contrast between his football shirt and the waiter's old-fashioned uniform, New World against Old, was as violent as his demeanor. When he shoved him backwards, the waiter crashed into a table.

Jake jumped up. "Hey!"

Virginie's stomach flipped. "No, Jake." The aggressive skinny biker challenged Jake with a stare, and her insides turned liquid. Vitor was halfway to his feet, staring right back. Did he know them? Don't, she thought, either of you, please don't.

An older man burst out of the kitchen, shouting. A terse conversation followed, the bike revving all the time. At last, to her relief, the fat driver killed the engine, and the pair followed the older man back into the kitchen. The door shut. The waiter straightened the table. She slow-blinked. It was okay. All was calm again.

Jake took his seat. "What was that about?"

Vitor checked his phone, the blue glow lighting his face. "Who knows? Business, most probably."

"Funny way of doing business," Jake said.

Vitor locked his phone screen. "Things work differently here than in England, Jake. The more time you spend here, the more you will understand this. Fifty-some years of independence means many changes. You will see. And you will adapt, as did I."

It had certainly looked a bit off to her. But he could have a point. She and Jake were newbies.

Teresa was still staring after the bike. "Teresa, what do you think?" she asked.

Teresa turned back, eyes wide. "I do not know these men."

"Oh, I thought—"

Teresa shook her head vehemently. "They are strangers."

She sounded adamant. But Virginie knew what she'd seen. And she could tell from Teresa's even more forced composure, from the way she avoided Vitor's eye but met hers with an unwavering, challenging look, that she was lying, but that she didn't want Vitor to know. She could call her out on it, or she could let it slide, not get involved.

"Sorry, my mistake." As she spread her hands in apology, she knocked a glass. Jake caught it in time, righted it, then squeezed her knee gently. Time to change the subject, find something to talk about that wouldn't risk stepping on anyone's toes. "So when are you heading over to Amarante, Vitor?" she asked.

Vitor chuckled. "Me? To Amarante?" He put his phone on the table, facedown. "No, I do not go there. I am here for business. Why would I go to a place like Amarante? What could be there for me?"

She must have misinterpreted him earlier. Never mind. But his comment niggled, and she found herself wanting to justify her—their—decision, needing to explain her passion for a place she hadn't even seen yet but which already had her hooked. "You're kidding, right?" she said. "How about beauty? Nature, peace, time? How about the challenge of self-sufficiency, of isolation? The sheer adventure of it?"

Vitor studied her. She didn't care if she sounded sentimental—at least they weren't thinking about the motorbike anymore. And anyway, she believed it all, corny as it might be. She glanced at Teresa, who was watching Vitor watch her.

"I hear there is nothing there now," Vitor said. "You must make sure you are well prepared."

"We are," Jake replied, backing her up.

"All right, so we won't have all the comforts of home," Virginie said. "We know we'll have to make sacrifices." She leaned forward, into the light, to better make her point. Her tiredness had gone. "But it'll be worth it. After all, the best things in life always have some cost."

There was a pause, and she felt Vitor weighing her words, appraising her. "Very true," he said eventually, toasting her with his wine, as if he'd decided he enjoyed being challenged.

Just then, there was movement across the restaurant. The motorcyclists had come out of the kitchen and were strutting back to their bike. Vitor raised his glass at them, too. They ignored him. The driver mounted first, firing up as the thin man climbed on behind. The back wheel kicked sideways as they moved off.

A few minutes after the strangers had gone, Vitor pocketed his phone and stood. "Well, I have some matters to arrange. Good night." He kissed Virginie on both cheeks and shook Jake's hand.

Virginie, a little woozy from the wine, leaned in to Jake as she watched the enigmatic pair leave. Vitor's soft suede loafers made no sound as he guided Teresa across the courtyard, and only the crickets singing from the pandanus trees broke the silence.

10

"It's a shame they aren't coming to Amarante," she said when they got back to *Wayfinder*. The saloon was like a steam oven, so she pulled off her shirt and sat at the top of the steps, hoping to catch a little air.

Below her, Jake came out of the bathroom, brushing his teeth, his head level with her hips. "Why?" he asked through a mouthful of foam.

She shifted a little on the step; the nonslip surface was gritty against the backs of her thighs. "They seemed nice. Well, Teresa was a little quiet, but she might come out of her shell if we got to know her better."

Jake tried to reply, but even though he tipped back his head to speak through the toothpaste, she couldn't make out what he was saying, could hear only "Ill-ee?" He held up a finger, went back into the bathroom, and she heard him spit, followed by the squeak of the foot pump as he rinsed the sink. He came out, wiping his mouth with a towel. "Really?" he clarified. "Nice? Nice wasn't what I was thinking."

"What were you thinking?"

He flung his towel over one shoulder as if it were a jacket and posed like a catalog model. "Did you see those loafers? I mean, come on, how much must they have cost?"

"I thought they looked good on him."

"Oh, you did, did you?" He raised a teasing eyebrow. "He *is* hand-some. I have to say I wouldn't blame you."

"Not like that." He was such a clown. She stretched down to pull the towel off his shoulder and toss it at his head. "I meant that if he wants to spend eight hundred euros on a pair of shoes and he has the means, why not?"

He removed the towel and draped it around his neck like a boxer. "So many reasons, not least of all crimes against fashion. How about practicality? Suede—on a boat? Good luck with that. What's wrong with good old-fashioned five-quid flip-flops?"

She laughed and climbed down the steps. "I'll remind you of that the next time you stub your toes." As she slid the towel from his neck, he caught the other end and used it to reel her in toward him.

"Baby," he said, using his name for her, nuzzling her throat, "we don't need anyone else." She could smell the mint. "We're enough as we are."

The next morning, Vitor's catamaran was still on anchor in the bay as they filled up with fuel, did the checking-out paperwork, and made final calls home.

"You will be careful, won't you?" her mother said.

It was super late in London. She didn't want to keep her up. "I will, don't worry. I'll ring you when we have signal again."

"When will that be?"

"Three months-ish?" She counted forward. "Wow—in the new year!"

She was turning the mooring lines into slips when the harbor-master official, the one with the tricky name, came jogging over, his sandals slapping against the concrete.

"Miss!" he called, waving a carbon copy of a docket above his head. "Your papers." She made the line fast on the cleat and waited for him to reach her. "Port clearance papers," he said, breathing so deeply his stomach strained against his shirt. She was impressed he'd managed to run in his backless shoes. He flapped the paperwork again. "Very important. You will be needing them in your next port."

"In Amarante?"

"Not Amarante." He waggled a finger. "No customs in Amarante, I am telling you. After, after."

"I'm sorry," she said. "I was making a joke."

"Oh, very funny, miss." Out here, in the sunshine, N. Ahmad seemed a lot less stern than he had in his office.

Jake came onto the side deck, to see what was going on. "Problem?"

"Oh, no, sir. Just you are forgetting these papers." As he handed them over to Virginie, *Santa Maria* caught his attention.

"Beautiful, hey?" she said. "We met the owners last night. They seemed very nice. Although they didn't want to come to Amarante with us."

"No," he said. "They go to Anjouan. Very bad place."

N. Ahmad didn't seem to like anywhere other than Port Brown. She folded the paperwork in half. "Do you need anything more from us?" His eyes were back on *Santa Maria*. "Sir?"

"No, no. Is all." He wafted a hand, then dug in his pocket for his phone. "You go."

While they started their engine, untangled their fenders from the chained tires, and cast off their lines, the official remained on the quayside, talking into his mobile phone. As *Wayfinder* drew away from the wall, he pulled the phone away from his ear.

"Goodbye!" he shouted, gesturing as if to hasten their departure from the dock. "Fair winds!"

"Fair winds?" she called back. "Where did you learn that?"

"English sailor told this to me. For luck. Fair winds!"

Once they were past the last of the fishermen, and there was only sea, sky, and the horizon, she stripped to her bikini and let the breeze blow the sweat from her skin. The northeast monsoon wind was steady, and the sails had filled, heeling *Wayfinder* as the yacht picked up momentum. What awe there was in harnessing the wind, in knowing its power and yet still being in control; what freedom in being in command of their own self-contained little world, in tune with the weather, the tides, the phases of the moon.

The strain had half lifted the dodgy clutch for the foresail sheet, so she nipped forward and pressed it shut with her hand, then went to stand at the helm next to Jake. Behind them, the rudder churned the water into a creamy froth and the wake made a rushing noise, a sound she'd always loved, ever since family holidays as a child. Philippe still sailed, too, but her sisters had let seasickness get the better of them. Luckily, it rarely affected her. She breathed in the air. Wind in her hair and wide blue all around. Nothing to do but enjoy the ride; nothing behind them—nothing that mattered, anyway—and everything ahead. The future, and all that lay within it.

Idly, she pondered whether life would have turned out differently if, when Jake had first mentioned the idea of buying a boat and going away, she'd said no. He might not have proposed so soon after; they might not still be together. Not that she'd been looking for a proposal—far from it—but she found Jake so . . . *infectious* was the word. Sweetly awkward when they first met, although that had faded, and, oh, how he made her laugh. She smiled at the memory of the morning after she'd moved into his flat. He'd been tracing the freckles that peppered her arm, and he'd grabbed a pen and started to join the dots, pretending they were constellations. "The big frying pan," he said. "Bug-eyed goldfish." Then he'd drawn one that looked like the real thing. "Cassiopeia." That beautiful, proud queen flung up into the heavens and marooned in the night sky for all eternity. She'd pulled back the duvet to examine him for celestial patterns as well, and they both ended up high on laughter and covered in scrawls.

Life was easy with Jake. No need to worry about meeting standards or passing tests she hadn't even known about in the first place. It was a world away from what she'd had with Tomas. She'd tried to excuse her early concerns there: she was young; Tomas knew what was best; her father wouldn't have set her up with his best client and encouraged the match, especially given the age gap, if it wasn't right. She should have listened to her gut. Thank God there was nothing of Tomas in Jake, none of that stifling feeling in this relationship.

Just trust, mutual respect, and love. And plenty of passion, too.

What are you smiling at?" Jake asked.

"Oh, nothing."

Jake liked the dawn watches, but she preferred the first half of the night. Sunsets and sunrises were quick at this latitude, not much to see. The best light show was when the stars came out, and the Milky Way misted the sky. She took some pictures with her phone, but they were no match for the real thing, turned out a blurry mess or else a blank black screen. She couldn't post them anyway—they were way out of signal range already.

It was always warm, and her bikini was enough. Little shots of sea spray—not even that; zephyrs of salt water, too light to really feel— landed on her arms from time to time, whispered past her ears, settled on her lips. They'd left the lights of Port Brown behind them days ago, yet she still got a strong sense of the ritual of the day ending and people, thoughts, worries being put to bed. Out here, even the sounds of the waves and wind were softer at night, despite the Windex relay showing a steady fifteen knots, and the rigging was still. Almost as if the ocean were settling down for the night.

Jake had gone to their cabin to get some sleep before his watch, and the dim red glow of the chart table lamp was as comforting as a child's night-light. Apart from the tricolor way up on the top of the mast, the dimmed instrument panels were the only other source of light, and when she stared at them and then looked out to the dark ocean, the digital numbers that had burned into her retinas danced, in negative, in front of her eyes.

It was strange to think it was mid-afternoon back home right now. If it was a weekday—was it a weekday? She counted back to Port Brown. Yes, it was Wednesday. So there'd probably be a herd of schoolchildren at the museum right now, being shepherded through her exhibits by their teachers and assistants, pressing noses and fingertips to the display cabinets. In London Mum would be out in the garden, weeding, dropping clumps of plants into the basket she always had at her elbow. Papa—well, he'd either be painting or at the tabac. Her brother and sisters—she knew their routines well enough that she could assign each of them a specific place or activity right now.

Life everywhere else would be carrying on as usual, but for her and Jake, out here, there no longer was any *usual*. The clock meant little, other than for portioning twenty-four-hour sections into alternating watches. These watches became their tiny days and nights: four hours sailing the boat, four hours resting, through daylight, darkness, daylight again. There was nowhere to drop anchor in the open ocean, nowhere to stop, to pause. Instead there was only routine, taking care of the boat and each other. That *Wayfinder* was proving an easy mistress to satisfy helped enormously. And when they got to Amarante, there'd be even more freedom. All her time her own. She could choose to do what she wanted, whenever she wanted, and there'd be nobody to tell her otherwise.

Below her feet, inside the boat, everything was still. Jake was zonked, spread-eagled in their bunk. She'd stuck her head round the door to check on him when she last nipped down to fill in the log. She'd melted a little at the sight. On a crossing like this, when the other person was on watch, you left them in sole charge of every decision, every action and reaction—in charge of your life, really. Jake sleeping was a sign he trusted her wholeheartedly. And in a few hours, in turn, she would hand over her complete faith to him.

Resting in the cabin, she heard her name being called. She swam up through layers of sleep.

"It's time," Jake said, leaning over her, silhouetted against the daylight. "Five minutes, probably."

She forced herself to sit, rubbed her eyes, told him she was coming. It felt like no time since she'd come down from a night watch and crawled into a bed that still held the imprint of Jake's body. But if there were only five minutes to go, she must have slept for several hours while the log clocked up the sea miles.

A splash of water on her face, and she was more with it. She went up into the sunshine. The thin blue line of the horizon stretched all the way around them, complete and uninterrupted, creating the illusion they were the only people in existence, that the thirty-six feet of their boat contained the whole world.

Jake had engaged the autopilot so he could stand at the front of the cockpit, right by the small GPS mounted on the instrument panel. She looked at the numbers—the degrees were still zero, as they had been since last night—but the minutes were zero now also, and the seconds were decreasing. She caught his elation as he watched the GPS. Any moment they'd be over it. How many sailors before them had experienced this? She took his hand and started to read the seconds out loud, as if it were New Year's Eve, and Jake counted with her. But then he said, "Wait," and dropped her hand to pick up his phone and angle the camera at the GPS. Three . . . two . . . one. And there it was: 00:00:00 latitude. The equator. They were out of the north and into the south, had traded one half of the world for its opposite.

Although it was impossible, she half expected time to stop, or at least something to happen to mark this momentous change. But as with the turn of the year, there was nothing. She looked at her husband and then out to sea. All was the same, of course: Jake, her, the pitch and sway of the Indian Ocean and the unbroken line of sea meeting sky. The only difference was on the GPS, where the *N* had been replaced by an *S*, and the numbers kept ticking and climbing— now the seconds, later the minutes and degrees—as *Wayfinder* kept sailing toward her destination.

She didn't smell the land before she spotted it, like some dyed-in-the-wool sailors insist happens, and they were almost upon it before she could actually see it. The chartplotter had no useful information, so she didn't know what she should be looking out for—how tall it was, if it had a rocky peak at its center.

"Amarante, the paradise island—a faceless orange polygon on a gray-blue screen," Jake said, coming behind the helm to rest his chin on her shoulder.

"Cut the sarcasm, mister. It'll be worth it, you'll see." Her belief in Terry's promise hadn't faded.

"I hope you're right." He zoomed out to show the ocean's expanse, the Malaysian mainland and Port Brown almost off-screen. "Because it's a hell of a long way back."

She readjusted the scale. The little boat-shaped icon that repre-sented *Wayfinder* was edging closer and closer to digitized landfall. They scoured the horizon until they could see it for real—a dark blotch above a white strip that seemed, in shimmering mirage, to hover above the sea. Slowly, as the yacht sailed forward, the island grew in size and detail so that the blotch became a low-lying thicket of trees and the strip a stretch of pearly sand. Underwater, a mottled green shadow of reef formed a barricade, forcing them to stay some way offshore.

Jake bent to the ignition panel to start the engine. It coughed but wouldn't start. He paused, tried again. Still the choking sound but no firing. Well, it had been switched off for the best part of a fortnight.

"I'll bleed it," he said, going below.

"Third time lucky?" he said when he came up. This time she twisted the key and the engine rumbled on. How strange it was to hear a mechanical noise after two weeks of only wind, sea, and the sound of their own voices. They furled the jib, and she swung the boat's bow into the wind so they could drop the main. Sails away, she motored to the west, finding a gap in the reef, while Jake alternated between watching the depth sounder and peering at the wall of trees with the bank of sand at its feet. And then the thicket ended, the land looped away, and she was looking into the most beautiful bay she'd ever seen.

It was wide, like the inside curve of a crescent moon. Coconut palms leaned right over, and behind these, thick bush reached back. Ground-level creepers inched their way onto sand the color of old ivory, blurring the line between beach and jungle. The water, fractured and sparkling in the lowering sun, was calm, protected in the lee of the island. Just two boats were anchored, evenly spaced in the bay, pointing their noses to the shore. A wind scoop twisted slackly on its string above the bow of the nearest yacht. *Wayfinder*'s engine made the only noise.

Neither of them spoke, tacitly acknowledging that what they were experiencing was so sublime that to speak would be to spoil it. Instead she moved to Jake's side and wrapped her arms around him. His heart, beneath her palm, raced.

Amarante. They were finally here.

11

Dawn was taking an age to arrive. Virginie lay on her back in the bed, trying not to fidget or disturb Jake. She needed to change position but was conscious she'd been tossing and turning for a while, making him shift across to the far side of the bunk, so she forced herself to keep still.

After two nonstop weeks at sea, she should have been exhausted, but there was no chance she could sleep. Every inch of her was extra alert: coursing energy made her sensitive to the surface of her skin, the stale taste of her mouth, the pulse thrumming in the side of her neck. She stared out of the hatch above their heads at the night sky, at the thick spill of stars. During the crossing they had delighted her; now they were annoying, a barrier to starting their exploration of Amarante, to finding out if this place they'd be living in was as good as promised, good as she hoped. Come on, morning, she urged, hurry up.

Eventually the stars faded, the sky grayed, and morning tiptoed across the world. At the first hint of blue, she grabbed her discarded T-shirt and climbed through to the main part of the boat.

While she waited for the coffee to brew, she peered back around the door frame. Jake hadn't moved. He was lying on his front, arms above his head, face turned away, the muscles of his back contoured by the early light.

Partly hoping that either the scent of coffee or the creak of the wooden steps would rouse him, she went up to the deck and crossed the small cockpit. When they'd anchored the evening before, they'd been so busy sorting out the boat there hadn't been much time to take stock of their surroundings before darkness fell. Now she found *Wayfinder* had turned with the current, and they were side-on to the beach. The colors were not yet vibrant in the low morning light, the beach beige and the sea a slick steel. Within the hour, she was ready to bet, the climbing sun would change the sand to a dazzling shade of cream she'd need sunglasses to look at and turn the shallower water between the yacht and the beach aquamarine.

She sat on the side deck, cup nestled on bent knees, heels wedged against the toe rail, and surveyed the two other boats. They were older-looking yachts, like theirs—one to the left and one to the right, a dinghy streaming behind each. The boat to the left was white-hulled. A small painted board was mounted on the A-frame at the back, a red maple leaf on a white background. Canadian. The second boat had a dark green hull. There was a flag tied to its flagpole, but it had drooped in the absence of wind, so she couldn't discern its nationality. The yachts were close enough that she would have been able to see their owners if they were on deck, but not so close that there was no sense of privacy. It'd be good to have other people to talk to, she supposed, as long as they weren't weirdos. Or, like Terry, bores. Still, in a way, it was a pity they wouldn't have the island to themselves.

From below came the sound of doors opening and closing, and Jake stuck his head out of the companionway, holding on to each of the wooden handrails, squinting in the light. He was wearing only his underwear, the hair on one side of his head was sticking up, and he had the beginnings of a grizzly beard. He hadn't wanted to risk shaving while they were at sea.

"What time is it?" he asked.

"I don't know. A little before six?"

He blinked a few times. "A.M.? And you're up?"

"Couldn't sleep." She pointed at the island with her cup. The colors had, as she'd predicted, brightened to postcard-perfect hues. "Too excited."

"Yeah, me, too," he said, then yawned. "Or at least I will be when I've had some breakfast and a shower." He darted up onto the deck and made a show of stretching over her to reach his shorts. "Actually," he said, his armpit right above her head smelling of stale sweat, "now we've gone back to basics, I might give up washing and shaving. Go properly bush." There was a mischievous note to his voice. "In fact, I might go the whole hog, you know, become the wild man of Amarante." Turning to the stairs, he pulled down his underpants and stepped out of them, paused to scratch his bottom slowly. "Yessir, I might do just that." She laughed and threw a peg after him as he disappeared below.

She was dressing in their cabin when a loud knock reverberated through the hull and a female voice called, "Hello!"

Jake looked up from the pan of eggs he was cooking. He was still naked.

"I'll go," Virginie said.

The brightness was an assault as she emerged onto the deck and she grabbed at her head for her sunglasses, cursing silently when she realized she'd left them in the cabin. But it'd be rude to go back now. A woman was standing in a little wooden rowing boat, bobbing gently in the waves, holding the guard rail at the back of *Wayfinder* to stop herself from drifting away. She was about Virginie's own age, or perhaps a couple of years older, mid-thirties and athletic in a swimsuit, with a short pixie haircut and two sore-looking pink patches on the tops of her shoulders.

"Hi. How's it going?" The woman squinted in the sunshine as she smiled. "Saw you pull up last night, but thought we'd give you time to settle in. I didn't think you'd appreciate lots of new people rushing over as soon as you'd landed."

Virginie laughed, delighted to receive such a warm welcome, and the woman smiled again, and shaded her eyes with one hand. "I'm Stella. You can probably tell from the accent I'm from that boat over there." She nodded toward the Canadian yacht. "We've been here a couple of months. We come every year 'cause we love it." She rolled her eyes. "Sorry—here I am babbling away. It's because you're fresh company, you know. New arrivals are always very exciting." She stopped abruptly, putting her hand over her mouth. "Sorry. I haven't even given you the chance to tell me your names."

At the plural, Virginie looked over her shoulder. Jake was coming up the last step. Thankfully, he'd put on some shorts.

"I'm Virginie," she said, turning back to Stella. "And this is my husband, Jake."

Stella removed the hand shielding her eyes to give a quick wave. "Great to meet you."

"I wondered why I didn't hear anyone approach," Jake said. "You're a rower."

There was no outboard engine on her little boat. Instead a pair of oars were nestled in the bottom.

"More of a paddler, really. I like it. It's my daily exercise."

She didn't seem like a weirdo or a bore, more like someone Virginie would want to get to know. "Want to join us for breakfast?" Maybe this was what life would be like here—friends popping by as and when. Easy. Fun.

"I've already eaten, so you go ahead. But sure, I'll come on board. Thanks." She tied her dinghy to secure it and ignored the hand Jake held out, swinging her legs easily over the guard rail.

Stella sat opposite her and watched Jake as he put the drinks on the table and passed a plate of scrambled egg to Virginie. "Oh, wow!

Milk!" She touched a bead of condensation on the carton. "I haven't had real milk for over a month."

Jake nudged it toward her. "Knock yourself out."

She pulled her hand away. "Oh, no, I couldn't. It's yours. You should enjoy it while it lasts. In a month's time you'll be dreaming of milk."

From across the bay came the cruck-cruck of an outboard motor. It added a neighborhood feeling to the bay, like someone starting a lawnmower or running the engine of their car.

"You must have a lot of questions," Stella said, looking from Virginie to Jake and back again.

She couldn't think where to begin. "We've never done anything like this before," she said. "I don't even know what I need to know."

"Well, I'll start with the introductions. There aren't many of us, so it won't take long. I'm Stella, as you know, and my husband, over there on our boat, *Swallow*"—she pointed to the white yacht—"is Pete. We've been cruising for a few years. Made it this far from Vancouver."

Jake whistled. "Long way."

"Yeah, we did it in stages. I'm not sure we really knew what we were getting into when we set off, but we were so sick of city life, you know? Ten years of that shit, straight out of college. Pete was insurance, I was marketing. Full-on rat race, treadmill, right?" She laughed, a tinkling sound. "I burned all my office outfits before we left. Held a little ceremony. Now we're divers. We work when we can, then find spots like this. We like quiet places." She raised an eyebrow. "I know, right? But it's true. We got here as early in the season as we could swing it."

Listening to Stella was making Virginie a little breathless. It wasn't just the speed and volume of her words, although they were fast and many. It was also a sense of recognition, a homecoming almost—a feeling that she might have found her tribe, other people in the world who thought as she and Jake did, and who were also willing to set off into the unknown.

Stella swiveled to point at the green boat. "And that over there is *Ariel*, where Roly—Roland—and Gus live. Gus is his dog, not his partner, but I guess you'll realize that when you see him—although he does act like a human a lot of the time." She tinkled again. "Roly's an Aussie, and the font of all knowledge, kind of like the unofficial chief of our little village. He's been coming here for years. Used to be with his wife, Christine, but she decided to return to the city a while back, and since then it's been Roly on his own. You need to know anything—mending things, rigging up this or that—Roly's your man. Fixing up boats is part of what passes for entertainment here." She smiled. "But, hey, it's not as dull as it sounds. I mean—just look around!"

The sun was high now and the bay staggering in its beauty. In the center of the triangle formed by the three boats a ray's wingtips breached the surface, offering a gentle greeting.

Stella stood. "I bet you're dying to get exploring, so I'll leave you to it. If you need anything at all, just holler. We'll put on a welcome bonfire for you later. It's an island tradition for new arrivals. Have a few drinks on the beach, get to know each other, that kind of thing. Say around seven?" She blew air up her face. "It sure is hot here. The price we pay for shelter, hey? You might want to look at rigging up some awnings, get a bit more shade going on back here. The sun gets pretty fierce, and there's no respite. Does good to protect your stuff, too—things get worn through pretty quickly by the UV." She laughed and touched the blister on her shoulder. "And I should know!"

A couple of confident movements and she was back in her dinghy. Virginie envied her athleticism. Such a natural, as if she'd always lived on the sea.

Jake untied Stella's rope, while she knelt and picked up her oars. "Catch you later!" she called as he dropped the line, and she started to back her boat away from the yacht. "And welcome to Amarante." She held up her oars, a celebratory V for victory. "Now you've been here, life'll never be the same again."

12

The water was as warm as a spa when Virginie stepped into it, coming halfway up her calves and so clear that her feet were barely distorted. A school of sand-colored fish, each no longer than a thumbnail, darted out of the way as she waded against the resistance. Jake was in the water behind her. They were towing the dinghy toward the beach, where tiny waves barely whispered as they slid up and down, steady as breathing.

As the depth of the water lessened, the dinghy grew heavier, so they each took hold of a handle and hauled it a couple of meters up the slope, safe beyond the high-water line. It was hard work, and she had to dig in her heels, strain through her thighs. Hopefully she'd soon build up strength—she'd need it, doing this every day. The rope was hanging down—she picked it up and tossed it inside the boat, and her hands came away sandy. Dusting them off, she did a half circle to survey her surroundings, her soles sinking an inch with every step.

The beach swept away in a shallow arc. They'd landed the dinghy at one end, and she could see the other from where they stood. It was just as beautiful up close as it had been when viewed from the yacht— so beautiful, in fact, that it was hard to believe it was real, that such untouched places could actually exist.

"Terry wasn't wrong," she said, wiping the last of the sand onto her sarong. Its hem had dangled in the sea and was now clinging to her legs. "It's stunning."

"I was worried about overhype," Jake said, "but it's perfect." He looked at her, and it was as if someone had fired a starting gun: they shot off down the beach, hooting, weaving toward each other to grab for a waist, an arm, making contact for a moment before whirling away again, creating crazy meandering tracks with their footprints. Jake stopped, his feet planted wide; as she ran toward him, he tipped his face to the sky and whooped. She reached him, her cheeks aching from how hard she was grinning, and they high-fived. He pulled her in for a kiss. It was sweaty, and they giggled and kissed again.

Once they'd caught their breath, they set off to walk along the rest of the beach, every now and then passing driftwood logs that had been tossed high above the storm-surge line. After a few minutes they reached the other tip, where the beach merged with jungle. The sand was rougher under her feet than she'd expected. She let go of Jake's hand to scoop up a palmful and examine it, finding fragments of coral and minuscule shells. When she opened her fingers to let it fall, particles clung to the damp creases in her skin.

Jake had moved a little inland, where creepers were stretching their way into the light like sunbathers' limbs relaxing on the sand. His T-shirt was already sticking to his back, sweat forming butterfly wings across his shoulder blades. She followed him, and as they reached the shade, they found another rubber dinghy, gray like theirs, but patched in places and scarred with dollops of resin and glue. Inside was a speargun, long and sharp. Virginie hung back, fascinated, wanting to take a closer look, but Jake had moved on, so she turned away.

The jungle—should she call it jungle, or forest, bush, brush?—was multilayered and haphazard, plants growing wherever they could sustain themselves. At ground level were the creepers, then scrubby knee-height bushes and midsized plants that came past her head—some palms, some more like pine trees, with inches-long needles and tight, nut-like cones. More palms and other wispier trees towered overhead, some so tall it hurt her neck to look, fanning their leaves to create a canopy that sieved the daylight. At the foot of many lay coconuts, the hairy husks heaped in piles where they'd fallen one on top of another, year after year after year. She passed a baby palm, thin-trunked and barely knee-high, wearing its outsized seed like a toddler its mother's shoe.

The foliage grew denser the farther in they went. Underfoot, sand gave way to hard dirt and the clear patches grew smaller and smaller, until she found herself playing a kind of hopscotch. She stood for the third time on a scratchy frond. Silly idiot, leaving her flip-flops on the boat. That wasn't the only discomfort—despite the trees letting through only a thin dappling of light, the temperature and humidity were high, causing sweat to pill at her temples, trickle down her lower back. Insects susurrated loudly, their insistent song making the heat seem even more intense. A bird's cry went up but remained unanswered.

"I hope there aren't any snakes," she said, scanning the undergrowth. The thought sent a shudder up her spine, prickled her scalp.

Jake called over his shoulder. "Only ones big enough to swallow you whole."

She caught up to him, feeling safer by his side. "Very funny." She swiped him on the arm. "You don't have to make it worse."

He stopped and faced her. "Sorry, baby." He rotated her so he could massage her shoulders. She let herself relax, allowed her head to hang.

"Better?" She nodded, and her hair swung. "Come here." He let go of her shoulders and held her hips instead, moving closer, until the front of his body was pressed down the length of her back. His chest was hot through his T-shirt, the fabric damp against her skin. He slid a hand across her stomach and up along the diagonal line of her bikini top. His fingertips traced her collarbone, curved up the side of her neck, reached the sensitive spot just below her earlobe.

"Just imagine," he whispered, starting to sway, and she closed her eyes to concentrate on his touch. "What it would feel like . . ." She let out an uneven breath. "If one dropped out of a tree and wrapped itself round your neck!"

The V of his arm clamped over her chest. She shrieked and drove her elbows against him. Letting her go, he fell back laughing, pretending to be winded. She tried to put on an angry face, but a smile kept tugging at her lips. She loved his playful side.

"Come on," he said, grabbing her hand. "Let's explore a bit farther."

Ten minutes or so later, they reached a section of the island where the trees thinned out, although the canopy was thicker and the shadows darker. Here, thin palm trunks grew at skewed angles, breaking like scaly forearms out of the earth as they competed for sunlight.

The remains of a brick wall made them stop short. It was knee-high and almost completely overgrown with vein-like creepers. She went up to it and pulled, and they made a tearing noise as they surrendered their grip. Underneath, the brick was as red as any you'd find in England. How odd, coming across something manufactured in this untouched place, especially something so Victorian, so British.

Jake was frowning. "Weird, hey?"

She followed the wall a couple of meters to where a tree had fallen. Over time, the insides of its trunk had been scooped away by insects, and what was left chewed to a rough powder. A line of ants crawled along the trunk, the one at the rear carrying a leaf fragment over its head like a sail.

Careful not to disturb them, she climbed over the fallen tree. Jake did the same. On the other side were the camouflaged remains of another low wall, running perpendicular to the first. She traced its line with her eyes—a second corner, a third—and understood she was looking at a building, about a third of the size of their old one-bedroom flat. A tiny house. A little farther along, edged up against the bush, was another. There, a tree straight out of a Lara Croft film was growing from a wall, its nest of buttress roots snaking like Medusa's hair down to the earth. She counted four wrecked one-room buildings in all, placed at the corners of a rectangular clearing, laid out like the symbols on a playing card.

Stella had talked of Amarante as a village. Had sailors built this? But what would have been the point when they had their yachts? And how would they have even done it, where would they have got the brick? She picked her way from one ruin to the next and stood at its center, trying to picture how tall it had been, how many windows it might have had. Several trees had fallen onto this building, and the floor was littered with broken brick. Some years, she'd read, the southwest monsoon could be especially bad, bringing storms with winds near hurricane strength, and she imagined heavy uprooted timbers crashing through thatched roofs, smashing onto walls, shattering them into fragments. People fleeing for their lives.

Beyond the fourth house stood an upright column-like structure. It was about the same height as a person and covered in vines. A statue? She went over there and ripped off creepers. It looked not unlike a giant pestle and mortar mounted on a plinth, each part made from a heavy metal, iron most probably, painted black. A bar, three feet or so in length, jutted out from one side of the bowl, weeping rust where the paint had been worn away and the metal exposed.

"Vee," Jake called. He sounded way off. She turned toward where she thought his voice had come from, taking a moment to locate him. He was about two boat lengths away, toward the far end of the clearing, near where the bush thickened again, down on his haunches among the detritus of leaves. "Come and look at this."

To begin with, she couldn't work out what he was staring at, other than compacted ground almost entirely masked by leaves and creepers. But then the piebald light shifted and she was able to make out two rows of low, rectangular mounds, each five or six feet long, evenly spaced.

"God." She brought a hand to her mouth. "Graves."

Jake nodded somberly. "Seems so."

"Sailors?"

He pulled up the bottom of his T-shirt to wipe sweat from his face. "Surely there are too many. Could be settlers, from those houses." He scanned the jungle, as if expecting locals to emerge from the shade. He stood and picked his way between the two rows of graves, toward the trees.

"Careful!" Ever since she could remember, she'd hated the idea of stepping on a grave. In the churchyard, when her mother had taken her and her siblings to lay flowers for her grandmother, she'd never dared step off the path.

When he got to the edge of the clearing, he parted the brush and scanned the ground.

"Any more?" she said.

He let the branches drop. "Doesn't look like it, but it's hard to tell."

One person must have survived, at least—someone had buried the others. Which begged the question: What had become of him or her? She thought of the ocean and shuddered.

Jake must have seen her shiver because he asked, "Want to get out of here?"

"Yes." She wrapped her arms around herself. "Let's get back into the sunshine."

They turned their backs on the ruins and continued walking in the same direction they'd been heading before, what she approximated was northeast. Within fifteen minutes they emerged on the other side of the island. The sunlight was so dazzling after the shade of the bush that it made her blink and shield her eyes. Amarante was much smaller than she'd imagined. She wore no watch, but she estimated that, even with the stop at the ruins and their slow exploratory pace, the walk across the whole width had taken less than an hour.

This coast had a different kind of beauty, a raw wildness. There was wind here. It caught her sarong and made it fly. She tightened the knot to secure it. Just offshore, the sea was the telltale green-brown of reef, and the water beyond was far rougher than in the anchorage. Large rolling waves that had run free for a thousand miles reached the reef and, forced by the barrier to a stop, reared and broke.

"Not so good for your swim," Jake said, angling his head at the white horses.

"I guess we'll stick to the other side."

The beach itself was shorter, ending in a rocky point. Plovers picked their way among thin black lines of desiccated weed that trailed along the sand, stopping and restarting like interrupted lifelines. In places, the sea had tossed up flotsam and jetsam: large pieces of drift-wood, ghostly shells, the hole-riddled bones of dead coral. Even—she could barely believe it—a Coke bottle, its familiar curved sides scoured opaque by the ocean. She pointed it out to Jake.

"Maybe broke away from a gyre," he said.

"I thought that was smaller stuff, soupy?"

He picked up the bottle, dusted it down. "Or jettisoned off a tanker? Some people have no respect."

She put it in her bag to take with them. When they reached the ruins, she thought again of the inhabitants. There were no things in the buildings, no belongings—no cups, bowls, furniture. That plastic bottle had traveled hundreds of miles—perhaps more—and yet noth-ing of the villagers' had survived. It was strange to think people could leave so few traces behind. Sad, too.

What happened next happened fast. She heard a loud rustle, just behind her, something moving through the dried leaves. *Snake*. Jake, looking past her, froze as something shot out from the trees, moving toward them, dark as the shadows it had come from. Not a snake. A creature with countless legs. She screamed and cowered against Jake, eyes tight shut. From close by came a loud crash—God, were there more of them?—and a whoosh, a feeling of something slicing past. Then stillness.

At the sound of a very human exhalation, she opened her eyes. Across the clearing stood an older man, looking down the length of a speargun. His hair was long and straggly, and he wore only khaki shorts and a knife in a holder at his waist. Tattoos dotted his wiry arms, one a large compass rose. As she watched, he stretched up out of his huntsman's pose.

He marched to his prey and bent to start working his spear back and forth, easing it out of the body. The creature he'd shot was some kind of giant crab, almost alien or prehistoric-looking. Although half curled into a ball, it was clearly the best part of a meter in length. Long articulated legs formed a row on either side of its body, which was cased in a hard, blue-brown shell. Its claws were club-like, thick as a man's forearm. As she watched, its legs contracted, clattering in death throes. Her stomach lurched.

The hunter spoke as he worked. "You the new Poms?" There was a sickening crack as the spearpoint came free. "Saw your dinghy."

She tried to answer but struggled to find any words. It had been so close. If his aim had been off . . . She could only watch as the man pulled out the knife, raised it above his shoulder, and plunged it, hard, into the center of the crab. The legs stopped their hideous clacking dance. Next he took a length of thin rope from his pocket and strung its legs together in a noose. When he'd finished, he pulled the knife out of the body, wiped it on the side of his shorts, and slotted it back into the sheath at his belt.

"Roly," he said, offering a hand. She shook it mutely. "From *Ariel*." He jerked his head toward the anchorage.

Still, she was unable to respond. The man lifted up the creature by its string and hoisted it over his shoulder. It thumped as it struck his lean flesh. He extended his hand again to Jake, who shook it without saying a word.

"Right, then," Roly said, stooping to pick up a grimy canvas bag. He lowered the carcass to the floor briefly to pack the spear, tether, and gun into the bag, slung one load over each shoulder, and strode past them toward the anchorage, the regular crack of dried leaves and twigs fading quickly.

Virginie turned to Jake, who was as wide-eyed as she was.

"Fuck, Vee," he said, his breath coming out in a long, slow whistle. "We're not in Kansas anymore."

13

It was another world in the water, and she was another person. Virginie duck dived, then popped up to the surface and slicked back her hair from her face. Jake was in the shallows, near the beach, watching. She ducked again so she could glide toward him. She stood, thigh-deep. Rivulets of salt water ran down her body, tickling her skin.

"Better?" he asked. He'd ditched his T-shirt, but he looked pink with heat.

"Much. You sure you don't want to come in properly?" Lowering herself, she let the water hold her and fan out her hair. She did a lazy kind of backstroke, sculling with her palms. "It's very refreshing."

He smiled. "Looks it."

"This is a good place to try. It's shallow."

"Nah. This is enough for me."

She floated faceup, luxuriating in the feeling of weightlessness. She hadn't known about Jake's phobia of deep water until their first vacation, a week's sailing in Greece, a few months after they met. The boat had belonged to a member of the yacht club, who let them borrow it in exchange for Jake's looking over the rigging. When he didn't join her for a swim in the sea on the first day, she put it down to exhaustion from work, or that he needed time to relax, unwind, and get into the spirit of things. On the third day, when they found a small bay all to themselves, they were at the bow when she suggested diving in. When she surfaced, expecting him to be in the water next to her, he was still on the deck, walking back to the cockpit.

"Phone!" he'd called over his shoulder, by way of explanation.

At dinner that night, outside a taverna whose stone walls radiated the day's heat, he'd admitted the phone call had been a lie and told her about his fear.

She tilted her chin to look at him now—kicking a foot back and forth in the shallows—and remembered how he'd fiddled with his knife, sawing it in slow motion across his empty plate.

"Boats are in my blood," he'd said, referring to his family's business, "you know that. And I love being on the water. And near the water." He stressed the *on*, the *near*. "That's why I like to sail. I'm fine up to my knees. But every time I try to go deeper to swim, I panic. Maybe it comes from living near the sea my whole life, knowing the dangers, witnessing the tragedies. I've tried to control it—breathing exercises, telling myself there's nothing to be afraid of—but the reaction comes from deep inside. I can't stop it. I have to get out. I tried immersion therapy once—can you believe they call it that? Made myself do laps in the pool. I threw up." The knife clattered to the plate. "Obviously it's embarrassing, admitting you're scared of the water—especially when you're a boatbuilder. And a guy. People never understand. So if it comes up, I tell them I just don't like to swim."

That night was the first time he'd opened up to her fully, shown some kind of vulnerability. Tomas had never been like that.

Now she waded in to Jake and touched his shoulders. His skin was sizzling. She made a bowl of her palms and began scooping water onto him.

He let out a small moan. "God, that feels amazing."

"I know, right?" she said. "How are you going manage two months here without swimming? You'll frazzle."

"Not when I've got a willing handmaiden to douse me. My own water wallah."

She dribbled more water onto the back of his neck. Here on Amarante, with her help, he could try again. She took his hand in both of hers and started to step backwards. The waves lapped her calves. "Come on, just try it."

His feet were anchored to the spot. "Honestly, I'm fine."

She moved a little farther so he'd have to choose between pulling his hand away and coming with her deeper into the water. "It'll be okay, I promise. I'm here. There's no current." She halted, waiting for him to decide. Squeezed his fingers. "Just this once? For me?"

It was at risk of becoming a standoff, a literal arm's-length standoff. But then the resistance eased, and he came toward her.

"For you," he said.

She encouraged him as gently and patiently as she could, guiding him slowly out until the water was high up their thighs. Then she persuaded him to let it take his weight for a few seconds at a time. She got him doing a rough doggy paddle, and then she enticed him a little deeper.

"It's okay, we're still shallow," she said, standing, the water at her upper chest. "Look."

He was fighting against the fear—she could see it in the clench of his jaw, the way his replies to her were super short, as if it were taking all of his concentration not to freak out. Eventually, by leaning him back and supporting his head, she got him to starfish.

"Okay, I'm going to let go."

"Mmm-hmm." He was puffing out sharp breaths through his mouth, but he stayed on his back.

"You did it. You're doing it." She floated next to him and reached for his hand. "See? Fun, right?"

"Mmm-hmm."

The sound he made was still tense but at least his breathing had eased. She closed her eyes, enjoying his success—her success. They could take it really slowly, practice every day. Maybe by the time they left Amarante he'd be a full-on, confident swimmer.

Through the water came the whistling whirr of a propeller, that telltale urgent whine. Jake floundered, struggling to find his footing.

She looked out into the bay. There was a small boat, still some way off. "Jake," she called, but he was thrashing his way to shore. He was already on the beach by the time she got to him, angled away from her, drying himself with his T-shirt.

"Jake?" She reached for him.

"I'm fine, Vee." He pressed the T-shirt to his face for longer than was necessary.

"I'm sorry," she said.

"It's fine, honestly." He wouldn't meet her eyes. He rubbed his hand back and forth through his hair, raking the water away.

"You did really well—" she started.

"I said, it's fine. We're about to have company anyway." He inclined his head toward the approaching boat. It was a tender. "Look familiar?"

She let it go. And he was right. The man at the helm did have a familiar, confident stance.

"Our Brazilian-Mozambican friends," Jake said.

She picked up her sarong and wrapped it around her body, tucking it tight under her arms, wanting to cover up if they were no longer alone. Now she saw a catamaran had joined the trio of anchored yachts. "Wonder why they changed their minds."

Vitor stopped his tender a little inshore of where they'd been swimming. He grinned at them as he threw an anchor into the sea. His tender was elegant: longer than theirs, twice the outboard power, its dove-gray rubber immaculate. She caught Jake's appraising look. Teresa was perched in front, where the white leather seat matched the color of her bikini, lacy kimono, and sun hat.

"Good morning. What a place this is!" Vitor stepped off the boat in one fluid movement, his unbuttoned shirt sailing behind, and helped Teresa into the shallows.

Her greeting was as brief as it had been in Port Brown—"Hello"—her smile likewise short, sharp. She headed for dry land, where she stood a little way off and slipped on her sandals.

Vitor followed her ashore and shook Jake's hand. "You are surprised to see us?"

"A nice surprise," Virginie said. And it was. She kissed them both. Vitor accepted her kiss with ease, but Teresa held herself stiffly. Virginie remembered how reserved she'd been last time. It might be she needed a while to loosen up.

Vitor stooped and picked up a coconut, weighing it in his palm. "The perfect desert island, as they say."

Teresa pursed her lips, considering. "Like the Bazarutos."

"Bazarutos?" Virginie asked.

"Some islands off Mozambique," Vitor said.

Teresa nodded. "They are very beautiful."

Vitor hummed in half agreement. "Maybe. Before the South African hoteliers came."

"Or like Eleuthera," Teresa suggested.

"Yes," Vitor said. "Very much so." He looked at Jake. "Have you been there?"

"No."

"You should go. It is wonderful. Actually, not Eleuthera. Like San Blas. How about there?"

Jake's jaw tightened. "Not yet."

"It is near Panama. Also wonderful." He tossed the coconut to Jake as if it were a ball. Jake, taken by surprise, caught it, but awkwardly, twisted to the side. He took a couple of paces back, returned the throw. They kept up the volley, widening the gap with every pass.

Men. They could turn anything into a competitive sport. Virginie raised her eyebrows at Teresa, in a kind of half-joking sisters-in-solidarity way. Teresa met her eye, but her expression remained unreadable. Virginie decided to be charitable, put it down to tiredness after their crossing.

"Sounds like you've been to some amazing places," she said, trying again to break the ice. "Have you been living aboard long?"

"Vitor travels a lot for work. I go with him."

"Do you work for him? Is that how you met?"

"No."

Virginie kept up her friendly, encouraging smile until Teresa gave her a little more. "I worked in a bar."

"In the Bazarutos?"

"In Maputo."

"And were you a sailor before you met him?"

"No."

Just then Vitor missed a catch, and the coconut skidded into the sand, bringing both the game and the awkward conversation to an end. A relief—possibly as much as for Teresa as much as for her. Vitor clapped Jake on the shoulder. Virginie might have guessed he'd be gracious in defeat. He made a swift detour to his tender and pulled out two bottles of water, giving one to Jake.

"Thanks." Jake cracked it open and drank deeply before passing it to Virginie. The bottle was chilled. "So you guys had a change of heart?" he said.

Vitor spread his hands wide. The sun glinted off his watch's face. "My business in Port Brown finished early and so I thought, Why not? Perhaps it will be good to take a break. Get away from emails, the cell always ringing. I even left my satellite phone behind."

"What is your business, Vitor?" she asked.

He held a finger to his lips, playfully. "No work talk. Not when we are surrounded by all this." He turned in a circle slowly, as they had done when they first landed, taking in again the beach, the bay, the jungle. "You have already been exploring?"

Jake indicated the start of the trees. "We went through there to the center, walked through a bit of forest and past some ruins to a beach on the far side."

"Ruins?"

"A village of some kind."

"Old?"

"No way to tell, really. They're pretty ruined ruins."

"And," Vitor said, addressing Virginie, "you have been enjoying a swim?"

"Yes—the water's gorgeous."

"You like to swim?"

"Love it."

"Me also. I like to swim every morning, keep the heart healthy, the body strong, you know?"

Virginie was suddenly conscious of how close he was standing and of the warmth of his smile. She was also aware of Teresa's silence. She stepped back.

Vitor turned to Jake. "And you, Jake?"

There was a pause before Jake spoke. He'd be worrying that Vitor had seen him panic.

He cleared his throat. "It's more Vee's style than mine. I prefer to keep my feet on the ground."

"But you live on a sailboat. You are surrounded by water. And you do not like to go in?"

Jake coughed uncomfortably. She gave him the bottle. He swigged. "I'm more of an on-the-water man, if you know what I mean?"

"Ah. A true sailor."

Yes, he was, and she loved him for that, and was glad Vitor understood. "How about you, Teresa?" she asked, shifting the spotlight from Jake. "Are you a swimmer?"

"No . . ." Teresa looked sideways at Vitor, as if checking whether she should speak. Virginie's stomach tightened. She used to do the same thing with Tomas.

Vitor said, "She is a little shy," and put his arm around Teresa's shoulders.

"My English is not so good," she said, from beneath her lashes.

Virginie exhaled. The caution, the aloofness—just a little insecurity, that was all. She shouldn't transfer her own experience onto someone else. All relationships were different. "Teresa, your English is great," she said. "Honestly, you should hear my Portuguese." Shyness she could work with—be extra friendly, until Teresa got to know them better and gained a little confidence. "We met one of the other cruisers earlier," she said, directing her words at Teresa. "A Canadian woman, Stella." She pointed into the bay. "From that boat there. She was really nice, very friendly. They're holding a party on the beach this evening, just after sunset, in honor of our arrival. I'm sure you're invited, too."

Vitor clapped, once. "Then you must come to *Santa Maria* first for sundowners and we will celebrate making it to Amarante. Yes?"

She glanced at Jake. He was shifting from foot to foot, his face flushed, his eyes on the sand at his feet. So his opinion of Vitor hadn't improved since Port Brown. But this was a small island. There would be no escaping each other. They needed to get along. All of them.

Vitor seemed unaware of Jake's mood, but Teresa was watching him, eyes narrowed. "Maybe they want time alone."

God, she didn't want them to think she was—that Jake was—unfriendly. "Of course not. We'd love to," she said. "Right, Jake?"

"Sure," he said, to her relief.

"Great." Vitor checked his watch. "You are returning to your yacht now for lunch?"

Wow, was it that time already? "I guess we are."

Vitor turned, and Teresa turned with him. "As you English say," he called over his shoulder, "see you later."

As the other couple walked away, she wondered again about their dynamic. Vitor was so warm, so outgoing, while Teresa seemed even more restrained here than she'd been in Port Brown. But she could have her wrong—they barely knew each other yet. And maybe that's why they were a match: he was the extrovert to her introvert. Who could say what drew couples together?

The sun was at zenith, the light so intense that as Vitor and Teresa crossed the beach the white sand seemed to vibrate with energy. They reached the line of trees. Barely a moment later the dark jungle swallowed them up.

14

"You look beautiful," Jake told her as she came up into the cockpit. She'd chosen wide trousers and a strappy top that scooped low at the back. Her shoulders were sunburned and she wanted to let her skin breathe.

She hung her bikini over the rail and kissed him as she stood up again. "Thanks. It feels funny to be wearing clothes after a whole day in this."

"Want a beer?" He'd almost finished his.

"Are they cold?"

"Kind of. Enough to be refreshing."

"Then yes."

"Sit," he said. "I'll get them."

Despite the late-afternoon hour, the sun was still strong and she was thankful they'd followed Stella's advice and strung up canvases to cast shade over the boat. She'd seen Stella rowing over to the beach a little earlier with a man, presumably her husband. A second dinghy— the Australian's—had followed not long after.

When they'd finished their drinks, they set off for the catamaran, Jake running the engine slowly, a lazy smile on his face. He seemed happy; what a relief the reluctance she'd sensed when she first raised coming here had vanished.

Vitor was waiting at the back of *Santa Maria* to take their rope and tie their dinghy to a cleat. "Welcome on board my home," he said, offering her a hand. He'd changed into a fresh shirt and trousers, and she could smell the laundry powder on him as she passed.

She reached the cockpit. *Santa Maria* was in a completely different league from *Wayfinder*. Unlike their cockpit, where the narrow benches, wheel, and steering compass took up most of the space, *Santa Maria*'s was more like a room in a house. It had a hard top, like a ceiling, supported on poles, meaning three sides could be open to the air. The bench seats were wide enough for two and lined with padded taupe cushions. The starboard half of the space was dominated by a full-size dining table with teak director's chairs. A bottle of white wine was chilling in an ice bucket in the center, beads of condensation clustering on its neck, and olives, nuts, and small crackers had been poured into a shallow dish. Classical music played quietly in the background.

Vitor pulled the bottle from its cradle and poured a glass for her. He raised his eyebrows to ask whether Jake wanted one.

"Actually, Vitor, do you have a beer?"

"Of course. One moment and I will find one for you." His own drink was a cloud of dark brown and chinking ice.

While he was inside, she walked around the cockpit again, and Jake examined the instruments at the helm. She ran her hand over the chamfered, polished wood of the table. It was impossible not to feel elevated in surroundings like these. She stood a little taller, leveled her chin.

Jake came over. "What do you reckon? One million? Two?"

She ducked her head, avoiding the question. In the early days of their relationship, they'd been invited to a party at the house of a wealthy client Jake had hand-built a boat for, and he'd been uncomfortable the whole evening. She hoped he wouldn't take against Vitor just because he was rich. Jake had invested all of his life savings in *Wayfinder* and this trip—a sum that, under different circumstances, could have bought him a good-quality German car. He'd refused her offer to put in more than 50 percent if it would buy them a bigger, newer boat, promising that *Wayfinder* would be fine for their needs. And, the luxuries of *Santa Maria* aside, he was right.

He went to check out the system for lifting the tender out of the water. She watched him examining the steelwork. Over the year and a half she'd known him, she'd gradually learned how different their circumstances had been growing up. She didn't consider her family to be rich, but they'd had more than Jake, and sometimes this made her uncomfortable, such as when he'd talked about what he called "latchkey dinners" by himself as a kid or mentioned having to hold down two jobs during university breaks to get through the next term. She hadn't wanted to admit that for her there'd been the large, chaotic houses, summers spent sailing with her siblings and cousins or at her godparents' country place or, when she was older, traveling around Europe. She tried to keep references to such things to a minimum. It wasn't a life-changing amount, by any means, but she hadn't yet told him how much she'd inherited from her grandfather, only that she had enough to pay for her half of the boat and to be able to take a year or so off work. She wanted him to see how alike they were, not how different.

Vitor came out of the saloon through the double doors and extended a bottle of beer to Jake. "Teresa is finishing getting changed. Then she will join us. Cheers, as you say." They all took a sip.

"Your boat is stunning, Vitor," she said. "I've been on a catamaran before, but nothing like this. You have so much space."

"I am lucky," he said. "I have had successes in my life. *Santa Maria* is my reward to myself."

Teresa stepped through from the saloon, a dress of midnight blue rippling around her legs as she moved. Her hair was wet, and water dripped from the ends of her braids and soaked into the silk either side of the low neckline. It was something Virginie would never dare wear, certainly wouldn't have packed to go sailing, but on Teresa, on this boat, it worked.

"Gorgeous dress," she told her.

"Thank you." Vitor poured her a drink. She kept a measured distance and sat at the table, in the far corner.

"Come, sit," Vitor said to Virginie and Jake. He chose the helmsman's seat for himself, lifting a lever to swivel the stainless steel chair to face into the cockpit. It was upholstered in white leather, like his tender. "Let us get to know one another more," he said, once they were all settled, addressing Jake. "For example, I know you are from the UK, I know you have a beautiful wife and she is French, and I know you do not like to swim, but I know little else. Let us become friends. Tell me."

"What do you want to know?"

"Well, for example, what is your business in England, how long you have been sailing, where you met the beautiful Virginie."

Heat flooded her cheeks. Twice in under a minute Vitor had called her beautiful. Teresa's expression was neutral, but somehow Virginie doubted she'd missed the comments. She was watchful, this woman, and, Virginie imagined, a collector of information.

Jake summed up his work history for Vitor, telling him briefly about the twelve years at his dad's boatyard—"I mainly do carpentry and rigging"—about how the industry had changed so much as people moved away from maintaining the kind of smaller hand-built day-sailers and dinghies that Selkirk's yard had specialized in for three generations, and opted instead for bigger boats with standardized fiberglass hulls, straight off a French or German production line.

Vitor's boat was fiberglass. Not fully production, by the looks of it, but still . . . She shot Jake a look; she couldn't tell what he was thinking. Perhaps he didn't mean it as a dig.

Thankfully it seemed Vitor wasn't insulted. "You have been in Asia for some time before coming here to Amarante?" he asked Jake.

"No—we bought *Wayfinder* quite recently." He explained the refitting and that the trip to Port Brown had been their first major offshore passage together, and the one to Amarante their second.

Vitor laughed, a deep, throaty laugh, his head thrown back. "You English! You are so crazy! Ah, pardon." He pronounced his apology to Virginie the French way. "You Europeans, I should say. But truly, this is your first boat and your first trip on it, and you come here, to a place where there is nothing? You bring your wife here when you have so little experience?"

They had plenty of experience. She jumped in before Jake could reply. "Actually, it was my idea to come here."

"Your idea?" Vitor turned to her and his tone softened, although it was still playful. "How did your husband manage to persuade you to leave your home and come to live on a small, humble sailboat?"

"Thirty-six feet was enough for Joshua Slocum," Jake said.

She extended a hand across the table toward Jake. The fine gold bracelet he'd given her last Christmas pooled on the polished wood. "Jake was being modest," she said. "We're not exactly novices. We both grew up around boats, and Jake's very good with his hands. He can fix almost anything, so we feel pretty confident. And anyway, this is meant to be an adventure for us, and for it to be an adventure, it has to take you a little out of your comfort zone, right?"

Vitor tilted his head in inquiry. "You are not comfortable?"

She laughed. Clearly he liked to play devil's advocate. "Well, it's certainly more basic on *Wayfinder* than it is here, but I always loved to camp, so we're getting along just fine." Jake put down his drink to squeeze her hand. "And you, Vitor, Teresa?" she went on. "Why did you change your minds about Amarante?"

Teresa adjusted her skirt. "Vitor chose it. He . . . he decides where we go."

Vitor sat back in his chair, his legs crossed, a smile at his lips. "Who could resist such beauty?"

He didn't continue, and in the growing pause she became aware of the arrhythmic lap of the water against the catamaran's hull. He was right about the beauty: to the west the sky had turned lemony, and the sun had faded to a pale globe as it sank. A dark column of smoke was rising from the beach, a beacon summoning them to the party. Something about it felt ancient, primal.

"Come," Vitor said, standing and draining the last of his drink. "If we are guests of honor, we should go."

Jake released her hand to finish his beer. He had peeled the label off the bottle and dropped it onto the immaculate table. She put it in her pocket.

At the stern, Vitor helped Teresa into his tender, and she settled herself on the front seat. "If you want, I can take us all," he offered, extending a hand to Virginie.

"It's okay," Jake said, and jumped into their dinghy. "I'll drive Vee." He pulled on the starter cord, and the outboard sprang to life.

She flashed Vitor a thanks-anyway smile and got in beside Jake, untying the rope as she went and pushing them away from *Santa Maria*.

"See you over there," Jake added. She was expecting him to motor slowly now it was dusk, but he twisted the control to open the throttle fully, and the roar of the engine shattered the calm of the bay.

15

When Jake killed the engine and let the dinghy drift into the shallows, she could hear crackling and smell the spicy scent of wood. Three or four burning brands speared the sand, casting a semicircle of orange light. It felt cozy, welcoming. The torches led the way to a fire, where low flames had turned people into little more than shadows. Someone came toward them: Stella.

"Hi," she called. She was still in her swimsuit. By her feet ran a small scruffy dog. "You have a good first day?"

"Fantastic," Virginie replied. She crouched to extend a hand to the dog—Gus, wasn't that his name? He was some kind of border terrier cross, fur a wild mess of gray and brown curls. His nose was cold and damp where it made contact with her fingers. "The others are just behind us. That's okay, right?"

"Of course. I went over earlier to invite them. They were grilling some chicken off the back. My God, it made my mouth water! I almost snatched a piece right off. Managed to restrain myself, though. I don't think that would have been the best introduction." Stella mussed Gus's fur. "Pretty rich, from the looks of that boat."

"Yeah," Jake said. "It's fancy."

"You know them?"

"We met them," Virginie said, "in Port Brown. Just for an evening."

Stella stroked Gus's ear, slowly, from base to tip. "We don't really get people like that turning up here. It's not their thing. This is more a place for folks who want to get away from all that materialism, you know? Live a simple life, get back to basics. You wear the same swimsuit every day, you eat what you pull out of the ocean, and you make your own entertainment."

"Sounds pretty perfect to me," Jake said.

Stella laughed. "Good man!" She hollered toward the fire. "Pete! Come meet *Wayfinder*." A man, squatting low, unfolded himself and ambled over. He looked outdoorsy, capable, exactly the kind of person Virginie expected to find in a place like this. The peak of his baseball cap had worn right through to the stiffener, and the crinkles at the corners of his eyes were visible even in the low light. His palm, as he shook her hand, was hard and dry.

"Settling in all right?" he asked after he'd shaken Jake's hand, too. "Saw you head over here earlier today. I'm guessing you went exploring?"

"Such a special island, isn't it?" Virginie said.

"Sure is. How far d'you go?"

She told him where they'd walked that morning: along the path to the village, and through to the other side.

"Village?" he said.

"Those ruins."

"Ah. I guess you could call it a village of some kind." He pulled his hat down lower. "Well, you've pretty much seen the most of it. It's a quiet little place. Suits us." Pete looked at Stella and chuckled. "Well, suits me. I think Stella would appreciate more people to talk to." He had a can of beer with him and he took a pull. "You met Roly yet?"

"Yup." The voice came from behind; then the hunter from earlier eased through the gap between the four of them, coating the air with the smell of diesel, brine, and sweat. He reached to untie something that hung from the branches of a tree—the creature he'd shot. "Didn't catch your names, though."

Embarrassed, Virginie apologized for their reactions that morning. "You took us—me—a bit by surprise. You're Roly, right? I'm Virginie, and this is my husband, Jake."

Roly dropped a knee to the sand and began undoing the noose. It was a complicated knot, but he seemed so familiar with it he didn't even have to look to know what to do with his fingers. "Recognized your boat when you came in. Used to be *Lost Horizon*?"

"That's right," Jake replied. "You know her?"

"Yeah, I know her. You renamed her?"

"Wanted to put our own stamp on her, you know? Start afresh."

Roly pulled the rope free with a jerk. He still wore the knife at his waist—a sliver of steel glimmered in the firelight. "Bad luck to rename a boat."

Virginie laughed, assuming he was joking. "That's what the official in Port Brown told us."

He didn't laugh back. He coiled the rope into his pocket and stood, holding the creature, its legs dangling past his knees. "Not sure I'd want to take the chance."

"Yes, well," Jake said. "It's done now."

"True. Not much you can do about what's passed."

Pete patted the crab's shell. "Biggest coconut crab we've seen on the island so far. Should cook up pretty good."

"At first I thought it was a snake," Virginie said, "when I heard it moving toward us. I hate snakes."

"No snakes here," Roly said. "Not the reptile kind, at least."

Jake prodded a massive claw.

"You don't want to be doing that with a live one," Roly said, although not unkindly. "One this size, pinch as strong as a lion's bite."

Jake eased his hand away. "What does it taste like? Chicken?"

Roly looked at him. "Like crab and coconut." He walked off to the fire, the dog following at his heels.

Jake raised his eyebrows.

"For real," Stella said. "I guess a diet of coconuts means it takes on the taste of them. It's kind of like lobster crossed with crab, basted in coconut oil. Makes a nice change." She looped an arm through Virginie's. "I need to turn my yams. Come with me?"

Vitor and Teresa must have been held up, because by the time they arrived and another round of introductions had been made, the food was ready.

Teresa seemed as reserved with all the others as she was with Virginie, but she was thrilled to meet Gus, kneeling to be at his level and mussing his head.

"You got a dog?" Roly asked as Pete began passing around leaves, piled high with pieces of hot white flesh.

Teresa tickled Gus behind the ears. "I had to leave him in São Paulo." She got Gus to shake paws.

"Christ," Roly said. "Never seen him do that before."

She laughed, all wariness gone. "It is easy. I will teach you some time."

Teresa seemed like a different person around the dog. Maybe if you found common ground, she opened up. "What kind of dog did you have?" Virginie asked.

"I don't know the name," Teresa said, "of the, what do you call? The family?"

"The breed?"

"Yes. I don't know the breed. But he is a very kind dog, very loyal." She shook Gus's paw again.

"And you were living in São Paulo?" Virginie asked.

"For some time," Teresa said. "Before—"

"Teresa," Vitor interrupted, calling over from the fire and showing her he'd got her some food.

"Sorry, I must go . . ."

"Sure." Virginie stood aside to let her pass.

The group formed a loose circle on the sand, Vitor and Teresa to Virginie's left, Jake, Pete, and Stella to her right. Roly sat last, across the fire, pulling up a log to use as a perch. The crab was sweet and juicy, and certainly tasted a lot better than it had looked. She copied Vitor in sucking the meat out of a leg. Juice ran down her hand, her forearm, and she had to lick it off. Teresa was approaching it in a more ladylike manner, pulling the shell apart with her fingers. Pete went up for seconds and, when he'd finished that, bit into one of Stella's yams as if it were an apple.

"Right then," Roly said once everyone had finished eating and Stella was hand-feeding pieces of crab to the dog. "Seeing as we're all here and there's new people." He nodded across the fire, his face lit red from underneath. "The rules." He registered the quizzical looks from the four new arrivals. "What did you expect? Anarchy?"

"They're commonsense things, really," Stella said.

Pete chipped in. "Think of it as a gentlemen's code of conduct."

Virginie recalled Terry mentioning a few club rules, but Pete was making it sound like something from the days of the East India Company. "You bringing the conventions of the civilized world to the savages?" she asked.

"Kind of," Pete said.

Stella tossed a shell at him. "Hey, we're not the savages here."

Roly cleared his throat, like a teacher trying to get the attention of unruly students. Because he was sitting on the log, he was slightly higher than everyone else, and the position lent him authority.

"Rules," he repeated. He held up a pinch of his leftover crab meat. "First is food. If I catch, I share. Pete catches, he shares. You go out . . ." He put the crabmeat in his mouth, chewed, swallowed. "We each pull our weight. Anything that comes from the island or the sea is for the group to share. Fish, firewood, coconuts."

"This makes sense," Vitor said. "And I love to hunt."

Gus went back to Roly and circled by his feet, checking the safety of the sand before settling. He laid his chin on his front paws and sighed. Roly stroked his head. "Next," he continued, "what you bring to Amarante with you is yours. Be careful with it. No way to replace stocks out here. Bring your own drinks to the beach. Someone invites you to their boat, take your own. Might seem unfriendly, but we all do it. It works. There's no hard feelings."

Virginie's face grew hot. They'd accepted those drinks on *Santa Maria*. How could she have been so naive? She glanced at Vitor. She got the sense he knew what she was thinking because he flicked his hand outward. Forget about it, the gesture said.

Pete spoke up. "Same thing as drink goes with anything else you got on your boat—food, fuel, spares."

"Trade items if you want," Roly said. "Or your time or skills." His sentences were short, part formed, as if he wasn't used to speaking. He stopped stroking his dog to hook his arms around his bent legs. "We got no use for money."

Someone made a noise. It was quiet and quick, indistinct, but sounded to Virginie like a half sigh, half snigger. It came from her left.

Roly had pinpointed the source. "Teresa? You got a question?"

Teresa dipped her head. "No."

"It's okay." His look was encouraging. "All questions, all opinions, are welcome here."

"It is only . . ."

"Only?"

Teresa looked down at the fire. "Only in heaven is there no money."

Another noise—this time Stella slapping her hands delightedly on her thighs. "Exactly!"

A world where money had no value. There couldn't be many places left where that was the case. Virginie liked the sound of it—it made her and Jake equals in that regard, at least for a while. Actually, it leveled all of them—even Vitor.

There was a shift in the mood around the fire, and she was reminded of a schoolroom, of kids starting to fidget after sitting too long. Not that she felt lectured to, really, but there was definitely something authoritative about Roly—she could see why Stella had described him as a kind of village elder.

Jake flashed a hand. "Do you think any more live-aboards will arrive?"

Stella said, "I doubt it. Not this late in the season. We were a bit surprised to see both of you turn up, to be honest."

The fire spat, and Roly brushed at his skin. "The odd fishing crew comes from time to time, but I haven't seen any yet this year. Navy vessel patrols about once a season. Used to be they'd come more often. We'd trade with them for fuel, fresh provisions—a box of smokes or a bottle of whiskey. Now it's rare they pass through. We're on our own. And we like it that way."

He ran through a couple of smaller rules—no fishing on the far reef, no burning rubbish on the island. "As Stella says, basic stuff. Clean up after yourselves."

"Leave only footprints, that kind of thing?" Virginie asked.

He nodded. "You got it."

Virginie loved those memes about travel, even the cheesy ones. And so did Jake. If either came across one that really spoke to them, they'd screenshot it and send it to the other. Jack Kerouac was a mutual favorite.

Jake spoke up again. "And the no-fishing rule—is it a reserve or something?"

Pete answered. "Not yet. They want to make the whole island a reserve, stop us coming. But it hasn't happened so far, and we've got subsistence fishing rights for now."

"It's local knowledge," Roly said, "passed down from cruiser to cruiser. When Pete and Stella first came to Amarante, I told them the same thing."

Both were nodding. Stella said, "Bad luck, some say. You know how superstitious sailors can be."

"Superstition!" said Vitor. "When we crossed the equator did our time change as well as our latitude? Is it not now the twenty-first century?"

Roly smiled and sighed, a combination that suggested he'd heard it all before. "Some say superstition. Some, including me, say rules. They often come from the same place. Best thing is to follow them, whatever they're called. Reckon you'll be right, that way."

When it became clear he had finished speaking, Jake went off along the beach, presumably to pee. Virginie began to apologize properly to Vitor for the drinks.

"It was a party," he said before she could finish. "Relax."

"Still, I don't want to get off on the wrong foot."

"You can pay me back some other time." He leaned on his arms and stretched his toes toward the fire. "And is that not the point of being in a place like this, so that you do not have to live by someone else's rules?"

From his other side, Teresa called him—"Vitor?"—plucking at his arm until he turned back to her. Virginie felt guilty for having taken his attention away. It was like Stella said—the excitement of talking to new arrivals.

She looked to the sea, to the foam line, and then beyond, at the blackness. How right Vitor was about rules. She didn't want to live by anyone else's rules, not her father's, not Tomas's. It was high time to start making her own. You could be whoever you wanted to be in a place like this, so far removed from the constraints of normal life, from the expectations everyone had of you and your own habitual behaviors; you could be yourself. She closed her eyes and listened to the song of the insects, the melody of the frogs, the pop of the fire. Underneath it all, the metronomic rhythm of the sea was as soothing as a lullaby.

The sand shifted. She opened her eyes. Jake was back, sitting next to her. He leaned in. "Tired?"

"Mmm." The heat of the tropical air and the fire, aided by the earlier drinks, were making her drowsy. They'd only been here a day, yet already it felt longer because they'd done so much.

"Well, Mrs. Selkirk, before I take you to bed, let me show you something." He was fine with her decision to keep her maiden name, but still, when they were alone, he occasionally called her this. He was the only one she allowed to do so. He stood, pulled her up, and led her by the hand away from the group and toward the water's edge. He turned her toward the interior of the island. The tiniest amount of water lapped at her heels. "Look up."

Away from the loom of the fire, the night sky revealed itself in all its glory. It was the sky but not the sky: the sky transformed, so studded with stars that it seemed weighed down, hanging low above the earth. There was almost more light than there was darkness. Every time she looked at a gap, she realized there were other stars within it, too. Fainter, but definitely there. "It's beautiful."

"Yes, but look."

From the inflection, she knew he wanted her to notice something specific, something with meaning for their relationship. She surveyed the sky. Travel memes and Kerouac were still in her head.

"Everything ahead of us?" she tried. "We're rolling beneath the stars?"

Jake came behind her, to better point out what it was she should be seeing, aligning their vision. He took her hand, pointed her finger, and moved it down, up, down, up.

"*W*?" she asked. "For *Wayfinder*?"

"Nope. Well, yes, I suppose." He tickled her forearm. "Look again." He retraced the same stars. This time, as he joined the dots, she got it. The skewed *W* was Cassiopeia, that same proud figure on her throne that he'd inked on her skin, now pinned in the sky. Etched into their story.

16

Jake looked at home standing at the helm of Vitor's tender, legs wide to counter the movement of the boat, gaze concentrated on reading the sea surface for reef as he took them farther out. The apparent wind was whipping Virginie's hair across her face. She snatched at flying strands and twisted what she could in her fist to hold it out of the way.

Jake leaned toward her. "This boat is so much fun." Despite his shouting, the wind whisked off his words, so that she could only just make him out. "Miles better than the yacht club's back home."

On the other side of her, Pete called out, "About here's good," gesturing at the water with his speargun. He put it down and wrestled his arms into his wetsuit, angling in one thick shoulder and then the other, ready for action.

It was their third day on the island. Yesterday they'd done some more reorganizing on the boat, as Stella had advised, moving everything they could out of the sun, covering what they couldn't. Then there'd been another delicious dinner on the beach, a feast of buttery fish caught by Pete, Stella, and Roly, cooked on a fire built of driftwood collected by everyone else. There'd been a fair amount of drinking, and as they parted for the night, Vitor had suggested a group fishing trip in the morning. But there were only five of them in his tender now. When they'd swung by to collect Stella and Pete, Stella put a hand to her stomach. "Too much wine last night." Roly was already off somewhere with Gus. Now there was a man far happier in his own company than in a large group.

As the tender slowed and dropped off the plane, Vitor stood and opened a locker and began piling scuba equipment onto the floor: tanks, breathing apparatus, long fins. "I have two sets. We could hunt some big fish."

Pete was already pulling his own mask and fins from a mesh bag. "I'm good as I am." He picked up Vitor's speargun, which looked newer than his own. "But I'll happily play with this."

"Virginie? Would you like to dive?"

She'd never tried scuba before. "Wouldn't I need some training?"

"Not if you stay close to me. I can check your equipment before we go down, and then I will take care of you. You have heard of the buddy system?" She had, but she couldn't have said where. "I will be your buddy. I have done many dives. It is not difficult—you just have to be sensible and keep calm. It will be worth it, I promise."

She eyed the air tanks. "Well, I have always wanted to try."

"Great." He passed a wetsuit to her. "Put this on."

After Jake had stopped the boat, he came to help her fasten it and took a long time pulling up the zip at the back. "All done."

There was a tremor in the words. No one else would have heard, but she knew what it meant. She turned to face him and lowered her voice. "Are you okay with me doing this?"

He let out a shaky breath. "That obvious?"

She took both his hands and squeezed them. "I'll say no if you want me to."

He looked at the sea, which was choppier than it had been when she'd got him to try swimming. "No, it's fine. I don't want my fear to hold you back."

Vitor came over with a kind of waistcoat in his hands. He passed it to her. "Ready?" She looked at Jake, who nodded. She took the waistcoat, and Vitor picked one up for himself. "BCD. You wear it like a backpack once we attach the cylinder." He demonstrated, putting it on.

Pete spat into his mask and rubbed with his finger. "Teresa? You want to come with me?"

Teresa was lounging on her seat at the bow, watching Virginie and Vitor. "I will stay here."

"Okay. Catch you later." Pete slipped the mask over his face, hooked his fin straps over his heels, and rolled off the side of the tender. After taking a few deep breaths, he dived out of sight. He made it look so easy.

Once Vitor had run through some instructions, she put on the scuba equipment. It was unbelievably heavy and made walking even a couple of steps difficult. As she sat on the tender's rubber sponson and lifted her legs over the side, she almost changed her mind. But she didn't want Jake to see her being anxious, so she took a breath and dropped into the water, and immediately the constrictive feeling eased. Vitor jumped in and faced her as they trod water next to the tender. He was so close that their fins kept touching. He adjusted a dial on his watch. "Ready?"

She already had the regulator in her mouth, so she nodded, trying to remember everything he'd told her about breathing out, about equalizing the pressure in her ears, about the hand signals.

"You will love it," he said, putting in his own regulator and giving her a thumbs-down to indicate they should start to dive.

Vitor stayed right in front of her during the descent. She had no idea how long it was taking them or how deep they were going. Beyond him, all she could see was a thick blueness, cut through by fine shafts of sunlight, in which tiny specks danced, like motes in summer air. Her breath was a loud fizz and burble, bubbles streaming upwards after every exhale. Vitor kept his eyes fixed on hers as they went and his hand on her upper arm, his touch as reassuring as a safety line.

Once they were down, close to the reef, she found she was brave enough to be able to ease the grip of her teeth on the regulator. She sculled away from him a little distance and experimented, turning a full circle, getting used to how her body moved in the water, to the regular hiss and blow of her breath, the stream of bubbles she was making. If anything, scuba felt more natural than snorkeling—almost as if she were flying.

Vitor held his two index fingers side by side: *Stay together*. She moved with him, turning her head this way and that as they swam on slowly, drinking in the sights of the coral garden below. Now that the sun was overhead, the colors were as vivid as in a tropical hothouse: anemones, corals, and fish in crimson, yellow, electric blue. Different fish, some small and striped, others long and tube-like, weaved through the reef, going about their daily business, paying her and Vitor no heed. Squid propelled themselves across the bottom, bodies moving in fits and starts, the appearance of their skin changing in pulses to camouflage with whatever they passed over. She swam right through a school of hundreds of small silver fish, which parted for her, and the sensation was like watching a 3-D movie for the first time.

Vitor touched her arm again to get her attention, then formed a circle with his thumb and forefinger. *Are you okay?* She was more than okay; if only she knew a hand signal for euphoria. He showed her heavy, lumbering grouper and tiny clown fish hiding in puffy anemones. He brought her cowries from the seabed so she could stroke their velvety mantles, pointed out sand dollars and sea cucumbers and countless astonishing creatures that she didn't know the names of.

They were swimming toward a patch of seagrass when she saw a turtle just launching off from the bottom. A thrill went through her.

She started to follow it, glancing over her shoulder to signal to Vitor. He was checking the air gauge on his tank, and the light glinted off his mask as he looked up. She was certain he'd seen her, so she returned her attention to the turtle. It didn't appear to be alarmed, was happy to share its underwater space, even slowed so she could catch up. It backpedaled and angled its head to look at her with a heavy-lidded eye. She wondered if it was male or female, and how you'd tell anyway, and stretched out a finger to touch it, but it angled its body and dived sharply. She kicked hard to follow, but then, all of a sudden, she was swimming over the edge of a cliff as the seabed dropped away, and the visibility and temperature plummeted.

Immediately she lost her bearings. She spun around, moving so fast that she crashed into an outcrop of rock on the underwater wall, and as she opened her mouth to cry out, the impact knocked the regulator from her mouth. A rush of bubbles clouded her vision. She clamped her mouth shut, to keep in what air she could. She cast her arms about wildly, trying to find her regulator. As she searched, kicking, her fin struck something hard, and she spun, and more bubbles vortexed around her. She couldn't see, couldn't see. Her fin hit something again. She clawed at her mask with both hands, ripping it up her face and off her head.

Her jaw muscles screamed from fighting the impulse to inhale. She had to get out of the water. She scrabbled about with both hands, kicked as hard as she possibly could, and shot off in the direction of what she hoped was the surface. She'd barely gone any distance when something gripped her calf, and then the side of her waist. She yelled, losing precious air, and thrashed to get free, but it was no use. What was it? The water was so churned up that all she could make out was a dark shape. Shark?

She braced herself for an attack, but then the turbulence stilled a little and she realized it was Vitor who had grabbed her, and that he wasn't letting go.

What was he doing, holding her down here? She looked up at the surface skin way above and tried to writhe out of his grasp, but he held her firm.

Blood drummed in her ears. He pincered her cheeks in one hand and brought her chin down, so her face was level with his. His eyes were open wide, the mask magnifying them. Her chest started to spasm. She needed to breathe. Anything, even water.

Vitor fixed her with his gaze, and then he took his regulator out of his mouth and wedged it into hers. She bit down, fierce, and hauled in air. He let her suck three fast, hissing breaths, took it back for one, gave it to her again. Eventually, he let go of her cheeks and retrieved her regulator from where it was floating behind her, tethered by its hose. After checking it was firmly in place, he took hold of both of her shoulders and started to move her steadily up.

As soon as she broke into the air, she wrenched the regulator from her mouth and gasped, trying to breathe for real. Her hair was in her eyes, her mouth, glued to her skin, and she scrabbled at it.

Vitor had also surfaced, and he turned to locate the tender and waved one arm. He twisted back to her. "Are you okay?"

She nodded, but the movement pushed her mouth below the surface, and she took in salty water. She coughed.

"Virginie, listen to me. Just breathe."

"I—" Another wave hit her.

He held her upper arm, keeping her steady, higher in the water. "The others are coming. They will be here any second. You are okay, I am with you." He turned her so her back was to the waves and cupped her skull with a palm. "Keep your chin up."

When the tender reached them, Jake took one look at her, and then he was leaning over the side, hauling her out of the water and into the boat in a single movement. He snapped open the clips of the BCD and wrenched it off her, unzipped the back of her wetsuit and yanked the top half down her body. Freed, she doubled over and panted. She was light-headed, and her legs began to shake. She was aware of Teresa coming from the bow to see what was going on.

Jake put his arms around her and lowered her into the helmsman's seat. He crouched in front. "Are you hurt? Where's your mask?"

She felt sick, from the salt water and from trying to catch her breath as well as from the panic, and all she could do was shake her head.

He moved her about between his hands, checking her body for injuries. "What happened?"

There was a thud as Vitor dropped his dive tank to the bottom of the boat. "She panicked." He reached behind himself for the zip of his suit. "She swam away by herself and—"

"By herself? What do you mean?"

Vitor peeled his wetsuit down, tugging the sleeves off his hands. It hung loose and low, like a partly shed skin, exposing a paler band at his hips. "It was only for a moment. I caught up with her as soon as I realized she was in trouble."

She opened her mouth to try to explain about the turtle, but a coughing fit overtook her.

"Trouble?" Jake's voice was rising. "How could you let her get in trouble?"

Vitor spread his hands. "She is okay. Just a little spooked because she dropped her regulator. It happens with beginners."

"Christ!" Jake's hands went to his hair.

This was the last thing Virginie wanted—fueling Jake's fear. She cleared her throat as best she could. "It was my fault." The saltwater burn made her croak. "I'm fine now. Honestly, Jake."

"It shouldn't have happened," Jake said, through clenched teeth, to Vitor rather than to her. "For fuck's sake, this was her first time. You should have been with her."

"Jake, she said she is fine."

This was getting out of control. "I can look after myself."

"That's not the point, Vee," Jake said. "Your buddy is supposed to be there for you." He jabbed a finger at Vitor. "You're the expert. You should have made sure she didn't go off!"

"If you were so concerned, why weren't you down there with her?"

At that, Jake got right up in Vitor's face, and she thought for a moment that he was going to hit him.

Teresa lunged forward, her sun hat falling to the boat's floor. "No!"

Just then a brace of fish landed in the bottom of the tender. Pete was treading water by the back of the boat. Indentations on his face marked where his mask had been pressed tight against his skin. "Dinner!" His grin faded when he saw their faces. "What's going on?"

"Vee nearly drowned," Jake said.

Vitor threw up his arms. "She did not. She lost her regulator for a moment, that is all."

Pete hauled himself up the ladder. He transferred his catch into a bucket and then squatted in front of her. "You all right, Vee?"

She looked into his eyes, sea-glass green, steady, calm. How foolish she'd been. Vitor was completely right—she shouldn't have gone off by herself, shouldn't have panicked. If he hadn't been there to help her . . . "Yes, I'm fine."

Pete patted her knee. "Attagirl."

Vitor drove the tender to the anchorage, Teresa keeping close by his side, as if standing guard. Jake stayed at the rear with Virginie, an arm around her the whole way, and by the time they were in sight of the yachts, her embarrassment had faded. They dropped off Pete first, and Jake held the tender against the side of *Swallow* while the Canadian transferred his speargun, catch, and dive kit onto the deck. Stella came up from below. Looking into the bucket, she clapped delightedly. They arranged to meet on the beach at six.

Wayfinder was next, and although Virginie was feeling better, she was glad to be nearly home. As they drew alongside, Jake stepped onto the inflatable's tubing, anticipating the tender coasting in. But just as he did, Vitor put the motor into reverse, giving a blast on the throttle. The change of direction threw Jake off-balance and he rocked on his heels, and for a split second Virginie thought that he was going to fall backwards over the side. He windmilled his arms, trying to catch hold of the rail again, but he couldn't reach. She made as if to grab him, but he was too far. She saw him being sucked into the rotating propeller blades, and her breath caught in her throat. And then, before he could tip all the way over, Vitor shot out a hand and seized him by the shoulder.

Virginie rose, to check Jake was all right. He waved her away and threw a hard look at Vitor. "Wasn't expecting you to reverse."

"My apologies. I thought you would realize I was kicking in the stern to get closer. Better hold on next time, hmm?"

The tender was now tucked tight up against *Wayfinder*. Jake grasped the yacht's stanchions with both hands and climbed onto the deck.

She moved forward to follow. "Thank God you caught him," she said to Vitor.

"I am glad he is all right." He lifted his sunglasses onto his head. "And you also. I am sorry if I scared you earlier."

"I'm the one who should be apologizing, Vitor, not you. It was stupid of me, swimming off. Thank you for showing me all of that, and for, well, you know. And I'm so sorry about losing your mask. Please, let me know how I can pay you back for it." His skin, when she touched him on the arm, was still cool from the water. She became aware of Teresa watching closely, and even though she'd meant it only as a quick touch of thanks and apology, the kind of gesture she'd make with any friend, again she felt she'd overstepped a boundary. She pulled her hand away.

Vitor showed no sign of realizing Teresa was put out. "I have more masks," he said. "Do not let what happened stop you from trying the dive again. You loved it to begin with. You are a natural. I will take you anytime. Just ask me."

She wanted to say she'd like that—because it had been wonderful, for the most part. But she was still conscious of Teresa. "Maybe," she said.

She stepped onto the sponson, the rubber bouncing beneath her feet. Although she didn't need help getting up onto the yacht, she accepted it, Jake taking her hand, Vitor pressing gently against her lower back. Both guiding her, reassuring her she wouldn't fall.

17

"Jake?" she called through to the saloon from their cabin one morning a couple of days later. "Have you seen my sketch pad?" Rummaging through the bag wasn't working, so she started lifting things out one by one, stacking them on the bed. She found her tin of pencils and put it to one side while she carried on removing jeans, a jewelry box, unworn dresses rolled up tight like cigars. What a fool, thinking she'd need all of this. Already she was getting used to not really caring what she wore; it was always so hot and humid that as little as possible was the key. As she removed another handful of clothes, she got a clearer view. Ah, there it was.

She pulled out the sketch pad and flicked through it. There were some still lifes at the front, vases of flowers, collections of fruit, things she'd forgotten she'd done. God, look at this old self-portrait. It wasn't finished, no fine details added yet, and that meant the face looking back at her was too unformed, too blank. And so young. She traced a finger along the curve of an outlined cheek.

She'd drawn it back when she still thought she had a future ahead of her as an artist. She even remembered the date, because it was the day before her twenty-first birthday, just after her wedding to Tomas. He had moved her into his Paris apartment, but he was away, and she took his mirror through to the salon and pulled back the heavy drapes from the tall windows. He would have been furious if he'd known she'd done this, because he said the light faded the antiques. She sat on the floor in the sunbeams and sketched. Later on, she wouldn't have dared.

How much had changed since then. She closed the book and slipped both it and the tin of pencils into her waterproof bag.

Jake was finishing off the washing up, drying a bowl and putting it away. "Find it?"

"Yes."

"What's sparked this urge to draw?"

"I don't know." The muse had been gone for years, had vanished not long after that sunny self-portrait. A few days—actually nearly a week now—in Amarante and it had returned. "Could be the magic of this place?"

He put down the tea towel and kissed her. "Well, I think it's great." He drew back. "Give me two ticks and I'll be ready."

She went up into the light and untied the dinghy rope, pulling the boat forward to the boarding ladder. When she heard Jake bound up the companionway steps, she turned. He had a machete in his hand.

"What's that for?"

He swished it through the air, like a boy pretending to be a pirate. "For swashbuckling." He made two fast arcs through the air, left, then right.

"So it seems. But really?"

He stopped fooling around and slipped it into a leather sheath. "Thought I'd have a go at a few coconuts. Get fully into this hunter-gatherer lifestyle. Do my bit for the commune."

"Commune? What is this, some sort of socialist utopia?"

"Hopefully." He winked and jumped into the dinghy.

She drove this time, guiding it to the usual place. It was funny how quickly you formed habits when you moved somewhere new. All this expanse of sand to choose from, yet she gravitated to the same spot, as if parking their car in the street at home.

Roly's dinghy was already there, and human and canine footprints led a trail across the beach and into the jungle.

"Where are you going to be?" Jake asked.

She looked around. "Not sure. Maybe on the north side. I'll take a walk."

"Meet back here later?"

"Sure." She kissed him. "Be careful."

"With what?"

"The coconuts. That knife."

He drew the machete again, angling it so the sun bounced off the blade. "Baby," he said, "I was born for this."

There wasn't much of a beach on the northern shore, just a short patch of sand strewn with sea-smoothed rocks, and then a view of the open water ahead. The reason she'd stopped was because there was a break in the jungle here, and the gap, together with the overhanging branches of the taller trees, created a natural frame for the seascape. She settled on the ground, leaning against a trunk with bark that peeled like sunburned skin. She slipped her pad out of her bag and rested it on her knee.

The first stroke, gray line stark against the blank paper, was the hardest, and she gave up only a few minutes in. She turned the page and began again. As she became more familiar with the view, and with the image in her mind's eye as it would appear on the page, she looked up less frequently. The sea here, breaking over and over against a barrier of reef, was louder than in the anchorage, and she lost herself to its constancy and focused on her work, on the strokes of her pencil, the soft scratching noise as she made her featherweight touches.

At one point she saw something from the corner of her eye, and the change in the scene startled her. She looked properly—it was a dinghy on the water. She'd been so absorbed, she hadn't realized how much time had passed. Was it Jake, come to find her? She wasn't sure she was ready yet to stop. The boat came closer. It was Vitor's tender, and there he was, sitting at the center console, scanning the shoreline. He must have seen her at the same time she saw him because he stood and waved, angling the bow toward her tree-fringed frame. Waves were breaking all over the reef—it would be difficult for him to find a safe way through. Twice he attempted it, but he deemed it too risky, and aborted, circling away. He aimed at her a third time. God, she didn't want to be responsible for flipping his tender—or worse. She ran to the water's edge to warn him not to come, it was too hard, but this time he found a gap and surfed the boat through, and once she knew he was out of danger, she allowed herself to feel a little fillip at the thought she was worth the effort.

He jumped out, into the shallows, and buried the anchor in the sand. "I saw you from the reef. You were framed by the trees, like a movie." He made a rectangle from his thumbs and forefingers and closed one eye to peep through.

She smiled and sat back down. "So were you."

He flopped next to her. "I was going to go fishing, but I think it is still too early in the day." He checked his watch. "Or too late." He looked at the sketch pad, which she had closed and put on the ground. "You were drawing?"

She wouldn't normally let people see, but she felt comfortable in Vitor's presence, as if she'd known him a lot longer than she actually had. She picked up the pad, folded it back to the page she'd been working on, and passed it over. "Trying to."

He examined her sketch, comparing it to the view, as she had done. Instantly, she regretted handing over the book and looked for an opportunity to take it back. But then she reasoned that he wouldn't necessarily criticize or tear her work to pieces.

He went backwards through the pages leisurely, appraising each one. "So you are an artist?"

"I wanted to be." Vitor looked at her sideways, under a lock of hair, in a way that encouraged her to go on. "I studied history of art at college, tried to draw and paint as well. But I wasn't ever any good. People told me so." It had been one person, really. "And I knew it, too. So I went into something else." She wasn't sure why she was being so honest. Usually she just told people she worked in a museum and left it at that.

"And Jake is a lover of art also?"

Jake was always out of place in art galleries, and even at the museum. He'd gone to the exhibition where they first met, he told her later, because he assumed it was "going to be about boats, not about *pictures* of boats." She'd noticed him when he walked in—the thick hair, his fit build, the healthy color in his cheeks that spoke of an active life—and watched him from across the room as he went from painting to painting. He'd examined the labels, the frames, the wires the frames were hanging from, even his trainers—anything but the art works themselves. Not taking it seriously, not even taking it in at all, was a welcome change from what she was used to, from the judgment and intensity of Tomas and his gang, from her obsessive father. Whenever she wanted to visit a gallery now, he'd kiss her at the entrance and arrange to meet her an hour later.

"No," she said, smiling at the memory. "Jake is not a lover of art."

Vitor flipped back to the old self-portrait. He touched the drawn hair. "I like this one." He held up the book to the side of her face, comparing one to the other. His brown eyes scanned her features, measuring her forehead, her nose, her lips. Hot under his scrutiny, the intimacy, she reached for the pad, closed it, and put it in her bag.

She stood, brushing imaginary sand from her thighs, and tied her sarong tighter at the waist. "Where's Teresa today?"

He shrugged. "She is on *Santa Maria*. She is reading some magazines." He stood, too. "Want me to take you around in my tender?"

He was so kind. The sort of man who pulled out a woman's chair, rang frequently, just to see how she was. It was possibly a generational thing, a form of manners that older men—especially well-educated, worldly men—seemed to have been taught. Even Tomas had been like that, and she'd have been lying to herself if she denied it had been part of his initial appeal.

She smiled at Vitor. "Thanks, but I'd like to walk. Stretch a bit after sitting." She shook out her legs to prove her point.

"Okay, then. But soon I will take you diving again." He gave a little bow, already stepping backwards into the water to dig out his anchor. She waited until he had made it through the reef and driven out of her picture frame, and then she picked up her bag and set off for the beach, humming as she went.

Coming from the north, the way to the anchorage led her via the ruins. Actually, no matter where she went, she always had to go via the ruins. All the tracks looped back there; they were a crossroads, the nub of the whole island.

Whoever built the village must have also created these tracks, hacking through the brush with knives, she supposed, tramping down plants, compacting the ground with the repeated passage of their feet. This, she thought, was how all towns and cities must begin, even somewhere like Paris or New York: a clement spot attracted first one family, then another, the position of their homes and the regular movements of their lives providing the blueprint for what and who would follow, so that each generation was towed in the slipstream of all those who had lived there before.

The brush darkened, and just ahead she could make out rusty red-brown between the overgrowth of leaves. Although she tended to steer

clear of the graveyard, she quite liked seeing the remains of the buildings; they made her think of the English saying *gone to ruin*, and how
that was often applied in an almost romantic way to describe some
loveable rogue or once-distinguished lady who'd fallen on hard times.
Sometimes as she passed, she would linger, imagining an Edwardian
woman in tattered organza waving away mosquitoes with a gloved
hand, or a gent in breeches digging in his vest pocket for his watch.

Invariably, as she dawdled and daydreamed, she would come across
something interesting. Today, as she reached the nearest tumbledown
wall, she spotted a centipede, green as a peapod. As she watched it
frilling its way along one of the roots of the Lara Croft tree, she heard
a bark. A moment later Gus bounded over. She mussed him, and he
licked her hand in return, then got up on his hind legs, wanting to see
what was so interesting. Just tall enough to reach the caterpillar with
his nose, but cautious enough not to touch, he sniffed, the tiny hairs
on his snout quivering.

She patted his flank. "No, Gus. Leave it." He wagged his tail and
yipped. Now she could hear leaves crackling underfoot. A shadow
emerged from the jungle, morphing into Roly in the daylight. He
tossed a ball for Gus, who immediately forgot about both the caterpillar and Virginie and raced after it.

Roly had a bag on his back, filled with sticks for the fire. When he
reached her, he dropped his bag to the ground, seeming to welcome
the opportunity to put down his load. He pulled out a canteen and
drank deeply. "Running rings round me, that one." Gus came back, the
ball in his jaws. Roly threw it again. They both watched him scurry off.

"He seems to love it here."

"He'd be happy pretty much anywhere, long as he had the space to
run about. Thinks he's still a pup." He drank again, his Adam's apple
bobbing.

She'd quickly worked out that, like with Teresa, small talk wasn't
Roly's thing. He'd come along in the evenings to throw his catch into

the pot, but he'd mainly keep himself to himself, and leave with Gus as soon as the meal was done. She wondered if he used to be more outgoing when his wife was still around, if being on his own had changed him. She certainly got the sense he'd decided there was as much value in being quiet as there was in speaking—perhaps more so.

She didn't have that level of self-containment; she was so full of curiosity about this new world that thoughts, questions, theories were constantly filling her mind. "Roly," she said, "do you know how long ago this village was built?"

He'd just taken another swig of water, and he half choked, as if she'd said something shocking. He brought the back of his hand to his mouth while he swallowed. "Village?"

"Yeah"—she swept an arm wide—"this. I keep thinking about the people who might have lived here."

He gave her a long look. "Who was it told you about Amarante?"

"Terry. On the mainland. Terry . . ." She tapped her chin. She'd never asked him his last name. But she did remember what his boat was called. "From *Shangri-La*."

"Ah." He nodded to himself, as if she'd confirmed a suspicion.

"You know him?"

"Yeah. I know him." He capped his canteen, slid it back into his bag. She caught his smell. "Let me guess—he gave you his spiel about how beautiful it is here. But he never told you the other half of it. Am I right?"

"Other half?"

At her expression, he snuffed. "No need to look so worried. Terry's harmless. Loves it here, or did. When he still had the strength to make the crossing. Used to be a fair few of us back then . . ."

She waited, but he seemed lost in private memories. "I don't understand, Roly," she said, bringing him back to the present. "What other half?"

He began rotating on the spot, surveying it all. "It's not a village, Vee. It's a prison."

His back was to her. She stared. "No . . ."

He kept turning. "Penal colony, really. Extension of a prison over there." He waved a hand northeast, in the direction of the Malaysian mainland. "They sent people over to farm copra."

"They?" He was facing her again. At her question, he turtled in his chin and raised an eyebrow. You really should know better, his expression said.

She sighed. The British. Who else?

He saw she'd worked it out. "Rounded up people opposed to British rule. Freedom fighters and the like. Shipped them out here and set up a hard labor camp."

"When? How many?"

He scratched a bite on his arm. "Hard to know. Started a hundred years back, a hundred and fifty? I'm going off hearsay, really—never heard of any records. But you can see for yourself."

"And the graves?"

"An attempted rebellion, someone told me when I first came. They shot the ringleaders."

What a punishment, to be sent so far away from home, from everyone and everything. Her breeches-wearing sea captain dissolved, replaced by a British Army officer. At his feet, a group of Asian men, shiny with sweat and brought to their knees by exhaustion, starvation, dehydration—and by the muzzle of a gun.

"Be pretty brutal," Roly said, "processing copra manually. Extracting the oil. Especially in this heat."

She swallowed, feeling stupid. Of course there wouldn't have been a village here, so far from anywhere else. Amarante had never been on any trade routes—she knew that. She'd bloody written about the trade routes for the museum.

Roly shouldered his bag, in the same way he had the crab on the day they'd first met, flexing his knees to help settle it into place. "That's your good old empire at work. Makes me glad my ancestors were of

Irish stock." He called for Gus. When the dog came, he fed him a treat. Then they left.

Alone again, she trailed a hand across the creeper-choked brick of one of the houses, as if through her touch she could come to terms with its new meaning. She shouldn't think of them as houses anymore. But if not houses, then what were they? Storerooms? Or . . . cells. She pulled her fingers away as fast as if she'd been burned.

18

Closer to the beach the brush was less dense, and light beamed through. There was more life here, and after what she'd learned at the ruins, the movement of the island creatures was more than welcome: the wink of tawny wings as a butterfly crossed her path; the stop-start motion of a gecko scuttering up a tree trunk when it thought it couldn't be seen, freezing motionless when it decided it could. Above it all, the chitter of unseen birds. She focused in on their calls—some were slower and more regular, others fast and chaotic, but occasionally their syncopated notes aligned, and for a moment, less than a moment really, their cacophony turned into unexpected harmony. Then she heard a distinctive human sound: a whistle.

Jake. It came again, from directly above. She followed the line of a thick-trunked palm, craning her neck right back. He was near the top of the tree, ten, maybe even fifteen meters up, knees by his shoulders, legs splayed like a frog. A tree frog, right at home. He'd taken off his T-shirt, and his skin blended with the jungle. There was no way she'd be so relaxed if she were that high, but this was an everyday occurrence for Jake, although usually he was hanging off a mast rather than a tree. His work had given him a rock climber's physique, lean but laced with muscle, and she knew he was strong enough to hang out in that tree for hours if he wanted to. Still, it made her heart jump when he lifted one hand off the trunk to twist free a coconut, and she couldn't help but think of the graves not that far away.

He put the stem between his teeth and shinnied down, making a hopping motion: both hands together, then feet, then hands again. At the bottom, he presented her with her prize. "Ta-da!"

"Thanks." It was heavier than she expected, its green skin taut.

"You've been gone ages. Are you thirsty?"

"Sure."

Her taciturn replies prompted a quizzical look. She wasn't being fair—he was having fun. And so had she, earlier. She needed to shake off this weird feeling. She gave him a quick smile.

The next tree along was smaller, younger, and had branched low, creating a Y-shaped trunk. He retrieved his machete from its resting place in the dip of the Y, took the coconut from her and placed it on the ground, holding it firmly with one hand. She gritted her teeth as he lifted the blade, both in fear that he might injure himself, and also because she couldn't help but think of the parallels between what he was doing and what the prisoners had been made to do. He brought the blade smartly down, chopping at the top of the nut, turning, chopping again. While she'd been sketching, he'd apparently mastered the machete.

There was energy in his movements, joy even. In no time Jake was all the way round the coconut; then he was hitting and prizing off the top, exposing the thick white husk inside. His eyes gleamed as he gave it to her.

She thought she didn't want it, that her moral objection was strong enough to override her thirst. But Jake was beaming at her expectantly, and she scolded herself again for being ridiculous. There was no escaping history. She worked in a museum, for God's sake—and museums by their very nature traded on both the triumphs and the dishonors of the past. She raised it to her lips.

The coconut water was deliciously sweet—and gone too soon. She tipped the shell, trying to get at the last drops, and they ran down her chin.

"Want another?" he asked, moving back to the tree. He braced his feet against the bottom, ready to go.

"Jake, you don't have to—" She stopped as he pulled a bamboo pole from where it had been hidden behind the trunk and waggled it, a magician revealing his trick. Rather than climbing the tall palm, he took the pole to a shorter one and used it to knock at a bunch of lower-hanging coconuts. She laughed.

"What?" he said, deadpan. He caught a coconut as it fell, bowled it to her. "No way am I going up there every time, the rate you drink them." He came over and swiped at her chin. "You threw half of it over your face." He licked his fingers. "And besides, I'm on holiday."

He bent to work the blade once more. She watched his muscles flexing as he hacked. Terry had been to Amarante twelve times; its dark history certainly hadn't put off Roly. If she and Jake had already known, would it really have stopped them from coming here, from experiencing moments like this? It must be possible to enjoy everything else the island had to offer and still remain respectful of its past. She didn't have to forget, and she didn't have to forgive, either.

By the time a fourth coconut had been fished down and opened, the preoccupation had gone, burned off in the rays of Jake's vitality like a mist by the sun. How she loved him and his ability to make everything all right.

The moon was rising as she and Jake motored over to see Pete and Stella on *Swallow* later that evening. The temperature was down a merciful couple of degrees from the daytime high, and the anchorage was still.

Virginie climbed up from the dinghy first, taking from Jake a cool bag and a coconut, its top sliced off and put back in place again, like a lid.

"It's the Amarante equivalent of bringing wine for your hosts," she said to Stella, passing it over.

Swallow's cockpit was even smaller than *Wayfinder*'s, and she had to bob to pass under the low awning that Pete and Stella had rigged up to give them shade during the day. Patterned cloths were draped over the bench seats, and a string of solar lights lent a chilled-out vibe to the evening. Not that she needed any help in chilling out on Amarante.

She sat next to Jake and passed him a beer.

He popped the ring and raised the can in a toast. "To a good day." The others copied him.

"Every day here is a good day," Pete said.

Jake sat back, and Virginie nestled into the arm he'd put around her. She'd told him about the prison over dinner. He'd listened, respectfully, and agreed with her about how awful it was. Then he'd naturally moved the conversation on to something else, and she'd been glad to let the matter go.

He drank from his beer. "How many times have you been here?" he asked Stella and Pete.

Stella stood to root around for something in one of the cockpit pockets, pulling out bottles of sunscreen and bungee cords, collecting them under an arm. She was wheezing.

Virginie leaned forward. "You okay?"

Stella pulled a plastic inhaler from the pocket and took two puffs, holding the medication in her lungs. "Yeah. Just a little breathless tonight. It'll pass." She waited a couple of beats, then sat down.

Pete took the sunscreen and bungees from her and tucked them back into the pocket. "This is, what, our fourth time here, Stella?"

She nodded.

"How'd you hear about it?" Virginie asked.

"Through Roly," Stella said. She sounded better. "We met him and Christine around Port Brown, got talking to them in a bar. We were all set for Thailand."

"Us, too. Except our old Aussie was called Terry, and our bar was a few days' sail farther south."

Stella laughed that tinkling laugh of hers. "They came here for years, Roly and Christine. They met late in life. After she retired, they bought a boat, set off to explore. When they found this place, Roly was in his element."

Pete tweaked his cap. "There's not much that guy doesn't know about hunting or fishing."

"You said she moved back to the city?"

Stella adjusted the cushion beneath her. "It's a hard life, being on a boat for a long time. Roly's from the bush, worked his whole life on farms. He's used to the outdoors, to the emptiness, the quiet. But Christine was from the city—Melbourne—a teacher. I guess she decided she just wanted a bit more normality."

"Why didn't he go with her?"

She drew her eyebrows together. "You'll soon learn that Roly's not one to share his emotions. And I bet that didn't help the situation with Christine at all. But I could tell, when we saw him a year later and he was on his own, that actually he was devastated. I don't think he ever wants to go back to Melbourne again. Living wild has always been his thing, his roots, his dream."

"Something certainly keeps drawing you all back here," Jake said.

Pete nodded. "Yeah, it's almost physical, like a pull deep within you. It's more than the beauty, though. It's like it's something basic, instinctive . . . primal? Man, I can't find the right words to describe it."

She wanted to tell him he didn't need to explain it to her. She'd felt the same thing, this unnameable pull, this desire for something, this need to fill a lack inside herself that she didn't even know was there until she'd looked at that chart.

"It's the call of the wild," she said.

Pete's face widened in recognition. "That's it! That's it exactly! Right, Stella?"

But Stella, toying with the ring pull of her can, seemed distracted.

"You all right, Stella?" Jake asked.

"Don't get me wrong," she began. "I love Amarante, but . . . well, I've had other things on my mind, things that sometimes stop me realizing how lucky we are to be here." She placed one hand on her lower belly and exchanged a look with Pete. "They say you don't know how much you want something until the opportunity is gone. Well, that's a load of BS. Wanting something desperately can hurt just as much before all hope is lost as it does after." She put a hand to her mouth and looked out to sea.

Virginie made a move to go to her, but Pete waved her down. "We thought coming here might help," he said, addressing his can of lager. "They say stress can make these things harder, and we wanted to give it our best shot. Can't be a much more relaxing place on the planet. But it just isn't meant to be, I guess." He adjusted his cap, looked up. "It can tear some couples apart, that kind of situation." He looked at Stella, who finally turned back and gave him a small smile. "Not us, though."

Virginie and Jake hadn't talked about children in depth yet, had only made occasional references to what their kids might look like, whose mannerisms or personality they might inherit, if they'd be more like him or take after her. She assumed Jake wanted children, and she assumed she did as well, although she hadn't yet had a strong tug or urge. She'd kind of been waiting for a moment of revelation, when she'd become certain she was ready to be a mother, or a happy accident. Or even both at the same time.

A clattering sound came from the direction of *Santa Maria*, loud in the stillness of the evening, and all four turned toward the catamaran, glad of the distraction. The cockpit lights were on, and Vitor and Teresa were spotlit as they moved around the table. They'd dressed for dinner, even though it was just the two of them.

Pete spoke, his eyes on *Santa Maria*. "He tell you what line of business he's in?"

"No," Jake said. "Although he seems to get around a lot. Mentioned India, the Bahamas, South America. Apparently he's due in a place called Anjouan."

"Really? It's a bit rough there, kinda lawless. Doesn't seem his kind of scene. Although I wouldn't have picked him going for a quiet place like this, either."

"Yeah, I thought so, too. Hey, maybe he's hiding."

"What do you think? Drugs?"

"Could be."

Virginie stared. How could they even think such a thing? The pair of them were being utterly ridiculous. "Oh, come on. That's hardly likely. Just because he's got a big boat doesn't mean he's dodgy."

"Oh, Vee," Jake said, hugging her into his side. "You're so trusting; you can only ever see the good in people."

She pulled back so she could see his face. "And what's wrong with that?" Her voice was rising, and she tried to modulate it. She didn't want to seem shrill. "Vitor could be anything, he could be, oh, I don't know . . ." She searched for an idea. She still wasn't sure what he did for a living. After their first day she'd never thought to ask again. "He could be an accountant?"

Stella huffed. "Very successful accountant."

"Whatever their business," Pete said, "people with boats like that usually want to be in places with a bit more going on. See and be seen, that kind of thing. Especially—"

He stopped as Stella batted his arm. "Pete!"

"What? You don't know what I'm going to say. I might be about to say something nice."

Stella gave him a long look. "Except you're not."

Pete grinned. "Fifteen years together—she knows me so well."

He caught Jake's eye, and Jake started laughing. The other three exchanged conspiratorial looks. What was she not getting? "*What?*"

"Pete's just saying," Stella explained, "that it might not be a genuine love match under it all."

"Under all what?"

Pete thrust out his chest. He and Jake dissolved into schoolboy giggles.

"Oh, come on," Virginie said. "Just because she's much younger—and, yes, gorgeous—doesn't mean she doesn't love him." That prickliness she sensed from Teresa, the way she'd leapt in to break up the almost-fight between Vitor and Jake—what else could that be but defense of the man she loved?

Jake pulled her to his side. She resisted at first, but then she softened against his shoulder. At least the mood had lightened. "You lot are awful."

Pete popped open a second drink. "We had a boat here last year, a group of young turks. The boys had long hair, they all wore ethnic clothes. You know the type. Decent, though, and mainly kept themselves to themselves. But Stella here"—he took his wife's hand and swung it—"decided they were a bunch of wife-swappers."

"No!"

Stella swatted Pete on the chest this time. "They were."

"How did you know?" Jake teased her.

"That's what I asked," Pete said.

Stella winked. "Let's just call it women's intuition. Although I saw one of them come out of the water naked. There was no way I was going to trade what I have here for that."

Virginie laughed. "Speaking of trade," she said, "I hear you need to change your masthead anchor light. Jake's great at climbing. How about we winch him up there tomorrow, then you can take us out, show us the best places to fish?"

Jake's face lit up. She knew that the idea of catching their own food was a big part of the appeal to him of coming away—he loved the idea of providing for them, he'd told her months before, while puncturing the wrapping of a tray of pre-prepared chicken breasts and spearing one with a knife. "Real food," he'd said. "Not this."

"Great idea," Pete said. "It's a deal."

As they drove slowly back to the yacht later, Jake was still smiling.

"What are you grinning about?" she asked.

"Nothing really." He reached back to knock the engine into neutral, and they coasted the last few meters over the black water in silence. "Just really glad we came."

19

Stella put down her kayak paddle and held up two onions, one in each hand. "Can I swap you these for some flour? Ours has got a serious weevil infestation."

Virginie leaned over *Wayfinder*'s guard rail. "Really? Gross."

Gus was with Stella in the kayak, perched on the other seat, standing lookout and tasting the air with his tongue.

"Occupational hazard," Stella said.

"Sure. Give me a sec, and I'll get you a bag."

"Thanks. But no rush." She tossed up the onions one at a time. "Say, I'm going ashore to take Gus for a walk. Want to come with?"

At *walk*, Gus angled his eyebrows at Virginie, turning his whole face into a plea.

She laughed. "Who could resist?" Jake had gone over to *Swallow* to climb the mast, and she was alone. If she went with Stella, she could collect some firewood.

As soon as they beached the kayak, Gus was off, sniffing his way around the base of the trees, happily cocking his leg here and there. They padded after him, letting him beetle about and burn off some energy. Virginie stooped every now and then, putting sticks for the fire into her bag. She had followed Stella's lead and given up on shoes, and now that she was getting used to the sensation, she enjoyed feeling the different textures against her skin, the graininess of the seabed in the shallows, the slipperiness of the dry sand where it heaped high like flour at the top of the beach.

In this area the tallest trees were hosts to air plants that nestled like roosting birds in the crooks between branch and trunk, high up near the canopy. She peered at one. A remnant from a long-ago school lesson came back to her: *epiphytes*—that was the word. They used taller trees to get their spiky leaves closer to the nourishing sunlight.

There was a lowering of both the light and the birds' chatter as they reached the ruins. They were so far into the dry season now that fine cracks had appeared in the ground, crisscrossing the earth like wrinkles mapping old skin.

Gus brought her his ball, sodden with saliva. She tossed it. He hopped off and brought it back, tail wagging. She threw it again, farther this time, and he scooped it up in his jaws and scampered off, hopping over one of the low prison walls and into the jungle.

She approached the odd metal structure, curiosity itching like a day-old mosquito bite. It occurred to her that the bar that projected from one side might be a handle. She curled her fingers over it, finding her palms landed naturally on the worn places, making her think that many pairs of hands had gripped it before her. "Stella?"

Stella was fanning her face with a leaf. "Yeah?"

"Do you know what this thing is for?"

"Not sure." She wafted herself. "Roly'll be able to tell you."

Virginie shoved; it clanked but didn't budge. As she stood there, holding on, she had the growing sensation of layers of the past gathering around her, almost as if she were trapped in the center of a Russian doll of souls. Gooseflesh rose on her arms. She hadn't felt like this since she'd been a teenager, trying out a Ouija board with a couple of girls from school. She let go of the handle, and the movement released an odor from the metal, ferrous, blood-like. Being spooked at thirty-one was silly, but she could feel the presence of the prisoners so keenly it was hard to believe she and Stella were alone.

She needed to speak, to break the eerie silence. "How long ago did people last live here?"

Stella was a little farther on, blithely watching a bird flit about the canopy. "I'm not sure. Eighty years? They were long gone by the '70s for sure. That's when cruisers started coming, and it was wild again by then." She absentmindedly swiped at some perspiration at her hairline. It was such a normal movement—mundane, human, alive—that the strange feeling that had gripped Virginie eased. "You used to be able to visit Amarante for as many months as you wanted, before the Malaysian government wised up and introduced licenses," Stella said. "Roly told us when he and Christine first started coming, they used to find things from time to time—a sandal, a plate. But he thinks the prison officials took almost everything with them when they left. And when the sailors followed, they did the same. It was the early cruisers that set the island rules. They wanted to ensure it worked, that people could make it through the season with enough resources to live. And that Amarante stayed pristine."

One of the things she loved about Stella was how she always lived in the moment. Take right now, for example—she wasn't fixated by history; she just saw it as a progression toward life here today. Without even being aware, she had slid them easily from the past into the present, from the prison to the sailors' paradise.

Virginie eyed a freshly fallen coconut. "I wonder why people didn't settle here properly? After the prison, I mean. There are plenty of coconuts—someone could have continued to farm."

"Maybe life was just too hard. I mean, we're effectively living in the same way, but we brought our homes with us, right? We have shelter. We can make water, and electricity, and we can store food, as well as catch fish and hunt. Imagine what it must have been like back then, a week or two's journey away from anywhere, with only a few tools. You'd have to fend completely for yourself. A broken bone, I guess, could prove fatal, or a particularly dry season, or running out of fishing gear, or rice. Imagine waiting, helpless, while tropical infection set in."

"There's really no help? What about that navy ship Roly mentioned?"

Stella dropped her makeshift fan to the floor. It spun as it descended. "That only used to come once in a blue moon, and we haven't seen it at all this year. Budget cuts, I heard."

Despite the heat and Stella's equanimity, the gooseflesh was back. Virginie wrapped her arms around herself, letting it really sink in, for the first time, how isolated they were, with only one another to rely on. If you died here, no one might find you. She thought of the prisoners' families, waiting back home—possibly for news that never came. They might have gone to their own graves not knowing what had happened to their parents, to their children. She had a strong impulse then to catch up Gus in her arms, to bury her nose in his bitter-smelling fur and press his warm body to her chest in order to feel him wriggle against her, to feel the life in him.

"Gus!" When he didn't come, she strained to listen for him running through the brush. The insects had stilled, and nothing moved in the thick air, not even a leaf. It was as though the island—and its ghosts—listened and waited with her. Then came a bark.

"This way," she said to Stella.

Gus was by the graveyard. He'd lost interest in the game of fetch and was scrabbling in the dirt, cutting a scar into the earth.

"Jeez," said Stella. "We'd better get him away from here." His ball was lying in some undergrowth, the rubber a shocking pink against the dusty greens and browns. Stella bent to pick it up and grimaced in disgust at the spit-sogginess. "Weevils I can just about handle, but that really is gross." She flicked off her hand, and waved the ball, held gingerly between finger and thumb, at the dog. "Gus, come! Come on."

He gave up his digging. Stella drew her arm back and flung the ball deep into the jungle, away from the graves. All four legs left the ground as he leapt after his prey.

"That's it. Good boy," Stella said, making to follow. "Leave those poor guys to rest. I think they've been through enough, don't you?"

Stella wanted to swim back to her boat, so Virginie offered to return Gus to Roly in the kayak. Roly was using his compressor, and as she paddled over, the bay was filled with the sound of it hammering away. When he saw her approaching *Ariel*, he shut off the compressor and screwed the cap of the dive tank tight. Virginie lifted Gus up onto the side deck, and he loped over to his master.

"Morning," she said.

"Afternoon."

Instinctively, she looked for the sun. It was lower than she had expected.

"Good walk?" Roly asked.

"We've worn him out, I think. Or, more accurately, he's worn me out." She rolled the ball onto the deck.

Roly stroked Gus's ear. "Yeah, he'll do that to ya." He put his hands on his knees, ready to get back to work. "Between you and Teresa, I barely need to walk him myself these days. Popular guy."

"Roly?"

"Mmm?"

"There's this thing, in the ruins, some kind of structure. Black, a statue or something."

He crouched again. "You mean the oil press?"

"Is that what it is?"

"Yup."

"From the prison?"

"Yup. They made the men turn it. Bright men, decent men, many of them, I would've thought. Reduced to mere cattle."

"Cattle? Why do you say that?"

"It was a job for oxen, normally."

"Christ."

An eyebrow lifted. "Don't think he had much to do with it."

When she got back to *Wayfinder*, she was restless, her skin irritated by salt and sweat. She had a swim, then took a shower, hoping the cold blast would also rinse away her unsettled mood. It helped a little, but not completely. She put on a clean T-shirt and stretched her neck from side to side, trying to release the tension. In the galley she drank two glasses of water, one straight after the other, then sat at the chart table to comb her hair.

Jake came out of the rear cabin, humming. He had showered before her and was still wearing his towel. He put on some music—slow, sultry jazz. Normally that would relax her, but tonight the discordance set her teeth on edge. The comb caught and ripped at her scalp. She gasped.

"I felt that," he said. "You all right?"

She tried again, but the knot was too tight. No matter how much conditioner she used, the seawater always tangled it into a mess. She pulled the whole lot forward, forming a curtain around her face, so she could see the knot. It was huge. No chance of untangling that.

"Can you pass me the scissors?" she called through her hair. She heard the scrape of the galley drawer being opened.

"Here." He placed them in her lap. The steel blades were cool against her thigh.

"Thanks." She slotted the scissors just above the tangle and cut. The knot landed on the chart table. It was far paler than it used to be, after all this time in the sun—Amarante was leaving its mark on her. When she flipped her head back up to finish combing, long wet strands clung to the side of her neck like seaweed, an echo of the panic she'd felt when she lost her mask diving with Vitor. She clawed at her skin. Neither of them had had a haircut since they left England two months ago. Jake's had reached his shoulders at the back.

An idea came to her in a rush. "Jake, will you cut it?"

He was rummaging in the fridge. "Hmm?"

"I'm serious. Will you? I'm tired of it. I look at Stella with her pixie crop, and she looks so cool. In both senses of the word."

He straightened to look at her. "But you love your hair long. And so do I."

She opened and closed the scissors slowly. Her hair had been long ever since she was a teenager, through college, her first marriage. It was high time for a change. She stood and swung the scissors round, so that the closed blades were in her hand, and extended the handles toward him. "This is driving me mad. If you won't do it, I swear I'll hack it off myself. At least you can see what you're doing."

He crossed the space between them, but instead of taking the scissors, he picked up a spanner from the chart table, dropped it into the toolbox, and carried the box away to put it back in its place. He took his time. She knew he'd be building a case against it in the forepeak.

"Vee," he protested, coming back through, "I have no idea how to cut hair."

"Neither do I." She locked her eyes on his. It was such a great idea—she didn't know why it hadn't occurred to her before. It would make her feel better. She made a determined movement with the scissors. "Please, baby," she said, using his name for her.

Finally, persuaded by the nickname, he took them. She pulled off her T-shirt, so that she was just in her bikini bottoms, and stood in the small space between the galley and the chart table, facing the companionway steps, shoulders set.

She could hear Jake fidgeting behind her. "Seriously, Vee, you really want me to do this?"

"Just lop it off straight. As short as you can at the back." He rested his temple briefly against the top of her head, and when he lifted it, she looked over her shoulder. "I trust you."

He swallowed audibly and she turned away again. He stroked her hair from crown to ends, worked his fingertips through the strands. He lifted a piece. She could feel his hand trembling as he slid the blades into place, hesitated. She focused on the steps in front of her. A metallic slicing filled the saloon, and a bolt of hair hit the floor. She looked at it—a question mark of gold against dark mahogany, a piece of her old life now separate from her. No going back now.

He worked quickly after that, and when he pulled away, she brought a hand to the naked skin of her neck. She ran her fingers through her hair, as Jake had done, from her crown to a silent thunk at the truncated ends, marveling at the new sensation. She was lighter. Years gone, just like that. Laughter bubbled up her throat.

Jake was looking at her as if he still wasn't sure whether she'd been testing him.

She laughed again. New short-haired Virginie was in control of this, was in control of everything. New short-haired Virginie cupped his face and kissed him for a long time, pushing her body against his, telling him through her touch what she wanted. She turned around, and he pressed his lips against the exposed nape of her neck and began working his way down. She opened her eyes. Above them, beyond the companionway, stars glistened like beads of sweat.

20

Time was liquid on Amarante. Each sun-filled hour felt long, brimming with possibility, but somehow sunset still seemed to descend unexpectedly. The days themselves were so similar, in weather, in what they did—swimming, walking, gathering coconuts and firewood—that if Virginie tried to think back, to pinpoint when some little thing had happened, it was difficult to distinguish one day from another. Two weeks passed, three. The earth turned, the constellations rotated across the sky, and the moon waned, then waxed gibbous again. Languorous mornings tipped ever so gently into lazy afternoons, just like on vacation, when it seemed you'd pressed pause on life, that you stayed still while the rest of the world scurried helter-skelter around you. Of course that was one of the main reasons people took vacations—a break from life but also a break from time. Sleeping through lunch, devouring a whole book in one gulp, spending an hour watching—really watching—the sun go down. It was such a luxury to be able to shut the door against the never-ending demands of the modern world and just let . . . everything . . . stop.

After a while, she felt she needed a change of scene from the same old beach bonfire supper. She was conscious that she wanted to repay Vitor for his initial hospitality, and also that the others always seemed to provide the fish for the communal dinners. Yes, she and Jake helped sometimes—Jake driving, she porting the catch back to whichever tender or dinghy they were using—but they hadn't actually pulled the fish out of the ocean themselves yet. Their initial pledge to learn had been stalled by a hangover, and then, when Roly, Pete, and Vitor had had a run of success, there hadn't seemed much point. But she wanted to do something.

"How about we throw a party?" she said to Jake.

He was reading, lying along one of the cockpit seats, his legs bent so he could fit. He put his book on his stomach and sat up. "Good idea. Here? When?"

"Yes. Tonight? Tomorrow?"

"Hang on, let me just check my diary. I'll have you know I've got a busy schedule." He picked up his novel and dragged a finger down the page. "Seems I have a nap penciled in for this afternoon, but"—he turned another page—"after that I'm free." He lay back down and carried on reading.

"Great." She took hold of the dinghy's rope and began to pull it in. "I'll go and invite everyone." Before she climbed down, she tugged the book out of his hands and rested it, spread open, over his face. "Better bring your nap forward so you can help me prepare."

Roly and Gus turned up first, just after sunset. She was pleased he'd come—she hadn't been certain he'd turn up once she'd used the word *party*—although she noticed he tied his dinghy to the toe rail rather than the cleat so he could make a quick getaway.

"Nice boat," he said, clambering aboard.

"Thanks. Can I get you a beer?"

He lifted a small cool bag. "I'm good."

The rules. She held up her hands. "Of course."

Stella and Pete weren't long behind. "Pretty," said Stella, coming into the cockpit. They'd taken down the overhead awnings for the evening, exposing the sky, and Virginie had tidied away what she could from the cockpit, setting out some cushions and sarongs in an attempt at decoration. Jake had carved a couple of coconuts as if they were pumpkins, even though Halloween was long past, and put torches inside so the faces glowed white.

"And you," Virginie said. In honor of the party Stella had put on a dress, a short floaty tunic. Stella twirled, and the hem ballooned. It was the first time Virginie had seen her in anything but swimwear or a T-shirt. Pete had spruced up, too, in a short-sleeved shirt creased from being crammed in the back of an overfull locker.

The guys—even Gus—went below. Chatter drifted up the companionway, followed by music, as Jake ran his playlist through the stereo.

Stella stayed in the cockpit with her, sitting high on the coaming and looking out into the dark bay as Virginie tipped olives from a can into a bowl. Not quite a *Santa Maria*–standard spread, but they'd have to do.

"Here comes trouble," Stella said.

Virginie was concentrating on trying to find somewhere to put the bowl where no one would sit or stand on it. "Hmm?"

"Vitor and Teresa are on their way." Stella pointed at a low red light moving toward *Wayfinder*.

"Why's that trouble?" She offered the olives to Stella, who held up a hand to say no thanks. Honestly, they were all such sticklers.

"Well, *he's* trouble," Stella said.

Virginie laughed. Not this silly talk again. "Vitor's not trouble."

"Really? You honestly think that?" Stella looked at her for a long time, and then she blinked and looked past, angling to see down the companionway. "Where's my husband got to with my beer?"

"Right here," Pete said, climbing the steps, the others following, Jake with a coconut for Virginie.

She was below when Vitor and Teresa arrived, and when she came back up and sipped from her drink, she found its water had been laced with rum. As she took the straw from her lips, startled, she caught Vitor watching. He aped innocence. Perhaps this was what Stella had meant by trouble—his mischievousness. She tipped her coconut in reply. It was a party, after all.

It was tight in the cockpit with so many there, but fun and kind of homey, too, almost like cramming in the family at Christmas. They were quite like a family, she supposed, in the way they all came together despite their differences, and in how they looked after one another, helped out. But instead of being joined by blood they were linked by what they loved: sailing, travel, adventure—their esprit de corps was an esprit de découverte. More specifically than that, they were joined together by all being here, in the same place at the same time. Amarante was their bond.

She took a moment to look around at her husband and new circle of friends: Vitor sitting behind the helm, leading a conversation, Stella on one side of him, Teresa on the other, pressed close. Could she consider Teresa a friend? She might have to accept that this was as deep as their friendship was going to get. Pete was opposite Virginie, resting against the coaming, his usual laid-back self, baseball cap in place. The only time she ever saw him without it was when he was diving. Above him, Jake perched on the coach roof. Roly was at the back of the boat, standing against the pushpit, in the spot always favored by skippers because it provided the best view of the whole deck. Gus had plonked himself in the center of them all, happily panting away.

She breathed in the warm air. What would she and Jake have been up to if they hadn't come away? She pictured their lives trundling along just as usual, following the set path. Work, home. Work, home. Same routine, same conversations, same thoughts, feelings. She examined the downy night, the stars with their cliques that were so different here from the familiar patterns of a Mediterranean or English sky. Jake had taught her more constellations. Brilliant Canopus gleamed, marking Carina, the ship's keel. She picked out Vela, traced the luff and leech of the sail. Together, as the False Cross, he'd told her, their stars had lured many a confused sailor off his path—but they had also guided countless others to new lands, new lives, new opportunities.

The party had been going for a while. Pete was building a tower of empty cans, and the rum had eased all worries about rules and responsibilities from her own mind. Stella popped open another beer. It fizzed, squirting liquid onto her thigh. Vitor teased her for being drunk and offered her a paper napkin.

She accepted it, and after dabbing at her leg, she tapped his arm. "Let's play a game." It came out as *lezz*. "Get to know each other better."

"What kind of game?" Jake asked.

"Strip poker!" Pete called out. Roly rolled his eyes.

Jake pointed to his bare chest. "Be a bit of a short game."

"Never Have I Ever?" Pete tried again.

Stella tutted. "We're not in high school, Pete."

"Blackjack." This was from Teresa.

Stella pointed a finger at her. "Ooh, I like that idea."

Vitor raised his eyebrows. "Be careful. She is very good. She will beat you every time."

Teresa smiled shyly. "I . . . I worked in a casino once."

"Then you can teach us a trick or two," Jake said. "Oh, hang on, we don't have any cards."

Roly pushed off from the railing. "Reckon I've got a pack on *Ariel*."

They all knew that this was his way of saying he was thinking of heading home—if he left now, there was a good chance he wouldn't come back.

"No, Roly, don't worry about it," Stella said. "Hey, here's one for irony. What about name the one thing you'd take to a desert island?"

Jake groaned. He hated these kinds of games, the ones that forced you into making choices. He was so logical, and always complained they were silly, would protest that no one knew how they'd react until they were in that situation for real.

"No objections?" Stella said. "Great. Pete, you can start."

"Why me?"

"Because I'm your wife and I said so."

Pete brought a hand to his cap's peak in salute. "All right, but I'm introducing a rule. You're not allowed to take your spouse with you. Or"—he pointed at Teresa, then Vitor, heading them off—"your partner, whether you're married or not. No other halves. Understood?"

Vitor grinned and crossed his legs. "Fine by me." Teresa held up a palm, as if to say sure, she'd play by the rules.

"Dogs?" asked Virginie quickly, on Roly's behalf, hoping making light of it would spare him the pain of thinking of the wife who'd left.

"That's me out, then," said Stella. "'Cause I'd wanna take Gus." At his name, Gus thumped his tail. "Come on," she prompted Pete. "If not me, what are you taking?"

"Or *who* are you taking?" Vitor said.

Stella poked Vitor in the arm and shook her head in an exaggerated way. "Nuh-uh. He'd never take anyone else."

Virginie caught the smile Pete gave Stella. They were so sweet together.

"So, Pete," Vitor said. "If not *who*, then *what* do you take?"

"Easy. My speargun."

"Figures," Stella said. "Sometimes I think you love that thing more than me anyway. Roly?"

He waved her off. "I'm too old for this."

"Fine. Teresa."

"Too easy, this game." She straightened her spine. "My son."

This was the first they'd heard of any children. Stella gaped at her. "You have kids?"

"One. A boy. Musa. He is six."

"And he's not here with you?"

Vitor put a hand on Teresa's knee. "He lives with his grandmother in Maputo."

Stella leaned forward in her seat so she could see past Vitor to Teresa. "Not with you? How can you stand to be away from him? God, if I—"

"Stella," Pete said, gently but firmly.

Jake intervened, although he did it kindly. "Maybe Teresa thinks a boat's not the best place to raise a child. Or maybe he's in school."

Teresa smiled at him, but Stella's eyes were wide. "A boat is a great place to raise a child!"

Pete shifted across the bench and took her hand. Stella tucked herself into a ball, pulling her knees right up to her chest.

Even in this light Virginie could see her eyes were welling. "Teresa," she said, to draw attention away. "What's Musa like?"

"Here," Teresa said. "I will show you." She had a little bag with her—she pulled a phone from it. Virginie hadn't seen her own phone for a couple of weeks. She'd taken some pictures the first few days on Amarante, but with no signal it was largely useless, and she'd quickly lost the habit of carrying it or charging it. It was chucked in the back of the chart table.

When Teresa unlocked hers, the blue light of the screen seemed alien. She passed it around. "He loves football. Always he is playing. Day, night, until bed." She glanced at Stella, who was still hunched up. "Musa's papa, he was . . ." She consulted the sea, as if searching for the right words in the darkness. "His woman, his other woman, was always knock-knocking on the door, always she demanded money." She spoke slowly, her accent putting the stress on the end of *demanded*, so it became *demand-dead*. "He had two babies with her. Then one day he was gone. Poof!" She turned back to the group and her fingers made a silent explosion in the air. "I do not know where. Some say South Africa, working. I found casino work, bar work. But I was out every night while Musa stayed sleeping with my mama."

"This is how we met," Vitor said.

The phone reached Pete. He offered it carefully to Stella, in case she didn't want to look. But she took it and smiled at the picture. When it got to Virginie, she saw a small boy in a polo shirt, a thin neck, a cheeky smile. He'd lost one of his front teeth. Six. Teresa was young now—she must have been very young when she fell pregnant. When she spoke of her son, it was the longest Virginie had heard her speak. She passed the phone back. "You must miss him very much."

Teresa gazed at the screen. "My mama sent me this photo when we were in Port Brown." She stroked the glass. "He grows so big." She kissed the phone and slipped it into her bag.

Pete was murmuring something to Stella, presumably checking she was okay, possibly asking whether she wanted to stay. She nodded at her knees, and then she sat forward again, rubbing her eyes.

"Sorry, ignore me," she said. "Too much to drink." She blew air up her face. "Okay. Jake, you're next."

"Knife," he said immediately.

Surprised, Virginie turned. He winked at her. "It was a toss-up between a knife and some matches." Ah, here it was—the logical reasoning. "If I had a knife, I could make other tools, build shelter. I'd need fire to signal for help, but if I knew I was going to be stranded, I'd have been on a survival course, so I'd know how to start a fire and I wouldn't need matches."

"No prior knowledge," Pete declared. "You're just tossed out of a boat and get swept there by the sea."

He mulled it over. "Still a knife."

Virginie reached for the nearest bowl of olives. Slick with brine, they slid around as she tried to spear them with a cocktail stick. She'd give anything for the crunch of a salad right now. Most of their fresh vegetables had gone, and she wasn't particularly looking forward to the canned ones. When asked, she might say she'd take a giant fridge with her to this hypothetical island.

"Vitor, you're next," Stella said.

Vitor flicked a loop of hair off his face. "I take what I always take, wherever I go." He picked up his drink from the floor. "Money."

Pete snorted, but Vitor grinned leisurely, his mouth taking a long time to stretch to its full width.

"On a *deserted* island?" Stella said. "What on earth would you do with it?"

"Not much call for it here," Roly said. "It's one of the reasons we all came. Get away from all that."

Vitor was still smiling. He dipped his chin in polite concession. "If you say so."

Now Jake spoke up. "But there's nothing to spend it on here, no need for it."

"I find," Vitor said, stirring his drink, "that there is always need for money."

"Sure there is," Jake continued. "In normal society. Where there are shops selling you stuff, bills to pay, and oh, I don't know, people to hire. But not here, not on Amarante." He was angled right forward. Why was he getting so riled up? It was just a bit of fun. "I haven't picked up my wallet since we left Port Brown," he insisted. "Don't even know where it is."

Vitor casually put his hand into his trouser pocket and came out with a thick stack of notes, folded and held in place with a clip. He placed it on the binnacle, and the clip clunked against the glass of the steering compass. The fold was nearly an inch thick, the outermost note a hundred-dollar bill. If they were all hundreds, there could be tens of thousands there. Stella gasped.

Vitor was looking at Jake, still smiling. "You think this isn't 'normal society'? That Amarante is different from anywhere else in the world? I wish, for your sake, Jake,"—he swung his glass wide—"and for all of you, that this could be true and such a place could exist. This has been the dream of many people for many years, maybe even for all the time of mankind. But everything has a price. Surely you understand that?"

To his right, there was movement. Teresa nodding. "This is true."

"This"—Vitor picked up the money—"is just one form of currency. It is only paper. But it represents something real. Your currency here is your fish, your onions. You agreeing to climb Pete's mast, and Pete saying he will show you where to fish—this is currency also. You think that you come to Amarante and stop trading these little pieces of paper and that makes life different?" He riffled the edges of the notes. "No, my friends, it is no different. I am sorry to say money, power—all of life, its rewards, its games, its problems—they are all here on this island in the middle of the Indian Ocean just as much as they are in London, in Toronto, in São Paulo. They follow you everywhere. If you came here thinking it would be different, then I am afraid you will be disappointed. If I have money, or"—he held up a hand—"okay, let us not say 'money,' let us say if I have a currency of some sort, if I can trade, then I can get what I want, when I want it. It is the way the world works—the whole world, including this little piece of paradise. I learned this lesson when I was young, and I have been successful because of it. So"—he gestured at Stella—"if I go to your desert island alone, I still take money. Because I do not know who I will meet there and if they will have something that I desire." He picked up the notes and slipped them into his pocket again. Teresa took his hand and whispered into his ear.

Pete started clapping. "I've got to hand it to you, Vitor. You really do put your money where your mouth is."

Stella sniggered, but with real mirth, as if signaling that she didn't believe a word of it but was pleased he had taken on the challenge of the game.

Virginie was also impressed with his powers of persuasion. No wonder he had a boat like *Santa Maria*. "Bravo!" she called.

Even Roly was chuckling. Only Jake was silent, staring at his beer, swirling what remained of it inside the can.

Later, after the others had gone back to their own boats and she and Jake were in the galley washing up, he asked her about Vitor's money. "How much do you reckon there was?"

"Don't know," she said, rinsing a glass, thinking about those dead American presidents, fixed in turtle green. She didn't want to say so to Jake, because he'd been so strongly opposed to Vitor's argument, but she could understand Vitor's reasoning. Money talks, after all— especially the US dollar. But further discussion of the point was not what she wanted to get into right now, after such a lovely evening.

"Like you said," she told Jake, "there's no use for it here. It's just pieces of paper."

"Yeah, you're right." He dried the glass and put it in the cupboard, then put his arms around her and kissed the top of her head. "And anyway," he said, his words muffled against her hair, "what on earth do we have that Mr. Moneybags Vitor could possibly want to buy, anyway?"

21

Pete steered *Wayfinder*'s dinghy beyond the northern tip of the island, not far from where Virginie had sat sketching the morning Vitor came across her. They had finally got round to the fishing. The sea was different in this area from the anchorage, where there wasn't a whisper of breeze and the water was flat calm. Here, out of the lee, it was bumpy in the rougher waves, and the dinghy, laden down with the four of them, was so low that every now and then a little water came over the side, wetting their feet, bringing relief from the heat. As soon as they stopped, Stella slipped into the water. Two kicks away from the boat, two back toward, and then she was hauling herself back in again, showering everyone with droplets.

She pinched water out of her nose. "That's better."

Pete handed her a towel for her face. "Real water baby, this one."

They turned their attention to the task ahead. On the floor of the dinghy the hand reel Jake had bought in Port Brown waited. It was a simple design in green plastic—a plain sheave-like ring about a hand's span in diameter, already wound with wire and primed with a hook.

"We tried it on the passage over," Jake said, picking it up. "Didn't catch a bean. Not a bean, not a sausage, and certainly not a fish."

Pete had brought a box of lures with him. He showed them the right kinds to use, the ones he said the fish would be most interested in, and Virginie and Jake took it in turns to handle the line, unspooling the long wire from the reel, letting it run behind the dinghy for a while as they drove about, and then winding it back in again, reaching for length after length between thumb and two fingers. It always felt there was more to pull in than she'd let out. Every time the hook came up it was empty.

"You can try adjusting your speed if they're not going for it," Pete said when Jake was taking a turn, twisting the tiller throttle a touch. "You'll get a feel for what works."

"How do you know where the best places are?" Virginie asked.

"Fish move around," Stella replied, "so it's not like you can just go to one spot every day and land the same number."

Virginie checked behind them. Still nothing.

"Then why don't we try somewhere else?" Jake asked. He nodded toward the far reef. "How about over there?"

"Best not," Pete said.

"Why not? Is there nothing there?"

"There's plenty."

"Then let's go!" He started to wind in, ready for the drive over, but Pete kept the tiller straight, the dinghy over the first section of reef. Jake snorted. "You honestly believe that superstitious stuff Roly spouts?"

Virginie shot him a look as he wound the line: *Play nicely*. She was frustrated, too, but there was no reason for him to be so obvious about it.

"Sure you don't want to try spearfishing?" Pete asked him. "I mean, I rarely troll like this. Doesn't land you the big ones. You get much more bang for your buck with a speargun."

Spearfishing meant getting in the water. Jake was saved from answering by Stella pointing at a school of small fish that had leapt clear of the surface.

"There!"

Pete steered toward the fish. Virginie took the reel from Jake and unspooled the line once more.

When it went taut, she didn't quite believe it. She'd been disappointed so many times already, thinking there was something on the end when really it was just the pressure of the water. This time, though, the line was bar tight. "I think I've got something."

Pete dropped off the engine revs and knelt in the floor of the dinghy beside her. Stella stayed where she was, but Jake stood, and the dinghy rocked. "Don't lose it!" The fish took another leap and the reel skewed sideways.

Pete was calmer. "Go steady. Just pull it in bit by bit, like you did before."

The reel wobbled in her hand, but she kept a tight grip. The line seared the pads of her fingers, but she kept on winding, loop by loop, inching the fish closer to the boat. As she pulled again, there was a rush along the top of the water and a flash of orange. No! It was gone; she was just pulling in the lure. Then she saw that the water behind the dinghy was ruffled—the fish must still be attached to the hook beneath the lure. Now it had been dragged to the surface, it was angry.

"It's there," Stella said. "Show it who's in charge."

She forced herself not to pay attention to the pain as she played the line like a kite string while the fish surfed in and out of the sea.

"That's it, keep going," Pete reassured her, and she did, pulling and winding and resisting the fish with all the strength in her hands—and then, with a pop she felt but didn't hear, it slid out of the ocean, into the air, and into the bottom of the dinghy.

"Nice one!" Pete said. "Rainbow runner. Decent size, too."

She looked down at the fish, which was as stunned as she was at its appearance in the boat. It was sleek, with a sky-blue back and a yellow tail.

Stella was beaming. "Way to go, Vee!"

No praise from Jake—he was already bending, wrenching the hook from the fish's mouth, desperate to try again. As she watched, waiting for him to say something, anything, a rush of blood spattered his arm. She drew away.

Hers was the only one they managed to catch, despite going at it for another hour. Back on *Wayfinder*, Jake told her he wanted to go ashore in plenty of time, that he was excited to start cooking. Once they were on the beach, he carried their bucket over to the fire, and she assumed he'd got over his fit of pique. Roly's offering was already there: a speared tuna, strung from a tree, and a small coconut crab. She picked up a filleting knife, but when she turned round to pass it to Jake, she saw he was walking along the beach alone, tossing shells into the shallows. The dead fish lay dulled and rigid in the bottom of the bucket, unblinking eyes staring. She did the gutting herself.

"All right!" Stella called out later when they were all gathered by the fire, raising her voice over the beat of the music playing from a speaker that Teresa had wedged into the sand. Stella was wearing a crown woven from palm. Together with the music, it created a party atmosphere. "Who wants a piece of Vee's first catch?"

"Virginie," Vitor said, holding the *r* sound of her name for a moment in his throat. "You caught this?"

She looked at Jake sideways before she replied, trying to read him. He was examining his feet. Why was he still being weird? Was he jealous? Was this another silly competitive man thing? "Well, really it was a group effort," she told Vitor.

Stella overheard. "Nuh-uh." She waved her barbecue tongs. "Not really. Vee hooked it and landed it."

"Well then," she protested again, "it was beginner's luck."

"Honestly," Stella said. "You Brits are just too polite. Why don't you claim the goddamn thing?" She put a hand to her hip. With that crown, she looked like the queen of the night's proceedings. "Okay, if you're so insistent on being fair to everyone, I'll rephrase. Who would like a piece of *Swallow-Wayfinder*'s first cooperative fish?"

"I will take some," Teresa said, holding out her hands for a loaded leaf. Gus followed her, frisking around her legs as she moved to the seating area on the sand. Vitor ushered Virginie in next; then he went, then Pete, Roly. Jake was last, motioning to Stella that she should eat before him.

After they'd all sat, Vitor leaned in. "You must not worry, Jake. You had bad luck. Try fishing in a different place next time?"

Gus was trying to get at Teresa's dinner, edging his nose up to her leaf. "Here," she said, tossing him a morsel. He caught it midair with a snap of his jaws and immediately started begging again—he knew a soft target when he saw one.

Roly called him away so she could eat in peace. "It'll come easier soon," he said, to Jake. "You'll see. Just need more practice."

Jake, who had chosen to sit farthest away from the fire, merely stared at his food.

When Virginie had finished, and thrown her empty leaf into the flames, she decided to offer an olive branch. She knelt in the sand next to him. "Not hungry?"

"Sorry. Miles away." He took a pinch. The face he pulled told her it was cold.

"We'll go again tomorrow," she said. "Just the two of us. Practice some more, like Roly said." By way of reply, he put a coconut to his mouth and took a long drink. She'd seen him spike it earlier with rum. "Come on, Jake, it's just a fish." She tried to be gentle, teasing almost, aiming to get him to snap out of it, but she couldn't keep a sharpness from her tone. He mottled at her words, drank some more.

She made herself look away, clamping her jaw tight, not wanting to draw attention to the friction. They shouldn't be fighting; they ought to be celebrating this small triumph. And they were bound to get better at it. Her fingers came to her new hairline, stroked the tingling spot where the whiter skin kept being burned by the sun. Jake's patience had evaporated, for some reason. Back home, he was nothing but patient, would spend an age fairing a hull, filling and sanding over and over, until the planks were seamless, beautiful. She'd always admired him for that—she didn't have the temperament.

Teresa turned up the music—a Latin version of a familiar song that it took Virginie a minute to place. Stella hooted and stood. She grabbed Pete and they began to dance, their bare feet kicking up a sandstorm. Gus scampered over and skittered in circles around their ankles, excited by the commotion. Without stopping her dance, Stella bent and ruffled his scraggy head. Pete swept her round in a half circle, reeling her close for a few beats, then out again.

Teresa went over to where Roly was sitting on his usual driftwood log. She took his hands and swayed her hips, trying to entice him to his feet, to dance with her. "Come, Roly." He resisted, but smiled, and it was sweet to see how he melted a little, clearly touched at the effort she was making. "Come," she said again, tugging, "relax," and this time he did get up. He shuffled his feet and bobbed his shoulders almost in time to the music. It was great to see; Teresa was kind to have done that.

The speaker was only small, portable, but it was good quality, the bass strong, the lyrics clear, even though Virginie couldn't understand their meaning. If she closed her eyes, it was as if she could almost see the music, and it sparked a kind of energetic nostalgic awakening in her body, a physical remembering of teenage raves and a craving to feel now the way she'd felt then. Although she was sitting, she couldn't help her body starting to move with the beat. She turned to Jake. "Dance with me?"

A few notes passed.

Everyone else was enjoying themselves—even Roly, even Teresa. "Jake?"

"Maybe in a while."

Vitor was suddenly standing in front of her, extending a hand. To Jake, he said, "You do not mind if I borrow your wife?"

She glanced at Jake. He rotated his coconut on the sand. "Go ahead."

She let Vitor pull her to her feet and lead her toward the area where everyone was dancing.

"Everything is okay?" he asked her, stopping.

She pushed past. "Everything's fine." She knew she was hiding behind that standard British response that the French half of her had always found a little odd, but she didn't want to get into it, just wanted to dance.

Right then, Stella swooped by, and as she passed, she lifted the palm crown from her own head and placed it onto Virginie's. Immediately she whirled away again, drawn into a spin by Pete. The crown wasn't quite level, and it started to slip. Virginie grabbed for it as it fell, and Vitor caught it as well, so that they both ended up holding it at the same time. They laughed at the same time, too, and he relinquished his grip. She put it back on her head, but at a rakish angle. He reached up and adjusted it, looking into her eyes for a beat too long.

In that moment, what had started as a white lie became the truth. Everything *was* fine. *She* was queen of the evening now. She was going to dance. And Vitor was the one who wanted to dance with her.

She raised both arms above her head, moved with the music. "Actually, everything's great."

He was a good dancer, fun, singing along in Portuguese. Sometimes he changed the lyrics to French so she could join in with the chorus. To begin with she was conscious of Jake's eyes on them, but it was tricky keeping track of him in the dark, and eventually she gave up and enjoyed the moment, losing herself in the whirls that Vitor was casting, letting the tension spin off away into the air. The sand was cool under her feet, and she went up on tiptoes. This was exactly how it had felt, at sixteen, at eighteen, in those smoky warehouses with the lasers and the whistles and the bass so loud you could feel it pulsing in your chest more than you could your own heart. The night alive with possibility. He flicked her away and pulled her back in tight against him. Their whirling created a wind that lifted her new short hair. The air kissed her face, skimmed her lips.

"You make a great partner," he said when they eventually stopped, breathless and warm.

"So do you."

He excused himself to get something from his tender, and she went into the bush to pee. The music changed to a slow song. When she came out, Pete and Stella were holding each other tight, swaying in the firelight. She looked around for Jake, and it took her a moment to locate him in the semidarkness. He was still on the sand, but Teresa was with him, her legs curled to one side, her long skirt tucked around her shins. They were talking. Laughing—really laughing, Teresa's head thrown back, throat exposed, Jake's chin down. Each had a beer. They were glass bottles, not the cans from *Wayfinder*'s stocks, so Teresa must have provided them. They were sitting close together—possibly to hear each other over the music? Should she be jealous? Or was Teresa just one of those women who preferred the company of men? Look at Roly, at the dancing. She scratched a bite on her shoulder as she studied them, trying to read Jake's body language. It appeared he'd loosened up quite a lot.

Just then Vitor reappeared, walking fast from the fire toward Jake and Teresa. As soon as she saw him, Teresa sprang up, and Vitor pulled her away into the dark.

When Jake was alone, Virginie stood where she was for a moment, trying to judge if she needed to steel herself for a continuation of his bad mood, and wondering whether she should ask him what he'd been talking to Teresa about. Her own anger at his churlishness was gone, and the last thing she wanted to do was risk pushing him back into a funk.

But as she approached tentatively, he disarmed her with a big smile, and thoughts of misunderstandings and Teresa vanished.

"Vee, let's try again," he said, slurring a little.

She dropped to the sand beside him. "What?"

"Let's try the fishing again. I'm sorry about earlier. I guess I just wanted to be good at it."

She leaned over and kissed him. He tasted of beer. "Just the two of us," she said. "We'll do it together. Teamwork."

He kissed her back. "Always."

22

The tap made a rumbling noise and spat, refusing to give her water. She hit the lever a few times, in case there was an air lock, but it was no better, just a hiss and a violent belch of damp air. She sighed and put the espresso maker back on top of the stove, but in her early-morning clumsiness she misjudged the gap and it fell off-balance, landing on its side and tipping coffee onto the cooker. Shit. She gathered up the fallen grounds as best as she could, scraping them back into the aluminum casing.

"Jake! We're out of water."

His voice came through from the cabin. "We should still have one tank left. Just switch it over at the manifold."

The coffee granules were sticking to her fingers, and she couldn't rinse them off. She swore again and wiped them on the front of her T-shirt.

They'd run the watermaker on a few occasions after reaching Amarante. Two full tanks lasted them about a fortnight. They'd replenished just after arriving and topped up three times over the month since. The stopcocks for the water system were under the saloon floorboards, and it was tricky balancing on the ribs of the bilge while trying to turn the stiff levers. The handle was so unyielding that when it finally came free in a rush she stumbled backwards and jarred her heel. She cursed again. Baseboard back in place, she tried the tap. After a couple of hiccups, it flowed. She smiled at the minor success and knocked the remaining coffee grounds off the burner before she lit the stove and put the espresso maker on to boil.

As she washed her hands at the sink, Jake came through and rested his chin on her shoulder. His stubble was sharp, and in the heat of the morning he was too close, his body heat merging with hers and intensifying in the humidity. She wriggled free and backed up against the short end of the L-shaped counter, putting some air between them.

"You get the tanks switched over okay?" he asked.

"Yes." The coffee was bubbling too fast. She turned down the gas. "I'm going to run the engine so I can power up the watermaker."

"I'll do it."

The movement of his body climbing the companionway steps created a tiny downdraft of air, and she closed her eyes to feel it better. It was deathly still in the anchorage again today, like it had been for what felt like forever, and the stillness made the heat almost unbearable. She reached up to try the new fan again, flicking the switch back and forth, but it refused to work. Cheap piece of rubbish.

From on deck came the familiar beeping noise of the ignition as Jake turned the key one notch and waited a few seconds before starting the engine. The motor churned. Time to get up on deck before the temperature rose even higher in the galley.

As she grabbed the cups in one hand and the coffee pot in the other, the engine shuddered and stopped. Through the companionway she could see Jake trying to get it going. It churned but wouldn't catch.

"I'll try bleeding it again," he said. "Come up here and turn the ignition when I call, will you?"

She waited by the helm, attentive to the sounds of work below, the chink of a spanner against the engine head, the scrape of wood as Jake removed another of the access panels. Across the glossy flat water, the three other boats sat loosely on their anchor chains. The current had turned *Ariel* and *Swallow* to point one way, and *Wayfinder* and *Santa Maria* in the opposite direction. From the air, with their dinghies tailing behind, their little fleet must look like the four of spades. There was no sign of Vitor or Teresa on *Santa Maria*, although their tender floated lazily next to the catamaran, indicating they were on board. Knowing Vitor, he would have already had his morning swim. She bet they were enjoying the air-con inside.

Every time Jake called up to ask her to try the key, she anticipated hearing the cough and eventual choke into life. But it refused to start. She drank her coffee, then Jake's, too. At the companionway she peered into the gloom. Jake had removed the stairs to get at the engine. Oil and fuel filters were strewn around him. The tendons in his forearm rose as he tightened something.

"What do you think it is?"

"Not sure." He put down his spanner. "Got me stumped, actually. I was thinking I might go over to *Ariel*, see if Roly's got any ideas."

"Want me to come with you?"

"Sure."

Over at *Ariel*, the solar panels on the A-frame glinted in the sun. The blades of the wind generator sat motionless. Gus, who had been lying in the shade, got to his feet and scurried toward them.

They stayed in their dinghy. Roly emerged from under the awning as they neared, bending almost double to pass under it. "G'day."

Jake got straight to the point.

"Any smoke from the exhaust?" Roly asked.

Jake raised his eyebrows. "Yes, actually, come to think of it."

Gus was panting, grinning, turning his head as each man spoke, following the conversation. Virginie reached between the guard rails to ruffle his fur.

"You check your tank for bug?"

"Shit."

"What's bug?" she asked.

Jake rubbed his head. "Bacteria in the diesel. It can grow out of control, clog up the system."

"Seems like your boat was on anchor for a good while on the mainland," Roly said. "Half-empty tanks. Hot tropical weather. Perfect conditions for it." He fished a treat from his pocket and offered it to Gus. "Messy, dirty job. Not easy out here, either."

Jake wouldn't meet Virginie's eye. His head hung low, making him look like a schoolboy chastised for failing to use his common sense.

"Let me know how you get on," Roly called over as she let the line go so their dinghy could drift away from the yacht. "Give us a shout if you get stuck again."

It proved a hellish job, removing all the lines from the engine, pumping out the tanks, and scrubbing everything down, and the boat, filled with the stench of diesel, was even more claustrophobic than usual. And it made no difference. It still wouldn't start.

She was up in the cockpit, taking a break from the oily tight darkness below, when she heard Jake yell, "Fuck!"

She rushed to the companionway. "What is it? Are you hurt?"

A clatter of tools, then a repeated groan: "No, no, no, no, no!" The clang of a metal object being hurled. She craned her neck—Jake had disappeared from view, but she could hear him stomping across the sole boards. A moment later he was up through the hatch in their cabin and pacing the cockpit, clasping his hands round the back of his head as he did when he was stressed.

"What is it?"

"I think I've fucked up," he said to the sky.

She moved to him. "Fucked up? How?"

In reply, he spouted words so fast she couldn't follow.

"Jake. Jake!" He stopped. His eyes were wild.

She pulled his hands from his head. They were blackened. "Slow down. You're not making any sense."

He held her gaze for the longest time, then wrenched out of her grasp and slumped to a bench. Hunched over, he looked defeated. "It's not diesel bug. It's never been diesel bug. When I checked the oil just now, I saw there was some residue under the cap, and I remembered I'd seen that before—and not just once, but twice—when we were giving everything an overhaul and in Port Brown, when I did an engine check before the crossing."

She reached for his fingers again and gave them a shake. "I'm sorry. I don't understand what that means."

"It's bad, Vee, that's what it means. It means the head gasket is blown. It means the engine is fucked." He closed his eyes and made a noise through gritted teeth. "If I'd been paying attention, if I'd realized, I could have got it fixed in Port Brown, then everything would have been okay. But no, stupid me, I didn't."

His entire body vibrated with frustration. He stood and paced. Her calm, capable Jake had vanished. Her stomach knotted. With Tomas she'd learned to make herself small, to not only reduce the amount of physical space she took up, but also to shrink everything else about her—her movements, the sound of her voice, her words themselves. She found herself retreating into that pattern now. "So, it's really broken?" she whispered.

"Yes."

Her mind went into fast-forward. "How long will the batteries hold out?"

He stopped pacing and his shoulders sagged. "A couple of days."

Power for the lights, instruments, and fridge didn't matter so much; what was more pressing was the need for water, and because the engine powered the watermaker, without the engine they couldn't make any more water. They were fine for food—they had plenty of canned supplies, supplemented by the group fishing—but they must be careful with their water or they might easily work their way through their remaining tank within a week. Rain would come after the turn of the monsoon, but there had been no sign of any change in the weather: just hot, clear, and windless, day after day. Shit, the wind. With no engine and no wind, they couldn't get *Wayfinder* out of the anchorage. That's why Jake was so worked up. He'd already realized the extent of the problem.

"What are we going to do?"

"Only one thing to do—I've got to fix it."

"What about the others? Can we go back to Roly? And Vitor has a watermaker. We can ask—"

Jake cut her off. "No. I don't want their help. I don't want anyone's help. This is my problem and I'm going to sort it."

"But Jake—"

"No, Vee." Steely confidence had replaced the anger. "I can do this, I'm sure." He went below.

Left alone, she stared out to sea as she twisted the ring on her finger. Carpentry and rigging were his specialty at the yard; he and his father outsourced any motor engineering. He knew more than most people, but this didn't compare to a broken kettle, or a temperamental car, and she wasn't sure he had the skills or equipment to repair an engine from scratch here, in the middle of nowhere, with such limited resources—and with no phone signal, they couldn't even look things up, or call anyone for advice. What if he couldn't fix it, couldn't get them back to Port Brown, couldn't make precious drinking water?

She took a deep breath. It was no good spiraling out of control. She needed to think logically, take things one step at a time. He could do it—really he could. Look at her car. And she'd help and surely the others would, too. Marriage was supposed to be about trust, about having faith and offering support. Yes. They'd be fine. She was over-thinking, fearing the worst. Things wouldn't get that bad. She wiped the sweat from her upper lip. Everything would be okay.

•   •   •

That night, she woke alone, jerked out of sleep by noises: a metallic clink followed by the slow rumble of a bolt rolling across the sole boards. Climbing out of bed, she felt her way through the cabin to the galley. Jake was at the chart table, books cast all around him, reading using his head torch. He looked up at her, and the light seared her eyes. She sucked in air over her teeth, sharp.

"Sorry." He switched his head torch to red mode.

"What's going on? Are you all right?"

He picked up a book and waved it. "I think I've found a solution. It's not going to be easy, but if I can work out a way of cutting a new gasket, I reckon I can replace it. All I've got to do is take the engine apart, copy the existing gasket, fabricate a new one."

He sounded odd, hyper. "All? That sounds like a huge job."

Her doubt didn't seem to register. He went to the starboard settee, the red dot cast by his head torch bouncing ahead of him. He knocked off the cushions and rummaged in the locker behind. "I think there's a sheet of metal in here somewhere." He lifted out pieces of wood, put them to one side. "Somewhere . . . somewhere . . ."

"Jake. It's still dark."

"Sorry. It's just . . . I mean . . . Sorry, Vee. I'm excited."

"What time is it?"

He looked at the clock. "Just gone three."

This was crazy. She felt gluey with tiredness—she half wondered if he was sleepwalking. "Well, you can't do anything till dawn. Come back to bed, just for a couple of hours. You'll need all your energy. I'll help you tomorrow."

"Can't sleep." He abandoned his search for the metal sheet and went back to the chart table. "I want to go through this, read up on it. I'll get started at first light." She began to tell him that this was madness, but he interrupted her. "I'll be quiet, I promise."

A mosquito whined by her ear. She batted it away. "You're sure you're okay?"

"I'm fine," he said. "I just want to get going."

She stood in the doorway of their cabin, watching. He was oblivious to her presence as he dropped his books and went to the engine, switching his head torch back to white mode. With the steps and side panels unbolted and removed, the engine was exposed, and she was struck by how much, with its red protective paint streaked with black grease and fine tubes coming off the side, it looked like a mechanical heart. She prayed he could get it beating again.

Over the following few days she and the others kept asking to help, but he insisted he could handle it himself. And to begin with, she had hopes that he could. Then the hours began to stretch long as she waited for the breakthrough to come. She hovered, expecting him to call her to come do this or that, lend a hand, but he never did. She was torn between two loyalties—to him and *Wayfinder*, and to her obligations to the wider group. The first day she stayed on board, but the next two she went out, to collect firewood or help fish, and even though she left the yacht for the shortest time possible, she felt guilty for leaving Jake, and made her excuses as soon as she could to return. The bonfire dinners continued without them.

When Vitor and Teresa dropped her back after fishing on the second day and Vitor offered assistance, Jake couldn't hide his impatience.

"Know much about engines, do you?"

"Only the basics," Vitor conceded.

"Well then, thanks, but I'll manage." He dropped through the hatch before anything else could be said.

To an outsider watching Jake rig up the boom as a crane to lift the engine head off the block, dashing from winch to winch, it might seem he could cope by himself. But he couldn't, not really. Several times she caught him staring into space, lost. She knew that retreating inside himself was his way of trying to take control, but she also knew that two heads, three, four, would be better than one. And with more hands, the work would get done more quickly.

On the fourth morning she decided to approach the others. Mechanics not being Vitor's forte or, she presumed, Teresa's, she opted to ask Pete, Stella, and Roly. She'd have to take them something in return. They didn't have much to spare, but she could bake bread. There was yeast and flour in the galley, and it would only use a little water. No one could resist a fresh loaf. Even the thought of the aroma of baking set her mouth watering.

Stella squealed with delight when handed the bread, wrapped in a cloth for the journey over in the dinghy. Virginie had to row across the bay because Jake had taken off the outboard to preserve the petrol for the generator to power his tools.

"You didn't have to do that," Stella said, accepting it. "Of course we'll help."

Next she went to Roly. "Keep it," he said, pushing the loaf toward her. "I'll meet you over there." Such kindness. She felt a bloom of warmth toward them all.

But the warmth, when they were all crowded in *Wayfinder*'s saloon, wasn't returned by Jake. "Thanks for the offer, but I can manage," he insisted.

"Come on, mate," Pete said, squatting down by the engine bay and flipping his cap round, ready for work. "We'll get through it quicker together."

"He's right," Roly said when there was no answer.

Jake reached for a rag to wipe off a valve, and she saw that it wasn't actually a rag but his blue T-shirt, the one he'd worn on their third date, the date when she'd realized she was falling in love. He yanked on the generator start cord and the rumble of the generator and the screech of the drill biting into metal drowned out the chance of any more talk. At the dismissal her gut twisted, as if a shadow hand from the past had reached into her body and wrenched her insides.

"I'm so sorry," she told them, leaning over the rail as first Pete and Stella and then Roly climbed back into their dinghies. She knew her cheeks were flaming.

Roly laid his hand on her arm. "The man's gotta do what he's gotta do." He untied the rope and drifted off.

She went below. Jake was hunched over the still-screaming drill. She shouted his name until he switched it off. "What did you do that for?"

He picked up a metal punch and measured it against the shape he'd perforated in the gasket before he replied. "I could ask you the same question."

"What do you mean?"

The punch wasn't right—he discarded it and chose another. He gave it a peremptory tap with a hammer. "You know."

She had no patience for riddles. "What do you mean?"

"I said could handle it by myself. I made that perfectly clear. Next thing I know, you're bringing people round, so obviously you don't trust me." He smacked the punch again, harder, then harder still. He was making dents, but the central piece refused to pop free.

"I do trust you. But it's been four days." Yes, they were using less water than ever before—drinking little, not showering—but every day depleted the tank further. "This isn't a game, Jake."

He placed the hammer and punch on the floor with deliberate care and reached for his drill. Before he switched it on again, he said, "I know it isn't a game, Vee. I hope you realize that."

Anger and frustration at his behavior, guilt and shame at hers, drove her up on deck. The loaf of bread was sitting on the seat by the helm. She held it on her lap for the longest time. Jake loved her bread. Back home in Lymington she set the machine running every Friday night so that the weekend began with the scent of baking. All she could smell now was petrol, oil, and sweat—her own nervous animal sweat. She reeked of it. She stood and hurled the loaf as far as she could into the sea.

23

She needed to get off the yacht. Thankfully, Anchorage Beach was deserted. She ditched the dinghy, grateful she didn't have to pretend to anyone that everything was fine. She dreaded to consider what the others must think of them. Damn Jake for being stubborn, for being so blind to the fact that his pride shouldn't be a factor here. Getting this resolved was the important thing.

She set off into the island's interior at a furious pace, stomping past the ruins without lingering there as usual, but soon the heat got to be too much and sapped the energy from her limbs. She'd eaten nothing all day. She sought some shade near the north, lying on the ground and letting the afternoon's heat draw her down into sleep, thinking that perhaps it would help her mood. But when she woke, bathed in sweat, her mouth thick with thirst, nothing in her had shifted, so she made her way back to the anchorage and sat on Roly's log under the fringing trees near the scorched patch where they built their fires. Around her the air was filled with the noises of natural life, carrying on as normal: insects in the middle of their steady chirruping song, the crackle of leaves as they dropped to the ground or were shifted along by a procession of ants. A tiny transparent ghost crab skittered across the sand in front of her. She thought about the prisoners, about how stretched for resources they must have been and about how little control they had over their own fate. And the one time they had tried to take control, in the rebellion, it hadn't worked.

She found she was biting at her nail, worrying the skin at the side with her teeth. She pulled her hand away from her mouth and jammed it under her thigh, hearing Tomas: "Disgusting habit. You're not a child." Her hand throbbed under her leg.

The jungle rustled behind her, and she turned sharply as someone emerged from the shade. The angle of the head was so like her ex-husband's that for a mad moment the old adrenaline kick of alarm booted her low down in the gut. But it was Vitor, alone, with a backpack slung over one shoulder.

"Ah, the beautiful Madame Durand."

"Hello." The word came out too stiff. Oh well, perhaps he'd leave her alone to wallow in self-pity.

He didn't get the message. Instead he opened his bag and lifted out kindling he'd collected and stacked it next to the fire for later. When he finished, he flopped to the sand in front of her, obscuring her view of *Wayfinder*. "How are you? How is Jake?"

She was in no mood for Vitor's brand of uncreased urbanity. Everything seemed to go so smoothly for him—had he ever had a problem in his life? "If it's okay with you, I'd rather not talk about it."

Vitor leaned back on his arms, the hem of his open shirt skimming the sand, that lock of hair falling across his forehead. He gazed idly around at the beach, the sky, the fringe of trees above them, as if he were a tourist pleasantly taking in the view for the first time.

A rough piece of cuticle was biting into the back of her thigh, where she still had her fingers wedged tight. She pulled out the hand and gave in to the urge to rip away the skin with her teeth. It didn't bleed, but the raw patch smarted in a satisfying way.

"What were you doing?" he asked her, after a while. "Drawing again?"

"What?" She glanced down at her bag by her feet, where one side of the canvas had drooped, exposing the unopened sketch pad and pencil tin. She'd forgotten she had them with her.

He slicked back his hair. "You could draw me." When she didn't answer, he put a hand to the back of his head, elbow out, and tilted his face to the sky, striking a pose. "I make a very good model." He winked.

Despite herself, she half smiled. Vitor never winked. He must have picked up on her mood after all and was trying to coax her out of it. If that was the case, he was going about it the right way—and certainly doing better than Jake.

He took her half smile as a sign of encouragement and flexed his biceps. She weakened further and started to giggle. He leaned across her to fish the sketch pad out of her bag and lay it on her knees. Next he slid a pencil into her palm, and she let him wrap her fingers around it. Then he was back on his feet.

"Come, draw," he said, hands on his hips, pushing out his chest. In this position, with his torso arched, his stomach muscles stood proud. She watched them move in and out with his breath, conscious of the dark hair trailing a line from his navel down.

He winked again, and the final resistance in her gave way—she might as well join in. She pantomimed a portrait artist, holding out her pencil at arm's length and tilting it, measuring angles and distances, then drew quickly, strokes flying, sketching a caricature: Vitor as Superman, with his shirt billowing behind him like a cape, and that lock of falling hair, but instead of a costume and boots she put him in miniature bathing trunks and espadrilles, inscribed a *V* symbol on his chest.

After a few minutes she said "Voilà!" She pulled the page from the pad and held it aloft. When he went to take it, she jerked it just out of reach a couple of times before relenting.

His eyes were sparkling as he looked up. "I like it," he said. "No one has made for me my portrait before. I think I will hang it in my boat. There is just one thing missing. The signature of the artist."

She took it back, leaning on her sketch pad to scrawl her name up the side. If was as if Vitor had known that persuading her to pick up her pencil, making her concentrate, would help her to feel better. This was the most fun she'd had in days.

He took both the drawing and the pad from her, and flicked back through her sketches, as he had done that other morning on the north side of the island. When had that been? It felt like yesterday, but it must have been weeks ago, not long after they arrived here. Since then she had added more, including a picture of Gus and a little study of Stella and Pete. He reached an outline she had started of Jake when he'd been relaxed enough to give in to her requests to let her draw him. It was the last in the book, and he flicked backwards, stopping at a self-portrait that was even older than the one he'd told her he liked before.

"This is my favorite. You look so fresh," he said, and looked at it for a long time. She'd liked it, too, when she'd drawn it—how full of hope for her future she'd been when she'd put pencil to paper—but her father had made it clear how bad it was, how it lacked technique, was both too simple and derivative.

"My honesty might hurt now," Papa had said, "but you'll thank me one day, when you realize how much time I've saved you, how much rejection and embarrassment you've avoided." She'd kept her head down and nodded mutely as he patted it. "Now," he had continued, his voice lifting easily, as if he were trying to get a small child to move on from a well-worn comfort blanket, "don't you think it's time you put all this behind you and reconsidered that job at the gallery? Much more suitable, no?" She'd done as she was told. And three months later, at the Paris gallery his friend had owned for two decades, Papa had arranged something else for her: an introduction to one of his most important collectors. Three big commissions for her father followed their engagement.

Vitor shut the book with a snap. "I almost forgot. Payment." He reached for his rucksack.

"No, Vitor." It would be awful to see that fold of notes again, here, now. It would ruin their game. "You don't need to pay me. It's just a silly sketch."

He rummaged in the front pocket of his backpack. "I insist. It was a commission. And I always settle my debts, as I expect others to settle theirs with me." He found what he was searching for and straightened.

"Seriously," she said. "It's enough that . . ." She stopped when she saw what he was holding out to her. Not money, but a crisp green apple. "My God." She took it from him, turned it in her hand. "I haven't seen one of these in months. Since we left home." Her mouth was already salivating, her taste buds anticipating the first bite. An apple. Here. He couldn't have bought this in Port Brown, or anywhere nearby—it must have been on his boat for a long time, traveled thousands of miles. How had he managed to keep it so fresh? A miracle. She shook her head and gave it back to him. "I can't."

"What?"

"I can't take it."

"Virginie, not this again." He sighed. "It is okay, a trade. Your art for my fruit." She hesitated. "Virginie. You are being ridiculous. Come." He held the apple almost at arm's length. "Relax. Take it. It is not a gift. It is a deal."

Her empty stomach pinched. Vitor was standing his ground. She took a half step forward and reached for the fruit, marveling at it before she took a bite, and its juice, as it flooded her mouth, was sweeter than she could have hoped for.

The air had taken on that thinning quality that signaled the switch from day to night as she and Vitor stood at the helm of his tender. She liked how he took control, and how that made her feel. No, *control* wasn't the right word; it was more that he made her feel self-assured, secure. Or safe. Yes, that was it—he made her feel safe. It was like when you reached harbor and found a place that offered shelter against whatever winds might come.

They were towing her own dinghy, to save her from having to row back. She presumed he was taking her home, so she was surprised when they drew alongside *Santa Maria*, not *Wayfinder*. She'd have no choice but to step on board with his line, secure his tender, then retrieve her dinghy and go home.

"Come," he said, overtaking her and heading for *Santa Maria*'s cockpit. He pulled out a chair for her at the table. "Sit." His tone and manner had switched from the playful Vitor she had seen on the beach to something a little more commanding, something more akin to how he'd been when he'd given his speech about money during the boat party. He disappeared inside, and she hovered at the edge of the cockpit, but he came straight back out with a bottle of wine, rattling in an ice bath, and glasses. He raised a hand to ward off any objections as he poured. "Consider it a second part of the payment."

There were only two glasses. "Where's Teresa?"

"She has a headache. I gave her some medicine and she is resting in the forecabin."

She dithered, not wanting to do the wrong thing. She looked across the water to *Wayfinder*. No sign of Jake. His pigheadedness did him no favors. She'd have been there with him now if he'd just let her in a little, but no. She stepped forward, took the wine, and sat.

The sun was setting, and night was cloaking the boat. Vitor went inside once more, and this time returned carrying a thick white towel. "I thought you might appreciate a shower."

She laughed, presuming he was joking, and was about to ask if she really smelled that bad when she realized he was being serious, and the words died on her lips.

He continued to stand there, waiting. She couldn't think of a way to refuse that wouldn't seem churlish, so she rose and followed him into the catamaran, let him lead her through the saloon, down a few steps, through a turn, and toward the back. Soft floor-level lighting showed the way along the dark corridor. Thick carpets hushed the sounds of their feet, and her bare toes sank greedily into the pile.

He flicked on a light. They had reached a wide stateroom, as large as *Wayfinder*'s cabin, saloon, and galley combined, where a high broad bed dominated the space, the sheet on top loosely crumpled. She saw it and instantly thought of sex—of Vitor and sex. God, no, she mustn't think of him in that way.

Vitor pushed at another door and continued holding it open at arm's length, so she could pass into an en suite bathroom. She looked at the narrow doorway—their bodies would be very close if she went forward, intimately close. Seconds ticked by. She swallowed. Still he held open the door.

And then he stepped inside and turned on the shower. "The temperature should be correct, but you can adjust it if you wish with the top lever." She followed him in. He draped the towel over a rail and withdrew, closing the door behind him.

At the click of the handle, she let out a long breath. What was she doing in another man's bathroom? This wasn't right. She pushed the crumpled sheet from her mind. She would find Vitor, thank him for his generosity, and go home. She leaned in to switch off the water. In those moments, she had probably wasted the equivalent of half of what remained in *Wayfinder*'s tanks.

As she opened the cabin door, she heard raised voices, rapid-fire Portuguese, coming from another part of the boat. Mortified about overhearing an argument, she tiptoed out through the cabin and along the corridor, wanting to jump into her dinghy and row over to *Wayfinder*, get out of this whole awkward situation. The voices stopped. She paused at the steps up to the saloon from the corridor. Ahead, all was dark. She strained to see better.

Overhead, lights flared. Vitor was there, coming into the saloon from the catamaran's other hull. In the sudden brightness she was conscious of how little she was wearing, even though she had spent all day, like every day, in nothing more than her bikini. She crossed her arms over her chest.

Vitor stopped between her and the tall glass doors that led to the cockpit. "I thought you might need something to change into." He was carrying a light cotton robe. He crept forward. "Virginie, please. Teresa gave me this to give to you. She says she is sorry she has not been able to greet you earlier, but she is feeling better now, and when you finish your shower, she will join us."

Something wasn't right. She'd heard them arguing. And Teresa had never been especially friendly to her before. She looked from the robe to Vitor's face, but his eyes, as she met them, were soft, the gold flecks molten.

"She says please be our guest and make yourself comfortable." He looked out of the window toward *Wayfinder*. "I know you have some problems over there. I know nothing about engines. But I make water from the ocean. Let me help you in this small way. Really, it is nothing."

She touched her hair. How matted it was, even though it was now short. She had to admit, it would be wonderful to wash in fresh, warm water, get properly clean for the first time in ages. Even before their engine broke down, a shower had been a quick, cold affair. She studied Vitor, who was still holding out the robe. He was right: it was a small gesture, not a big deal. She was overreacting. Whatever pride was holding her back surrendered.

"All right," she said, closing the gap between them and accepting the robe. "But just the shower. And then I will have to go back to *Wayfinder*. To Jake," she added. Best to cover all bases.

"But of course," he said, stepping back, holding up both hands. "To Jake."

In the bathroom she locked the door, took off her bikini, and looked at her reflection in the full-length mirror. They didn't have a large mirror on *Wayfinder,* and she hadn't seen her naked reflection for a long time. Not since home—nearly three months. Was she thinner? She turned sideways and back again. Yes, she was; her hips and collarbones were more pronounced. The heat and humidity had halved her appetite, and recent worry had shrunk it further. Tan lines made ghosts of her breasts and bum, and a dotted track of mosquito bites trailed down one calf. Her hair was a mess, stiffened with salt so it stuck up every which way. She wasn't exactly looking her best. In fact, she didn't really recognize herself at all. It had been a while since she and Jake had had sex—since the engine problem. No, even before then, come to think of it. She rubbed her forehead. She'd put it down to the unbearably hot nights here. But was this why, really? She thought of Teresa's curves, and that led her back to Vitor's sheets, and a hot, lonely ache started low in her belly.

The warm water flowing over her head and shoulders relaxed her almost instantly. Automatically, she reached out a hand to turn off the tap as soon as she was wet, but then stopped. Vitor had said it didn't matter. She should just enjoy the experience. Bottles of shampoo and gel were lined up on a ledge. She picked them up and sniffed at them, one by one, savoring their rich aromas of citrus, of cedar, and took her time massaging them into her hair and skin.

The robe was too long and wide—one of Vitor's, not Teresa's—and she needed to cinch it tight at the waist. A thick towel made quick work of rubbing dry her hair, and now that it was clean her fingers slid easily through it and she was able to style it into place. She wiped the steam off the mirror. Much better. As she walked back along the corridor to the cockpit, her bikini in one hand, she hummed.

Vitor was laying out a platter of meats. He stood tall as she approached. "Better?"

"Much," she replied, with a happy sigh.

Despite what he'd said, Teresa didn't appear, and Virginie was glad. Her improved mood blunted her earlier determination to get back to *Wayfinder*, and she acknowledged she selfishly wanted to enjoy Vitor's attention a while longer. In a way it was a relief to let someone else make the decisions; it helped ease the burden of worry. And she couldn't deny it was great to be spoiled. Although, really, having a drink, accepting a friend's hospitality—this would be normal back in England, in France, where Roly's rules didn't exist, and she wouldn't have thought twice about it. She allowed Vitor to top up her glass again, and the alcohol buzz quickly became a warm glow.

They talked about all kinds of things—mutual places they'd been, artists they admired, books they'd read, switching easily between English and French. At one point, at a natural lull in the conversation, a clank of metal against metal sounded across the bay, and she looked out through the darkness to where she knew *Wayfinder* was. The lights were off, but she could make out a dim glow flickering through the portlights: Jake's head torch. He was still up. A strand of guilt tugged at her stomach. She'd been here ages. Time to leave.

She went into the bathroom to change into her bikini, and when she came out, Vitor was waiting by her dinghy with a surprise: two white plastic jerry cans nestled in the bow.

"Water," she said.

"Yes."

There must have been fifty liters there—several days' worth. It'd be pointless to say no when she'd taken so much from him already tonight. She'd been feeling so helpless. This could be her way of contributing.

"Thank you," she said, and his cheek was smooth under her lips as she kissed him good night.

Her journey back across the silken water was slightly less direct than it had been in her anger that afternoon. She giggled first as she missed the sea with an oar, and again as the dinghy clunked against the yacht as she made a clumsy arrival. She tried to heft one of the containers up onto the side deck, but she wobbled under its weight and put it back into the dinghy. They could stay where they were until tomorrow—it wasn't worth the risk. She'd bring Jake out to show him. He could relax a little now, knowing that they would be fine for water, that Vitor was genuinely offering to help. It would take the pressure off. He might even open up a bit more. In the warm night things were better than they had been for a while. Yes—Jake'd soften, and she, Roly, Pete, and Stella could all chip in. They'd get it sorted way before the monsoon came and they really had to leave. That was weeks off yet—and with Vitor's offer of water, she'd bought them some time.

The moon was full, and its light enough that she could see the companionway steps hadn't been fitted back into place, so she went into the boat the same way she had come out of it earlier: through the bedroom hatch. All was quiet below, but a faint glow came through from the saloon. Good, he was awake. She could show him the water, then entice him into bed. She skipped through the galley.

Jake was asleep along one settee, an arm dangling down into the air, his head torch still on. She watched him for a moment, thought about waking him, but he looked so peaceful. She bent down and kissed him softly and switched off the torch. He didn't stir.

It could all wait till morning. She tiptoed back to the aft cabin. She'd surprise him then.

24

Footsteps overhead woke her. It was light, the sun fierce. What time was it? Afternoon, after a nap, or morning? Her head was pounding. Oh—she'd had wine the night before, too much wine. She must have slept well past dawn. Well, it wouldn't hurt to stay here a little longer, until her headache eased. Suddenly she remembered the water and knelt to put her head through the hatch, her hangover pushed to the side. Jake was already climbing into the dinghy. She launched herself up, stepped to the side deck, and leaned over the rail. Jake was in the dinghy's bow, crouching by the jerry cans. He'd unscrewed one of the lids, and through the open mouth the contents sparkled.

"Surprise!" she called down.

He looked up. "What's this?"

"Wa-ter," she said, teasing, drawing out the syllables.

"I can see that. Where did it come from?"

"It's a gift." She swayed her hips.

Wordlessly, he screwed on the lid. He climbed back onto *Wayfinder* and swerved the good-morning kiss she tried to land on him. She pulled back. Not the best start to the day, but she could still turn it around. "I'll make breakfast," she said, and headed for the hatch.

Jake dropped through behind her and leaned against the chart table as she worked at the galley. She felt his eyes following her as she opened the cupboard, cracked and beat eggs, fired up the gas.

"What did you get up to with Stella yesterday?" he asked.

The cups chinked as she set them down on the counter. "I didn't see Stella."

"Oh?"

As she pushed back her hair, it released the spicy scent of Vitor's shampoo. "No. I spent the afternoon with Vitor."

"Vitor gave you the water."

She poured two coffees. "He wanted to help." She started to turn, his drink in her hand. "He saw that you, I mean we, were having problems."

His voice sparked. "We are *not* having problems."

Coffee spilled onto her hand, seared her skin. "I–I mean the engine. The watermaker."

Jake came right in front of her, holding his thumb and finger two inches apart in front of her eyes. "I'm this close to a breakthrough. It'll be a couple more days, that's all. We can last a couple of days, can't we? Don't you believe in me?"

They were close, close enough to kiss, but all she could see in his eyes right then was fury. Her heart contracted.

He moved back to the chart table. "And last night? While I was working here? Were you with Vitor then?"

That half-forgotten reflex, the urge to keep quiet, kicked in. She tried to fight it. It wasn't the same . . . *He* wasn't the same. She took her time putting his drink back on the galley counter, stirring the eggs in the pan.

"And Teresa? What did she make of this? Presumably she was there? Not off shopping at the Amarante mall?"

"She . . ." She paused. "She was asleep. She had a headache."

He snorted. "I bet she did. You don't think he's just waiting for his chance to get his paws on you? And that he's not dying to get one up on me, prove he's the better man?"

She stared at the watery eggs and switched off the gas. This couldn't just be the old insecurity about money talking. What had got into him? She turned back toward him, the wooden spoon in her hand, and his face was screwed tight, a mask of fury.

"And what exactly did you give him in exchange for it?"

"What? Nothing!"

"Come on—I know you're not that naive."

"Jake! How could you even say that to me?"

"As if a man like Vitor would do something out of kindness."

"What do you mean?"

"You know how it works here as well as I do. Hell—he even gave us a lecture about it!"

She snapped. All right, if he wanted a fight, he would get one. "Yes, I do know. We work together, we help each other out. At least *I* do." She jabbed the spoon at him. "You're the one who's hiding down here day after day doing nothing."

"Nothing? You think I'm doing nothing?"

She pointed at the dead engine. Parts of it were strewn all over the floor. "Well, whatever you're doing, it's not working, is it? And yet you won't accept any help. You turned everyone away."

"Yes, because it's not their problem to solve."

"Well, what if you can't do it? Why do you have to be so stubborn? Shut us out? Shut *me* out? I'm trying to help, too. Vitor said—"

He cut her off. "Oh, I know very well what Vitor will have said." He put on an accent. "'Let me help you, let me be your knight in shining armor. I am wealthy and you are poor. I have so much more than I need.'"

She threw the spoon back into the pan. Bits of egg flew up. "I told you, it was a gift. He gave the water to both of us, not just to me." Despite her best intentions, her voice rose. "I thought you'd be pleased. I thought if I accepted the water, it would take the pressure off, buy you some time. Buy *us* some time."

His hands went to his head. "For fuck's sake, Vee. How could you accept things from Vitor without bearing my feelings in mind? How stupid does it make me look, having to rely on handouts from another man, putting me in his debt? We have water, don't we? I already told Vitor I had everything under control, and now you've undermined that. And what the hell were you doing spending all that time with him anyway?" He didn't give her space to respond. "I told you, I can fix this. I don't need any help. You said you trusted me—was that a lie? Is that we're doing now, lying to each other?"

His words stalled her. Were they? Were they lying to themselves as much as to each other?

He turned to go back to his work at the engine bay. "I won't be anyone's charity case." As he spoke over his shoulder, his voice cracked. "Take those water cans back. I mean it, Vee. Take them back."

Santa Maria was quiet as Virginie drew alongside. Her palms were stinging, and she eased her grip on the oars one at a time to examine them. The skin of each was red, white marks at the center indicating blisters would soon form. She flexed her hands, wincing at the soreness. Stupid, really. Rowing so fast hadn't solved anything.

"Hello?" she called, knocking on *Santa Maria*'s hull. "Anyone home? Vitor?" The tender wasn't there, but she knocked again anyway. "Teresa?"

No one came. *Swallow*'s dinghy was also gone, as was Roly's dive gear from the back of *Ariel*. They must all be fishing without her—getting up so late, she'd missed them. She'd have to ensure she was ready in time tomorrow. She sat back and let the dinghy take her weight. The underside of the catamaran reflected the sunlight, and she watched it dancing in swirls and whorls, flickers and curls, nothing settling in one place for longer than a heartbeat. After the fight, she was glad of the peace.

That argument was by far the nastiest they'd ever had. Sure, Jake was on the defense, but what an unfair conclusion to jump to. What was worse was his tone. That was the first time he'd ever ordered her to do something. She knew very well what it was like to be ordered around, to have a husband who expected, demanded even, to be obeyed. Please let it not be coming to that. She wouldn't be able to stand it again.

There wasn't one big thing that triggered the end of her first marriage, one unforgettable argument; it was more a gradual wearing away of her sense of self until she became aware, on what had started as just another normal day, that there was almost no Virginie Durand left. She hadn't packed a case, hadn't even known she was actually leaving him until the story came out, through hot tears, in her mother's kitchen. The distance between London and Paris had helped, and she'd begun to understand that she didn't have to go back. "You do have a choice," her mum said. When she did finally return—only for her things—her mother had stood, like a guard dog, inside the entrance to the apartment. Once she was free of him, she'd sworn to herself that she would never let a man—or anyone—control her like that again. So there was no way she could sit by, waiting, while Jake called all the shots. She'd worked so hard to build herself back up: the new country, the rent she paid herself, the job that she'd found, applied for—even though she had no experience—and won. She'd considered her and Jake to be partners, two halves of a team. She had to do something now, whether he liked it or not.

The two containers, wedged tight against the sides of the dinghy, were immaculate, as if they'd never been used before. An idea came to her: she wouldn't give them back to Vitor; she'd keep them. Yes! She *would* keep them—they were a gift; she was within her rights. But how could she decant the water into their tanks without Jake noticing, when he was always on board? She could hide the containers on the island. Then he wouldn't be angry, wouldn't know she'd gone against him. And if it did turn out they needed them, if they got really desperate, she could produce them, and he'd be relieved and pleased. It would be her effort for the cause, and might go a little way toward repairing the damage done. She looked over at *Wayfinder*—he was still below deck, so if she was going to do this she'd have to go now, while he couldn't see her. She let go of *Santa Maria*, picked up the oars, and began to row.

The cicadas screeched relentlessly in the noon heat, building toward a peak that never came. She was on her knees, grabbing and scooping handfuls of sand at a speed to match the insects' urgency, clawing so hard that she almost pulled herself off-balance.

Here at East Beach everything was louder: the crash of the waves, the crackle of creatures moving through dried detritus in the tide lines. What creatures they were, she didn't know and wasn't about to pause to find out. Things on this side of the island were harsher, too. The grazes on her knees from digging were proof of that.

As she scooped away another handful of sand, her fingers came into contact with something hard. She probed, searching for the edges of whatever it was she'd found, until she was able to hook underneath and prize it away. It was the bottom half of a kind of bowl made from a polished coconut shell, with edges jagged as teeth where it had broken. Brushing it clean, she turned it over in her hands. The outside was carved with a sea scene: wavy lines depicting the ocean, fish leaping, even a turtle swimming. It was old, and exactly the kind of thing they'd had on display in the museum, lined up in the cabinet alongside monkeys' fists and pieces of scrimshaw. The detail was exquisite, every scute of the turtle's shell delineated. Judging by its age, it must have belonged to one of the island prisoners or guards. But she couldn't imagine a British guard bending to carve, hour after hour. A prisoner, then. So beauty had mattered, even during such an ordeal. Did beauty always matter? Did it make incarceration any easier to bear, being imprisoned in a place like Amarante? Did seeing the sky, feeling the sand beneath your feet, help in any way at all? Or was it even worse? It dawned on her that the authorities might have chosen Amarante for a reason: Here's paradise, bringing you pain.

She put the pad of a finger against a point of the broken edge; it was so sharp it almost pierced her skin. If she used it now as a scoop, it would make her work quicker. She went to dig, then hesitated. Perhaps it had belonged to someone whose bones now lay beneath the earth by the ruins. She pictured an older man watching her with wary eyes. Silver hair, knuckles already thickened by arthritis. She saw him searching through piles of discarded coconut husks, finding one that would be the right size and shape for his needs. Looking for a sharp stone with which to carve. Turning the oil press, leaning into it, driving his feet into the ground. Afterwards, dipping the bowl into the ocean and pouring the contents over his head to cool down. On another occasion, bringing it to his lips, drinking tea.

She flipped the bowl in her hands. It was beautiful, yes, but practical, too. In her mind's eye the silver-haired man flicked a hand at her, as the fisherman who had taken them out to *Wayfinder* had done. *Pergi, pergi.* She started to dig.

At last she finished her task and stood up to look around for something to mark the position. A fly buzzed around her face and she waved it away. There: a few small sticks, their bark long gone, soft insides bleached and hardened like bones. Stooping, she placed two on the vague mound, crossing them over each other. X marks the spot. No, too corny. She stood them on end, pushing them partway down into the sand. Far better.

As she stood, her skin prickled. She looked up at the jungle line, waited a moment for her eyes to adjust to the depths of the shadows. She scanned along the fringe. There was no one there, of course.

Thinking of the prisoners was spooking her. It was hard to believe you were ever alone on this island.

She knocked some sand off her knees and stepped back to survey her handiwork. Disturbed by the movement, a swarm of flies that had been working away at something on the beach lifted for a moment, and then settled back to their task.

It didn't look quite natural, to have the sticks jutting up like that. Someone might know they'd been deliberately placed there, might think to look underneath. She scolded herself again. No one was going to come looking. The containers belonged to her now. Vitor didn't need them. And they weren't hidden, as such. They were just under the sand for protection, to stop the sun's glare from degrading the plastic, like Stella had warned, to keep the water inside cool and fresh. They were stored, that's all. Safely stored in case they were ever needed. For an emergency.

She picked up the bowl, to take it with her to *Wayfinder*. As she turned to head back to Anchorage Beach, she caught sight of what the flies were eating on the sand. Trapped between two strands of blackened weed was the head of a seabird, lying on one side, the crawling flies giving its oily feathers the illusion of movement. Its beak was partly open as if it might at any moment make a sound, but its eye was already gone, and putrescence pooled in the socket like tears.

When she got to *Wayfinder*, Jake was conciliatory.

"Thanks for taking them back, Vee. I know it's silly, but it means a lot to me." He pulled her into a hug. "Sorry I shouted. Forgive me?"

His skin smelled of grease and sweat, of hard work, of commitment. Apologies were supposed to make you feel better. This one only made her feel worse.

25

The air was even more oppressive than usual the next morning when she tied her dinghy next to Roly's off *Swallow*'s stern. She didn't think it was possible for the conditions to get more cloying, more stifling, but they had, and even Gus, sprawled in *Swallow*'s cockpit, was slow to get to his feet and amble over to greet her. Pete and Roly were on the foredeck. Her hand was heavy as she gave them a wave. Neither man returned the greeting.

Stella came up from below, arms full of snorkeling kit. "He's not coming then?"

"No." Virginie eyed the two spearguns propped on the cockpit bench, standing on their butt ends, the sharp shadows they cast against the coaming making it look like there were four guns stacked there, an arsenal ready for battle. She still hadn't told Stella about the argument. How could she when Pete and Stella were so tight, so perfect? She'd never even seen them bicker. Her own marriage was on the verge of broaching, overpowered by all kinds of forces she couldn't control. Jake was acting fairly normally around her as he worked on the engine from first light until beyond sunset, yet she jumped at the clang of every dropped spanner, shrank at every uttered swear word, even though they weren't directed at her. When he spoke, she analyzed his words, looking for meanings she might have missed, second-guessing everything, trying not to add to the pressure. She couldn't ask him again to come fishing. She just couldn't.

She pulled a smile across her face and met Stella's eye. "He's making progress, actually."

"That's good," Stella said, neutrally. Virginie fiddled with her bikini ties, unsure whether the tension she was feeling this morning was real, or if she was imagining it. Stella dropped the masks and fins onto the cockpit seat. "You know, Vee . . ." she began.

Right then Vitor came alongside *Swallow* in his tender, skewing it sideways to an abrupt halt like a skier. Teresa was sitting on the seat, brim of her hat angled down, masking half her face.

"Good morning," Vitor called. "Ready?"

Virginie looked at Stella, waiting for her to continue with what she had been saying, but Stella had picked up her fins and was handing them over the guard rails to Vitor. Pete was already climbing down, the peak of his cap hiding his face. He still hadn't said hello. Virginie rubbed her cheek. She was reading too much into everything. She was tired; they all were. It was too hot to sleep properly, and getting harder to collect coconuts and driftwood for the fire—they'd used up the resources nearest the beach and were having to trek farther and farther each day into the bush, carrying heavy loads longer distances.

She bent to pat Gus. "Good boy," she said, ruffling the fur on his head. "Stay here in the shade. Back soon with some supper for you." He panted at her, hope in his eyes. Unswervingly loyal, dogs. As Vitor pulled away, driving a semicircle around *Swallow*, Gus trotted along the deck until he reached the peak of the bow. His barks followed them as they headed out to deeper water.

The swim wasn't working its magic today. Exhaustion rolled over her, and she signaled to the others that she was going to return to the tender. Below her, Roly, the sea thick beyond him, kicked hard to shoot away almost before his thumb and forefinger had formed the okay symbol. Stella, in scuba kit, deepest of all, doubled back, twisting her body around easily, supple as a seal.

"You didn't have to come with me," Virginie said, treading water after they surfaced by the transom of the tender, taking off her mask and snorkel. She lifted the trio of fish she was carrying over the side, followed by her fins. Teresa, sitting on the bow, didn't come to help.

Stella undid her BCD and let it slide to the floor. "I was done anyway." She took aim at her dive kit with the snub-nosed gun of the shower head. Virginie watched the fresh water streaming down the valley at the bottom of the boat and along the gully toward the drain. Such waste.

Stella finished her task and came over to the double seat. Virginie shifted over to make room for her. She didn't sit right away—first she glanced over her shoulder at the bow. Virginie followed her gaze. Teresa wasn't flicking through pictures on her phone as normal, but was staring out to sea.

Stella lowered her voice. "Look, Vee, there's something I wanted to talk to you about earlier, but then Vitor arrived and it wasn't really the time."

So she was finally going to come out with whatever was bothering her. Virginie waited.

Stella sighed. "I don't really know where to start. We had a meeting last night."

"A meeting?" Since when did they have meetings on Amarante? And if they did have them, why weren't she and Jake invited?

Stella rested her forearms on her thighs and looked at her out of the corner of her eye. "You know when you arrived at the island and Roly gave the little welcome talk, about how everything works here? Well, someone else gave us the same one the first time we came to Amarante. I remember thinking it was so formal to have these rules, considering where we were. I mean"—she arced an arm, taking in the open sea—"who's going to enforce them? Anyway . . . The thing is . . ." Her sentences became uncharacteristically short, as if forcing them out was breaking them into pieces. "There have been concerns." She placed her hand, fingers cooled by the shower water, over Virginie's. "About you two not pulling your weight."

Before Virginie could say anything, Stella continued. "I know it's difficult for you, given the problems you're facing. Everyone understands that. Look, I know Jake isn't good in the water, so he isn't going to catch as many as Roly, Pete, and Vitor. But he needs to show willingness at least. He hasn't been out for a week—not helping with the firewood, driving, collecting coconuts, cooking. Nothing."

Virginie felt blood rush to her cheeks. Of course she knew they had to work together. She'd tried her hardest to persuade Jake, and she made sure she was out here, joining in. She snatched her hand out from under Stella's. "But you know our engine's broken. Jake needs to spend his time—"

Stella interrupted her again. "Of course he does. But Vitor gave you some water, so surely he can spare a few hours, right?"

So Vitor had told her about the containers. Or Teresa had. Virginie hadn't been able to bring herself to; she'd felt too ashamed, or guilty.

"Look," Stella said, glancing again at Teresa, "it's not me saying this, but there is a point. We're a group here, a tribe, and we have to all work together."

"Who started this?" Virginie demanded. She lowered her voice to a whisper. "Teresa?" Was that why Stella kept looking at her? Was it some weird kind of revenge because Teresa was jealous of the friendship she had with Vitor? Was she pissed off that Vitor had given them the water?

"No."

"Roly then." She didn't want to think that of him, but they were his rules—at least, he seemed the biggest proponent of them. Maybe he'd got to the end of his tether.

Stella pressed her lips together in denial. So not Roly. But that would mean it was her and Pete. She couldn't get her head around what was going on. Stella was supposed to be her friend. They all were. She turned her head away, afraid that she might start crying.

"Vee, it's not an issue with you. You're fine, you're here, contributing. It's Jake. We've all offered to help him get your engine working again, and he's knocked everyone back—and kind of rudely, too. It's not how we roll here. We thought you both understood that. Why doesn't he commit to doing one, two hours a day of fishing?"

She shot a look at the bow seat. "Teresa never fishes."

"No, but she comes out. And Vitor does his share. You know that. Jake doesn't have to get into the water if he doesn't want to. He can do it from your dinghy. Whatever. Look." She took a breath. "No one is going to say anything to him yet, it's just grumbles. But grumbles can flare up pretty big around here. I know—I've seen it."

Just then a large fish hit the bottom of the tender, flung over the side by Roly. The tender rocked as Teresa scuttled over with a bucket and took his speargun. Virginie seized the commotion as an opportunity to cut the embarrassing conversation short. "Of course. Whatever you think best."

As they headed back to the anchorage, Roly at the helm, she watched the horizon. A lot of what Stella had said rang true—she'd told Jake herself that he had to get more involved. But they needed the engine for water, for power, to get them away from Amarante by the end of the season. The others didn't have these problems, so it was unfair of them to complain. But then again, if Jake would let them all help, as they'd offered . . . She was going round in circles, not sure whose side she was supposed to be on, or what she was meant to be defending.

Vitor came over. "Everything is okay?"

Had he been at this so-called meeting? She found it hard to imagine he had—he was acting just like normal, making sure she was all right. She tried to relax her frown. "Yes."

From the corner of her eye, she saw Teresa turn in their direction, holding her sun hat to her head. "Vitor," she called.

He ignored her. "You have everything that you need? You need fuel, you need more water?" He touched her arm. "Virginie. You know I can give these things to you."

How white Vitor's shirt was. Unbuttoned, it billowed behind him, white and clean and freshly pressed. What life must be like on that boat, how comfortable he and Teresa must be, wanting for nothing. All she had to do was ask. But Jake's reaction to her accepting anything from Vitor had been so strong that she didn't dare risk rocking things.

"No, we're fine," she said, and looked out to sea once more. How many times had she used that word to him, and how many times had she not been telling the truth? "Thank you, though."

Teresa called his name again, but still he lingered, as if deliberating about trying to change her mind. Finally he moved away, leaving her on her own.

For the first time in a long time, she felt like an outcast. She'd always been excluded like this when Tomas got together with his friends. Oh, they had been polite, kissed her hello, asked how she was, but then they dismissed her, even if she remained in the room.

After Vitor dropped them all at *Swallow*, she rowed back to *Wayfinder* as quickly as she could, not caring about the pain from her blisters or the building sweat. Even if he was still angry with her, she wanted to see Jake. She needed to be with her husband, to feel that she was still on someone's team, that she wasn't in this alone.

She shifted their basil plant out of the way so that she could peer down the companionway into the dark bowels of the boat to find him. The plant was lighter than it should have been, the soil in the pot dry as sand, the leaves desiccated to brittle ribs. Jake was squatting by the engine, plucking at his lower lip, lost in thought. As she watched, he scrubbed his head hard, and then he blew out air, put his face in his hands, and stayed like that. He seemed so forlorn, so diminished, that she wanted to go down there, put her arms around him, to pull him tight against her and tell him everything would be okay. But she knew she was witnessing an intensely private moment, one he didn't intend her to see.

She shifted her weight, deliberately making noise, hoping he'd assume she'd just arrived back. "Jake?"

His head snapped up, focus back in his eyes. "Hi. Productive morning?"

Is that all it had been—a morning? "Yes." How much to tell him? He picked up a piece of sandpaper and folded it to fit inside the cutout in the metal plate he'd crafted. "How about you?" She kept her voice neutral. "Things going well?"

"Yep." As he rubbed, a regular shh-shh-shh filled the boat, a steady muted rhythm like a snare drum.

"Actually, Jake . . ." He was a long way down. She shuffled forward in a squat until the tips of her toes reached past the lip to the air below. "Actually, Stella had a word with me."

"Oh yeah?" He pulled the sandpaper out of the plate and refolded it to expose a fresh surface.

She waited for the grainy noise to come again before she continued, speaking quickly, her words surging as she told him about the fishing trip and Stella's revelation, being careful to edit her story, to say *we* rather than *you*, clarifying that they weren't singling out him, but accusing the two of them together.

The sanding stopped. She expected a string of expletives, but instead he remained still, his head bowed. The paper fell from his fingers. He placed the gasket down, carefully. When he looked up, he looked adrift. "What am I supposed to do? Fish or fix this?"

"I know, I—"

"Who was it who complained? Roly? I had a feeling he didn't like me."

"No, I don't think it was Roly . . ."

"Vitor, then." He hit the floor with the side of his fist so hard that the gasket jumped. "He's always had it in for me."

"Not Vitor. He's . . ." Now wasn't the time to try to convince him of Vitor's loyalty. She looked away, her lips twisted shut.

"It's bullshit," he said. He stood abruptly, raking both hands through his hair, leaving a black smear on his temple. He strode to the front of the saloon, out of her sight, and back again, his hands still at his head. "What happened to share and share alike?"

She wanted to say that that was kind of the problem, that not sharing was what had caused this issue, but she didn't want to escalate things. Below her, he marched into the galley, disappearing from view again. A moment later he was up through the hatch.

"Come on," he called down through the companionway. There was steel in his voice. Through the space she saw him open the cockpit locker and lift out a bucket and a long, sharp filleting knife. "We're going fishing."

26

Amarante shrank as they blatted across the ocean, slicing a rucked gash through the flat water and shattering the peace with the outboard's loud drone. Jake meant business—he'd reattached the motor, was sacrificing some of the petrol. Virginie clutched at the dinghy handle like a rein and pushed her feet more firmly against the floor of the boat so her thighs could better ride out the shocks. She thought about those motorcyclists in Port Brown who'd come right into the restaurant. What was it about men and machines? Did having some throbbing engine under their control make them feel like gods?

When they reached the place where Pete had taken them to fish, Jake dropped the revs and yanked the kill cord from its slot, stopping the outboard dead. There was the rushing surf of the boat's wake and then, as the dinghy lost its forward momentum, nothing. She eased her grip and worked some feeling back into her fingers. Her legs were trembling, and the racing of her pulse was even faster in the stillness. "Feel better now?"

"What?" He was already scrambling past her, reaching for the reel.

"Was that really necessary, going so bloody fast?"

"It was fine. I was in control."

She watched him untangle the lure. Technically, they *were* fine, and he *had* been in control. Damn him for being right.

They trolled for an hour in silence, sitting on opposite sides at the back of the dinghy, Jake fishing, Virginie steering. He barely looked at her. She became convinced he was holding her responsible for their situation. After all, if they'd been anywhere else in the Indian Ocean right now, not Amarante, the engine problem wouldn't be such a big deal. They'd have had access to mechanics, could have put *Wayfinder* in a marina while everything got sorted out.

Jake's shoulders were reddening under the sun. She started to say something, then thought better of it. In their haste to leave the yacht they hadn't brought any T-shirts or sunblock. Oh God, it was difficult to know what to say, what to do, to know whether she actually *was* being blamed for something.

Jake threw the reel and empty line to the bottom of the dinghy. "For fuck's sake."

A week or so ago, when they'd gone fishing with Stella and Pete, whether they caught anything or not hadn't really been important. Nor had time mattered—not that day, or the week before, or the one before that, all the way back to when they stepped off the plane. But now, every day without the engine counted for so much. They couldn't afford to waste hours here, catching nothing. Something Vitor had said to Jake on the beach the night she'd caught her fish came to her— try somewhere different. She steered north.

Jake had to shout over the roar of the outboard. "Where are we going?"

She indicated with her head, raised her voice as well. "To the far reef." He'd object, she knew, but she had her answer ready. "Sailors' stories and superstitions be damned. And that goes for rules and regulations, too. They've got us nowhere so far."

A shadow of greenish-gray under the surface told her they'd reached the spot. He had the lure in the water as soon as she slowed, and this time the line went tight within minutes, the reel clunking his hand against the back of the boat.

"Vee!" he called, but she was already throttling right back.

The muscles in his jaw worked as he wound in the line. "Come on, come on," she urged under her breath. He needed to land this fish; she needed him to land this fish. It was more than just food now. The moment, its significance, mushroomed. It was as if she were watching the ball clatter around a spinning roulette wheel, waiting for it to drop into a slot. Come on, come on.

If Jake landed this fish, he'd fix the engine.

If he landed this fish, they'd have water; their friendships would be repaired.

Land this fish and their marriage would survive.

Come on, come on.

Land this fish and—

Yes! There it was. Shining in the sun, dangling from the line. She closed her eyes for a moment, afraid she'd imagined it. But then he whooped, and she opened her eyes, and there, flapping about in the bucket, was a huge silver fish, far bigger than the one she'd caught before, bucking and glorious. He'd done it.

He was already checking the hook and casting it back into the sea. "Why'd Pete say not to fish here?" His grin was wider than she'd seen it in ages—here was her old Jake; she'd lured him back to her.

She eased her grip on the tiller. "It's a great spot."

"Sly bastard probably wanted to keep it a secret for himself."

Moments later the line was stretching tight again. He caught two more after that, trolling backwards and forwards across the reef as she tried different speeds to see what attracted the fish the most. As she scooped up the third, spinning on the end of its line, Jake looked up at the sky.

"Sun's going down," he said. "We'd better get going."

•   •   •

The fish bounced as Jake thumped the bucket onto the sand, next to Vitor's icebox. Roly looked up from laying the fire, surprise on his face clear, even in the dusk.

Stella peered into the bucket and clapped. "Bravo!" She seemed genuinely delighted at their success. Virginie let her shoulders drop. At least that was one problem solved.

"Nice work," Pete said.

Jake raised a bottle of cheap Thai whiskey in a mock victory toast— aping the kind of thing Vitor did—and took a deep swig. He'd already made a significant dent in it in a short space of time. She'd known, when he grabbed the bottle from the chart table to take ashore, that this was on the cards. How she'd been able to predict it she wasn't sure, because he didn't usually use alcohol like that, as armor. The look on his face she had recognized, though: it was the same one her father wore when he was between commissions, worrying he'd never paint again, when he sank into a bottle like a melancholy genie who wanted to be trapped, be insulated from the world.

She edged away, taking the bucket with her. Let him get it out of his system this way if he must, but she wasn't going to watch him drink himself into oblivion.

Pete came over to her. "He okay?"

"He's fine." She jiggled the bucket by way of changing the subject. "What's the best way to cook these, do you think?"

She was kneeling on the sand, using the light of the fire to follow Pete's suggestion to thread their catch onto sticks to roast, when Vitor appeared.

He crouched next to her. "Yours? You went fishing this afternoon?"

Jake spoke from behind them. "That's right." She heard the challenge in it. She turned. Jake eyed Vitor, looking along the length of his bottle as if it were the barrel of a gun.

Vitor rose and slapped him on the shoulder. "But this is excellent news." She caught Jake's wince. With his sunburn, the slap must have smarted. Vitor gestured up at the night sky, where the full moon hung, fat and glistening. "I also made a good catch today. It is the effect of the moon. It draws up the fish. Makes it easy."

She closed her eyes against the pair of them.

"Let us celebrate," Vitor said. "Have a party. It has been too long." The chink that followed was of bottle against glass, but somehow it sounded like a key turning in a lock.

She didn't want any alcohol. After all that time in the dinghy in the sun, she needed to rehydrate. She dug in her bag for a bottle of decanted coconut water. It had rolled beneath everything else in there—the drawing stuff she hadn't felt like using since she'd sketched Vitor, the carved bowl she'd found on East Beach. After taking a couple of deep swallows, she screwed the lid tight, keeping the bag with her so Vitor couldn't lace it with rum. At dinner, she sat on the opposite side of the fire from Jake. Stella was the last to sit, plopping down uninvited next to her. She made a point of taking one of their fish, holding up her leaf to show Jake. "It's good," she called over.

To his credit, he sent her a proper smile back. In the firelight he looked flushed.

Stella leaned in close to Virginie. "Everyone really appreciates it, Vee. Thanks for talking to him."

She didn't know what to say. She poked at her fish, unable to eat. The way their eyes had blistered to an opaque white while they were roasting made her feel sick.

"Hey," Stella nudged her. "Look."

Virginie followed the line of Stella's thumb to the edge of the trees. Vitor and Teresa were there. One look at their body language— Teresa with her hands on her hips, Vitor jabbing a finger in the air— and she knew they were arguing. They were quiet with it, though, their voices little more than a hiss, different from how she'd heard them that night on *Santa Maria*. That had felt fresh, passionate; this was frayed.

He made a grab for the little bag she often carried, tipped it upside down so something fell to the sand. Teresa picked it up, and there was a flash of blue. Her phone. She tapped at the screen, waved it in his face. He threw up a hand and began to walk away. She ran after him, pushing the phone at him again. He shook her off. She followed him into the jungle.

"What do you think?" Stella said. Gus came over, and she fed him a scrap of her fish.

Virginie clawed her toes into the sand. She had the feeling Stella was prying, that she thought Virginie had insider knowledge or was even somehow to blame. She didn't want to get involved in village gossip. There must be something in the air today. Accusations, arguments. "I don't know. Couples argue." First she and Jake were fighting, now Vitor and Teresa. Only Stella and Pete were immune. The claustrophobia was getting to people. "It's not our business."

She took herself off for a walk, her bag thumping against her hip. The moon lit the way ahead, turning the sandy track silver, a glimmering trail. She was like Gretel, following the way, except the way was leading to the prison ruins, not to home. The soundtrack she'd heard on their first night here—the crickets, the tree frogs, the waves on the beach—was playing, as if on repeat. It struck her that anyone—everyone—who had been to Amarante—fifty years ago, a hundred, a thousand—would have heard exactly the same thing. She reached the clearing, pressed on to the fourth building. Time did strange things here. It concertinaed, contracting at some points, like now, expanding at others. A day that felt like a month; a century held in a moment.

She stopped at the graves. There was no eeriness; the air was still, calm, with more moonlight breaking through than she would have expected. Hot, she reached for her drink.

Sometimes school seemed so close. How had ten years gone like that? Christ, not ten—thirteen. Could that really be? She drained the bottle, slipped it into her bag. Is that what it was like for the prisoners, too? Did their lives at home, with their families, feel as if they were just yesterday, or had being here extended time, opened a chasm between the past and the present? She took out the coconut bowl, flipped it over and over. The silvery light threw the carvings into relief, making the turtle look as if it were following a moonbeam into the ocean. It belonged here, not in a museum. She stooped and placed the bowl toward the top of the nearest grave. An inadequate gesture, she knew, but it was all she could do.

Back at the beach, she found only the dying embers of the fire. She was bone tired and wanted to go home, but she'd lost Jake—he'd wandered off somewhere. She walked to the dinghy parking spot in case he was waiting. Theirs and Vitor's were the only ones left.

Vitor was ankle-deep in the water, unburying his anchor. "Everything is okay?"

"Do you know where Jake's got to?"

He shrugged. "You want me to take you back?"

"I should find him, really." She did a couple more turns on the sand.

Vitor's gaze was still on her. He cleared his throat. "Well, I was just about to return to *Santa Maria*."

No sign of Jake. Maybe he was sleeping off the rum under a palm tree. If she let Vitor give her a lift and left their dinghy on the beach, Jake'd still be able to get back to *Wayfinder* when he woke up—and sobered up. "Okay then, yes, please." She was knee-deep before she thought to ask where Teresa was.

Vitor was facing away from her as he pulled on the line, drawing the tender closer toward them, into the shallows. "Roly took her back earlier."

He must be right—Roly's dinghy was gone. After their row she'd probably wanted to go home, too.

They rode in silence, the bay charcoal gray, the reflection of the moon barely wrinkled. When they got halfway, Vitor slowed the engine to an idle and offered her a nightcap on *Santa Maria*. "You have not been yourself lately. Tonight should have been a triumph. And Jake . . ." He let his words tail off.

She thanked him but asked him to take her home. "I really just need to be on my own."

What time Jake came back, she didn't know. The unfamiliar vibration of the dinghy propeller woke her, and when she heard him clattering about on deck, she held her breath. Would he join her in the cabin? Her pulse quickened in anticipation, but there was a thump as he dropped through the forehatch onto a saloon settee and then nothing. She lay awake, staring out at the stars, for the longest time.

27

Frantic knocking woke her up. Light filled the cabin, and the clock on the wall showed it was gone eight. From outside, someone—a man, Pete—was calling her name. Before she could clamber off the bed and get through the galley, he had already come on board and dropped down the companionway, despite the lack of stairs. He looked crazed: wide-eyed and unable to stand still.

"It's Stella," he said, lifting off his baseball cap, putting it back on again.

Her stomach dropped. "What is it? What's happened?

He eyed Jake, who was asleep on the port-side settee, his feet jammed against the chart table. "She's really sick. Vomiting, headaches, chills. I can't get her to keep anything down, not even water." His cap came off, and he worried the peak with his hands. "I've tried everything I can think of, but I've never seen her like this."

It wasn't like him to be so panicked. "I'll come." She moved the steps and bolted them in place. From the settee came a groan as Jake stirred. Alcohol fumes rolled off him as he levered himself up to sit. A triangle of sunlight seesawed back and forth across his sunburned shoulder with the tiny movements of the boat.

He rubbed his face. "What's going on?"

"Stella's ill." She strained to keep impatience out of her voice. Not in front of Pete, not now. "I'm going to see if I can help."

"Wait." He stood, teetering. "I'll drive you."

"I'll go with Pete," she repeated, putting a hand out to push him back onto the settee. She wasn't going to let him try to make amends that easily. She wanted to talk to him, properly talk, but that would have to wait. "You come when you're sober."

She nodded at Pete and they headed up.

The first sign that something was seriously wrong was the state of *Swallow*'s saloon. It looked like it had been ransacked: locker doors hung open, and the back cushions had been ripped off the seats, exposing the maws of the storage holds behind. Bandages, blister packs of medication, and first aid manuals lay scattered across the chart table.

Pete led the way to the small forward cabin. Stella lay crossways on the wedge-shaped bed, twisted in a white sheet, her hair stringy with sweat. Pete was right—this didn't look like a hangover. As she watched, Stella uncurled to scratch at her forearm, scouring white lines on her skin that reddened quickly. On the floor next to her, a bucket filled the air with the stench of vomit.

"Stella," Virginie said, skirting the bucket and reaching for her friend. Stella's skin was gray, sodden, and at the contact she jerked away and hugged herself tightly, as if to keep warm.

"How long has she been like this?" Virginie asked Pete.

"Came on halfway through the night. She said she had a headache and felt dizzy, and then she started throwing up. Her whole body was convulsing."

"Has she drunk any water?"

He nodded. "A little. But she couldn't keep it down, and now she keeps pushing me away, telling me it'll make her throw up. I don't know what to do." He hurled his cap onto the settee.

She knew only the basics of first aid, but enough to understand that dehydration was a real risk in a hot place like this. Touching him on the arm, she slipped past to the chart table, where she rooted among the first aid kit until she found a sachet of rehydration powder. The paper packet was crinkly between her fingers, and when she turned it over, she saw the expiry date was long past. She raked through the kit again; it was the only one. It would have to do.

"Boil the kettle," she told Pete. "Put a cup of water in your freezer to cool it down as quickly as you can, and then mix this in." He came to take the sachet. "Let's concentrate on getting that into her while we work out what's wrong."

The gas ignition on the stove clicked as she returned to the cabin. Stella hadn't moved from her fetal position. Virginie smoothed back the hair from her fevered forehead. "Stella, I'm here. Let's get you onto your back, see if we can cool you down."

Stella shook her head and pulled the sheet tighter around herself. "Cold." Her teeth chattered on the word.

When the boiled water had cooled, and Pete had stirred in the powder, Virginie coaxed Stella into a half-sitting position. The tremor in Stella's hands was so bad that some of the liquid sloshed from the cup onto the bed and wet the sheet, turning it near transparent. She helped her hold the cup steady and guided it to her lips, encouraging her to take a sip.

Stella gasped and pushed it away. "It's boiling!"

Pete had only just taken the cup out of the freezer. It'd had long enough, shouldn't still be hot. Virginie dipped her little finger in to check. Definitely cool. She looked up, ready to get her to try again, but Stella lunged for the edge of the bed and vomited. After she collapsed back on the mattress, Pete picked up the bucket to take it on deck and empty it over the side.

She wrapped her fingers around the handle. "I'll do it," she said. "You stay with her."

The fresh air and sunlight were a welcome relief after the confines of the cabin, and she inhaled deeply. Up here, everything looked just as normal. Calm, bright, focused. She tipped the contents of the bucket into the sea and rinsed it with salt water, trying to ignore the fish that swarmed up to feed. Could it be a stomach bug, or food poisoning? For the second time since they'd left Port Brown, she wished they had a phone signal, so she could google how to best treat Stella, or ring a doctor for advice.

At a noise she looked across the bay. Vitor was leaving *Santa Maria* in his tender. He was alone. When he saw her on *Swallow*, he waved and pointed the boat's nose toward her, but he must have known from her expression that something was wrong because he asked what was going on as soon as he came alongside.

"Stella's really sick," she said.

"Do you think it is something contagious?"

God, that hadn't occurred to her. "Are you all right?"

"Yes," Vitor said.

"And Teresa?"

"We are fine." A pause. It looked like their argument was still ongoing. He pushed his sunglasses up the bridge of his nose. "You?"

"I'm okay. Jake is, too." Apart from his hangover.

"And Roly?"

Virginie looked over to the Australian's boat. His dinghy was still tied to the back of it. "I haven't seen him this morning."

"Well, perhaps it is some kind of food poisoning and it will soon pass."

"I thought that. But the fish was well cooked—you saw." She remembered how the skins had blackened on the fire, and those blistered eyes. "Oh, I don't know. She's pretty ill." She peered down the companionway. "I'd better go. Pete's not dealing with it very well."

Vitor started his engine. "Let me know if you need any help."

She took a deep breath and went back down below.

•   •   •

A knock came through *Swallow*'s hull—but she didn't dare leave Stella to see who it was. She had got worse over the past hour—there was now a wheezing that the inhaler didn't help, and she was alternating between shrieking and muttering to herself while her eyes roved round the cabin, following something only she could see. Virginie held her hands and tried to calm her, but nothing she did had an effect anymore. She felt useless, as wrung out as the washcloth Stella had knocked from her hand onto the floor.

From behind came footsteps on the stairs, then Jake's voice. "What's happening?"

She looked over her shoulder. "She's hallucinating."

"What?"

She turned back to Stella. "We think it's some kind of bug, or food poisoning."

"What kind of food poisoning causes hallucinations?"

Pete edged past them into the cabin and sat on the bed. "You're going to be all right, honey," he murmured, reaching for Stella's hair. She jerked away, as she had done earlier with Virginie. He recoiled, as if she'd physically hurt him, but when he tried a second time, Stella allowed him to touch her. He didn't let go of her again.

Virginie looked for Jake. He'd come closer and was just on the other side of the doorway. They locked eyes.

"Are you feeling sick?" he asked her.

She shook her head. "You?"

"No. What about everyone else? *Santa Maria*? *Ariel*?"

Pete said, "Vitor and Teresa are fine. No one's seen Roly yet."

Here was something useful she could do. She pushed herself up to standing. "Will you be okay here with her if I go check on Roly?" she asked Pete, who nodded. She backed out of the cabin, Jake right behind her, and Stella's cries followed them up the steps, only fading when they reached the sunlight.

•   •   •

Ariel floated green and serene on her bed of crystalline water, the sea so clear that the sun had thrown a shadow of the outline of her hull onto the white sand below. The stillness, after the drama of *Swallow*, was uncanny.

Virginie sat right on the bow of the dinghy, as if by being as far forward as she could, she'd get there sooner. Jake had already removed the outboard again, so he heaved on the oars, driving them deep into the sea. As the dinghy lurched across the bay, she tore at a hangnail with her teeth, ripping it away and rolling the husk of dry skin between her fingertips, circling it round and round.

They made their final approach, and Jake pulled the oars out of the water to coast. Something was off. She couldn't quite pinpoint what it was, but *Ariel* was definitely different. As soon as the dinghy touched the yacht she climbed aboard. "Roly?" There was no response. Please don't let him be huddled up in his bed, hallucinating like Stella—or worse. Christ, don't think like that. She tightened her jaw and headed for the stairs.

Roly was standing in his galley, pouring water from a pan into a yellow plastic bowl, the picture of health. She released the breath she'd been holding. "You're fine! Why didn't you answer me when I called?"

Jake came down the stairs, and still Roly didn't reply. He didn't look up, either, just carried on pouring the water.

"Roly, Stella's sick," she said. "It's pretty bad. We came over to check on you, make sure you were okay. Obviously you are." Silence. What was the matter with him? "Roly? I said Stella's really ill—"

She stopped as he pushed past her, the familiar tang of sweat trailing. He bent over the saloon table, his back to her, his body obscuring what he was doing. A rasping noise was coming from somewhere.

Lost for what else to say, she looked around the saloon. It was bare as a monk's cell: no photos of family on the shelves, no trinkets from past adventures hanging from the walls. The only spot of color came from Gus's pink ball, wedged next to a toolbox on a shelf underneath the window.

"Come on," Jake said to Roly. "I know we've had our differences, but don't take this out on Vee. Or Stella." Roly ignored him, too.

She slipped round to the far side of the table, Jake following. And then she saw what Roly was doing.

Gus lay on the table, his ears back, body shaking, tremors coming in waves. The rasping noise was him gasping for breath. Roly cradled his head and tilted his muzzle, letting a couple of drops of water fall from the bowl onto his tongue. Gus swallowed, and the effort of doing so cost him. He slumped, exposing a patch of neck that had been scratched so raw that the gray skin welled with beads of dark blood.

That was it. That was what was different when they pulled alongside *Ariel*. No little dog running up to greet them, barking a welcome. She reached across the table and cradled a paw. It was so limp it was almost weightless.

Roly stroked Gus's flank, his compass rose tattoo flexing every time he lifted his hand. "Poisoned," he said. "Looks like ciguatera. Must have been the fish last night."

"Pete thought poisoning," Jake said. "But the fish was all cooked through."

"You can't kill ciguatera by cooking." Roly sighed, his eyes fixed on the dog. "Always a risk, in a place like this."

Gus's paw quivered in her hand as he tried to work up the energy to scratch himself again. She stroked his leg and laid it gently back on the table.

"Don't understand it, though," Roly said. "I fed him my leftovers and I'm fine. But if Stella's sick, too . . . reckon that must be it."

The cabin walls rushed in. Virginie stumbled, and Jake's hand came to her back. Were they to blame for this? Stella had taken one of the fish they'd caught and given a little of it to Gus. He'd licked his lips afterwards, hoping for more. She glanced at Jake, but wasn't sure he'd worked it out.

"Roly . . ." She stopped. Made herself carry on. "Stella gave him some of her fish."

He looked up. "How much?"

"Only a small piece."

"How much is small?" He leaned in. "A fillet? A half?"

She held out her little finger.

Roly regained a little of his composure. He stroked Gus tenderly. "He's a strong bugger. Always has been. Used to take on mutts much bigger than him when he was a pup." His eyes were soft as he lost himself in reverie. "Christine got him for me. Meant to leave him in Aus when we set sail. Little girl next door took a liking to him, told me her dad had said she could have him. 'Course he changed his mind." He laughed sharply. "If he'd even known about it in the first place. Little minx she was. So Gus came with us, stayed with me when Christine left. Took to sailing well, never got seasick, even on the ocean." He chucked Gus under the chin. "We've had some adventures, haven't we, mate?"

"Roly," she said. "But Gus will . . . I mean, surely he's going to . . . ?"

"Die? Survive?" He offered the dog more water. "I'm no vet, Vee. You tell me. He might fight his way through. What else can you tell yourself? What else can you let yourself believe?"

She looked wildly to Jake. His eyes were widening—now he'd made the connection with their fish, with the far reef. She gripped the edge of the table, knowing she had to ask one more thing. "Roly," she said, "Stella ate much more of it. The same fish as Gus."

"And how is she? Like this?"

Her stomach tightened. "Worse."

28

Virginie hung back as they boarded *Swallow* again. "Just wait a minute," she told Jake. "Can we think this through?"

He had lifted the awning so they could pass into the cockpit. He let it drop. "Vee, we have to tell him."

"And we will. In a second. It's just . . ." Everything was real and unreal at the same time. Time had sped up—she couldn't gather her thoughts quickly enough. "It's just I don't want to scare him unnecessarily."

"Unnecessarily? I think it might be beyond that."

"We don't know that. Not for sure." She stopped. Wiped her clammy palms on her thighs. How to explain what she meant, that she didn't want to break Pete's heart if there was even the slightest possibility that they might be wrong about the severity of the poisoning? They might be catastrophizing. There was a chance it wasn't as bad as it seemed. The way those two looked at each other. All that they'd been through.

"Look," she said. "I just mean we need to gather the facts. I'll get the first aid books. We'll look it up, see what we can do to help her."

His hands went to his head.

"It'll only take a few minutes."

"Fine. But then we tell Pete."

She ducked under the awning and crept down the stairs. Pete was on the settee near the forecabin, fiddling with the same piece of hair over and over, and she could see through the cabin doorway that Stella had at last fallen mercifully asleep. Maybe she'd got it out of her system, was already getting better.

As quietly as she could, she picked up two first aid manuals from the chart table and went back up to the cockpit, to where Jake was waiting, staring at the compass.

"Here," she said, passing him the top book. She skimmed through the index of her own manual, checking first under *S* and then, realizing her mistake, *C*. Ciguatera. The pages sent up a puff of air as she flicked to the correct section. *Marine neurotoxin*, she read, *accumulating in fish that live in coral reef waters*. Sweat ran into her eyes, making the words swim on the page. She blinked it away. *Undetectable. Cannot be destroyed by cooking*. So Roly was right, there. She ran her finger down the page, searching for the section on symptoms. *Vomiting, fever, temperature reversal, hallucinations*. Stella had all of those. She jumped to the heading *Prognosis*: *Rarely fatal*. Thank God. She held the manual to her chest for a second like a prayer book.

But when she started to read again, a section of text caught her eye. *Can cause respiratory failure, especially in susceptible patients*. Stella's asthma. She dropped to a bench. *Seek immediate medical attention*. How immediate was immediate? They were two weeks from Port Brown, and at least five days from anywhere else. No doctor, no air ambulance, as the official in Port Brown had made clear. An image of the prisoners' graves in the center of Amarante came unbidden into her mind.

"Jake . . ."

His expression was grim. He must have read the same thing. "We have to tell him right now." She swallowed and nodded.

"Tell me what?" Pete asked, so close that she jumped. They hadn't made an effort to keep their voices down.

Pete came up the last few steps into the cockpit, and Jake faced him. "Gus is poisoned, too," he said, quietly. "He's in a bad way, shivering, gasping for breath. Roly thinks it's ciguatera."

"How did we end up with a fish with ciguatera?"

Jake and Virginie exchanged looks. "Actually, Pete," she said, "they both ate our fish, Stella and Gus."

He jerked, as if punched.

Jake took a deep breath. "We got it from the far reef."

"The far reef? Where I told you not to go?"

"We . . . I assumed it was just a silly superstition. Surely the ciguatera could have come from any reef, any fish—"

"Silly?" Pete advanced toward them, flushed a dark red, enormous in the tiny cockpit. "Why would you take the risk?"

Jake held up both of his hands. "There's something else."

"What?"

Virginie stood. She would tell Pete. Jake had already been the fall guy for what had been her decision to go to the far reef, her choice to take the risk; she couldn't let him take all the blame. "Stella's asthma makes her more vulnerable."

Pete searched her eyes for the longest time, and then he crumpled onto the seat. She knelt on the floor next to him. "Listen," she said. "It doesn't mean that Stella will . . ." She couldn't finish the sentence. "She's strong, she'll fight it."

Pete's head was hanging low, his face turned away from her in the direction of the coach roof and, beyond it, the cabin, Stella. He shook his head.

"But the book does say that there's an extra risk for people with respiratory problems. So we need to get her to a hospital. Sri Lanka's the closest." Not that close—it was six hundred miles, and with the currents *Swallow* could probably only manage a hundred, a hundred and twenty miles a day. She didn't know how she was managing to keep her voice level, to sound so matter of fact, when inside her mind was screeching, Five days away, *five days*. There was no other option—they had to set sail now and pray they got Stella to land in time. Surely Sri Lankan hospitals were good, experienced at this sort of thing? She reached for Pete's sleeve. At her touch, he sprang from his seat and jumped down the stairs, taking the whole lot in one go. He understood.

She spun to Jake. "Can you go back to *Wayfinder* and grab me a bag of clothes and my passport?"

"What? Why?"

"Pete can't sail the boat and look after Stella. I'll have to go with him."

"To Sri Lanka? How will you get back here?"

"I don't know," she said. "I'll figure something out." She glanced down the companionway. She hugged herself, suddenly cold. She'd forced Jake to go fishing. She'd taken them to the far reef. Stella had picked that fish to please her. She needed to do something to help make it right. "Please."

Pete came rushing up the stairs, barreling into Jake in his haste to get to the engine panel. *Swallow* came to life immediately.

"I'll go with them," Jake told her, raising his voice above the noise. "It was my fish that poisoned her. I can sail the boat while Pete looks after her."

"You can't and you know you can't," she said as Pete barged past them to go downstairs again. "You need to fix that engine. You have to stay here. So it's me." From his expression she could tell he was desperately seeking a counterargument. But she had to do this. "Please, Jake." She kept her eyes on his. He wiped his mouth and she took that as agreement.

Pete returned with the control for the anchor windlass in his hand and started for the bow. He couldn't manage by himself. It was madness. She ran after him. "I'm coming with you." She clutched at his arm.

"No," he said, shucking her off and striding forward.

She tried again. "Pete—"

"I said no!" He was shouting now. "And I mean no. You've both done more than enough." He hurled the words over his shoulder, and when she saw the fury, the blame, on his face, she stopped.

She turned and ran, past Jake, down the steps, into the boat. There was no way she was abandoning Stella. Pete would have to physically throw her off this yacht. She'd told him herself: Stella is strong, Stella will fight. Stella would survive this. They'd get to the hospital, and everything would be fine. He'd see. It'd all be fine.

It was dark below, and noise was coming at her from two directions—from behind, the engine roaring; from forward, the chain thundering up through the windlass and crashing into the locker as Pete raised the anchor. It was overwhelming, and halfway through the saloon she faltered. Her hand was at the mast; the aluminum was cool, and she pressed her forehead against it, letting it temper the spot between her eyes. She took a steadying breath and lifted her head to look through the doorway into the forepeak cabin.

Everything dropped away.

29

Afterwards, they fought with Pete about what to do with her, with her body. He wanted to take Stella home—but Jake pointed out, as delicately as he could, that that wasn't possible. *Swallow* didn't, as he put it, "have the facilities." In the end, Pete dug the grave himself, carried her over there, covered her again. He forbade anyone from stepping foot on Amarante while he worked, but Virginie kept a vigil from her cockpit all afternoon, staring at the line of trees so long they blurred. She wasn't sure she'd ever forget the sight of him emerging from the jungle onto the beach, head hanging, tread heavy, shovel in hand.

The next morning, when she woke, *Swallow* was gone—and so was *Ariel*.

"They went at first light," Vitor told her. "Roly took Teresa with them."

It was inevitable, really, that Roly would go. And, to her shame, partly a relief. She wasn't sure she could have faced him again after Stella, coped with the look of blame that would have been plain on his face. He'd have had every right, of course. He'd made the rules perfectly clear.

She realized Vitor had said *them*. So Gus was alive. It was small consolation, but something at least. And Teresa gone, too. Their argument must have been a big one for it to come to that.

Vitor answered before she could ask. "She wanted to leave."

"Are you okay?"

He looked away. "Things were not well with us. And she is free to make her own choices. She and Roly were friends—you saw. I told her, 'Go, if you want.' So she did—she packed her suitcases and she went."

Vitor seemed remarkably sanguine about it, but perhaps reality hadn't kicked in yet for him. In a way, she could understand his flat reaction—she didn't have the energy to feel upset that no one had said goodbye, that they had slipped silently away in the dawn. She didn't deserve anything more. First there were four boats; now there were two.

Time moved treacle-slow, and the thick, never-ending hours weighed on her as heavily as mounded earth. In her dream it was she who lay buried in the dry dirt of the island, not Stella; she who burrowed laterally through the ground seeking the osseous hands of the other prisoners.

But in another dream, she, Virginie, was sailing, off, off, off, away toward the thin blue line. Stella wasn't there, nor Pete, not even Jake; it was just her, alone. That was the best dream, because of the release it brought. When she woke there was half a second of relief, where everything was normal, before reality set in, hard as bone.

Vitor came over to see how they were. "Fine," she said, not meeting his eye.

Jake wasn't fine, either; he was anything but, and she didn't know how to reach him. The day the others left mania had come over him, even worse than before, and he spent hours in the engine bay, working long past sunset, so that the white light of his head torch swung across the saloon like a miner's searching for a seam of gold. The next morning was the same, until he dashed up on deck and tried the ignition and got nothing, and then, gradually, the mania had worn off, replaced with despondency. Her attempts to talk to him were rebuffed or, worse, ignored, and she gave up, too numb to care.

• • •

It was mid-afternoon when she woke, gluey-mouthed and sticky-skinned, from yet another nap. In the galley she pumped the floor pedal to get water from the tap. It came out in a series of thin spurts, and when she brought the glass to her lips, the plastic taste told her their last tank was all but empty. The realization hit her as hard as a slap and jarred her into action. She'd dig up Vitor's water containers now, and deal with Jake's anger later.

Anchorage Beach was abandoned, the only sound the never-ending screech of the insects. A single set of footprints going into the jungle and out again told her Vitor had been there since the high tide. It could only be him; there was no one else. She left the dinghy in the usual place and headed inland.

Every part of this island was so familiar to her now that when she reached the ruins the mound of dirt was immediately obvious. Pete had picked a spot on the nearside of the other graves, midway between two palms. She tiptoed closer. He'd done his best to pack down the earth and had fashioned a crude cross from young branches bound together with palm fronds. Beetles were already chewing it away. She'd brought nothing, and there were no flowers to pick. For a while she remained there, as the insects chanted their plainsong all around. She searched inside for feelings of grief but found only a blankness.

At East Beach there was no pair of upended sticks, but she was confident she remembered the right place. She picked her way between the lines of dried weed and rubbish and dropped to the rough sand. The first dig yielded nothing, even though she gouged deep with both hands. She stood up to survey the area, and now she was looking at it, remembered that lately this had become one of Roly's favorite areas for collecting firewood. Shit. No, she couldn't let herself believe that he might have taken her markers. She just had it wrong. They'd fallen over, that was all. She went to the nearest stick, knelt, and burrowed, expecting to see the plastic tops of the containers any minute. Nothing. She tried a few inches farther along, scooping faster this time, sand flying backwards as she worked. A fingernail ripped right down to the quick. Nothing there, either. Perhaps she wasn't going deep enough. She redoubled her efforts, digging again and again in different places, moving on every few minutes when she hadn't found what she was looking for.

By the time she quit, the surface of the beach was pockmarked with scoured pits, and the skin on her hands and knees red raw. She sat on her heels, panting, and tried to get her mind to work properly— Think, Virginie!—but nothing clicked into place.

She stood, wiping her brow with the back of an arm, and moved to the shade at the edge of the jungle. Bringing the damaged nail to her mouth, she gnawed at its rough edges until she tasted blood. God, she was thirsty. She whirled around, searching for fallen coconuts that she could carry back to Anchorage Beach, where Jake kept the machete at the Y-shaped tree. Even though she'd never tried cutting open a coconut before, she'd attempt anything right now. But only the fibrous remains of old husks littered the ground. She'd have to knock one down from a tree.

A surge of energy came from nowhere, and she ran back across the island. Jake's bamboo pole, the one he used to poke the coconuts out of the palms, was there, along with the machete. Staggering a little under its weight, she went to the nearest fruiting palm, extended the pole upwards until its tip brushed against the bottom of the lowest of a cluster of yellow coconuts, and then drove both arms upwards, as hard as she could. The pole skewed sideways, knocking into the trunk of the next tree along. The second time the tip skidded off into a palm leaf. She had to admit it—it was too much for her; she couldn't control it.

The short burst of energy drained away. Her head was heavy; the inside of her mouth ropy, brassy. She let the pole slide through her grip, but when the bottom hit the ground, the force jarred her hands

and brought her round a little. She'd try again. She had to. Widening
her stance, she took a few deep breaths, let out a cry, and rammed with
all her might, channeling everything she had, everything she'd been
feeling for weeks—for years—through her arms and up into the tree,
over and over and over again.

And then Vitor was there, in front of her, taking the bamboo from
her to toss it aside and grabbing her by the shoulders. His lips were
moving. He was shouting her name, but she couldn't hear because she
was still howling. She brought her hand to her mouth, began to sob.

He pulled her into his chest. "Virginie. What is wrong?"

She couldn't answer. So much was wrong. Stella, their water supplies, the engine. Trying to be strong for Jake, not letting him know
how worried she was, not adding even more pressure for him to get
the job done—they were all taking their toll.

Vitor held her tight. She closed her eyes and listened to the lullaby
tone of his murmured words, relaxing against his chest, inhaling his
scent. Eventually the tears stopped.

"Virginie," he said, in a low voice, "you know I want to help you. I
do not like to see you like this." He rubbed her shoulder. "Now is not
the time for pridefulness. Come with me."

She pulled back enough so that she could look into his eyes.

"I mean it," he said. "Leave Amarante and come with me."

The world tracked out and zoomed in again. Could they? *Wayfinder* was their home. Their life savings were invested in her—if they
left her behind, they'd lose everything. And not just their belongings
and their money but also their dream. The life they wanted to build
together. Their future. It would crush Jake.

But things had gone too far. She'd been offered a way out. It was
madness to turn it down.

"Thank you," she said, pressing her cheek again to Vitor's chest
and squeezing him hard. "Really, thank you. How soon can we go?"
She was light-headed with relief. "We'll repay you once we get back

to Port Brown, or wherever you want to drop us. If you want to go tonight or first thing in the morning, we'll pack a bag and we'll come to *Santa Maria* as soon as—" His posture stiffened. She stopped.

He drew back and held her at arm's length. "We? I did not mean the two of you. I meant you alone."

The ground rocked under her feet. She stared at him.

"What?" Surely he didn't mean to maroon Jake?

He didn't answer, and in the silence she felt idiotic. Of course not. How could she even think that of him?

At a crackle, she looked away, grateful to be released from Vitor's gaze. A coconut crab was inching slowly up the palm trunk, testing the way with a scrape and tap of an extended claw like a blind person with a cane. All that armor—that bone-hard shell, those giant club-like claws, the saw-toothed edges on its leading legs as sharp as a serrated knife—and yet here, on this tree, it was so vulnerable. One well-aimed blow with Jake's machete was all it would take.

"Virginie," Vitor said as she watched the crab, "why do you think I stay here, day after day, in this place where there is nothing? I am here for you. I am waiting for you. I thought you understood that. I thought . . ."

The crab was at shoulder height now, lifting its legs gingerly one at a time, as if it understood the jeopardy. Yet it continued to climb determinedly toward the coconuts she couldn't reach.

She turned back to Vitor. What did she think of this man, really? What did she feel for him, if she was truly honest with herself? A few times—more than a few—she'd sensed something from him, she knew, but she'd always dismissed their mild flirting as a form of friendly playfulness. But it was more than that, for him. Had she wanted it to be more, all this time?

"Vitor," she said, and when he heard the sympathy in her voice, he hung his head, nodding as if he'd already known what her answer would be. The hem of his shirt fluttered, flickering like a luffing sail.

She watched it for a moment before she understood what she was seeing. Breeze. She looked out to sea. Were those cirrus clouds above the
horizon? Was the monsoon changing? No, it wasn't due yet. It couldn't
be cloud. It was a reflection off the reef. Or a mirage.

She rubbed her eyes with the heels of her hands. She was so tired,
it was hard to keep her focus and work out the meaning of what he
was saying. "But what about Teresa?"

"What about her?" he said to the ocean. "She is gone—I told you."

"And Jake—"

He snorted. "You know, surely," he said, "that Jake is never going
to fix your engine? That it is lost?"

The change in his manner threw her. "Lost?"

"A—how do the English say it? A lost cause."

"He says he can do it." Even she knew she didn't sound convinced.

"I am sure he does." He tipped his head to one side, eyeing her.
"But do you really believe that?"

She wanted to defend Jake, but a lump had formed in her throat,
and it choked down the words.

"Can you really trust," Vitor said, "that he will not let you down?
This boy who wants so much to be a man like Pete, like Roly, a man
who can build, who can hunt, who can provide." He swung an arm
around, taking in the island and, with it, her. "But he cannot fish, he is
frightened to swim, he cannot even take care of his wife."

Her fingers found her wedding band. Looser these days, it had
slipped down to her knuckle.

"It is a nonsense anyway," Vitor continued, "a silly childhood
dream, like Pinocchio. A real man knows how to get the things that
he needs, that he wants, he takes care of the woman he loves. If he
loves her."

She slid her ring back into place. "Of course he loves me."

He fastened his eyes on hers. "Are you sure? He has deserted you.
He has endangered your life. He has—"

"What? What has he done, exactly? Apart from try his best?"

He came right up to her. "You should ask him. Ask him about Teresa. Ask him about the beach, the night with his drinking, the night I took you back."

A drop. A disconnection from reality. Like on *Swallow*, before Stella.

Then a landing, a plugging-in. Teresa and Jake? Lies. Jake would never. Vitor was twisting things to get his own way. "I don't believe you."

He laughed dryly, and in it she heard her father's laugh, Tomas's. "Believe what you want."

She slapped him. Hard, across the cheek.

And then she ran to her dinghy, dragging it backwards down the sand into the water, scrambling to get away as quickly as she could, off Amarante, away from Vitor and, most of all, from his words.

30

Jake was in the saloon, but not where she'd hoped he would be, crouching by the engine bay, working, fixing it for them, like he'd said he would. His tools were out, jumbled all over the place, but he was lying listlessly on a settee, his toes on the floor, the back of one arm shielding his eyes.

In two strides she was across there, shaking him. "Get up, get up, get up!" She hissed her words, didn't care if he was sleeping. When she grabbed his arm and yanked him to a seated position, he didn't exactly resist, but his limbs were heavy, torpid. "What are you doing?"

"Nothing," he said.

"I can see that." Fury was making it difficult for her to breathe. "How dare you? How dare you! I've been out there all day, trying to find water, trying to help us. And I hoped you were doing the same, down here. I thought that you were . . ." Words failed her. Vitor's comments echoed through her mind—that Jake would let her down, that he couldn't do it, couldn't fix it all this time. And now he didn't even seem to want to try.

At that, her anger fizzled out. She looked around the saloon, at all their things, at what might have been. Their flip-flops, unworn for weeks, were under the chart table. They'd bought them on that first holiday in Greece, picking out identical pairs in separate stores without knowing, and she'd taken that as a sign of how good a match they were. Somehow, despite the rest of the mess, they were still neatly lined up. They looked absurd to her now, as if they belonged to two other people, the kind of people who tidied their shoes, who agreed on things, who had their lives sorted.

When they'd lain in their bed in Lymington, fingers entwined as they planned this adventure, it had never occurred to her that it could come to this, that it could force them apart. It would be such fun, sailing the world on their own boat, they'd agreed. They'd be masters of their own universe, free to do what they wanted, when they wanted. What could be better? All this trip had done was chain them down, lock them into these roles they seemed to have created for themselves—and trap them in this place, this god-awful place that they needed to leave.

She took a long look at Jake—his gaze fixed on the floor, his body motionless. On the shelf behind him was their wedding photo. The memories tumbled in. Their happiness and love for each other, the vows they had made, the faith she had promised. For better, for worse. In sickness and in health. Maybe Jake was depressed, not lazy. She shouldn't be so harsh. She wouldn't give up.

Kneeling, she took his hand and made her voice gentle. "We're out of water, Jake. I know you feel awful, about Stella, about the engine and the watermaker. I do, too." Even the tiniest of words were too big for her mouth. "There's not even a cupful." Fear rose in her again, but she attempted to smother it—falling to pieces wouldn't help either of them. She thought of the breeze, felt another knock of adrenaline. "The wind's building already, Jake, listen. The monsoon's coming. There's almost no time left. We need to find water and get out of here fast."

He hadn't moved; his fingers were limp in hers. Was she even getting through to him? "When I went ashore earlier, it was to find those containers that Vitor gave us." Her face burned with the lie she'd been keeping. "You told me to take them back to him, but I didn't. I took them ashore and buried them, hid them."

She willed him to jump to his feet and demand how dare she lie to him—even fury had to be better than this pit of despair he'd fallen into and was unable to climb out of. But there was just this hunched-shoulder silence, the same glassy stare. She slumped back onto her heels. "I couldn't find them, Jake. I looked and looked and dug and dug, but they weren't there. See my hands." She turned the palms up, to show him how red they were. He glanced at them briefly, then returned his attention to a spot on the sole boards. This couldn't just be despondency. "What's wrong?"

"Nothing," he said to his toes. Then, "Vee, I . . ." He stopped, hung his head even lower.

Something in his demeanor, his body language, sent her core cold. Was what Vitor said true? Jake and Teresa? They'd been so close at that other party. Had she seen the beginning of something?

Everything stopped. She scrambled away from him, until the galley counter bit into her back. Images reared—Jake and Teresa in the moonlight, Jake and Teresa on the sand. She could hear Vitor: *Ask him*.

"Where were you," she said, "the night we caught the fish?"

Now he looked up. "What? I was on the beach, with you."

"After that. After I came back here. You were gone a long time."

He was making his face long, as if he couldn't follow what she was asking him. Or as if he were pretending not to follow.

"Come on, Jake, it's not that hard. We went fishing, we ate, you got shit-faced." The hinge of his jaw worked as he clenched his teeth, swallowing a retort. "What happened next?"

"I took myself off for a walk. Think I passed out for a bit."

Was that defensiveness in his words? Deliberate obfuscation? "And?"

He searched the saloon, as if thinking he'd find the answers among the cupboards and shelves.

Damn him, she would get the truth. "Was Teresa there?"

His eyebrows rose. "Yeah, actually, she was. She found me."

"And?"

"And I took her home?"

Was he asking or telling? He was hiding something. "Then why were you so long?"

He stood and paced away, to the forepeak, paced back again, a hand rubbing the back of his neck. "Look, Vee, I don't really know why you're asking me all this. Or what this has to do with now."

Such a cliché! He was trying to buy time, to work out if he needed to confess. She crossed her arms.

He exhaled, a jagged sigh. "I promised not to say anything. Teresa was upset. She was crying, worried about how she was going to provide for her son. She and Vitor had had a fight, a serious one. About something that happened in Port Brown, some guys Vitor owes money to—she says he's into a lot of shit, and mixed up with some scary people, that he's lying low out here. Remember how he told us he'd switched off his sat phone?"

She huffed a laugh. Lying low! He needed to get real, to stop twisting everything back to Vitor and to stop avoiding the subject. She pulled it back. "So Teresa was crying about her awful boyfriend and you consoled her. How, Jake, how?" She knew it was small fry compared to the engine, to the watermaker, but she needed to know—because it was looking increasingly possible she might die here as a result of her loyalty to this man. This man who probably hadn't been faithful to her and who couldn't get her out of here, either. All of her faith in him was crumbling at once.

He shoved his hands in his pockets, looked to the side. "Great. So now you don't trust me about this, either."

"Vitor told me—"

"I don't care what Vitor told you. You shouldn't care about what Vitor tells you, either. You should care about what *I* tell you." He stepped closer, tapped his chest, full of the energy now that she'd needed to see in him earlier. "You should trust me."

"Trust you!"

He registered the sarcasm and his features hardened. "Actually, let's talk about trust. How many times have you pushed my trust in you? Those late nights with Vitor?"

She twisted away, but he got into her eye line, moving so she couldn't not look at him.

"Choosing him over me—leaving me in the sand, when I felt so awful, to dance with him, like you didn't give a shit about my feelings? Coming back smelling of his shampoo. I told myself, It's not what you think, Jake. She wouldn't." He backed off abruptly, put his hand over his eyes, scrunched up his face. "This fucking place! I wish we'd never come here. I wish we'd never bought a boat, never heard of Amarante."

They'd already had this fight. Would they keep having it, over and over? "Vitor," she said, speaking slowly, "has repeatedly offered to help us." Like when she told him about Stella's ambush over the fishing, she was careful to use the plural in *us*. "Which in your pigheadedness you've refused. He's given us water, stayed behind, when he could have left at any time. And God knows he didn't receive the warmest of welcomes, from you, or Pete, or even Stella. All three of you, ganging up with your holier-than-thou judgement, just because he's not nobly poor. You set yourself against him from the start, and now you won't admit you're wrong. So you're trying to shift the blame."

"I'm not trying to shift anything. I'm just trying to get you to see things for what they are."

"Oh, my eyes are open. It's yours that are closed. I don't care that you want to do this all by yourself, Jake. I don't even care about the boat. It's gone way beyond that." Too far. She felt a tightening in her body, a gripping of resolve that she would find a way out.

She took a breath, ready for action. "I'm going to Vitor." He stared at her. "Jake, did you hear me? I'm going to Vitor."

31

The light was failing as she drew alongside *Santa Maria*, draining life from the sea and sky, bleaching everything gray. She attempted to tie up her dinghy, but her hands fumbled with the line, and it slipped off the end of the cleat. Finally she had it, and she stepped onto the catamaran.

Vitor was sitting at his cockpit table, playing solitaire, as if he'd been filling time, knowing she would come. He put down the card in his hand to regard her across the cockpit, scrutinizing for so long that her skin started to prickle. In her haste to leave *Wayfinder*, she'd forgotten to grab a sarong. She took hold of her own shoulders, crossing her arms over her body, covering up. Then she thought such a position might make her seem vulnerable. She couldn't have that. She needed to look strong. Take control. She let her arms drop.

"So?" Vitor said. He took a slow sip from a glass of water. She heard the ice chink. Clearly he wasn't going to make this easy for her. She considered the best way to start: Begin by apologizing for slapping him? Or get straight to the point? After all, there was nothing to be gained by delaying.

As she moved closer, her cheeks started to flame. "You were right," she said. The dusk was deepening, but enough light remained that she could see his eyebrows lift. "About Jake."

Still he said nothing, but continued to watch her, judge her, making her small under his gaze. She didn't know what to do with her hands; she settled on clasping them in front of her.

"I've come to ask you." She swallowed tightly. "To beg you, really, to take us, both of us. Back to Port Brown. Or to anywhere." She swallowed again. "Please."

He looked at his drink on the table, adjusting its coaster to line up with the edge. Above them, a rope, caught by the wind, began a steady clank that matched her heartbeat.

"I thought when I saw you rowing over here," he said, still focusing on the coaster, "that you had changed your mind. That you had decided to acknowledge that you felt something for me, that you had decided to come to me. I thought I had sensed these feelings in you, Virginie, many times. On the island, here on *Santa Maria*." He stopped fiddling with his drink and looked at her. "But you must be a very good actress because you do not have these feelings, do you?"

"Vitor, I . . ."

He sighed and stood. "No, you do not have these feelings for me. You play along, pretend that you do, because you want something from me. You come here now to ask me to give you something. Again. Virginie, always I am giving you something. You take and take—from me, from the others. Food, water, wine."

That wasn't fair. He'd always offered those things. She'd never asked him directly for anything before.

"You know the rules of the island as well as I do," he continued, "but still you take. And what do you give in return? Nothing. You have accrued quite a debt already. Let us say I agree to what you propose. How would you pay your debt to me this time?"

Debt? Okay, so he'd given them more than they had him, but a few snacks, a few gallons of water—what did they matter compared to saving two lives? This was insane. The situation was far past petty island rules. "But—"

"But!" he mimicked, and his face turned sour, and she saw no tenderness there, only resentment at not getting his own way. "Look," he said, softening. "I am not cruel. We will leave him food, water." He walked past her to the back of the boat, opened a cockpit locker, and pulled out two white containers, already full, identical to the pair he'd given her before. He placed them just in front of the steps that led down to the sea.

The waves were growing with the wind, slapping against the underside of the catamaran, making it skittish and unstable. He came to stand in front of her, took her hand, and stroked the skin with his thumb. She stayed quiet, thinking. She needed to persuade him to have mercy. "The answer is still no, Vitor," she began. "I'm sorry. Jake is my husband. I love him and I won't abandon him here."

"Love?" He dropped her hand, tapped his fingers on the lid of one of the containers. "What is love, really?" As he talked, he began to unscrew it slowly. She wondered if he was going to pour a glass for her. She licked her cracked lips. "Two halves," he said, "hunting around for all eternity in the hope of making themselves complete?" He sounded objective, philosophical. "Passion and adoration, and a big white wedding? Or security, support, and taking care of the other person?" He lifted the can higher, rested it on the coaming. She cast around but could see no empty cup. "And let us not undermine the prosaic but important elements of obligation and social responsibility." As he said *social responsibility*, he looked at her, and she felt an internal lifting with relief—he was going to help them after all. But then he tilted the container, pouring the water not into a cup, for her, but over the side, into the sea.

She lunged forward, arm outstretched, and screamed, and her scream filled the bay. "Wait! Stop, please stop!" He tipped the container back to cease the flow, but kept it angled over the edge, ready to pour again. "Let me think," she said. "Please."

There would be no more favors, no more gifts, that much was clear; with all his talk of debt and obligations, he was demanding a deal. They had a thousand dollars on *Wayfinder* from their honeymoon fund. She pictured the roll of cash Vitor had flaunted; their money would mean nothing to him. The clanking of the line overhead was louder now, faster, thrumming with agitation. If they were back in the real world, she could have found something to offer, but here she had nothing. Even her words held no value. Amarante had stripped her right back, until she was just a body, utterly powerless to control anything.

Since she'd come on board, *Santa Maria* had swung on her anchor and *Wayfinder* was now in front. She stared at the anchor light, vivid against the background of stars, Cassiopeia just visible beyond.

Overhead, the line continued to frap rhythmically, and a single thought also began to echo in her mind: a body, just a body. Her stomach jolted. Just a body that Vitor wanted.

When she'd faced Jake in the register office, she'd meant every word. But marriage vows weren't written for situations like this, when remaining faithful meant putting lives at risk. There was too much at stake. And Jake wouldn't even have to know. She could at least spare him the kind of pain that he'd caused her, with those thoughts of Teresa.

Before she could change her mind, she squared up to Vitor. "I'll trade with you."

"I do not want your money."

"That's not what I meant." She went to the control panel at the helm and switched on the overhead spots, which shone down on her like stage lights. Hoping she seemed self-assured, she walked right up to him, until they were so close that her skin tingled and blood began to pound in her ears. It was just her body. Everything would be okay; she could live with it and try not to think about what her decision might do to her and Jake—if there even was still a her and Jake. Vitor remained completely still. She couldn't decipher him.

"I do have something you want," she said. Keeping her eyes on his, she straightened her spine, then stood motionless. She couldn't bring herself to say it out loud, but she had to make her intention clear. She only had this one chance. But if she was going to give him this, she wanted more than water in exchange. "One time. And then you take both of us away from here."

In the brightness of the ceiling lights, she saw his pupils expand and knew he understood what she was offering. Everything started to slowly spin. It was fine; she could do it. She had to. "Vitor," she asked, fighting to keep a tremor from her words, "is it a deal?"

He put down the container and reattached the lid. He took her wrist. "Yes."

All kinds of memories from their time on the island flicked through her mind, a stilted silent movie. A glass of wine, condensation bubbling on the bulb; the roll of money; his bed with the crumpled sheet. She made herself think of the good times: the scuba dive, the sketching on the beach, the firelit dance.

He kept hold of her wrist and started to lead her across the cockpit, and as they passed the table, she saw the card that he had been playing in his game of solitaire was the four of spades, and she remembered when all four boats had been there, how she'd thought of them as all being in accord, a fleet. How naive she'd been. Two steps later they reached the threshold, and he piloted her across it, through the double doors and down into the boat.

The chilled air in the stateroom caused her skin to stipple. Her feet sank into the carpet as she followed Vitor in, but this time the pile felt artificial against her soles. The high bed was neatly made. Draped over the back of a chair was a kaftan Teresa had left behind. Had she been wearing it that night, the night when Jake . . . ? She couldn't remember. A discarded lipstick rolled back and forth on the dressing table as *Santa Maria* rocked.

Vitor stopped at the side of the bed and gestured for her to sit. She did so, hyperaware of every part of her body, of how the mattress dipped beneath her, and of how little she was wearing. She kept her knees clamped, her spine straight, and tipped backwards until she was lying down. Above her, the ceiling was covered in square-shaped panels, lined up precisely, edge to edge. When he left her to go and close the door, she slipped under the sheet and put her head on the pillow. She kept her bikini on.

The overhead light went off, and the ceiling panels disappeared. Her heart thumped against her breastbone. She tried to calm herself. If it stayed dark like this, she could try pretending it was Jake she was with. Would that be less of a betrayal? It might be worse. It'd be simpler if she'd stopped loving him, but she hadn't. Couldn't.

Footsteps padded across the cabin toward her. She stiffened. The side lamp came on with a click. She didn't look at Vitor but focused on the seam where one of the ceiling panels adjoined another, where there was a slight smudge, an excess of glue or residue left by an insect. She heard a clip, and then a rattle and a clunk as Vitor took off his watch and laid it on the dressing table. A rustle and the sound of fabric dropping to the floor. A creak as he got onto the bed. The sheet slid across her thighs, her middle, her breasts as he pulled it away, until she was exposed. She squeezed her eyes shut.

He started by kissing her mouth. His lips were fuller than Jake's, wetter. He tasted of rum—a hit of sugar at first, then a bitter aftertaste. He worked his way down her throat, taking his time. When his lips touched her ribs, her stomach, she fought the urge to recoil, reminded herself that she had chosen this. It was just a body, just a transaction, that's all. She was playing him at his own game, just had to focus on what she and Jake would get in return. It would be worth it.

Vitor's hair had fallen forward, and it tickled her stomach. She could hear him breathing; she could hear her own pulse; she tried to swallow, but her mouth was dry, her throat thick. He moved his way leisurely back up her body and then raised her arms above her head and held both of her hands in one of his own. With the other he untied the string of her bikini at the back of her neck, reached beneath her to pull at the second bow, drew the top away. Gradually, he lowered some of the weight of his body onto her, laid his chest against hers. He'd taken off his shirt, but he still had his shorts on; the fabric pressed into the front of her thigh. He didn't make a move yet to take off her bottoms. Realizing he might draw this out for a really long time, she kissed him, urgently. He responded immediately.

At the sound of a yell, she opened her eyes. Jake was there, wrenching Vitor off the bed. He drew back his fist and drove it forward, connecting with Vitor's face, hard. Vitor staggered back and crashed into the wall. He brought his hands to his nose, and one came away smeared with blood. He wiped it on his shorts. She snatched up her bikini top and retied it as quickly as her shaking fingers would allow. Jake was breathing deep and fast, his ribs pushing out and in. He shook his fist and cradled it in his other hand. He turned to her. He was dripping—water was running off him, onto the carpet; his hair was plastered to his skull. Her brain was sluggish, slow, unable to make connections. Why was he wet?

"Are you all right?" he asked her, and she knew from the way he said it that he must have asked her more than once. "Vee, are you hurt?"

She looked from him to Vitor, who was still propped against the wall. She couldn't form a thought.

"Vee," Jake said again, extending a hand to her. "Baby, come on. Let's go."

Couldn't move.

Vitor began to laugh. The laughs got louder until they became coughs, and he brought the back of his hand to his nose again, to dab away more blood. He looked at it, and then he looked at Jake. "You are making a mistake."

"A mistake?" Jake said, his voice rising. He stepped away from the bed and curled his hand into a fist. "You force yourself on my wife and I'm the one who's in the wrong? How's that, exactly?"

Vitor stood. "I did not force anything. She came here of her own accord. She asked for this."

Jake turned away in disgust. "Come on, Vee." He came back to the bed and held out a hand. "We're leaving." Still she couldn't get her limbs to move. It was as if she wasn't really there.

"She did ask." Vitor sounded so reasonable. "She came here. She wanted to trade with me. She understands how things work."

"Trade? Trade what?"

"You want to leave Amarante," Vitor said. "And I want to f—"

Jake was on him before any more could come out of his mouth, slamming him into the wall. "Shut the fuck up," he spat. He backed away, and Vitor slid down. Blood trickled from his nostril.

Vitor coughed. "Virginie," he said, the edges of his teeth dark with blood. "Was this, or was this not, your idea?"

She looked from Vitor to Jake. It was all going so wrong. What had Amarante done to them?

"She screamed," Jake said. "She shouted, 'Please stop.' Why would she do that if this was her idea?"

"She was screaming about something else. A little misunderstanding. But she came round to my point of view. The island rules—surely you have not forgotten those, Jake? She wants something, and I want something in return. So we struck a deal. It is a trade that will benefit you also, I must point out."

"In what possible way could this benefit me? You're a lunatic. I thought I was cracking up, but what kind of sick logic is this?"

Logic—to reason through words. She should speak, convince him. "We need to get out of here." Her voice came out as little more than a croak, but it was enough to make Jake stop, listen. "Vitor can take us."

"We don't need him. There's wind now. We don't have to use the engine. We can just cut the anchor lashing and sail."

She looked straight at him. "We don't know that, Jake. What if the wind hasn't really come in? We could be drifting for weeks. We might not make it. And we don't have any water. I tried to tell you earlier."

"Fine. We'll pay him for our passage." He walked over to Vitor. "How much do you want? Name your price. The moment we get to Port Brown, I'll transfer it into your account. I'll borrow it if I have to. Go on, name it. A thousand? Five? Not bad for giving someone a fucking lift."

Vitor, still in a crouch, smiled at him. "I do not want your money. I just want what she offered. That is my price."

Jake pulled at his hair. "No one's making any sense!" He came back to her. "Vee, please," he pleaded, taking her hand, "let's go."

She let him guide her off the bed, walk her across the cabin. At the narrow doorway she let go of his hand so he could pass through ahead of her. The tips of his uncut hair had formed into damp curlicues that brushed the base of his neck. One curl released a droplet of water, which ran down his upper back, arcing like a shooting star through the cluster of new freckles that had bloomed there. She wanted more than anything then to pause time, to memorize each of these new marks, to press her body against the length of his, to touch that drop with the tip of her tongue and feel it roll into her mouth. To rewind and go back to that faraway morning when they'd been in bed and he'd traced the heavens onto her skin, and into her heart, and made her feel celestial, the beloved queen. To return both of them to the people they had been. That was paradise, there, then.

But instead she stopped on the cabin side of the door, holding the handle with one hand, the other against the frame. "I'm sorry. I have to do this," she whispered, and pushed the door. He tried to wedge his foot in the way, but he was too slow.

"I have to, Jake," she said again, sliding the lock home. "It's the only way."

32

She pressed her shoulders against the door and flinched as Jake hammered against it from the other side. She checked where Vitor was—he was going into the bathroom. The sound of a tap, water running free.

Beneath her fingers the handle moved as Jake rattled it. "Vee! Don't do this." Thick wood muffled his voice. "Come on. He's crazy. We'll talk him round somehow."

There was a pause, and then he slammed so hard against the door that it moved in its frame, knocking against her bones—he was trying to shoulder it open—but he was weaker these days, as was she, and *Santa Maria* was made of sturdier stuff than *Wayfinder*. The door didn't budge. He stopped slamming to plead with her instead.

"Vee," he begged again, "don't do this. You don't have to do this. We'll find a way. Please. There has to be another way."

Vitor came out of the bathroom, holding a damp towel to his nose. He tossed it to the floor, sat on the bed. Watched.

There was no other way, not that she could think of.

She stood her ground and eventually she heard Jake slide down the other side. Imagined him crouching in the corridor, his hands to his head. She reached behind her, grasped the hard oval of the lock, ready to twist it open. But then she saw the footprints that he'd tracked across the cabin and the darker patch on the floor where water had dripped from his hair, his skin, his shorts, and soddened the carpet. He'd been absolutely wet through. Wait—was it finally raining? She looked to the portlight above the head of the bed for confirmation, but the glass was dry. Then the realization hit her. He'd *swum* across to find her.

The bed, the dressing table, the window—all blurred. She laughed, once, and sniffed back tears. If Jake could do that, push aside his crippling fear, for her, for them, then what was this in comparison, really?

Blinking cleared her vision. Vitor was on the bed, his expression unreadable.

Her skin flushed hot, then cold. "Do we still have a deal?"

He pushed out his lower lip. "My offer stands if yours does."

She raised her chin. "Yes." The edges of everything were sharper now.

"Good."

No one was forcing her into anything; it was her choice, her decision. She started to loosen her grip on the lock. Vitor pushed up and off the wall and walked across the cabin toward her. Despite his efforts to wipe it away, blood had dried in the lines around his nose and mouth. She could handle this. She was the one in control. She lifted her thumb free of the still-twisted lock, then her fingers.

He put his hands to the door on either side of her head and leaned in. She could smell the blood. He kept coming and she braced herself for the kiss, but at the last moment he pulled away, put his mouth close to her ear. His breath tickled, sent a chill slicing all the way down the side of her body.

"I told you once that everything has a price. Do you remember? And that I expect everyone to settle their debts. I am glad that you understand this. Not everyone does." He looked at her, and the gap between them was so small that all she could see were his eyes. They were flat, contained no hint of sympathy or humor. "I am also glad that you were not a pushover. I enjoyed the challenge. But I knew you were intelligent enough to change your mind. We are similar creatures, you and I." Keeping his arms framing her, he moved to her other side, her other ear. "We understand the game and we know how to get what we want."

She'd heard enough. The glossy refinement was gone—here was the real Vitor, the serpent exposed. Before he could touch her again, she slammed her heel into the top of his foot and then lifted her leg on the rebound and kneed him in the groin, ramming as hard as she could, connecting with soft flesh.

He let out a surprised grunt, a rushed oof of air. As he stumbled backwards, doubled over, she turned the lock, opened the door. Jake was in the corridor, starting to get to his feet, but nausea overwhelmed her, and she dashed past him, a hand to her mouth. She kept going, along the corridor, up the stairs, through the saloon, only stopping when she reached the back of the boat. She kept her hand over her mouth, trying to breathe, fighting waves of panic. What had she done?

Jake thundered out after her. He cupped her shoulders and rotated her so that she faced him. "Did he hurt you?"

Her eyes were locked shut. The hand over her mouth was shaking, and the trembling started to work its way through her whole body.

"Vee! Say something! I need to know you're all right."

Slowly she shook her head, forced her eyes open. She spread her fingers to whisper between them. "I'm so sorry." He pulled her tight against him, and she could feel his heart racing as fast as hers. "Jake, now how will we—"

An engine rumbled; a second started. Then came the telltale whirr and chink of a windlass winding up an anchor chain.

Vitor was at the helm station, flicking switches to turn on the chart plotter and navigation lights. He knocked the throttle into forward tick-over.

"I'll make him take us," Jake said, letting go of her.

She pulled him back. "Don't." She couldn't stand to be here any longer, near Vitor. She knuckled the tears from her cheeks. "Let's just go." She climbed down the aft steps and got into their dinghy and untied the rope, ready, holding fast to *Santa Maria* with one hand.

But Jake didn't come with her this time. He went up to the wheel. Addressed the back of Vitor's head.

"I always thought you were a fucker, but this is just evil. What kind of a man would do this? Abandoning two people here to die? It's murder."

"Jake," she rasped, "please don't. I can't." Whatever either of them said to Vitor, he wouldn't allow them to win a single hand, let alone this whole game he'd set up.

Jake must have heard the urgency in her voice because he turned and took half a step toward her, but then he stopped, his attention caught by something on the other side of the boat. She followed his eye line. The cockpit overhead lights were still on, illuminating every-thing on board. Right at the back of the far hull, the jerry cans of water shone in the night.

Jake moved fast, but Vitor was quicker, yanking Jake off the con-tainers and throwing him to the deck. Jake struck out with his legs, and the two of them were down on hands and knees, grappling. Jake punched Vitor on the cheek, and a spray of blood arced through the floodlit air. Jake staggered to his feet, breathing hard, stumbling back onto the guard rail, sagging against it as if it were the rope around a boxing ring. Before Virginie could react, Vitor rebounded from the punch and was on his feet, too, yelling furiously, ramming his shoulder against Jake's chest, and Jake, off-balance, skidded backwards, past the jerry cans, Vitor chasing him down like an enraged bull, crashing into him two, three, four times, the force of each hit tremoring through the deck and up into Virginie's arm as she clung on. He drove him back-wards, down one stair, two, never giving him the chance to recover, and now they were right at the rear of the boat, opposite her, and Vitor shoved a final time, and Jake's arms were windmilling in the air, his mouth open in an O of surprise, and then, as his soles slipped off the deck, he brought a flailing arm down on the back of Vitor's neck and both men hit the water and were gone.

Virginie moved fast—too fast, so that when she tried to loop the dinghy painter around the cleat as she leapt on board, she missed. She didn't have time to try again—she needed to stop *Santa Maria*—so she dropped the rope and let the dinghy drift away. At the helm she jabbed the engines into neutral and sprang to the starboard side, where Jake and Vitor had fallen into the water. Frantically, she scanned the surface, looking for any sign—bubbles, a raised hand.

"JAKE! JAKE!" she screamed into the empty air. Behind the boat the water had been flattened by eddies scooped up by the propellers. Wait—what if they'd gone right under the hull, into a prop? "Jake!" Oh God, oh God, oh God.

The catamaran was still creeping forward, driven by the momentum it had gained before she stilled the propellers—not by much, but enough to move the light's loom and sink the area where Jake had gone under into blackness. She dashed back to the helm and hovered a hand above the throttles. To put the engines in reverse to stop the boat completely would risk killing him. She grabbed a flashlight instead and ran to the rail, raking the beam over the sea, flinging his name repeatedly out into the dark, as if throwing him life rings. Back and forth she swung the light. Back and forth. Back and forth. On the next back, she caught sight of something, and dug around in the darkness until she found what she'd seen. There! A domed back—someone in the water.

The dinghy was gone, and Vitor's tender already stowed on its davits. So she dived, surfaced, heaving air into her lungs, and began to swim, ripping handfuls of churning water out of her way. Out past the semicircle of light cast by the boat it was hard to see, and she had to wait for her eyes to adjust. White flank. A motionless body. What if it was Vitor? She faltered, and her legs sank. But what if it wasn't? She kicked hard and carried on, adrenaline driving her.

When she reached him, he was facedown in the water, and she wasn't sure it was Jake until she jerked up his head. Heat went through her. His face was bloody, his eyes closed, his limbs dangled. With effort she turned him onto his back, and then she clamped her forearm over his chest, angled her body beneath his, and started to kick them toward the boat.

It was hard going, and when they were halfway her energy plummeted, and she doubted that she'd be able to get him there. She was so weak these days. But then he started to cough, and the knowledge that he was alive was enough to spur her on. "I've got you, I've got you," she kept saying, timing her kicks to the words, using them as a mantra to drive herself on.

When they reached *Santa Maria*, he was with it just enough to respond to her command to beach his chest on the bottom step, but that was all he had left, and he lay there, spent, blood diluting in seawater to pool pink on the deck beneath him. The boat was seesawing on the waves, the underside repeatedly rising and dropping with a slam. She kicked furiously to tread water. He needed to be all the way on board before the motion shook him loose and he fell back into the sea. If that happened, she wouldn't be able to lift him out by herself. On the next crest she stretched overhead for a cleat, pulled herself on board, and bent to take hold of his armpits to drag him completely clear. She was exhausted, but like on that day with the coconuts, she gritted her teeth and screamed and dug into her heels, her thighs and shoulders white hot, and eventually she managed to get him into the cockpit and onto his back.

He was in a bad way. A dark gash on the right side of his head leached blood where something—a rudder, a propeller blade, a jagged coral outcrop—had ripped open the skin. Blood was welling dark in the cleft, pooling and overspilling, running down his face, his neck, his collarbone, onto her thighs, her knees, the deck. She put her hand to the wound and felt the hot, thick spread of it bubbling beneath her palm. He was conscious—just—his eyelids flickering. She left him for the briefest amount of time possible, to wrench open drawers in the galley to find cloths and towels to stanch the flow and bind his head, and even though only eight or ten seconds had passed, by the time she returned to him the dark tide was worse than before.

Kneeling, she set to her rudimentary first aid. The first towel quickly became sodden, and she tried her best to ignore what it might mean that it was so heavy with Jake's blood. She got a bandage on. He was still now, unconscious. She pressed two slippery fingers into the dip beneath his jaw, searching for reassurance, waiting to be certain that the movement was more than the trembling of her own hand. There! A flutter . . . two . . . another. Alive.

She knelt back on her heels. Sweat and salt water were running down from her hairline; she dashed the back of her hand across her forehead. She had to get them out of here, and she would—she just needed a moment. A moment to breathe, to steady herself. She sucked one breath in, pushed it out. One, two. One. Two.

A hollow clang came from the back of the boat. She cocked her head to listen. There, above the slap of the sea—a rhythmic squeaking like the scrape of a metal hinge with every fall of the hull, and a bang at every rise. Was the boat damaged? Were they taking on water? She pushed herself up to standing, her knees stiff and hot. Squeak, bang, squeak, bang. She moved backwards across the cockpit, following the noise. Squeak, bang, squeak, bang. It was coming from the starboard hull. She went up onto the side deck, easing round the water containers. Yes, it was definitely louder now. Her feet found the lip of the first stair, the second, the third. She was at the rear of *Santa Maria*, where the very last part of the deck was just centimeters above the water, rearing and dropping with the waves. If she took too long a step, she'd be off the boat and into the ocean.

Because the cockpit lights were on, everything beyond, out at sea, was flat and black, and Amarante was shrouded. The squeak and bang sounded again, from just beyond her toes. The boarding ladder. It was designed to be folded up and stowed flat along the step when not in use, but it was out of its cradle and hanging vertically, the rungs disappearing down into the water. The movement of the catamaran was making the frame swing on its hinges, the ladder squeaking as it lifted when the hull dropped, and banging as it smashed against the fiberglass on the upwards ride. It was regular, like the ticktock of a clock, or the pump of a heart: Lift . . . squeak . . . fall . . . bang. Lift . . . squeak . . . fall . . . bang. Lift . . . squeak . . . fall . . .

Vitor was there, in the water. Right at the boat.

He reached up and clamped her ankle, manacle-tight. She yelped and tried to leap back. The sudden movement cost her the grip of her other foot, and the deck skidded away beneath her. She was going in.

As her body reeled, she scrabbled at the air, but there was only emptiness, and then her fingers found the tender hoist line, and she snatched at it and managed to steady herself. Below, grimacing, his face was tight with fury as he strengthened the grip on her ankle and started to lift his other hand to take hold of the top rung of the ladder. She struggled to break free, but it was no use. Once he came back on board, what would he do? Rape her? Throw Jake overboard? At the very least, strand them here, let Jake bleed to death?

She wouldn't take that chance. Before he could get onto the ladder, she leaned into her fettered leg, tightened her grip on the tender line, and kicked him in the face with her free foot. His head snapped back, and he swung away from her, holding tight to her ankle. It had all been for nothing. He was going to pull her in. But as he continued to pivot out, his fingers slipped on her bones, and he dropped away into the night.

She turned and fled up the steps. The fucking water containers were in her way, and the quickest thing to do was bulldoze them over the side, into the sea. She was back at the helm within seconds, her heart in her mouth, her breath coming in heaving gasps. Both throttles forward. More, more. The boat leapt. The course, the lights, the sails— she'd sort all of that out later. For now, all that mattered was to get Jake to safety, to put as much distance as she could between them and Amarante. She rammed the throttles again, making sure they were all the way to max. The engines roared in protest, and their roar matched the scream of blood in her ears.

PORT BROWN

33

Hour after hour had passed while Virginie and I were sequestered on the stationary *Patusan*, and the air in my cabin was extraordinarily still when she finished her story. I put down my pen. Beyond my portlight the calm afternoon had melted serenely into the golden hour, all traces of the night's storm gone, and the sky was ombré, honey deepening to bronze above the horizon.

Before I'd heard her speak, I'd asked myself who this woman was. Now I had answers. I'd been wrong to distrust her. My first guess, back when Yusuf told me about the flares, had proved correct: she was practical, well versed in the ways of the seas. She was determined, adventurous, confident, and capable of making decisions. But she was also too quick to see the good in people, and this social naivete was to her detriment. Although perhaps that's the cynic's view. I'm always aware, after what has happened in my life, that I'm trapped in the quicksand of suspicion. And which is the better way to live: to trust, with the risk of an occasional fall, or to shut yourself off from hope? I know what Maria would say.

Yet now that I felt I knew Virginie better, I couldn't believe such a woman, without a backward glance, would leave a man to die. Whether that belief came from me or her, I couldn't tell. By listening to her story, had I got to the heart of who she really was, or was this intuition actually being driven by some need within myself for her to win through? Whatever it was, as we sat there amid the hum of the engines holding us in position, I knew there was more.

"Virginie. Tell me the rest."

She glanced up from the beads she still clutched, frightened into immobility, but when she saw that I was looking at her with encouragement, she sighed and settled my wife's rosary around her neck. The cross sat high on her chest, framed by the hemmed V of the scrubs shirt she wore.

"You went back?" I asked.

She plucked at the beads. "You have to understand—Jake was so ill."

I reassured her that did understand, and she loosened a little. "I'd throttled forward, as I told you, and was taking us out of the bay. It was cloudy, and fully dark by then, and I couldn't see much, but I had Vitor's entry track on the GPS to follow, and I used that to guide me out so I didn't hit any reefs." Clever. "We were about to reach open water when I knew I had to turn the boat around. I needed to see if . . . if he was dead, if I'd killed him. After all, he'd been trying to get back onto the boat and I'd . . . well, I'd stopped him."

She gnawed at the side of a fingernail. "I got *Santa Maria* back into the bay. I made a wide U around *Wayfinder* and reversed toward the beach. The catamaran only draws a meter and a half, you know, so I could get fairly close, closer than we'd been when he and Jake went in."

I could almost hear the blast the engines would have made as she did a quick reverse to stop the boat, feel the rock of the aborted momentum beneath me.

"I was able to make out the silver line of the beach, but that was about it. I still had the flashlight—it was a searchlight, really, you know one of those high-beam ones for man-overboards?"

"I know the kind." I'd used one to look for *Santa Maria* the previous night.

"I took it to the back of the cockpit. I daren't go down the steps again, not after what happened before, but I got as close as I dared. I switched on the torch and aimed it at the water. I think I was holding my breath. I was expecting to see a body floating, and I was both hoping for it and dreading it, because I hadn't yet decided what I'd do if I did see his body in the sea, if I'd be able to leave it there, or try and . . . I don't know—rescue it? Recover it?" She swallowed. "I started closest to the boat, trying to ignore the fact that this was probably foolish anyway, that he could have drifted in a current to any part of the bay by now, and that I couldn't possibly search everywhere. I was wasting time—the important thing was to get Jake to hospital. I kept telling myself, One more sweep, then I'll go, and I was so nervous my palms were sweating, and I think my hands were shaking as well because I lost my grip on the torch—not completely, but just enough that the beam jumped ahead, from the water onto the beach, and there he was. Vitor."

She stopped talking so abruptly that in my mind's eye I saw him as deathly still, a washed-up corpse, and my heart started to sink—for her, and also, somehow, for my family.

"He was crawling up the sand from the waterline. And he had with him one of those water containers, using it as an anchor almost, casting it ahead a little way, then hauling himself up behind it. How he'd managed to find it in the dark, I don't know. It must have been pure luck."

Alive. I breathed a little easier.

"When the torch beam hit him, he stopped crawling and sat on the sand, blinking in the light." A hesitation; eyes fixed on the bedsheets. "Captain Tengku, I honestly think that if he'd looked at me with the slightest bit of contrition, if he'd pleaded with me, I'd have launched his tender and gone to pick him up. But he just stared and stared, with this expressionless face, and I was so frightened, still so scared of what he might do, that I . . . ." Dry, heaving sobs overcame her. She doubled over on the bed, rocking, as she had when she'd first started to talk.

My heart went out to her. Finally we'd got to the core of what was troubling her, of what I'd sensed when we first found her: this was fear and guilt combined—fear *of* guilt—so pronounced it was palpable. And I was very familiar with the self-destruction that brings.

It's all my fault, she'd said hours earlier, when the sun was at the meridian, before she'd finally opened up to me, and throughout her retelling this was a steady beat, like the frap-frap-frap of a loose halyard against a mast: it was her fault they went to Amarante in the first place; her fault Jake reacted to the pressure the way he had done, that he'd fought with Vitor and gone into the water; her fault they went fishing on the reef, poisoned Stella and Gus, marooned Vitor. Her fault. Paradise ends when guilt begins.

There's always an if-only. I know so well how that goes. If only I hadn't been working away that December day. If only I'd gone with my family to the beach. If only I'd taught Maria how to read the water better. Self-blame is an addiction. The logical part of you knows you need to kick past, but it's a long way to the surface, and the effort needed is too frightening, the suction and gravity of guilt too great. And what if someone sees you trying to cast off that guilt? Easier to stop and stay submerged where you belong, down there among the silt and muck, among the rolling bones and the monsters of the deep.

Still she cried and rocked. I went to sit near her and reached to rub her back, soothing her as I had Farah, whenever she wept. Farah's problems had been far lighter than Virginie's—a broken toy, a quarrel with her brother—but she'd always felt injustices deeply, had taken them so much to heart.

"He's probably still alive, you know that?" I said, once her sobs had subsided and her breathing had regulated.

She lifted her head. Her eyes were bloodshot, her lips swollen. "But what if he isn't?" Her voice was thick.

International maritime law states that it's the duty of every master to render assistance to everyone found at sea in danger of being lost, although you could argue that Vitor was on land, not at sea. But the finer points of any legislation, spiritual or civic, were not what she was getting at—she wanted absolution, and I wasn't sure I was the right person to offer that. Back when I still had a faith, I might have counseled that failing to help someone whose life was in danger constituted a mortal sin. And yet the church—and the law—permitted killing in self-defense, if it saved your life. Where did this—Vitor abandoning Virginie and Jake, and her abandoning him in turn—fall on that scale? And did the scale even matter, anyway? To my pre-2004 self, it definitely had done. But at that point on the *Patusan*, after everything, I wasn't so sure. She was asking me for absolution, but absolution I couldn't give, because in order to give it I had to believe.

"We will go back for him, okay?" I said, in a father's soothing voice, a voice I hadn't used for so long. "We'll get Jake to a hospital, and then we'll return for him."

"And Stella? I shouldn't have taken us to that reef."

There it was again, the plea for forgiveness. "Ciguatera is not location-dependent. It might not have been your fish. It is not necessarily your fault. Just an act of . . ." I nearly said *God*. "Luck."

I kept my eyes locked on her face, until she had no choice but to look at me. At first she couldn't do it, but eventually she met my gaze and nodded.

Sensing she needed some time to herself, I collected up the radio Umar had brought me, the *Santa Maria* papers and passports, and told her she could have a shower, sleep. I was giving her directions to the mess in case she wanted something to eat when a hiss interrupted me. The radio.

"Captain." Umar's voice filled the room.

I picked up the handheld to answer, speaking in Bahasa. "Go ahead, Umar, over."

"I've fitted the radar reflector to the catamaran, as you asked, and gone through the boat."

"Understood, Umar. Out." I was impatient to find out if we'd been given permission to leave, so I released the transmit button almost before I'd finished my last word.

"Wait, wait, Captain," Umar continued.

I clamped down. "Yes, Ensign, what is it?"

"One of the forward cabins is locked."

"And?"

"You ordered to me to pass through the whole boat. Everything looks normal. But one door is locked. Shall I leave it?"

I was tempted to tell him to forget it, but what if Jake had been right about Vitor dealing drugs and that cabin was full of heroin? I pictured stacks of bricks mummified in multiple layers of plastic, sealed with duct tape against the corrosive effects of the salt air. If I abandoned that boat and it was found later, with a haul on board, I would lose my job. And my job was all I had.

"Can you force the lock?"

A delay, a crackle of static. "No, sir."

I watched Virginie pick up a bottle of water. She cracked the top and brought the neck to her lips.

I looked at the top passport in my hand, the one for Vicente de Sousa. I spoke into the radio. "Can you force the door itself?"

"I can try." He must have kept his finger on the transmit button while he shouldered it, because a thud issued from the VHF and reso- nated through my cabin. There was a pause, then another thud. Vir- ginie stopped drinking to listen, the half-drained bottle by her mouth. Umar grunted with every impact he made, louder each time. The thuds got bigger, harsher, too, and I realized he had switched from shoulder- ing to kicking the door, and I was hearing the wood splinter with every blow from his boot. There was a loud bang, and all went quiet.

"Ensign, are you receiving me?" I tried. "Umar?"

Just that same soft crrr marked the distance between us. And then the radio blasted into life again. "Sir, sir! There is someone in here! A woman!"

My insides flash-froze. Virginie had told me they were the only two people on board.

"Sir, sir!" Umar was shouting into the radio, and as long as he was transmitting, I couldn't question him, because he couldn't receive me. "Sir! There is a lot of vomit." His breath was stertorous. "She is not moving, sir!" He cursed. "Sir, sir, what should I do? Her skin is gray. I think maybe she is dead."

He finally stopped transmitting, and I could speak. My training took over. "Umar, feel for a pulse." My own blood surfed.

"Sir, nothing."

Too quick. "Try again, Umar." Purposefully, I slowed my words. "Take your time. Remember to try at her throat, not her wrist."

The break in contact was longer. I eyed Virginie. She was motionless, staring at the radio. I still didn't think she could understand our words, but she could hear the tension in our voices.

"Sir!" he came in, "I think I have it. I think she is alive."

"Check again, Umar. Be sure." The surf was now a pounding in my ears.

He returned to the line. "Yes, sir. I can definitely feel it. She is alive."

I took one breath in, one breath out. I reeled off a list of instructions to him; then I called the bridge and ordered two crew to take the support boat over there and help him bring this woman back. I called Yusuf and told him to meet me at the tender loading bay.

When I clicked off, Virginie's eyes were fixed on me. "What's going on?"

How to answer that? I had no idea. Had I let myself be carried away by Virginie's story, let my own fate and feelings, my memories of my family, be mixed up with it? All I had to go on, really, was an overall impression I had of her, partly shaped by some tiny similarities to my wife, to my daughter, and a courtly need to be gallant.

But now it seemed she had lied to me. Two people were fighting for their lives. And I was standing here while chaos broke all around. It was time to act.

34

After Tengku left, Virginie filled the bathroom sink with water and plunged her head into it, hoping the shock of the cold would revive her. She opened her stinging eyes and stared at a clutch of tiny bubbles on the plug, keeping her face immersed until her lungs burned. The sensation was so like that she'd felt on the dive with Vitor, when he'd held her down, that she immediately threw up her head and gasped for air. The mirror showed her red eyes, sunken cheeks. She turned away to find a towel, to get back to Jake and to find out what was going on.

Captain Tengku's officer had brought a pair of scrubs trousers in the same shade of green as her borrowed shirt. She put them on. Too long and too big. She rolled them at the waist and turned up the ankle hems. They were anonymous clothes, and she didn't feel like herself in them. Right now that was a good thing.

The passageway was deserted when she opened the door of the cabin. Which way to go? Dim lighting, sounds of activity in both directions. She took a tentative step out, metal grating cold and rough under her bare feet.

She turned left, passing closed doors and storage lockers labeled in Malaysian. No windows. It was disorienting, not knowing where she was in the ship, which way was forward and which aft, even whether it was night or day. A door opened, and the loud ring of the handle startled her. One of Tengku's men came out, and she shied against the wall. After he'd passed, she took a few moments to compose herself. She was being ridiculous. These men meant her no harm. She just needed to find Jake.

At the end of the passageway, she recognized where she was. The door to the sick bay was closed, but there was a small round window riveted into it, and she went up on tiptoes to look through.

Jake was lying on the operating table-cum-bed, where he'd been when she followed Captain Tengku out yesterday. His eyes were closed, his face slack, and her gut lurched, but then she saw the peaks and troughs of his pulse on the monitor and her own heartbeat steadied. She pushed on the door.

Inside, the room was cold, the air antiseptic. The beeps of the machines were frightening and reassuring at the same time. The medic, busy in the far corner, gave her a small smile, which was also reassuring. She went to the bed, took Jake's hand. It was warm, but his fingers were unresponsive to her touch.

The medic came over. "Your husband is okay." Haziq—wasn't that his name? She hadn't known he could speak English—he'd never addressed her; had used rapid Malaysian with the captain, like the rest of the crew. "We take him to Port Brown hospital soon. They have good doctors. Take very good care."

She stroked the back of Jake's hand. You hear that, Jake? Just hang in there.

The door slammed back on its hinges, and two officers ran in with a stretcher, followed by the captain. As they laid it on a second bed, she caught a glimpse of a face. Dark skin, braids.

Teresa.

Haziq and Tengku talked in rapid Malaysian. Haziq drew the curtains around the bed, and the captain and the two officers strode out of the room.

She chased after them into the corridor. "Captain Tengku, that's—"

Tengku turned on his heel, so fast she nearly slammed into him. "Stay here." His expression was so severe, it was as if he'd cut her. He pointed at a spot outside the door. "I will be back to deal with you."

While she waited outside the sick bay, the cadence of the engines changed and she had a slight feeling of takeoff. The propulsion had kicked in—the *Patusan* was on the move, on its way to Port Brown. With far higher engine power, the journey back would be much shorter than the two weeks it had taken them in *Wayfinder*, yet she found little solace in this. Four days was still a hell of a long time to wait to get Jake to a proper hospital. She thought of Pete setting off to seek help for Stella, none of them knowing it was already too late. Thinking of Stella made her picture that mound of fresh soil, of how she would forever lie, like the prisoners, in that parched earth so far from home.

The door opened, and Haziq stuck out his head. No smile for her this time. "Captain wants you to wait in here now. He is coming soon."

She followed him in. Her eyes went straight to Jake, scanning him for any changes. There were none that she could see, no horror like that she'd found in *Swallow*'s forecabin.

Teresa had been placed in the neighboring bed, the sheet pulled up almost to her chin. Her braids spread over the pillow, their normally neat edges rough under the fluorescent light. Her skin was ashen, her face slack like Jake's. A plastic tube curved from her mouth. One arm, above the sheet, was bandaged. Teresa, here, on the *Patusan*. How?

"She is very . . ." Haziq searched for the right word. He settled on mime instead, his hand descending from his mouth in an arc, fingers splaying on the descent to mimic the rush of vomit. "After Umar found her, I tried to make her stomach empty, but she is making it empty first. This is very good."

As they stood at the bedside, Teresa started to surface, fluttering eyelids progressing to repeated blinking until she was able to hold them open. Recognition broke; then her pupils widened in panic, and she half croaked, half gagged, bringing a hand to the tube at her mouth. Trying to talk.

Virginie stood aside to let Haziq get to her.

"I will tell the captain," he said.

By the time Tengku arrived, Haziq had Teresa propped up against a buttress of pillows. He'd removed the tube—out of embarrassment and courtesy Virginie looked away and tried to close her ears against the gagging noises. He'd taken her vitals and poured her a cup of water, from which she took tiny sips, wincing as she swallowed. Dark smudges under her eyes matched the purple emerging from the bandage on her arm.

Tengku looked more formal. He'd changed out of the fatigues he'd been wearing when she told him her story and was dressed in a crisp uniform with golden stripes and a coil on the epaulets. With all of them, plus Jake, in the sick bay, the space was suffocatingly small. Virginie stood, intending to leave.

"No," Tengku said, pointing to the foot of the bed. "You stay." As in the corridor, there was ice in his voice. She pushed herself into the corner.

When the medic had eased away, Tengku pulled a chair up to Teresa's bedside. He opened his notebook, ready to begin questioning. "What is your name, miss?"

"Teresa Mabote." Her voice was weak, and it sounded as though it hurt her to speak. Tengku noticed, and as he went through the story he'd covered with Virginie, writing notes in his pad, he phrased many of his questions so that all Teresa had to do was answer yes or no. Much of the time she kept her eyes closed, nodding or shaking her head as her replies.

Although he was skimming it, going fairly quickly, still the retelling dragged. Virginie just wanted to know one thing, and when he got to what had happened to Stella, she couldn't hold it in any longer. She pushed herself out of her corner. "Vitor told me you'd gone with Ro—"

Tengku silenced her with a hand. "I will ask the questions." He was brisk, terser than he had been before, at least until his crew had called him on the radio. Clearly she'd lost his trust, his sympathy. She found her corner again, chewed her nail.

Tengku turned to Teresa. "Virginie told me that Vitor said you had left the island after this, with the Australian. Clearly you did not."

Her hair looped on the pillow as she shook her head. "Roly said he can . . . could take me," she rasped. "And I wanted to go. Vitor said no."

"Why did you want to leave?"

"Vitor . . . we were fighting. Many times, many days. It was very bad."

"What were you fighting about?"

Teresa looked at Virginie, and Virginie thought, Don't say me, don't let another thing be my fault.

"Some men . . . businessmen, in Port Brown. They are looking for Vitor. One time, when I was alone in Port Brown, they found me. I know that soon they will find Vitor, and I am afraid."

Tengku looked up from his notes, his eyebrows drawn together in concern. "They threatened you, these men? And you were afraid they would harm Vitor?"

Another shake of the head. "I am afraid for Musa."

"Musa?"

"My son."

Tengku riffled back through his pad. "But he was not with you on the boat?"

She brought a hand to her throat and Virginie stepped in. "Musa lives with his grandmother in Maputo." Tengku let her speak this time, but whether solely out of kindness for Teresa's discomfort, she couldn't tell. "Vitor supports the boy. That's right, isn't it, Teresa?"

Teresa slowly rubbed her brow. "At first, he sent money. Musa was growing so big, healthy. But then he stopped. Always he promises—'I will do it soon, tomorrow I will wire.' I think it is my fault, he will find another woman soon." She didn't look at her, but all the same, Virginie's throat dried. Had Teresa's child suffered because of her? Shame razored up her cheeks, thinned her skin.

"My mama told me Musa need more money for school," Teresa continued, "for uniform, for food. If I don't send more money, she cannot buy these things." She took a mouthful of water. "These men found me. They wanted information on Vitor, on his business. They offered money, not lots, but some. Enough for school, for shirts and shoes. They told me what to look for, in Vitor's papers, in his diary, and they gave me money." Her eyes flicked again to Virginie. So that was what she'd witnessed outside the restaurant loo the night she'd first met Vitor and Teresa. She remembered how jumpy she'd seemed, how she'd kept touching her little bag.

Teresa closed her eyes against either the pain or the memories, perhaps both. "On Amarante Vitor . . . Vitor discovered what I did. He looked at my phone, at a message. I thought I deleted all, but I missed one. He was searching everywhere for the money, but it was gone. It is small money to him. I tell him I already sent it my mama. He is getting angry, he wants to know what I told the men. He throws me in the cabin. I hurt my arm." With the fingers of her free hand, Teresa gingerly probed her bandage. "He lock the door with a key—I hear it turn. I hear him take it away, and I am scared. I scream—'Open, please!' I try to climb through the . . ." She pointed up.

"The hatch?" Virginie suggested.

"Yes. The hatch. It was closed. Locked also."

"How long were you in there?" Tengku asked.

"I do not know. Mostly I was not awake."

She broke off for water. Tengku was scrawling, his pen scratching in haste to get it all down. Sickness was growing in Virginie's stomach. Teresa must have been in that cabin the whole time, not only the days after she'd taken *Santa Maria* but before then, too, even a whole day more. She was probably already locked in there when Virginie was in the stateroom with Vitor. She'd heard no banging or screaming, so Teresa must have been unconscious. If only she had heard something, known somehow, seen through Vitor's lie, she could have helped her. The nausea worsened.

Teresa lowered her cup and resettled against the pillows. "I could hear him moving. I screamed through the door: 'When I get out, I am telling everyone what kind of man you are.' Then I swore never to speak one word. I begged: 'Free me.' Nothing."

Virginie thought of Jake shouting through the door of Vitor's cabin, pleading with her to come out, banging, and she almost felt again the wood rebounding against her back.

Tears were brewing in Teresa's eyes. Before they could fall, she swept them away with the pads of her fingertips. Tengku studied his notepad, giving her time to collect herself. When he spoke again, it was even more gently than before. "Teresa, my medic informed me you took pills. Tell me what happened."

She slumped a little. "I found the bottle in my robe. In the pocket."

"What kind were they?"

"Temazepam. A doctor gave them to me." She sighed a whistling sigh. "He came, once. Vitor. He looked at me through the, the hatch. I told him: 'I will take all the pills.' I took some—maybe . . . maybe more than some. I only wanted to scare him, to make him open the door and free me."

"But he did not?" Tengku asked. He had stopped writing, had an appalled look on his face.

"No," Teresa said. "He watched me swallow, and then he walked away."

A few days ago, before Jake went in the water, Virginie wouldn't have believed such stories about Vitor, would have been sure he wasn't capable of this. But now she had no doubt Teresa was telling the truth. Another thought made her stomach roil. If she'd gone through with her deal with Vitor, what would have happened after, to her, to Jake, to Teresa? Would they be here, now, on the *Patusan*, safe? She turned to look at Jake, so still there in his bed, and hoped to God that he *was* safe.

When she twisted back, the captain was looking at her as he had in his cabin, when she'd started to cry the second time. He was on her side again.

"Teresa," Tengku said, "I need to ask you about Vitor's business."

She fidgeted, staring at his pad. "What is this you are writing? A statement? Are you police?"

He adjusted his position in his chair. "I must make a report to my superiors. But I am not the police. Although they will want to speak to you when you get to Port Brown."

"Port Brown?" Teresa shrank into the bed. "Where is Vitor? Is he here on this ship?"

"No, he is not here," Tengku said. "He was not on *Santa Maria*. But we know where he is. And we will arrest him."

Virginie flinched. Arrest? He'd said he'd return for Vitor, not arrest him. If they meant to arrest him, would they not arrest her, too?

Teresa was also panicked—she looked as if she might try to bolt from the bed. "And in Port Brown? What will happen to me there? With the police? And how will I have money, for a place to sleep, for leaving?"

"I will contact your embassy. It might take a few days to arrange everything, but we will look after you. These last few questions, and then I can leave you to rest. I promise."

She ignored him, instead seeming to notice Jake for the first time. "Did Vitor make Jake like this?"

"Yes," Tengku said. "Teresa, tell me, please, what is Vitor's business?" She closed her eyes against him. "You don't even have to say it out loud," he said. "I will ask you questions, and you can nod or shake your head, like before. If you tell me what his business is, who these men are, I can help you, get the police to help you."

He leaned forward, and Virginie couldn't help but do so, too. "Illegal?" Teresa didn't move, but her lashes grew wet. "Drugs?" He inched closer, and although he took care to keep his voice level, his eyebrows rose high. "Worse?"

Teresa covered her face with her hand. "Please."

Tengku drew back. He must have decided to let it go because he recapped his pen. He took his time gathering his things, standing and lifting his chair. While its legs hovered above the floor, he asked her, "How old is your son?"

She uncovered her face. "Six. Seven next month."

He gave a small, private smile. "It is a good age."

After he left, Teresa's eyes brimmed again. Virginie automatically reached for her hand, but stopped when her fingertips brushed hot skin, not knowing whether the gesture would be welcome. She hadn't touched Teresa since that first day on the beach on Amarante, when she'd gone to kiss her hello and she'd tensed at the greeting. She let her hand rest on the bed instead, the sheet cool against the inside of her wrist. "Teresa, I'm so sorry. For all of it. For Musa, for not knowing what was happening to you. For Vitor . . ."

Teresa gave a sad smile. "At first it was not so bad, with Vitor. It was fun, I traveled the world. Of course I would rather be home, with Musa, but we cannot always have what we want. As long as he is safe, he is well, I am happy. So I stayed, and it was okay. Good. But things cannot stay good forever. I know that in your language the people say 'too good to be true.' Vitor taught me this English." She pinched the bridge of her nose. "I cannot stay in Port Brown, Virginie. Vitor owes people."

Virginie refilled her cup with the jug. "I'm sure it can all be sorted out. We can tell the police, report these people. They'll have Vitor, anyway, the police. And I'm sure Captain Tengku will help you."

"Tengku? This man? A sailor? What can he do?" Teresa looked straight at her, and this time she didn't wipe away the tears, but let them spill onto her cheeks. "My son. How will I care for him now?"

Virginie took her hand. Teresa turned her face to the wall and gripped her fingers tightly as she wept.

35

Four days later we reached Port Brown. Through the harbormaster I'd asked for ambulances to be waiting. Ahmad was also there to greet us, and I shook his hand and thanked him for his assistance in arranging this. By this point it was six days since Jake had gone into the water, and he was still unconscious. He was taken ashore on a gurney, Haziq wheeling along the dockside a drip stand that squeaked with every rotation of its casters. Virginie, looking like a medic herself in full scrubs apart from her bare feet, guided Teresa along the *Patusan*'s gangway, a hand supporting the elbow of her undamaged arm. Teresa seemed worried, looking about her like a bird checking for predators. I was distracted by a small crowd of dockworkers and fishermen who had gathered to see what all the fuss was about and were astonished to see three foreigners emerge from the bowels of my vessel. "Captain," one man, of Indonesian descent, called out to me. "What happened? A shipwreck?"

I suppose, really, that it was a shipwreck. It certainly had all the hallmarks: a boat adrift, later abandoned; a marooning; perhaps, along with all the injury and death, there might be some treasure at the end. Although I struggled to anticipate a happy ending for Vitor, and most probably not for Teresa, either. As for Virginie and her husband—well, that would depend on many things, not least the skills of the doctors at the Port Brown hospital. From what Virginie had told me of Jake, I imagined him as being not a little unlike myself in my youth: a proud man, moral but kind, fiercely protective of his wife, and I knew I'd like him. I was aware it was unprofessional of me, but I couldn't help but feel attached to them and to their story. They'd been tested, but it was still early days in their marriage, and I had hope they'd continue to build a future, maybe with children. Perhaps even a boy, a girl.

Jake was soon settled on a ward, and Teresa, who'd made good progress in her recovery during the passage, was checked over and discharged, although she was told she must rest and return for out-patient appointments. I found some temporary accommodation for her and Virginie—nothing fancy, just a couple of rooms at Mrs. Lee's guesthouse near the harbor, within walking distance of the hospital. I predicted Virginie would barely use her room, would instead snatch at sleep on a cot beside Jake's bed.

Once all that was arranged, I sent the *Patusan*, under Yusuf's command, back to Amarante for Vitor while I remained behind in Port Brown. Virginie and Teresa could do with an interpreter, and I had plenty to do there anyway—including going to report to the local chief of police.

The police station wasn't far from the harbor, so two days later I walked there, through the shipyard and down a side street lined with cars parked nose to bumper. These days there are as many Toyotas and Nissans edged up against the high curbs as Protons. At the edge of the cracked pavement waited a woman, her arms loaded with shopping, a child standing by her hip. The little girl's mouth was slack with boredom. Farah and Aadam used to do that, and Maria would tap the undersides of their chins to get them to stop.

I was nearing the fish shop. Ahmad, from the harbormaster's office, was coming out, a bulging plastic bag hanging from his wrist. I raised a hand in greeting, but he didn't see. He turned to walk along the street ahead of me. I looked in the shop window. Laid out on a slab were three evenly spaced sea bass, two whole, one partly filleted. I thought about Virginie gutting fish on Amarante, and about her, in turn, being gutted by the belief she was responsible for the death of her friend. Life is a game of luck. Sailors have always known this, and that's why they have so many superstitions, to try to turn their luck. Of course this works in reverse as well, allows them to shrug off responsibility, hang it instead on chance. I love my wife, but sometimes I blame her for taking the children to the beach that day; on the blackest days I even blame her for not sensing what was coming. Couldn't she feel a shift in the air, a thickening of fate? When the anger passes, the guilt always comes as a sharp stab in my belly. If the wound were made with the clean edges of a filleting knife, it would be easier to bear, but it is the waved blade of a keris that I have mentally adopted as the particularly agonizing weapon of my own self-torture.

There was another man on the pavement between Ahmad and me now—a Malay; very tall, very thin, youngish. Something about his proximity to Ahmad caught my attention. He was too near, and closing the gap too fast. He clapped a hand to the back of Ahmad's neck. In the time it took me to understand that I really was seeing such a thing—here, in this street, in the middle of the day—he shoved him against a car.

"Where is the orang putih?"

Ahmad didn't struggle. His face was toward me, his features distorted against the glass. He had an oddly resigned expression, as if this had happened to him many times before, and he knew resistance would be futile.

"Hey!" I broke into a run. "Hey! Let him go!"

I expected the attacker to be scared of me, to instantly drop Ahmad and run away, intimidated by my authority, by my Royal Malaysian Navy uniform. But he wasn't. Instead, as I ran, he found enough time to crush Ahmad against the car window once more—despite his thin frame, he was strong—and then he backed off, sneering. I had an instant decision to make: stay with Ahmad and make sure he was okay, or rise to the challenge and chase this thug down. I chose Ahmad and sucked back my rage as his attacker sauntered off down the street.

Ahmad had straightened. In a way he looked more frightened now I was there.

"Are you hurt?"

He passed a hand over his face, sluicing away sweat, but didn't reply.

"What was that all about?"

He looked hurriedly over his shoulder. "Nothing. Just a misunderstanding."

I eyed him. He didn't want to be seen talking to me. "Really? That's all? Because from where I was standing, Ahmad, it looked very much like he was threatening you."

"Threatening, sir? Oh, no." He tugged with his free hand at the hem of his shirt, leveling it out. Another swipe tidied his hair back into place. "As I said, a misunderstanding."

I edged closer, lowered my voice. "Look, Ahmad, if you're in trouble, I can help?"

But he'd shut down. "I don't want any trouble, Captain Tengku. I just want to go home and give this fish to my wife." He opened the bag. Inside, a pair of mackerel curled round each other, nose to spiny tail, like a yin-yang symbol. "She already made the sambal."

Clearly he didn't want my help. I let him go.

The run of restaurants and launderettes ended, and I reached the squat police station. Palms had grown in the dirt either side, a pair of sentries. Inside the lobby, Irene, the desk sergeant manning reception, was dealing with a visitor. I caught her eye and she waved me through.

The deputy commissioner was at his desk, on the phone, cradling the receiver against his ear as he typed on his computer. He acknowledged me—barely—with a lift of his eyebrows. I remained standing and examined the tips of my boots, which were dull compared to the water-like gloss of the floor tiles. I made a mental note to polish them properly when I got a moment to myself.

When the commissioner ended his call, he kept me waiting a little longer, finishing his typing. I didn't react—I was used enough to his petty power games.

Eventually he sat back, lacing his fingers over his lean belly. "Captain."

"Chief." I kept on my feet and got straight to the point, explaining about the foreigners I'd found, and the man left behind on Amarante. From my breast pocket I took the four passports, and, opening them all, I spread them out on his desk.

The deputy commissioner's chair creaked as he leaned forward. He picked up the three passports for Vitor Santos, João da Silva, and Vicente de Sousa, leaving Teresa's on the desk, and examined each in turn, shuffling them in his grip like a deck of cards.

"Do you recognize him?" I asked.

He rotated through them again. "Maybe." He pursed his lips. "Hard to tell. They all look the same, these orang putih."

"Do the names mean anything to you? Could you run them through the system?"

He put the passports down and looked at me. "Isn't this a maritime issue? The man you talk about isn't even in Port Brown. Why does it have anything to do with me?"

That raised a red flag. Normally, if he saw any opportunity to interfere, he would. Whenever we seized drugs from fishermen turned smugglers, for example, he petitioned to take over the case. Because of his record, he was, as he was fond of telling anyone who would listen, the youngest man in the Royal Malaysia Police to have made deputy commissioner, and he was on track to be promoted within five years.

I had no proof, but I decided to voice my suspicions. "He's mixed up in quite a lot of stuff, I'm told."

"Is that so?" The corners of his mouth rose a little. "By whom, Captain? Maybe I should speak to them? Don't you think I would have heard of this"—a pause as he consulted a passport—"Vitor Santos if he was some kind of master criminal operating in my territory?"

It was obvious he wasn't going to do anything on my say-so, and I knew the best I could hope for was that curiosity would get the better of him, and he'd look into Vitor once I left. I didn't want to expose Virginie and Teresa to this man. If he was so great at his job, he could figure it out by himself. There were a few days before the *Patusan* would return, anyway, with Vitor in naval custody. I held out my hand for the passports.

"I'll keep them for a time, if you don't mind," he said, slipping three into a drawer. I suspect he knew I'd have no valid reason to object.

"Of course." I was careful to keep my voice level. "Possibly something will come to light."

"Possibly." He held out Teresa's passport to me. "But you can take this one."

Luckily, I have a near-photographic memory—it was always useful in exams, both at school and in the military—and I could perfectly remember the spelling of the three names. On my way out, I stopped by the reception desk. The lobby was empty now apart from Irene behind the counter. I adopted a casual pose as I asked her how her husband and kids were, how her mother-in-law was doing.

"Much better, sir, thank you for asking," she said. "The doctors say she'll be home with us soon."

"I hope so." I genuinely meant it, but at the same time I was conscious of my scalp prickling with guilt. This wasn't me, breaking the rules, disregarding procedure, but I was about to lie to her anyway. "Oh, Irene," I said, widening my eyes in my best attempt at faking forgetfulness. "I forgot to ask the chief to run some names through the system. I know how busy he is. Such an important man." I fought to keep any sign of sarcasm from both my voice and my expression—he was her boss, after all. "I don't suppose you could . . ."

She frowned. "I'm not sure that's allowed, Captain. Let me check."

Before I could stop her, she'd picked up the phone. She held the receiver a little distance from her ear, and I could hear it ringing. I couldn't leave now—it'd look too obvious. Sweat started to bead at my temple.

The chief didn't answer, and Irene hung up the phone. This was my chance. I wetted my lips. "It doesn't matter, Sergeant." I used her rank to reassure her that this was all professional government business. "I can ring the base and get someone there to do it. I just thought it'd be more efficient, since I'm here now."

It was probably out of respect for position that she relented. "Okay, sir," she said. "Give me the names."

She had trouble with the unfamiliar foreign spellings, and after I'd corrected her a couple of times—"Santos, not Santas"—she motioned me to come round to her side of the counter, so I could check she'd entered it correctly. There were no hits for the first two names, but João da Silva had a result—a long result that placed him firmly within the interest and jurisdiction of the police.

I scanned it as quickly as I could. "I don't suppose I could have a printout of that?"

She reached for the computer mouse. "I really am sorry, sir, but I think I do need the deputy commissioner's permission for that. I'm not sure I should even be doing this." She minimized the window.

I'd had long enough. I swiveled and, ignoring Irene's protests, was back at the deputy commissioner's office within seconds.

"You again?" The chief, still behind his desk, sounded bored. "I told you, we have no reason to hold him."

"But I saw—" I stopped myself. I didn't want to get Irene into trouble. She had two kids of her own to bring up, plus her husband's brother's brood. "I checked," I said, hoping he wouldn't realize that I hadn't had enough time to look up the records via the navy's systems, "and there is a warrant."

The chief leaned back. His hands came to his belly again. "No, there isn't."

"There is. Under one of his aliases."

"Are you calling me a liar?"

I didn't answer. A creak of the chair again; he made a series of taps on his keyboard, paused, and rotated his computer screen toward me. On it was a search box showing the name João da Silva. Underneath, the words *No results found.*

I knew, as soon as I saw it, that I was wasting my time. Knew just how much of an effect money could have.

This time, the deputy commissioner escorted me to the door. I stopped, and looked down at the top of his head, to the place where his hair whorled out from the crown.

"How long has he been paying you?" I spat. It wasn't the first time I've been glad that I am taller than he is—and, I have to admit, I had perfect military bearing that afternoon.

Outside, I blinked in the midday sun. A bird flitted past at eye level and came to rest on the radio aerial of a police car, setting it swaying like a reed. The bird was a black-hooded finch, way off track. There hadn't been any mangrove in Port Brown for years, not since they'd cleared it all to create the commercial port. It assessed me and chirped, and as it took flight, I felt against my cheek the downdraft from its frantic chestnut wings.

36

One of the first things Virginie did when they arrived back in Port Brown was to borrow a spare mobile phone from Tengku and call her mum, who cried and cried down the line, then her brother and sisters. It was good to hear their voices, know now she was back in signal range she could reach them any time she needed after all the weeks of silence. When she spoke to Jake's dad, the crack in his voice nearly undid her.

For almost a week she shuttled between the guesthouse and the hospital as if on automatic pilot. Often the Port Brown air felt as thick as water, and she had to wade on with limbs as heavy as if they were weighted with lead lines. It didn't help that her shoes were too big. Teresa had picked the sandals—black rubber flip-flops—and guessed, wrongly, at her size. She'd also bought her a few clothes: jeans that were made from the thinnest cotton, yet armor-stiff after her months in swimwear, and some long-sleeved blouses.

She suspected where Teresa had got the money: their second day in Port Brown, Virginie had been walking through the shipyard on her way to the hospital when she saw a motorbike drive off as Teresa emerged from a gap between two stacks of shipping containers, a partly filled plastic bag in hand. It was a scene she'd witnessed before, except this time there was no sign of nervousness—Teresa's head was held high, her step confident, victorious.

Returning to the guesthouse the following morning, Virginie found the new clothes folded neatly on her bed, the shoes placed on top. She tugged the pinching trainers she'd been loaned by a nurse off her feet and slipped on the cool sandals. Such kindness. Especially from a woman who, by the sounds of it, didn't have much to give. Her chest tightened. She didn't deserve it.

"You need them," Teresa said, with a shrug, when she went to thank her and to pledge to pay her back as soon as she made it to the bank. "You cannot always be looking like a doctor."

The clothes were a parting gift, it turned out: two days later, on the day Tengku told them the *Patusan* would reach Amarante, she knocked on Teresa's door, ringgit in hand, and it swung open under the rap of her knuckles, creaking on its hinges. Inside, the drawers in the dark wooden chest were open, the bed neat, the passport gone from the side table. The only sign there'd been someone living in the room was a collection of price tags, some for children's clothes, scattered in the bottom of the wastepaper basket like fallen petals.

A silent leaving. It was apt, coming from a woman who spoke only when it mattered, who held her words tight, close inside her. She thought of that photo of Musa and of the last time she'd seen Teresa and wished them all the luck in the world. It was remarkable, a mother's love, how it demanded vulnerability and sacrifice but at the same time engendered a particular kind of battle-hardness, a fierce primal instinct to protect above all else.

On Christmas Day, Tengku came to the hospital to find her. After the fluidity on Amarante, time had solidified again back on land. She was aware of the days here, counted their passage, added them to the tally of how long Jake had been unconscious—twelve— knowing his chances of recovery dwindled each day. The doctors kept telling her he was making progress, and in good moments she believed them: thought she felt a pressure from his hand, or was sure something in his face had shifted. Other times—usually long after the hospital lights had dimmed to mimic the darkness outside, when the squeak of a nurse's clogs against the corridor linoleum only occasionally interrupted the beeps of Jake's machines, she found it harder to believe.

Tengku hadn't been around so much the second half of this week. He was in his formal white shirt again, and the gold stripes on his shoulders gleamed under the hospital lights like baubles.

"Do you know, it's Christmas today, Captain Tengku?" She couldn't feel less like celebrating. "Last Christmas, Jake and I were planning our trip away. We were saving hard, so we made a pact, to only buy each other one gift. We set a price limit—a tiny amount—but of course he broke it." The bracelet he'd given her was still on *Wayfinder*. She circled her bare wrist with thumb and finger. "I didn't think they'd celebrate Christmas in Malaysia."

"Some people do."

"Of course—you're Catholic. Do you?"

He looked up and away, at the clock above the door. She followed his gaze. It was an analog clock, the kind that showed the date as well as the time. It was wreathed in tinsel, and the air-conditioning lifted its fronds, like a palm leaf shifting in a sea breeze.

"The *Patusan* will be back in tonight," he said.

The sounds coming from Jake's monitors seemed to ring more loudly. She took a step toward the alarm button, poised to call for a nurse as she scanned the first screen, the second, the third—but the readouts were the same as usual. In the hours she'd spent staring at them, she'd learned by heart the patterns they traced.

Tengku was watching her check the machines. "Do not worry," he continued, and her anger flashed—he wasn't a doctor; what would he know about Jake's condition? But then she realized he wasn't referring to Jake, but to Vitor. "I will make sure he is taken into police custody.

I have—" He looked away, at the clock again, the door, the tips of his shoes. "I have already spoken to the police chief."

"Does he . . ." She trailed off as it occurred to her that Tengku's out-of-character distractedness might be because he didn't want to tell her she would also be arrested. What would a Malaysian prison cell be like? Christ, she might be held a long time—weeks, months. She'd have to find someone else to sit at Jake's bedside. But there was no one who could drop everything and fly out to Malaysia. His dad wouldn't cope well in a place like this. She wasn't even sure he had a passport. She needed to know what she was up against, if there was a risk Jake would be left by himself. She made herself ask the question: "Does the police chief want to see me as well?"

Tengku lifted his chin and met her eye. "He has not said so to me."

She breathed out, but at the same time she questioned whether that was right, whether freedom was what she deserved.

Tengku paused in the doorway on his way out, a look of deep concentration on his face. "You do realize, Virginie, that you saved Vitor's life when you pushed those water containers over the side?"

Their weight had instantly given when she'd cannoned into them; they'd plummeted into the dark. Her belly concreted. "But I didn't do that on purpose. I wasn't thinking."

"Regardless." His eyes went again to the clock. "That was more than he did for you and Jake. He was going to leave you for dead. What you did means something, even on an unconscious level. Mercy. It matters. And you should never forget that."

The next morning, after stopping by the guesthouse to change her clothes, she passed the harbor and saw the *Patusan*. This close to land it looked enormous, its bridge deck level with the roofs of the buildings edging the harbor, and also alien, the monotonic finish of its superstructure and hull so flat and dead, nothing at all like the ever-changing sky or sea it was designed to blend in with. She pictured Vitor barefoot, in the shorts he'd been wearing that night, shuffling toward a squad car with his hands cuffed in front of him.

At the hospital, Ani, the junior nurse on duty, was waiting for her. "Mrs. Virginie," she said, "Mr. Jake is waking up."

The corridor rucked. "What?" She'd only been gone an hour. Shock made everything around her constrict, lasered her attention to a fine point. "Is he okay?" She was already wheeling, starting to run.

"Mrs. Virginie!" Ani was on her feet, chasing her into his room. "He is sleeping again now. But the doctors say he is very well."

The tubes were gone, and he certainly looked peaceful. Ani left them, and Virginie pulled a chair up to his bed. As he slept, she examined his face. He looked so different from the Jake he'd been at home: leaner, his skin weathered and bristly, freckles peppering the edges of his mouth. What else about him had changed? His feelings for her? She brushed his hair with her fingertips. It was long; she should cut it.

He stirred and blinked open his eyes. When he saw her, he smiled.

"Hi," she said. And then she started to weep.

Later, while the doctors and nurses were doing their checks, she rang Tengku, but his phone went straight through to voicemail. She didn't leave a message; she'd tell him the good news in person.

When the last nurse left Jake's room, having sat him up, he said, "Come here."

Virginie climbed onto the bed beside him and put her head on his chest. His arm came around her. They lay quietly for a while, and she stared at the window. They were on a high floor; clouds were racing past.

When he next spoke, his voice vibrated against her cheek. "Vee," he said, "you know that I love you, don't you?" He paused, and she kept staring at the clouds. Jake took a staggered breath in. "When I think of everything I've done, taking you away from home, putting you through this. Being so full of pride that I wouldn't let you help, either with more money for the boat or with the repairs. Worrying I didn't measure up to what you wanted, to what you had before. Trying to fix that engine when I should have been fixing us. And Teresa, I swear nothing—"

She put a finger to his lips. "Shush. It doesn't matter now. You mustn't tire yourself." She couldn't handle regrets—his or hers, and God knew, she had so many. Regrets were about the past; think about the past, and you'd worry about the future. And she didn't want to worry about how long it would take him to heal, whether or not he'd make it back to the way he was, whether or not they'd rescue their marriage. She just wanted to be here, now, and take each moment as it came. She believed him now, about Teresa—another of Vitor's lies—but if they started to talk about that, then she would have to tell him what had happened in the cabin with Vitor, and she didn't think she could explain how she'd allowed him to him touch her, undress her. How do you tell the person you love that you let someone else do those things to you?

She settled her head on his chest; it dropped as he sighed. "We're going to be okay, you know that?" he said after a while.

She couldn't bring herself to raise her head.

"Vee, look at me." He crooked a finger under her chin, and she let him tilt it. "I mean it. And I'm not just talking about getting out of here. I mean you and me." He kept his finger under her jaw. She raised her eyes to meet his. "I'm not Tomas," he said. "I'm not Vitor, or your father. I'm not any of them. I promise you, I don't think you've done anything wrong. I don't blame you for any of this. Christ, coming sailing was my idea. Chasing some stupid boyhood dream. Beating myself up all the time, thinking, I should have spotted this, I should have known how to do that. Shutting everyone out. Shutting you out. But you're here, Vee. You're here."

For the first time in a long time, she felt the connection between them. She tipped her head to the side, so that her cheek slid onto his finger, and he opened his palm and cupped the side of her face, stroking his thumb from the corner of her lips to her cheekbone. The pad of his thumb was rough, worn hard by years of carpentry compounded by these months on the boat. It was a touch so different from Vitor's, unmistakably Jake's.

Something Terry had said to them in the yacht club came back to her, and she was finally able to give Jake a small smile.

"What?"

"Survive this," she said, "and we can survive anything."

He returned the smile. "I reckon so."

Ani let her spend the night with Jake, spooned against him in the narrow bed, but when morning broke, filling the hospital room with creamy light, she shooed her out.

"Go now," she said, not unkindly, sweeping her hands in the air, brushing Virginie away. "Mr. Jake has work to do."

"Work?" Jake asked.

"Many, many tests," Ani said, opening her eyes wide. "And cheating is not allowed." She grinned as she drew the curtain around the bed.

It was early enough that the streets were still fairly empty for Port Brown. A skinny dog jogged along the pavement, stopping to sniff at a balled-up roti wrapper. A single car passed the hospital entrance.

She set off in the direction of the market. She'd get a fresh pineapple for breakfast. No doubt her landlady, Mrs. Lee, would use up the leftovers for one of the fiery rojak salads she pressed on Virginie almost daily. Delicious, but so much chili! Jake would love it.

She turned the corner, to cut along the gravel path that channeled through the shipping containers and old warehouses in the shipyard. A little way ahead, a local man was leaning against one of the containers, vaping, staring at her. He was tall, skinny, a scarecrow in football shirt and shell suit bottoms. One leg was bent, a trainer cocked against the ridged casing of the container. She passed. The vapor, when it reached her, was super sweet: synthetic apples.

She heard him push off from the container and start to follow her. The fabric of his trousers rustled with every step, gravel crunching underfoot. She hooked her fingers around the strap of her purse. Her heart started to hammer. She tried to reason with herself. He was just walking in the same direction, that's all. He was going to the market, too, or he was a stevedore about to start work. She considered speeding up, not enough to cause offense, just a little, to put more distance between them. No—better to slow down, to find a cause to stop, like tying a shoelace, so he'd overtake her and she could keep an eye on him. God, no shoelaces. Damn flip-flops! She lengthened her stride, and her too-big shoes slipped on the gravel.

"Hey, you!" he called. "Hey, lady!"

Shit. Now she'd drawn attention to herself. Probably it was nothing; probably he just wanted to be friendly, pass the time of day. But probably wasn't definitely. She cast a glance over her shoulder as she continued speed-walking, hoping he'd interpret it as a "Who, me?" gesture. He'd moved closer to the containers. She couldn't quite see him.

"Lady!" he called. She was almost at the last stack of containers and could see the yard beyond. There was no one else about. The shoes were hampering her. She considered ditching them. Without them, she could break into a run.

It was too late. He was sprinting, and he was on her, grabbing her by the shoulder, flinging her round. Her bag hit the gravel. Was that all he wanted—her bag? She stumbled back against a container, expecting to see him snatch it up and escape off through the yard.

But the man remained facing her, only an arm's length away. His eyebrows lowered over his eyes. "Where is he?"

"Who?"

He shoved her again, and her skull ricocheted off steel.

"Your friend. With big ship."

Did he mean Tengku? "I . . . I don't know. On board the *Patusan*?"

"Not navy captain." He came in closer and pinned her against the container by her shoulders. He had a thick gold chain around his neck, diamonds in both ears. "Man with sailing boat. From South America." Before she could say anything, he pulled her toward him and slammed her once more against the container, which thundered at the impact. This time, she managed to stop her head from connecting, but the rough metal grated her shoulder blade through her thin shirt. "I see you with him," he said. "In restoran. With other English, with Africa woman. I see her later. She tells me he is coming here, but I don't see him. Where is this orang putih? Where is his ship?"

Breathing was difficult. "The police—" she said.

"Polis?"

He let her go, and she staggered forward. She lifted a hand to the back of her tender head. "The police have arrested him. But I don't know where he is. Or where his yacht is." Her hand came away clean. "We had to abandon it."

Her attacker turned his head fast, from her to the open end of the yard, and back again, the ear studs flashing. Someone was coming. He shifted his weight back on his feet, like a boxer, and she had a vision of him launching a kick at her. She tensed for the strike, but he must have thought better of it with a witness approaching because he spun on his foot and jumped onto a motorbike parked between the containers and the warehouse. The explosion of the engine firing into life jolted her heart. Gravel screed, and he was gone.

She slumped over, hands on knees, searching for her breath. It was okay; everything was all right. It was Vitor he wanted, not her. She was fine, unharmed, just a little bump on the head, a tear to her blouse.

After a few seconds she was able to stand properly. She picked up her purse. Dust from the gravel and sand had scurfed up its sides, and she patted at it and slotted it back onto her shoulder. No market now. She needed to go back to the guesthouse, take a shower, wash away the feeling of that man's hands on her. Mrs. Lee's was in a different direction, past the warehouses, along a street that would be busier. She started forward on shaky legs. Lifted her gaze from the ground. Ahead, halfway through the yard, someone was walking toward her. White clothes. A naval uniform. Tengku. Her heart lifted. She took a bigger step, passed a weedy patch, a shady gap between the two buildings.

A hand shot out from the alleyway, clamped over her mouth. The last thing she saw was Tengku sprinting toward her before she was hooked into the shadows.

37

"Virginie!"

It took me just a few seconds to reach the warehouse she'd been dragged into, but the door had already clanged shut. It was a heavy fire door, and there was no budging it.

Proper procedure meant phoning the police, but obviously that was pointless, given the corrupt chief, and I knew trying to call in navy resources would be a waste of time—this was out of naval jurisdiction. It was down to me.

I circled the building, looking for another way in. Every window on the front, down the alleyway and along the back, was barricaded with padlocked grilles, as was the rear door. The loading bay at the front appeared the weakest—no grille, just a padlock—but I'd need a crowbar or something similar. I cast around: a few links of chain, some rice sacking. Nothing of any use.

I sprinted back into the alley. The warehouse was as tall as a three-story apartment block. There was a fire escape scaffolded along its side, the type with an extending ladder telescoped up on the first floor. The ladder was hanging down partway. Boosted by a run-up, I grabbed the frame and swung from it. For the second time in a few days, I was grateful for the height my mixed ancestry had bestowed on me. But it didn't move, and I dangled. I couldn't recall this building being used for at least three years, and things decay fast in the salt air. I started to swing back and forth, even though I knew I didn't have a gymnast's strength to flip myself all the way up. But my penduluming worked off some of the rust, and the ladder started to jerk down. I let go just before it jolted to its full extension. It was still quivering as I climbed up to the first level. Only after I'd jumped onto the platform with both feet did I realize that that had been a stupid thing to do, blithely throwing my whole weight onto it without testing it first. Some kind of hero I was. Luckily, it held.

At this level there were two side windows. They, like the others below, were grilled and locked, and too cloudy to see through. Here at the back corner, there were stairs rather than a ladder to the top level, and I did a switchback, running as stealthily as I could, emerging at the front corner of the warehouse, high up. Same layout: two side windows, both locked. No way in. But the glass was missing. I strained against the grille diamonds. The smell of old oil greased my nose.

Inside, it was a vertiginous drop all the way down to stained concrete. From the ceiling hung hook-ended chains. Empty pallets and the carcasses of shipping crates lay scattered across the floor. To one side stood a barrel filled with filthy water. Because of the angle, I couldn't see the whole room, but I could hear voices, although they were all but drowned out by my own heavy exhalations. I forced myself to breathe more quietly, willed my heartbeat to slow.

There was movement below—a blur of limbs as someone was propelled into the center of the room. Virginie. I pressed my face harder against the grating. She skidded on a piece of plywood and staggered to keep her balance, then backed up, arms out to fend someone off. A person—the back of a person—came into view, advancing toward her. It was a man, a tall man, white. I didn't have to see his face to know that it was Vitor. I didn't have to ask myself how he was out of police custody, either.

Seeing them, I wanted to dash my forehead against that impass-able iron. I was useless. Just as I'd been useless to Maria, too, doing overtime a thousand miles away, tucked securely in my ship when she needed me most.

Below, Vitor said to Virginie, "You know I do not mean to hurt you." It didn't look that way to me. He had a length of piping in his hand. "I just need to know what Teresa told you about me. And I need to find her. Where is she?"

"I don't know."

"Where she is or what she said?" He was still moving forward, driving her back.

"Both."

"So she told you something. What?"

"Nothing."

He scoffed. "Nothing? Do you think I believe that? All those days you spent together, and you did not speak of me at all? I find that very difficult to believe. Tell me the truth."

Virginie shook her head as she retreated past the water barrel. "We don't get on, Teresa and I, you know that."

"Well then, let me put it a different way: What did she tell the others? And what did you tell them?"

"What others?"

"Do not pretend. I told you, I am sick of your pretense. Always you are feigning innocence, widening those eyes. You know what others. I saw you talking to one in the yard just now. What did you tell them about me? How much did you take from them?"

"Nothing!"

A high-pitched metallic clang rang out, the sound of steel hitting concrete. I couldn't stand to remain there, on that side of the grille, and watch as he hurt her. I had to get to him, somehow, had to get her out.

"Liar!" He yanked her off the ground and threw her against the barrel. His hand was at her skull, and he doubled her over the lip, forcing her head into the water.

I stopped breathing. Her legs, lifted clear of the ground, were thrashing, and I could hear the water churning. She screamed, a horrible, bubbling, gurgling scream—the kind of scream that has haunted my dreams for years. It must have been only two seconds, three, that passed, but it felt like hours before he wrenched her out again.

He held her by the head against the barrel as she coughed and gasped for air. The back of his neck was puce with rage. "Tell me!"

"Vitor," she spluttered, flailing her arms, but clearly unable to get out of his grip. "Let me go."

He dunked her again. "Why should I? You left me for dead. Why should I not do the same to you?"

Again that freezing of my innards. I saw two children, facedown in the shallows, and a wife, drifting with the current a fathom deep, water-filled mouth loose, glassy eyes unseeing.

He hauled her out and threw her to the ground. She lay there fighting for air, water from her hair and shirt darkening the concrete. Vitor paced back and forth, swinging the metal pole in front of him, the end striking against the concrete with the regularity of a tolling bell.

I gave up on God many years ago, when my family was taken from me. The last time I'd been in church was when we had a memorial service for my wife and kids. Like countless others, their bodies had never resurfaced, and so we couldn't give the reception rites or even have a proper funeral. Instead Maria's sister made a shrine at my house from that photo I carry in my cabin, draping Maria's rosary across it, lighting candles, and relatives wept and prayed over that instead. I hadn't been able to pray that night—or any night since. I'd watched the candles shrink hour by hour. That photograph was not my boy, not my girl, not my wife. They were not at rest. God was not in that room with us. God was not in that undertow.

Yet somehow, on that fire escape, I found myself pleading with Him. Help me, please. Please. Help *her*.

I suppose I'll never understand whether the idea that came to me was an answer sent to my prayer or not. A rational man would say my subconscious was working through the possibilities while my conscious mind was paralyzed. It was the phrase Virginie had used on the *Patusan*. *Orang putih*: the white man, the colonizer, he who has affected so much of my country's history and so many of my country's people. *Orang putih*—I'd heard someone else use it recently, too.

Damn the proper way, damn the rules. Look where being obsessed with the job had landed me. I slid away from the window, pressed my back against the wall, and called Umar. He's from Port Brown; he knows almost everyone. I told him what I needed.

"Be quick about it, Umar. There's a new phone in it for you if you get back to me within five minutes. Top of the line."

He'd never sounded so sharp in his life. "Sir, yes, Captain, sir."

My mobile vibrated less than a minute later. A text from an unregistered number. *You have information for us?*

My mouth went dry. I typed the response as quickly as I could with clumsy hands. *The man you are looking for is here*, I wrote, and gave the address. I sent a second: *Hurry*.

In my cabin, as we crossed the ocean, Virginie had asked me: What is guilt; what is blame? To put it another way: What is debt, and dues owed? What is one life weighed against another? What is one soul judged against three? Even now, I think I would have made the same choice.

I went to put the phone back in my pocket, but it slid out of my shaking grip like a jumping fish. I tried to catch it, but I was too slow, and it sailed into the air, arcing out and down, landing on the platform below with an awful clang that would have been heard streets away.

I was immediately back at the grille. Vitor had spun on the spot, and both he and Virginie were staring at the window below mine. He must have spotted my outline because his gaze raked up. I ducked.

"Jake?" he sneered. "Is that you? Are we to play this game again?"

Of course he didn't know how badly Jake had been injured. I'd be silhouetted against the sunlight; Vitor wouldn't be able to tell who it was. I lifted my head just enough to be able to see him, to see her. I hoped she'd guess it was me, that the knowledge would bring her some comfort.

From her position on the floor, she eyed Vitor. "It's the authorities." For the first time, I heard righteousness in her voice.

He reeled round. "The police will not touch me. I have ensured that. It is Jake. And once more he is locked outside, and he cannot get in. You would think he might have learned by now."

"It's not Jake," she said, pushing herself to her feet.

Vitor moved away from her and turned his face toward my window. "And how can you be so sure? You say that it is not your husband because you know that your husband will not come for you after what you did." He jabbed with the pole, but he was too far away to reach her. "I bet he cannot bear to touch you."

"It's you I couldn't bear to touch," she said. I was heartened at the steel in her. Now she really could see Vitor for what he was. She had prized loose those shackles of guilt. Something inside me settled, too, as surely as if she'd poured a little of that oil Maria used to speak of onto my own troubled waters.

When the end came, mere minutes later, it came fast and loud: the hellish buzz of motorbikes and cars swarming, a series of almighty blasts.

As soon as I heard the first discharge, I leapt for the stairs. By the third or fourth I was on the level below, tumbling down the ladder, aware that the door had been blown open and several people were piling into the warehouse. I was there the moment she came out, coughing and blinking in the cloud that had whirled up from the ground, scrabbling at the dust in the air in the same way a drowning person claws at the water. She barreled blindly into my arms, and I picked her up—she weighed more than my daughter, less than my wife—and I ran and ran, not looking back at what was happening behind me, at what I'd set in play. Maybe they would show Vitor mercy; maybe they wouldn't. It was a matter now of luck—luck that Vitor had made for himself.

"I've got you," I told her as I ran, and she clung to my neck. "I've got you."

AMARANTE

38

The chart tells me we'll reach Amarante by daybreak. I'd set night orders, and was all ready to retire to my cabin, but then I decided to stay. I like being on the bridge at night, when the ocean beyond the windscreen has all but disappeared and the red lights are on. Virginie once described it as being as comfortable as a child's night-light, and that comparison has stayed with me since.

Over the years, I've often wondered what it would be like to return to Amarante. Of course I was never actually there with Virginie—I came across her nearly four hundred miles to the northeast—but I always felt as if I had been. The tale she'd told me had been so rich, the images she created in my mind so vivid, that I could almost remember the musty smell of the fallen palm fronds in the brush, and recall leaving my footsteps in the sand.

I suppose, in my musings, I always thought that if I did go there, it would be on the *Patusan*, rather than on an unfamiliar vessel such as this. But civilian life suits me well enough. Earlier this evening, I was being a touch too military for Umar's liking, and my engineer Yamat fired me a salute. I had to laugh. I'm glad I brought them with me—and I think they are, too. I definitely know they're happier with the salary this side of the line. I only regret that Yusuf would not come with us, but he's not far off getting his own command now, and I'm delighted for him. He'll make a great captain.

We have an unusual passenger list this trip, to say the least, and we'll have an even more unusual cargo on our return. The world of academia was an unfamiliar one, and it took me a long time to learn how to navigate my way through it. In retrospect, that was a good thing—it kept me busy after I resigned. Ever the workaholic.

Eventually, I found the right university with the right team, one already working on gathering what they could on the histories of the freedom fighters. There were some records kept by the British, they tell me, but many were destroyed after the massacre, which won't make identification any easier. They'll try to piece together what they can. They suspect there are far more men buried on Amarante than anyone knew.

As far as landlubbers go, the research team have been an okay bunch to have on board. They've largely kept out of our way, and now that they've recovered from their seasickness, they pass the time between meals working in the mess on their computers, checking on their stock of tools and equipment, and running through their plan of action for when we get there. Excavation and exhumation is a complicated business.

I take out my phone and dial in to the satellite Wi-Fi system to check my messages. My phone habits have changed since my *Patusan* years—these days, I keep my mobile switched on. When it connects, there's a message sent a few hours ago: *What's your ETA?* I start to type, and as I do so, the phone vibrates in my hand: incoming call.

"I caught you," Virginie says. "I thought you might be in bed by now."

"Not yet."

"What time is it there?"

"Twenty-one hundred hours."

She laughs. "Ever the military man."

I chuckle. "Old habits."

"And when will you get there?"

"A little before daybreak."

"Great." A pause, then: "You will take care of her, won't you?"

"I promise."

She managed to track down Pete about six months ago. He was working in the South China Sea, diving on the rigs. When she explained what we were doing, he gave us permission to exhume Stella's body, and to take it back to the mainland. Virginie's still working on getting the funds together to return Stella to Canada.

She's quiet for a while, and I know she's crying. She's never been one to hide her emotions from me, either when we first met or through our years of friendship since. "You've seen me at my lowest," she said once. I believe I did—and I hope she never has to suffer like that again. But I've also seen her at her fiercest, and that's how I prefer to think of her, not as a victim, but as someone who fights for what she wants, and what she deserves.

To lighten the mood, I ask her about the weather over there. My English grandmother always told me it was a fail-safe topic among the British.

"Oh, you know, gray as always," she says, and her voice lifts a little. Aha! Granny was right. "We miss the sun." Kitchen noises down the phone, then: "Do you think it's changed much?"

"Amarante?"

"Yes."

From the way she says it, I know she isn't expecting an answer. Often in our calls, we are content to sit in companionable silence, connected across the ten thousand miles through radio waves in the way we were that first night on the ocean. I'm sure some things will have changed on Amarante—storms will have sculpted the beach differently and heaped new jetsam above the tidelines; trees will have fallen and others started to grow in their place; creepers will have claimed back even more of the ruins—but I imagine that, yes, it is still beautiful. A long time ago, I dismissed the way foreigners considered those golden sands a philosopher's stone. I have mixed feelings now. Because, despite all the darkness—and these days, for both of us, there's a lot more light than dark—I truly believe her experiences changed her for the better.

She doesn't ask about *Wayfinder*. As I ferry cargo from port to port, I always keep a weather eye out for her boat on the waves. I doubt it's still anchored off Amarante; I imagine it was long ago dragged away by monsoon winds, caught by oceanic currents. I've vowed to myself, although I haven't told Virginie, that if by some miracle I do come across it, I'll salvage everything I can carry. I haven't yet decided whether I'll scuttle the boat afterwards or leave it free to drift the oceans, a ghost ship forever finding its way.

Someone else is talking to her, and I hear her murmuring, then a rustle, and I picture her pressing the receiver of the phone to her chest as she listens. Another rustle and she's back. She's finishing a giggle, and when she talks, she sounds buoyant. "Jake's asking if you'll bring his machete back. He says he wants to crack open some coconuts next time we're in Malaysia. Reckons he hasn't lost the knack."

Always a joker, that man. He's good for her. There's more background noise, and I fear I've lost the connection, but then she's on the line again, clear as anything. "Someone else wants a word." I know who it will be, and a smile tugs at the corners of my mouth.

" 'Lo, Uncle Ten-koo," Izzy says.

"Hi, Izzy." She's still too little for phone conversations, and I can make out Virginie guiding her. I ask her: "What have you been doing today? Drawing?" I have one of her scribbles on the fridge in my apartment. That's where Maria used to stick Farah and Aadam's pictures. It's a different fridge, of course, and a different home, but it feels the right place to have put it.

"Mummy," Izzy says, and I can tell from the way the word is blunted that she's got her thumb in her mouth.

"You've been drawing Mummy? And how about Daddy, did you draw him, too?"

Virginie is whispering to Izzy again. "Go on, Isabelle."

Isabelle—it means God's gift.

"Baby," Izzy says.

"You drew a baby?"

"Baby," she repeats. As she says it, my phone double-buzzes against my temple. Virginie's emailed me a picture, and I'm expecting it'll be a snap of my goddaughter. But it's not that—it's a grainy sector shape framed in black: a sonogram.

Virginie has taken her phone back from Izzy. "A boy," she says as I marvel at the scan. There, a foot; there, a tiny upturned nose. "Adam."

Adam. A glimpse into the future: a life—and an echo to heal all wounds.

Author's Note on Amarante

When living on a yacht in Malaysia, I met other cruisers who told me of how, some fifty years earlier, they would spend months at a time living a self-sufficient existence in the Chagos islands, a paradisical archipelago in the Indian Ocean. These stories lodged in my imagination like the grit in an oyster, and over time I layered in other places, ideas, and experiences until I had cultured a fictional island, Amarante.

Although my Amarante shares an approximate location with the Chagos islands, which lie at 7° S, 72° E, it is an amalgam of other real Indian Ocean islands I visited on my travels, primarily the Andamans and the Seychelles.

Like Tengku being followed by the ghosts of his family, even as I wrote of beautiful sands and warm lapping waters, I was always aware of being shadowed by history, not only by the knowledge I was writing in a tradition of island stories that went all the way back to Daniel Defoe's *Robinson Crusoe* (1719), widely acknowledged as the first novel in English, but also by the pasts of the real islands I was borrowing from. On Ross Island, in the Andamans, which are now part of India, stands an utterly inhumane construction known as the Cellular Jail, now a museum, to which the then British government of India transported more than eighty thousand Indian and Burmese convicts between 1858 and 1939. The British Empire also had penal colonies in Malaya, at Penang, Malacca, and Singapore.

The Chagos islands themselves, which I haven't been to, are now officially known as the British Indian Ocean Territory. After forcing all Chagossians to leave in the 1960s and '70s, the British government loaned the islands to America for use as a strategic military base—an arrangement that continues to this day.

The records of brutalities committed in these places, and other penal colonies, are understood to have been largely destroyed.

If you are interested in finding out more about the histories of the real places that were spliced into the fictional Amarante, I recommend:

"The Andaman Islands Penal Colony: Race, Class, Criminality, and the British Empire," by Clare Anderson (available online via cambridge.org)

"Convicts in the Straits Settlements 1826–1867," by C. M. Turnbull, published in the *Journal of the Malaysian Branch of the Royal Asiatic Society*, Vol. 42, No. 1 (217), 1970 (available online via jstor.org)

In the Andamans and Nicobars: The Narrative of a Cruise in the Schooner "Terrapin," with Notices of the Islands, their Fauna, Ethnologys, Etc. by C. Boden Kloss, published by John Murray 1903 (available free online via Project Gutenberg)

"Britain destroyed records of colonial crimes" by Ian Cobain, Owen Bowcott, and Richard Norton Taylor, *Guardian*, April 18, 2012

www.chagossupport.org.uk

Acknowledgments

For help with all kinds of things in sailing *Deep Water* safely to harbor, from engine mechanics to plot and pace, and from oceanic physics to word choices, I'd like to thank the following people: Camilla Bolton, Jade Kavanagh, Mary Darby, Georgia Fuller, Sheila David, and Rosanna Bellingham at Darley Anderson; Alison Callahan, Maggie Loughran, Taylor Rondestvedt, John Paul Jones, Jaime Putorti, Kathryn Kenney-Peterson, Jessica Roth, Biana Salvant, Lucy Nale, and everyone at Scout Press; Suzanne Baboneau, Sabah Khan, Richard Vlieststra, Hannah Paget, and everyone at Simon & Schuster UK; Bobbie Darbyshire, Ellen Macdonald-Kramer, Julia Rampen, Karen Wallace, Joanne Rush, Sharon Brennan, and others at Writers Together; Giles Foden, Naomi Wood, Trezza Azzopardi, Jean McNeil, Yan Ge, Tasha Ong, Catherine Gaffney, Margaret Meyer, Polly Crosby, Nathan Hamilton, and others at UEA; readers Nicola Rayner, Julia Faulks, Lucinda Bampton, Vicky Page, and David Llewelyn; Dr. Spike Briggs of Medical Support Offshore; and sailors and adventurers Aaron Duffy, Paul Stringer, Ben Thompson, Sam Jefferson, Brian Trautman of *SV Delos*, Duncan Kent, Duncan Wells, Ian King, David Cusworth and Marilyn Mower. All mistakes and artistic licenses are my own—and I owe you all a tot of rum.

About the Author

Emma Bamford is an author and journalist who has worked for the *Independent*, the *Daily Express*, the *Daily Mirror*, *Sailing Today* and *BOAT International*. She spent several years sailing among some of the world's most beautiful islands and wrote two travel memoirs about her experiences, *Casting Off* and *Untie the Lines*. A graduate of the University of East Anglia's Prose Fiction MA, she lives in the UK. Her next thriller is due to be published in summer 2023.

www.emmabamford.com